ADVANCE PRAISE FOR

THE NEW ORDER

"Once again, Isenthal dazzles with her quick and biting portrait of a city in turmoil, and the human face of our most intractable conflicts. Sharp, as harrowing as a ticking bomb, *The New Order* explores both our darkest and our noblest impulses, and the complex intersection of the two. Page-turning, thought-provoking, indelible."

—I.S. Berry, author of *The Peacock and the Sparrow*, A *New Yorker* & NPR Best Book of the Year, Winner - Edgar Award for Best First Novel

"*The New Order* is a masterclass in high-stakes suspense and emotional depth—a razor-sharp, heart-stopping thriller that doesn't just ask tough questions, it dares you to answer them. With a pulse-pounding plot, relentless tension, and characters that feel strikingly real, Claire Isenthal proves why she's one of the most talented new voices in fiction today with another twisting, thought-provoking adventure that's perfect for fans of *Homeland* and *Divergent*. Everyone's going to be talking about this book . . . don't miss it!"

—Ryan Steck, The Real Book Spy and Author of *Ted Bell's Monarch*

"Sharp, propulsive, and terrifyingly plausible, *The New Order* cements Claire Isenthal as a master of near-future thrillers. With breakneck pacing and unforgettable characters, this book will leave you breathless."

—Bruce Borgos, author of Barry-nominated, *The Bitter Past*, and the Porter Beck Mysteries.

"Claire Isenthal gives you a ringside seat to a city under siege. The people of Chicago are living under the thumb of a ruthless terrorist group made up of white supremacists. The White Power Mafia group known as the "Reds" holds the entire city hostage after they gain control over a cache of nuclear weapons. The city's last hope is a courageous young woman who joins an underground resistance group that is willing to give up everything to stop the terror from spreading any further. The pages turn at a breakneck pace barely leaving you time to catch your breath."

—John Adams, author of American Legacy Book Awards 2024 Winner of Best New Fiction, *Second Term*.

"Isenthal does it again in her sophomore novel. This fast-paced, thrill ride drops you right in the action following *The Rising Order*. She brings a fresh look at the same characters you know, and beautifully demonstrates the complexity of human nature."

—Jensen Parker, contemporary romance author of the *Strangers* series

"Crafted with masterful suspense, Isenthal once again places you in the mind of each character like nobody else."

—Jeff Clark, Air Force Veteran, and Host of *Course of Action* podcast

"Isenthal brings the kind of depth and strength to her characters that will stick with you."

—Jeff Circle of *The Writer's Dossier*

THE NEW ORDER

Other Titles by
this Author

✶ ✶ ✶

THE RISING ORDER

THE
NEW
✶✶✶✶
ORDER

A NOVEL

CLAIRE ISENTHAL

Cover design by Brian Phillips Design
Cover images used under license from ©Shutterstock

Publisher's Cataloging-in-Publication data is available.

Hardcover ISBN: 979-8-9929955-0-3

Paperback ISBN: 979-8-9929955-3-4

eBook ISBN: 979-8-9929955-1-0

Printed in the United States of America on acid-free paper

25 26 27 28 29 30 31 32   10 9 8 7 6 5 4 3 2 1

First Edition

To Justin, who gives me strength.
& to William and Amelia, who give me hope.

"He who fights with monsters should be careful lest he thereby become a monster."

— *Friedrich Nietzsche*

AUTHOR'S NOTE AND
CONTENT ADVISORY

started this series almost ten years ago. It began as a way to process the
Orlando nightclub shooting, in 2016, and has since evolved to encom-
pass the growing violence that will now be interwoven into my children's
daily lives. I started writing this before the Manchester Arena Ariana Grande
concert. Before the First Baptist Church of Sutherland Springs Sunday service. Before Uvalde. There have been so many others in between.

Please take into consideration that this book contains acts of violence
and mass shootings, and it explores themes around trauma. My intention
is never to glorify this violence, but to instead depict how it is present and
inescapable in places and parts of our lives we once considered the most
sacred and safe.

PART ONE

✦ ✦ ✦ ✦

RISING TIDE

1

WOLF

I *have no problem killing a monster.*

Flynn's voice swished around Wolf's brain, as distracting and unrelenting as the sensation of water caught around his eardrum.

I tried to tell you, he wanted to scream. *I told you I was a monster.* A fangless, clawless monster. A beast with an empty black heart.

A monster who was all alone. Except for the bloody corpse on the floor.

Arguing with an imaginary Flynn was pointless. She and Nate had already fled her apartment, leaving him alone with Cori's lifeless body.

Cori.

Wolf labored to his feet. He gritted his teeth, a yell of pain surging against his throat, his shoulder aflame from Nate's bullet. Wolf knew, because Nate had fired at close range, the bullet had gone straight through the muscle. He took a deep shuddering breath, but his pounding heartbeat only accelerated.

He shoved his hands against his ears, but Flynn's voice still rang through his head.

We used each other...chasing each other around and around, until we collided.

She was right. They had used each other. And in the end, it got them nowhere. He'd failed everyone.

Himself. Spider. Flynn.

He'd been fully prepared to kill Cori in order to spare Flynn's life. Except when the time came and Spider, leader of REDS, demanded Wolf plunge the knife into her chest, he froze. Again.

He couldn't do it.

In the dark stairwell, Wolf staggered down seventeen flights and out of Flynn's building. He blinked into the stinging brightness, shading his eyes with his hand. The setting sun bobbed above the lake's horizon, as if deciding whether to dip in a toe or plunge straight through the water's glossy sherbet surface. Surrounding skyscrapers cast their elongating shadows over the city, carrying an evening chill and summoning a blanket of suffocating silence. But the quiet bubble burst, punctured by frenzied noise. Blaring honks from cars inching along the packed street. Impatient yells out windows. No traffic lights were functioning. Pedestrians wandered into traffic. Cyclists wove around cars. Wolf's zero-day virus had shuttered Chicago's electrical grid, transforming the highway into a dysfunctional sliding block puzzle.

How could he ever return to REDS now that he couldn't kill either Flynn *or* Cori?

The city spun. Wolf tried to steady himself, but every time he shut his eyes, Flynn's face swam before him.

Killing had always been easy. Essential to quenching his thirst for power. Until, suddenly, it wasn't. Compressing the trigger had taken on a different meaning once he finally knew the person facing the other end of his rifle.

And that one person had changed everything.

The ringing in his head intensified. He pressed himself to the building's cold glass.

REDS's chant pounded through him.

Redemption for the oppressed. Execution for the unjust. Deliverance for the guilty. Salvation for the lost. REDS. REDS. REDS.

It reminded him of the life he could never escape. A life he had devoted his entire existence to for the past decade. He couldn't think. His senses were in overdrive—the sunlight too intense, the quiet too pronounced, the noise too overstimulating.

Let him suffer alone. Don't let him change you, too, Flynn had told Nate when Nate tried to kill him.

Flynn had known death would be too merciful. Too easy. He wished Nate's bullet had hit a few inches to the right. Then he'd be gone. Then he wouldn't have to deal with this excruciating pain. He'd been so close to death he could taste its promise of blissful peace. The thought danced around him, laughing, spitting in his face. Why had Flynn stopped Nate from releasing the lethal shot? Why couldn't she just let him die? Maybe for the same reason he'd never be able to kill her either.

Don't become the monster he is—the monster he's turned me into, he heard Flynn say again. She'd drawn a line by keeping him alive. A line that would forever divide them. It marked her refusal to cross into his evil depths—the depths that had swallowed him when he first murdered a soul.

Beta.

He shook his head as if he could somehow fling Beta's memory out of it. But Beta's and Flynn's whispers followed him, starving animals lunging at his feet. He set off at a jog, desperate to outrun them. Unease had settled over Lincoln Park, an idyllic neighborhood just north of the downtown Loop. An unspoken, tense energy pulsed through the air. Wolf recognized it immediately—a precursor to panic. Quiet at first. Restlessness. People looking around to see how others were reacting to the dead silence, searching for cues to inform their own responses. Chicago had already been on edge after REDS's most recent attack on the downtown Loop. The power outage added a deeper layer of anxiety.

Wolf picked up speed. Three police cars and two fire trucks blew by. The concrete beneath him trembled. Leaves overhead, yellowing from the end of summer, shivered indignantly on their swaying branches. A blur of flashing lights and wailing sirens interrupted an unnatural stillness that accompanies a once vibrating city.

Wrong way, Wolf thought.

More sirens screamed by, blustery, self-important warnings. Only he knew their attempts were useless.

OOF.

Wolf collided with a middle-aged woman, sending her sprawling to the ground.

"Excuse me!" she screeched with indignation. "Watch where you're—Oh my god!" She gasped. "Sir, are you hurt?" Her hand fluttered to her mouth, eyes widening. "Do you need an ambulance?"

Wolf reeled back. The woman's face had transformed into Cori's, staring up at him with the same pleading expression.

Sweat prickled his brow, snaking down his temple.

"What?" he wheezed.

"You're bleeding everywhere!"

"Bleeding?" he repeated, his voice hollow.

The woman pointed a shaking finger to his chest. "I can't call anyone, m-my phone won't work. You need a hospital. Do you live around here? Can someone take you?"

Wolf glanced down. He clutched his shoulder, blood pooling through the V-shaped valley between his fingers in a steady flow. "No," he whispered, stepping around the woman, who was trying to get to her feet. "No one."

He tried to absorb the realization he had nowhere to go. REDS was his only home. But they no longer needed him. He'd served his purpose, hacking into Magnetic's system, and now he was of no further use to them. He needed to convince them otherwise. In a matter of hours, the next phase of their plan would begin, and REDS would commence their takeover of Chicago starting with the police department.

Ripping off the sleeve of his jacket, he wrapped the fabric around his shoulder, using his teeth to keep one end taut while he tugged the other into a knot. The wound burned like hot oil leaping from a pan, sending a fresh wave of pain sizzling through his arm.

People's gazes fell on Wolf as he hurried by, their blurred faces recoiling at the sight of fresh blood covering his vest. Wolf's fingers itched, desperate to reach for his handgun. The old Wolf probably would have just started shooting—really given them something to gape at. But this strange new creature slunk away from their scrutiny.

A hand caught his good shoulder, pulling him back. He spun around, reaching for his gun, when his mouth dropped open.

"S-Spider," he stammered. "I thought—I thought you'd left."

Spider must have followed him. A million questions spun through Wolf's head. But he straightened, attempting to pull himself together so he didn't appear as unhinged as he felt. Had Spider seen Nate and Flynn leave? Had he killed them and stashed their bodies? His insides collapsed on each other, triggered by a mudslide of panic. Was he next?

"Come, Wolf. We have places to be. Time for the new order to rise."

Wolf cast his gaze down. "But I failed you. I don't know—I don't know what's wrong with me."

"Yes," Spider agreed. "You're lucky I'm merciful. Besides, I know some ways you can make it up to me."

Wolf's gut gave him a kick, urging him to run. True, he had nowhere to go, but he knew what came next in REDS's plan. Threads of blackmail and propaganda, woven into a masterful tapestry that would forever change the world. It would be easy. Too easy. People were so fucking gullible these days. They would listen to anything social media and its algorithms spewed at them. They didn't question altered videos or manufactured stories. What wouldn't be easy was convincing Spider not to kill him. Nate's quick shot straight to the heart was one thing. A slow tortuous death at the hands of REDS was another.

Spider wrapped his jacket around Wolf's shoulders. "Scorpion's got a truck nearby. He'll patch you up."

As Spider guided Wolf down a side street lined with limestone mansions, the hairs on the back of Wolf's neck prickled, tiny antennae searching for a signal. Despite what he said, Spider was not merciful. Nor did he ever do anything from the goodness of his heart. Spider brought his lips close to Wolf's ear.

"You are more than the world has allowed you to believe. You are worthy. Among REDS, you serve as an integral part of our purpose. We were once lost, victims of an unjust system. Now, we stand as one, soldiers championing those oppressed by tyranny. We create a binding heart, pulsing fear into society..." Spider paused, prompting Wolf to finish REDS's manifesto.

Wolf tried to recover from his encounter with Spider so soon after Cori's death. Seeing him incited both a jolt of terror and submission, but also a promise of security and family. Wolf felt the familiar tug back toward what he'd always known. What had defined him for so long.

"De—uh—Des...Destruction must come before creation, and from the ashes of despair, a new order will rise." Wolf stumbled, the next words creating friction inside him that hadn't been there before, two stones grinding against each other to create a spark. "Together, we will rule."

2

WOLF

Six Weeks Later

The Windy City has become America's forgotten city, Wolf thought as he kicked aside an empty beer can. It bounced, pinged over the crater-pocked street, leaving a streak of watery residue in its wake. He watched it roll under an abandoned bus splayed in an intersection, the doors and windows gaping open. A useless traffic light swung from a wire above, stirred by gusts of wind. Its agitated creaking disrupted the heavy silence.

Wolf followed a pace behind Spider. They were intentionally late. A prompt arrival presented too many risks when meeting with an untrustworthy, revolting excuse for a human. It still felt surreal to travel the streets freely. After years of hiding and plotting their mission to take Chicago, REDS had finally gained control of the city. Society might have once dictated and controlled REDS's worth, but their insurrection turned everything on its head. Their patience had paid off. Wolf always knew it would. They all knew it would.

Wolf kept his eyes glued to Spider's taut back. His mentor's body seemed welded into a rigid pole, although Wolf could tell his gaze continued to scout the area. Over the past six weeks, Wolf had remained submissive, chained to Spider under his watchful eye. It didn't take long for Wolf to figure out why Spider kept him around. No one else came close to his hacking abilities, and

Spider needed Wolf's help to gain access to a nuclear reserve hidden beneath Lake Michigan. The one the US government had kept secret from the public.

Wolf always knew there had to be a strategic reason why REDS chose Chicago as its target and headquarters. Once he'd learned of the nuclear arsenal, everything made sense. If REDS controlled nuclear missiles, the military couldn't intervene. Traditional rules of war, or mutually assured destruction, had always kept other countries in check. But those same rules didn't apply to a group like REDS, and the rest of the country had no choice but to comply with their demands if they had any sense of self-preservation.

"Who needs Iowa anyway?" Spider had laughed.

The two men strode through a park wedged in the middle of what was once one of the wealthiest neighborhoods in the city. Gold Coast. Even the name triggered Wolf. Except now the ornate limestone high-rise buildings, with their prized lakefront views, sat vacant. Soot stained their façades and bullet holes peppered the brick walls—evidence of the Chicago Police Department's short-lived resistance. Despite the CPD's higher numbers, they'd been unprepared for REDS's onslaught and sophisticated weaponry. REDS took as many hostages as they could, attacking weaker parts of the city first. The CPD caved once the number of casualties climbed too high and the National Guard couldn't provide any sort of backup.

Gold Coast residents were the first to try to flee the city. They poured exorbitant sums of money into any possible method of escape. But cash can only get you so far when the world is going to shit.

Sheep flock together, Wolf thought. *Fucking cowards.*

Their heavy boots scuffed the concrete as they descended some stairs leading into a narrow tunnel, ducking below Lake Shore Drive. It led to a path bordering the lake that, prior to REDS's attack, drew crowds of bikers, runners, and pedestrians. He'd always thought it strange—packed beaches tucked along the underbelly of a bustling urban city. The sands were now desolate; the only sound was the calm swish of froth-capped waves peaking in the distance.

A lanky man waited for them in the tunnel's center. He shifted on his long legs, his head swiveling back and forth in anticipation of their arrival.

White and black tile lined the wall, from the damp, urine-stained ground up to the low ceiling. Orbed light fixtures mounted every few feet were extinguished. Chicago had been without power for weeks.

"Krammer." Spider's voice echoed throughout the confined space. He offered no apology for their tardiness. "It's been a while."

Brett Krammer cleared his throat, tugging at the lapel of his ill-fitted suit jacket that did little to flatter his gaunt frame.

Wolf stood slightly behind Spider, observing the politician. A screen of bright light at either end of the tunnel illuminated the underground haze. Cradling his rifle in his good arm, Wolf made sure to hold it in clear view. *If only he knew,* he thought, *I'm on thin ice with Spider too, and it's never a place you want to be.*

"I'm sure you've been very busy, given recent events." Above Krammer's angular chin, his abnormally tiny mouth gave him a constant sour expression. "I owe you a belated congratulations on the insurrection's wild success."

Wolf suppressed a leer. *Typical.* Krammer had always cowered on the sidelines, eager to reap the benefits of their work yet never willing to plunge his own hands into the muck. He'd run for Senate twice, desperate to advance beyond Illinois State Treasurer. After his second defeat, a crony from his party's administration connected him with Spider. He'd proved himself as an astute embezzler, funneling Chicago's tax dollars into REDS's coffers ever since, funding the organization's rapid growth. But, more importantly, he'd provided them invaluable information—information about the city's nuclear arsenal, their key to freezing the military and the United States government and forcing them into submission.

Spider nodded once in curt acknowledgement of the man's fawning gratitude. "We've taken over every hospital, central power plants, and the water management plant."

Krammer's jowls danced in excitement. He swiped a palm across his shiny, high forehead. "Well done."

As if we need your validation, asshole. Wolf ached to speak, to tell Spider that they didn't need this spineless slug anymore. But after he'd attacked Spider to save Flynn in front of the entire organization, REDS's Executive

Committee had voted him off the leadership council. His opinion was no longer welcome, and he knew Spider still didn't trust him. Even worse, after Wolf's most recent meltdown, Spider probably questioned whether he still felt a pull toward Flynn. He wished he could convince himself this wasn't the case.

"Did you experience much pushback?" Krammer asked.

"No. People reacted exactly as expected. Panic. Chaos." Spider shrugged one of his broad shoulders. His cropped head nearly brushed the cement ceiling.

"Those riots were something, let me tell ya. I expected the yuppies to abandon ship real quick, but not the rest." Krammer snorted a guttural chuckle before releasing a low whistle. "Boy, was I wrong. They wasted no time. Food went fast...gas even faster. Became a giant free-for-all, huh?" His voice carried an artificial twang, reminding Wolf of a rehearsed, overly confident salesman.

"Yes...The city unraveled at the seams. All we had to do was watch and wait." Spider fingered the machete hanging from his belt with fond strokes. In the gloom, Spider's sandy-colored skin was subdued to a gray hue.

Krammer glanced at the weapon, his back snapping to attention. "Well, let me tell ya, the stragglers are getting desperate. Desperate and frustrated. This whole ordeal makes the government look incompetent as hell. How've they responded?"

Spider's upper lip lifted. "Once the president learned we gained hold of the nuclear arsenal, it's been radio silence."

"HAH. Must be scramblin' for a response. It won't be easy for him to explain to the country that a reserve of nuclear warheads has been tickin' under Lake Michigan."

"Nuclear warheads under *our* control." Spider pointed to the end of the tunnel. "I'm in no rush to work out anything. The longer negotiations last, the stronger we get."

"I can't see how they're gonna get outta this one. What, are they gonna nuke the entire damn city to oust you? Yeah, right. People would overthrow the government for you. Oh, well, not our problem it's blown up in their faces...literally!" Krammer guffawed, slapping his knee. He fell silent when neither Spider's nor Wolf's cold stares wavered. He eyed Wolf's bandaged arm. "Any updates on the remainder of the CPD? We can't have them meddlin'."

Wolf bit down hard on his tongue. *"We"? Who does this prick think he is?*

"We're still scouting out what's left of them," Spider said. "They fell fast... or should I say, it didn't take much."

"Sure helps that we fudged some of the numbers last year. The state cut a fourth of the force! Brilliant idea, Spider, just brilliant."

"Never mind the numbers, they stood no chance against Hyena's weapons. We've spent years preparing for this, Krammer. It took far more than *cuts* to get to where we are today."

A pang of jealousy ricocheted through Wolf. Hyena, REDS's Executive Director of Weapon Advancement, was brilliant, albeit insane. If anyone matched Spider's thirst for mass destruction, it was him. His missile development had increased his rank and visibility within the organization over the past five years, and although Wolf's zero-day virus had successfully compromised the entire electrical grid, Hyena's Semtex bombs and grenade launchers were unrivaled. An ex-Army veteran free from the moral constraints of the military, he unleashed knowledge gained from his deployments, dedicating himself to uncovering unlimited methods for creating chaos.

"M-My only concern is people are gonna keep leavin'," Krammer stuttered. "We need more support if we're gonna expand past Chicago."

The goal had always been for REDS to gain access to more states beyond Illinois. REDS cells were active in other cities, just waiting for their signal to pounce, but Spider had hinted he had a plan for Wolf to help accelerate that process.

Spider sighed, visibly impatient with Krammer's shortsightedness. "Let them try. We're patrolling the main arteries leading out of the city. If they escape, we'll kill them."

Krammer's tight pucker loosened into a smile. "Ruthless. I've always admired your way of thinkin'. So black and white. Just don't kill too many, we need numbers."

"Speaking of numbers, it's time for you and your party to step in and do your part." Spider cupped the machete, massaging the handle with his thumb. "Stir things up a bit. Contact your friends in the media. Spread lies. The longer the government takes to respond, the more fear will build, and the easier the public will be to manipulate. Both inside and outside Chicago."

Wolf watched as the slight curve of Krammer's Adam's apple quivered against his long neck. He cleared his throat again with a phlegmy gurgle, trying to avoid glances at the blade at Spider's waist. "Listen, this is—uhh—my area of expertise. You know what I can do. This is where I shine."

"And you know where I shine. Nuclear weapons are not enough to secure the entire country. We need support from the masses. We need to create a following."

"Leave it to me." Krammer puffed out his chest. "I know what to do."

* * * *

Wolf waited until they'd returned to their truck before speaking. "Permission to offer my opinion, Spider?"

Spider pressed the ignition, awakening the vehicle. He considered the request for several seconds. "Granted."

Their breath hovered in front of them, like lingering ghosts, before evaporating into the crisp early October air. "I don't trust Krammer. He's a coward."

"Yes. That's easy to see. He'll be disposable soon enough. We need him for the moment. We need outside agitators. Krammer has ways of riling up underrepresented communities. He knows the right people. The moment is right to plant the seed."

Wolf leaned back in the passenger seat. He couldn't help but think of his shoulder injury as a physical manifestation of weakness—a torturous handicap. His patience had burned down to a stubby wick. He would do anything to tear the dressings from his skin, but the bullet wound still hadn't healed. Its deep ache was impossible to separate from Flynn and how she'd saved him from Nate almost shooting his brains out.

"If we want to create a domino effect throughout the whole country another sniveling politician like Krammer isn't going to do it," Wolf argued.

"Agreed. But someone has to set the stage."

3

FLYNN

op. Pop. Pop.

P Everything hurt. Flynn woke with a pain she couldn't shake, and it continued to beat across her temples. Deep and endless, it was a pain she could never get used to.

"Flynn, come on. We've got to keep moving."

Her breathing hadn't slowed and her heart raced, as if she'd spent the past half hour sprinting. Day after day, she and Nate had battled through the same routine, searching for fuel and risking their lives for crumbs to stay alive. She stayed doubled over, head braced between her biceps, avoiding Nate's scrutiny. Sometimes the sound of distant gunfire still had that effect on her.

Another person dead, she thought to herself. *Dead because of me.*

"You okay?" Nate pressed.

Swaying, she tried to swallow, but her tongue stuck to the roof of her mouth. She tried again, forcing her throat muscles to contract. She straightened. "Yeah, coming." She stumbled forward, eyes glued to the tiny scars sliced into her palms—a permanent reminder of the glass scattered around her best friend, Cori, another murder at the top of her growing tally. "Just a little lightheaded, that's all."

She saw the fight drain from Nate's face. "You hungry?" he asked.

"Yeah," she said, though she hadn't truly been hungry in weeks. "And tired."

Food was scarce. Once the power grid collapsed, REDS's insurrection moved quickly. They'd appeared from the most inconspicuous and innocuous places, gushing onto the streets like murky water from a storm drain after heavy rain. That's what had been most terrifying—the realization that REDS had been living among them this entire time. Hundreds of them, blending in with everyday people, waiting and planning for their moment to take control. She had known about Wolf. She had known about the blindness of her small hostage cell. She guessed some might consider it denial, but even she couldn't have predicted what would emerge from the darkness. And it was worse than she could have ever imagined.

Within days of REDS's cyberattack, they gridlocked Chicago, creating borders they patrolled ruthlessly. Some managed to flee early on, but escape was risky. Anyone caught trying to leave faced immediate execution, and no one from the outside could infiltrate REDS's perimeter.

No military, no communication, no relief, no aid.

Panic escalated. Vicious mobs raided grocery stores and gas stations, like medieval marauders pillaging their own beloved villages. Loss of electricity debilitated the city. Those who remained retreated into their homes, waiting for help that still hadn't arrived. Paralysis unfurled across the fractured neighborhoods.

"Let's head back to camp," Nate said. "No more cars around here to siphon from."

She nodded, already dreading the stale underground quarters that now served as their home. A cool breeze coerced moisture from the corners of her eyes. She wrapped her thin jacket tighter around her. Summer had slunk away overnight, replaced with fall's brittle chill. Their worn tennis shoes scratched over fallen leaves, curled and withered on barren streets. Eerie silence nipped at their heels, ever present. Flynn longed to scream, to cry, to sing, or to shout just to fill its void—just so she no longer had to feel its suffocating weight.

Nate kept quiet, as he had for the past few weeks. His thick brows permanently sloped into a deep valley. In his defense, Flynn hadn't done much to pry. She couldn't bear his confusion, or anger, or disappointment. Not knowing how he felt was better than knowing. In the distance, smoke snaked into the air, spat from buildings that had crumbled into rubble.

Gone. It's all gone.

Everything she loved about the city had disappeared overnight, including her two best friends. Cori was dead, and Nate barely spoke to her. She didn't know how to go about explaining herself to him. She couldn't reveal why she hadn't let him kill Wolf or why she'd been weak enough to succumb to terrorist blackmail. She couldn't bring herself to admit that this—all of it—was her fault. So, she didn't try.

"Listen." Nate stopped, throwing up an arm to block her too. Rumbling through the quiet, the purr of a truck mingled with the skitter of dead leaves skimming along the sidewalk, shoved forward by windy bursts. Only REDS still had functioning cars. "Come on, this way."

The dribble of gas they'd managed to extract from the nearby BP gas station sloshed in their jugs as they sprinted into the belly of an overpass. Its arch formed a bridge, straddling an exit that curved onto Lake Shore Drive. They crouched against the cement, gasping, trying their best to melt in the overhang's shadow. Unsupervised excursions without a REDS guard were strictly forbidden. Punishment was death on-site.

Wolf's green eyes flashed through her mind. She wondered if they'd ever stop haunting her. It'd been weeks since she'd last seen him. A stab tore through her chest. The thought of him provoked a strange mix of emotions, but rage smothered them all.

The car thundered toward them, the roar of its engine echoing off forlorn, empty buildings. Nate's body pressed against her, keeping them in the shadow. Even through the weeks of sweat and grime, his scent brought a brief breath of comfort, warming her fingertips. Speeding past them, the truck rocketed onto Lake Shore. Its headlights carved through the dark, illuminating the road, but not expanding far enough to reach them.

Nate waited a full minute, until the engine became a low drone in the distance, before creeping from their hiding place. In a second of weakness, Flynn almost grabbed him. She wished he would stay squashed next to her and absorb some of her loneliness. She wished he would hold her, like he had done after REDS's first terrorist attack at the Green Line concert.

How can so much change in just a matter of weeks? she asked herself.

"That's the fifth one today," he whispered. "It's getting harder to move around the city."

"There's not enough cover around here."

He stood slowly, then turned and offered her a hand. His ragged appearance mirrored her own. Hollow eyes buoyed by dark circles. Shaggy, unkempt hair. The bristles on his gaunt face had sprouted into a beard, darkened by lack of sun exposure. His skin had peeled and cracked, staining his lips with a rosy tint of fresh blood. She wrapped her fingers around his, allowing him to lift her to her feet. Even now he was handsome, a steadiness radiating from him that could never fade.

Please don't let go.

Dropping his hand to his side, he shifted his backpack and headed in the opposite direction of the truck.

"Nate..." Flynn stammered.

He looked back at her, his chin kissing his shoulder. "Yeah?"

She held her breath, summoning the courage to spill all the things she'd practiced saying to him over and over again. Except the words wouldn't come. They lingered on her tongue, refusing to emerge. Once again, she couldn't tell him the truth, her fear mutilating her ability to speak.

"Never mind."

His gaze dropped to the cracked pavement before he continued walking. Sighing, she followed, her legs wavering like a paper plane caught in a wind tunnel. Exhaustion seeped into every muscle fiber. Her sleep had been restless night after night, never bringing any relief. She feared it more than waking moments, terrified of what would spring out at her after she closed her eyes. She couldn't control her dreams. Relentless demons would appear when she finally drifted off, reminding her of what she'd done—reminding her she had to wake again tomorrow. And when she did, she was always alone.

4

FLYNN

Flynn and Nate checked both directions before pushing open the battered door of the old jazz club off Broadway. An hour of panicked skirting through alleys had brought them back up north to the Lakeview neighborhood. Looping, cursive letters scrawled on the marquee outside announced the abandoned venue's historic name, The Green Mill Cocktail Lounge. It had once lit up in a bright neon exclamation, but now the bulbs, void of light, blended into the backboard. Propped against a dimming sky, the words were nearly illegible.

A lanky man with square wire glasses leapt from one of the shadowed booths set into the wall. The barrel of his gun jumped back and forth between their foreheads.

"Antonio." Nate's hands flew into the air. "It's just us."

Antonio lowered his handgun when he recognized them. "Sorry 'bout that. I can't see shit in here. Any luck?" He nodded toward their gas jugs.

"Barely." Nate held up the weightless can, placing it on the chipped table. His shoulders drooped as if his arms were weighted by an anchor. "We're going to have to start pushing out even farther."

"Man," Antonio sighed. "We're running outta options. It's gettin' too risky. REDS trucks roll by here almost every hour."

"Yeah, we had to dodge a few too. Did Kerri have any luck with the weapon search?" Nate asked.

Antonio buffed his head with an agitated palm, poking up his coarse hair that had grown longer over the past few weeks. "Nope, nothin'."

Nate's mouth twitched. "Where is she?"

"Downstairs. Hopin' for some better news from you two."

"Well...today's not the day."

Positioned at the back of the dark room, a stage sat slightly above them, looking down forlornly. Now covered with stacked chairs, a tilting piano with one caster missing, and a drum kit without cymbals, it was smaller than Flynn remembered from the few times she'd visited with her parents when The Green Mill was still a functioning club. Her father loved jazz. When he'd come up to take her out in Chicago, they'd grab Chinese next door and then swing by for classic Manhattans, martinis, and live music. The room had once vibrated with life, jammed with people sitting around circular tables on the platform's perimeter or stuffed into booths crammed against the walls. Now, although still adorned in ornate framing, the stage no longer held the same impressive allure. A jolt ripped through Flynn, like ice pressed against a tooth's exposed nerve, at the thought of her family. She hadn't been able to get ahold of them since the grid collapsed.

Squeezing behind the wooden bar, Flynn and Nate shuffled sideways to reach a narrow trapdoor overshadowed by shelves of booze. Nate stooped and rapped a knuckle once on the doorframe's upper left corner and once on the lower right corner. It cracked open, revealing a man with a wide face squinting up at them, an AK-47 lodged against his shoulder.

"Just us, Vic," Nate said.

"Nate. We've been waiting." Vic peered around Nate. Catching sight of Flynn, he tilted his chin in greeting. "C'mon. Kerri's in the control center." Tugging at a grungy bandana wrapped around his tree-trunk neck, he pressed his body against the wall so they could descend the steep staircase.

Flynn and Nate inched past, down into a basement serving as the mouth to a network of underground tunnels. The resistance, now self-proclaimed as the Allies, had set up camp underground to avoid REDS's detection. The title seemed an appropriate homage to the WWII soldiers who'd fought and overthrown the Nazi regime. Originally, the tunnels were created to transport coal to the mill's boilers, until Al Capone's gangster outfit converted them into smuggling routes during Prohibition. This jazz club had been one of the notorious mob leader's favorite spots.

Flynn held her breath. She hated it down there. The stale air, the flickering fluorescent lights, the sound of the moaning, ancient generator. She swore the claustrophobic closet rooms and squat ceilings made her nightmares worse. Unable to escape the sensation that she was trapped, she wondered at times if she was going crazy—trapped in her own mind, trapped in the confines of four walls threatening to crush her at any second.

Battery-operated lanterns and colored chalk guided them through the passageways. All around them were stained concrete, rust-frosted pipes suspended along the walls by worn leather straps, and old knob-and-tube wiring held by porcelain insulators strung inches above their heads. Interspersed doors led to cramped rooms lined with cots and sleeping bags.

Stepping through a gaping hole in a demolished brick wall, they entered the basement of a neighboring abandoned mid-rise apartment building. A long time ago, during new construction, workers had sealed off some of the tunnels, but the Allies broke through in order to convert the large space into a control center. Flynn and Nate wove through the lines of other refugees awaiting their evening rations. The familiar, nutty smell of peanut butter reminded Flynn of a school cafeteria.

In the back corner, a short, curvy Scottish woman bent over a too-small chess table, a map of the city pinned to its surface. Kerri, the Allies' chosen leader, looked up as they approached. Oval green eyes dominated her pale face. Despite her miniature form, her presence filled the room, drawing people to her with magnetic force.

"Tell me you managed to squeeze out a few liters." Their grim frowns provided an answer. "Bloody hell," she muttered. Striking a fist on the table, her chin dropped to her chest. "We're dangerously low on supplies—food, gas, water, ammunition, medicine. We don't stand a chance against REDS without the basics."

"We can try tagging one of REDS's trucks...see where it goes," Nate suggested. "Trace them back to their headquarters. Once we figure out where they're based, we can plan a raid."

"They're no longer in one location. They've set up far too many stations. Hospitals, power plants. They just secured the water management plant." She slashed another giant X onto the map with a plastic marker before tossing it with a flick of her wrist. It skidded across the table, teetered on its edge, then fell to the floor. "At this rate, we're nothing more than a tick on a dog's arse."

"We can head back to the neighborhoods. Try and recruit more people. They might have resources they'd be willing to share," Nate said.

Kerri's cropped, dark red hair swished across her forehead. She tugged at a small silver pendant of a Scottish thistle clasped around her neck. "Too dangerous with REDS patrolling everywhere. Anyway...it's not enough. REDS propaganda is penetrating too deep. Their inside moles are spreading lies about the government. We can't risk exposing ourselves when we don't even know who's working for them. If word got back to REDS about us, they'd sniff us out and shut down our operation before we could blink."

Propaganda. An invisible shudder quivered through Flynn's bones. The seeds of misinformation REDS had planted were deadlier than a direct wound, spreading like an infection. They'd fabricated and twisted lies about the government, positioning the system as deceitful, corrupt, and intent on maintaining control over the public. REDS weaved stories about how the government had purposefully used Chicago tax money to house weapons of mass destruction without consent of the city's constituents. They distributed fliers, blasted from radio stations, and disseminated fake news articles about how elections had been rigged and manipulated. The citizens of Chicago—and likely beyond—didn't know what to believe anymore. Truth blurred and bent, a self-serving weapon both sides wielded with opaque motives. The longer the military took to interfere, the faster trust in the government's capabilities eroded, fueling doubt. Doubt, piled with layers of uncontrollable fear.

"I have an idea," Flynn said cautiously. Lately, she had remained stoic and aloof, silent unless spoken to. She'd been too worried about drawing attention to herself. She was the reason behind all of their pain, after all. But their desperation grew with each passing day.

Kerri eyed her with interest. "We're open to anything at this point."

"We've tried east, west, and north. There's still pockets we can scavenge, but we haven't gone far south."

Kerri's attention returned to the map. "We've discussed this. South is too unpredictable. Not to mention bloody dangerous. We can't risk the small numbers we have."

"Time is running out," Flynn pressed. "It's the area with the lightest REDS coverage, you've said so yourself. I know a guy there who trafficked guns. I bought one from him to…" She choked, unable to finish her sentence. Nate's expression soured.

Kerri studied her, brows high with intrigue. "*You* know a guy who trafficked guns?"

"Yes." Flynn ironed her lips shut.

Kerri's eyes narrowed, as if she possessed some superpower that allowed her to see straight into Flynn's thoughts. "I expect there's a story there… Regardless, no chance he has any left?"

Flynn shrugged. "Maybe. Maybe not. He could connect us to some of his clients."

"His clients are gangs and drug lords," Nate interjected.

"It's gangs or REDS at this point," Flynn argued back. "Let's be honest with ourselves, they know more about guerilla warfare than any of us. Might be worth seeing if we can form some kind of alliance…or, I dunno, a partnership."

"A partnership?" Nate balked. Glowering, he leaned his weight forward, kneading his knuckles into the chess table. "Chicago is the most dangerous city in the country because of these gangs. They're not interested in an *alliance*."

"Okay, fine, maybe not an alliance. An agreement. There is no way their business hasn't suffered. They're probably the only ones left out there who have a large network with the manpower we need, let alone the gunpower."

"I know you have a soft spot for scum of the earth, but I would've thought you'd have learned your lesson on that by now," Nate said, his eyes steely.

Flynn's head jerked back, the unexpected blow a powerful one. Salty tears blistered her lids. She opened her mouth to respond, but he had knocked the wind out of her.

Kerri rubbed her chin, glancing back and forth between them. "It's not a bad idea," she said, doing her best to diffuse the explosive tension. "I read the CPD used to form coalitions with gangs to stop some of the intergang violence."

Flynn tried to recover, but her breath continued releasing in short bursts, as if Nate had cracked open her ribcage and yanked her lungs straight from her chest.

Nate straightened, his reproachful glare softening. "Alright, look, maybe I went too far."

Still reeling, Flynn strode toward him. "Fuck you, Nate. You have no idea, *no* idea what I've lived through. No idea what I now have to live with." Before she could stop herself, her hand swung through the air, smacking him across the face. Red fingerprints instantly sprouted across his cheek. Palm tingling, she spun on her heel and marched from the room before she could see beyond his stunned expression. Although it was cruel, deep down a small part of her hoped the sting lingered.

5

WOLF

The Ferris wheel loomed over Wolf and Spider as they sped down Navy Pier. Without its obnoxious flashing lights, its thin spokes and swinging bucket seats appeared skeletal, like a mounted prehistoric fossil. Once the largest wharf in the world, Navy Pier had since devolved into the most frequented tourist trap in Chicago, lined with tacky restaurants stacked on top of each other, cheesy rides, and booths offering greasy fried food. Chicago's Children's Museum greeted visitors upon their arrival to the pier, but now empty, it adopted a menacing disposition. Panes of glass from its impressive arched entry were shattered or missing, and giant letters from the NAVY PIER welcome sign hung in crooked defeat.

Ten Pinzgauer trucks manned by armed guards spanned the width of the strip, blocking access to a building at the end of the long pier. Pincer-like steeples flagged either side of the building's enormous green domed roof. As they approached, Spider slowed, their engine idling. Shuttered concession stands, interspersed between the vehicles, were nothing more than hunched huts battered by the fierce Lake Michigan gale.

"Stand down. Spider and Wolf confirmed," a voice crackled through the radio in Wolf and Spider's Humvee. Invisible snipers, embedded in hidden positions, observed their every move.

Two of the trucks revved backward, creating an opening in the barricade. Spider pressed on the gas, accelerating past.

Wolf glanced at his leader. Spider's profile, as always, was stoic. Wolf had practiced mimicking his mentor's cold, impenetrable demeanor for a long time. One of these days he would master it. "Spider, permission to rejoin council meetings?"

Wolf gripped the handle above the passenger window, less for stability than to calm the nerves jittering about his abdomen. Spider whipped the car around at the end of the pier, slammed on the brake, and yanked the gear into park. He switched off the ignition. Silence stretched between them, creating an abyss as wide as the infinite lake behind them. Wolf had asked permission to reclaim his position on the Executive Committee every day for the past week. Despite Spider's doubts, he was still fully invested in their mission. He'd come too far and sacrificed too much to sever it from his identity. It was all he had left.

"No," Spider finally said. "You're not ready."

Disappointment shot through Wolf, torching his insides. "What else do I need to do to prove myself?"

"You've already proven yourself. You proved yourself when you couldn't kill the woman. Both women, in fact. We made a deal, and you didn't uphold your end of the agreement." Spider swung open the door, ushering in a surge of cold air. Torn flags whipped and snapped in the winds blowing over the lake. "You've changed, Wolf."

Wolf sighed. Spider had a pulse on everything and everyone, down to the smallest subtlety of a whispering breeze changing direction. Wolf was convinced Spider knew him better than he knew himself. He had imagined watching Chicago fall since he joined REDS a decade ago, and it had been every bit as gratifying as he'd hoped. Except, an emptiness spread around the bullet hole that had barely missed his heart, and Spider sensed it. Flynn had saved him. Even after she thought he'd killed her best friend, she hadn't let Nate shoot him.

"I still want the same things." Wolf's voice rose, fighting the gusts pummeling his ears. "REDS's mission is still *my* mission."

"You know what you need to do." Spider leapt from his seat, slamming the door behind him. Hungry waves crashed up over the retaining walls, reaching for him before retreating to try their pursuit again.

Wolf's stomach clenched, and he swallowed hard to prevent acid from rising up his throat.

Kill Flynn.

Fumbling out of the truck with his wounded arm, he followed Spider past guards stationed in front of the building camouflaging the Missile Launch Command and Control Center. It was laughable really, and maybe a tad brilliant—locating a nuclear command center below the biggest tourist attraction in the Midwest. No one ever would have guessed the American government would be so reckless, or strategic, with countless citizens' lives. A tiny part of him he'd never acknowledge felt bitter and resentful toward Spider for not sharing this piece of critical intel with him earlier.

"I have no idea where she is," Wolf said, tailing Spider into the building. "I'll never see her again. I got us access to the nukes. I've promised to make it up to you—to REDS—whatever it takes."

"You should have killed her when you had the chance." Spider made a sharp left, entering a stairwell with a sign marked NO ENTRY, RESTRICTED ACCESS. "It's never women. Never women who shoot up a school or rob a bank. Never women who blow up a movie theater." He swung around so they were practically nose to nose, spittle flying from his lips. "It's not that they aren't capable. No. *Men* underestimate them. Women have never been allowed into REDS, not because they don't possess the power, but because they can't be controlled. They're too unpredictable. They manipulate and destroy people. They know how to make you suffer. She used you." His eyes lasered into Wolf's, his pupils tiny pricks of black. "She. Won."

"She didn't win. I still took down this entire city's power source."

"She turned you against me!" Spider's voice echoed off the thick concrete walls. Wolf could see Spider's chest rising and falling in shallow bursts.

Wolf resisted the urge to cringe. He almost backed down, almost conceded, until unexpected anger flared inside him, an abused dog finally mustering the courage to fight back.

Fuck this.

"REDS wouldn't be in this position if it weren't for me!" Wolf shouted.

"I formulated the mission targeting the electrical grid. I infiltrated Magnetic. I created the malware responsible for overpowering its network." Wolf jabbed his index finger into Spider's chest. It jammed into hard bone. "*You* were the one who chose me to be your successor. *You* were the one who told me overcoming my weaknesses would make me stronger."

An invisible hand wiped Spider's face clean of fury. He straightened, scrutinizing Wolf for several moments. After a long pause, he exhaled. "Wolf." His voice dropped. "There's something I need to tell you." He turned and continued down the staircase. "About your past...about how we found you."

"What?" Wolf startled, unable to mask his surprise at their conversation's abrupt switch in direction. His grip slid along the metal railing, his palm suddenly humid. "What do you mean? You were the one who found me."

Spider descended each stair with slow, deliberate steps. "I've debated telling you for a long time now. I almost did after you attacked me to save that bitch. But I wanted to see what decision you'd make on your own." He stopped and glanced over his shoulder, his gaze resting on Wolf. His eyes were misty, lost in some memory. "My fear is you'll make the same mistakes as those who came before you if you don't know the truth about where you came from."

"Where I came from?" Wolf blinked, otherwise paralyzed. It was as if he had become mute, his brain unable to process words. He didn't have a story other than REDS. That was the point. He'd eliminated his past during the Naming Ceremony when he'd melted his fingerprints into the coals. "Why does that matter?"

"It matters because your father founded REDS."

6

WOLF

Spider's face and the stairwell around him blurred into a mass of gray. Wolf swayed and, for a brief moment, thought he might fall, face first, down the remaining concrete steps.

My father?

He had never thought those words applied to him. Never said them out loud, as far as he could remember, or even in his own mind. He'd never cared about who he came from. What good would that have done? It sure as hell hadn't done jack shit for him growing up.

A straitjacket squeezed his chest, constricting tighter and tighter until it hurt to breathe. He stumbled forward, his legs no longer able to support the full weight of his body. A part of him didn't want to hear what Spider had to say. It would be easier not knowing, because knowing would irrevocably change everything.

"It was your father who found me that freezing winter day I almost died. The one I told you about a few weeks ago." Wolf couldn't focus on what Spider was telling him. His voice sounded garbled, as though Wolf were listening to him speak while underwater. "As you might remember, I had just lost the last person I loved in this fucked up world. I was only twenty. Had nowhere to go. Your father...he saved me."

Feverish waves of nausea crashed over Wolf. His skin burned hot, followed by icy chills stampeding up his arms.

"Your father founded REDS when he was only eighteen. Not much older than you were when I recruited you. He left home when he became a legal adult. His father was an abusive drunk and his mother abandoned them when he was young, leaving him to fend for himself. He had no family. No money. No future. So, he built his own." Spider leaned against the wall and massaged his wide jaw with a thumb and forefinger. In the dim, shadowed light he appeared older, and it struck Wolf that he'd never wondered about Spider's age until this moment. The only signs of years passing had been razor-thin crow's feet splaying further from the corners of his eyes and specks of gray spattered through his cropped hair.

"His following grew large quickly," Spider continued. "So quick he needed to establish a headquarters, which is when he took over the church. A few years later, he found me." Spider stared at his boots, avoiding Wolf's gaze. "I became his most trusted advisor. Over the next several years, we grew REDS together. Your father at the helm, and me, recruiting new members into our ranks. Until it eventually came to an end."

Spider crossed his arms over his chest and withdrew into himself. Wolf waited for him to continue, but he didn't.

"Why?" Wolf pressed. Spider's head snapped up as though he'd forgotten Wolf was there. "Why did it come to an end?"

Something behind Spider's eyes shuttered closed and his demeanor hardened. "Your father met a woman. He fell in love." He spat the word "love" as if it were venom. Straightening, he watched for Wolf's reaction. "She became pregnant with you, and once you were born, it changed everything. For a few years he hid you, but as you got older it became clear he could no longer lead a double life. He tried to leave REDS. Go into hiding. Even though *he* had made the rule that members can never leave REDS after joining. I warned him, risked everything to warn him, but it was too late. The Executive Committee tracked him down. They killed him." Shock waves pulsed through Wolf. His hands began to tremble uncontrollably. "They went after your mother as well. That's why she fled. She knew they would inevitably track her down and kill her too. So, she left you where no one would find you. Except I did. Before he died, I promised your father I would do whatever I could to protect you. I promised I'd repay him for saving me. I owed him, you see. He transformed me into someone I never knew I could be." Spider finally met Wolf's stare. "Over the next fifteen years, I watched you, waiting. Waiting for the moment when I could do the same for you."

Wolf's fingers curled into tight fists and his nostrils flared like a snorting bull's. He'd been trained for years not to feel. REDS had branded that deep into his psyche while simultaneously destroying his past identity. But this blow almost brought him to his knees. He hadn't been abandoned. He'd been wanted. His mother had been trying to save him.

"Why are you telling me this now?" Wolf whispered. "After all these years?"

"No one within REDS knows about your father or your background. I didn't want to draw any negative attention or skepticism to your loyalty. Your father's mistakes are his own, and I know he would have wanted you to become one of us. It's what he would have chosen if he could've gone back and done it over."

Rather than reassuring him, Spider's words fanned the sparks of doubt that had exploded inside his mind over the past few months. "How did you...?" Wolf paused, forcing himself to exhale the pressure compacted in his chest. "How did you reconcile with the fact that REDS killed him? Your best friend. The person who saved you."

Spider raised an eyebrow. "You slit your best friend's throat too, did you not?" Wolf opened his mouth and then closed it, unable to speak. His neck flushed. "We all have to make choices. I didn't have you killed after you attacked me because I knew that wasn't *you*. Just like I knew that wasn't really your father at the very end. Your mother made him weak. She corrupted him." Spider yanked open a door leading to a dark hallway. "Don't make the same decision, Wolf. Kill the girl, before she gets you killed."

7

FLYNN

Flynn shoved her head under the thin sack she'd been using as a pillow. A whisper of relief trickled through her. It had felt good to speak up, to finally *say* something. That slap had been the manifestation of the voice she longed for, the disgust she held toward herself, the silent pain she carried.

She'd wanted Nate to feel its barbed sting, even for a brief moment.

Ugh, what is wrong with me? she thought to herself, groaning. *I'm such a freaking bitch.*

"Hey." From beneath her burrow, Flynn craned her neck, peering over her shoulder. Framed in the doorway, Nate's silhouette blocked the hallway's weak light from entering her cramped sleeping quarters. She hadn't expected him to follow after she'd run off like that. "Mind if I come in?" he asked.

"Sure," she muttered, pushing herself into a seated position. She crossed her legs, reconsidered, then settled on pulling her knobby knees to her chest.

He sat on the edge of her cot. Its old springs crunched and squeaked under his weight. "Look, I'm sorry. I shouldn't have said what I did. I deserved that."

Her handprint glowed red on his cheek. She wrapped her arms around her shins and squeezed. "No, I'm sorry. I don't know what came over me."

Familiar silence hovered over the invisible rift dividing them. Flynn examined the thin scars branded across her palms, her guilt always within sight. She wished she could transfer all the thoughts and emotions she couldn't articulate into Nate. Then maybe he would understand. Better yet, maybe he would be able to interpret them back to her. He was always better at that than she was.

"Are we ever going to be friends again?" she asked. "Is this...secret always going to be there?"

Rubbing his forehead, Nate propped an elbow on his knee. He seemed to have aged ten years over the past few weeks. "I don't know how to get over this, or through this, or even around this. I feel like I don't even know who you are anymore."

Nodding, she leaned back against the concrete wall. A damp chill slithered through her thin jacket, making her shiver. "That's fair. I'm not sure I know who I am anymore either, to be honest. I just...I'm in constant energy-save mode, you know? I'm always running on empty. It takes everything I've got to keep moving forward, to put one foot in front of the other. And if I even start to think about—" She gulped, unable to say Cori's name. An ember of guilt burned deep within her stomach. "I didn't know what else to do," she croaked, her voice hoarse.

"Flynn, I did everything in my power to be there for you, and you pushed me away. I couldn't reach you." Nate angled his chin toward her but couldn't meet her eyes. "I still can't."

"I didn't have a choice. Wolf almost killed you. What was I supposed to do? I would do anything to keep you safe. To keep—" She choked again, her vocal cords still refusing to form Cori's name. "I know I failed." Tears spilled down her cheeks, but she couldn't feel them. Her face was numb. "Don't you think I know that now? Don't you think I know it's all my fault she's dead? I sacrificed *everything* and look where it got me. I still failed."

Her breathing raced, jumbling alongside her erratic heartbeat. Right when she thought the pain couldn't pierce any deeper, a thousand shards shot through another layer of her skin. Her shoulders trembled.

Nate studied her. His jaw, clenched into a rigid line, loosened. "Look, no one has been through what you went through. No one can possibly know what they would have done in your shoes." He hesitated before shifting closer, guiding her into a tight embrace. "It's not your fault," he breathed into her shoulder. "This would have happened with or without you."

Sagging against him, she succumbed to an overpowering release. The tears kept coming, an endless stream of agony departing her body. Nate pulled back slightly and reached a hand toward her face. Brushing a thumb up her wet cheekbone, he glided it over her brows and down the length of her nose. Flynn followed the intensity of his stare, absorbing her features as if she might disappear without warning. She sat perfectly still, afraid to move, afraid to break the spell. The warmth of his fingers thawed a thick shell of ice that had hardened around her body. They lingered and then stopped on the upper tip of the scar that stretched over her collarbone, visible from the scooped neck of her shirt. She suppressed a shudder at the memory of how she'd gotten it—how she'd walked away from that attack on the Chicago Loop intact, unlike so many others. She placed a hand over his, resting it against her chest, squeezing as she tried to forget the exploded limbs raining down around them.

"I didn't want to leave you in the dark," she whispered, the salt from her tears stinging her chapped lips. Lifting her jacket, she wiped her face with the inside mesh fabric. "I wanted to tell you everything, to not be alone. I missed you."

"I know it wasn't easy. Or simple."

"I should've known I couldn't stop them. REDS, I mean. Fear...it paralyzed me. But I'm not afraid anymore." The air crackled between them, alive. "I know now nothing could have prepared me for this. Being on the other side of grief has changed me. I can't run from it. I can't hide from it. The only way to survive is to face it." She swallowed. "Face who I've become."

Nate's lips twitched into a hint of a smile. "My mom always used to tell me, sometimes when you're stuck, the only thing to do is to just sit in it."

"Sit in it?"

"Yeah. Stop resisting and just let it be."

"Let it be," Flynn repeated, cementing the mantra in her mind. She had to accept that broken was her new normal. That she would probably never fully heal.

She suddenly felt exhausted. How much of her energy had been depleted by trying to resist certain emotions, she wondered. She'd dug her heels in for so long, refusing to be dragged into an endless pit of despair, terrified that if she even acknowledged this pain, she'd lose herself in it forever. Except maybe it wasn't an endless pit. Maybe living through the pain was the only way to rediscover herself.

She scooted down on the cot, patting the narrow space beside her. Nate wrapped his arms around her body, tucking her close to his chest. "You think there's hope for me?" she asked.

His breath rustled her hair. "There's always hope."

Closing her eyes, she relaxed into his warmth, coiling her fists into his shirt. That way he could never leave her again.

8

WOLF

Alone in the stairwell, Wolf struggled to absorb Spider's lingering confession. At first, he'd felt shock, until the words gored deeper, piercing to his core. He'd lived his entire life thinking he'd been abandoned by both his mother and his father, like a defective toy neither were interested in. He'd had no idea his parents were taken from him by the very people he now considered his family. A million conflicting emotions boiled in his gut, fierce and devastating.

Ripping open the door, he careened into the hallway, head spinning. Spider had disappeared into a room with the remainder of the Executive Committee. Wolf choked back the yell of rage threatening to burst through his throat. He'd never been shut out from REDS, isolated like some recidivate inmate. Now, he had no one.

He was alone.

Blinded, he staggered into a small mess hall where the Executive Committee gathered for meals and grabbed the first thing he came into contact with—a metal folding chair. Using his uninjured arm, he arced it over his head and slammed it onto a nearby table. The crash shook his eardrums, but it didn't drown out Spider's voice.

Your mother made him weak. She corrupted him. Don't make the same decision, Wolf. Kill the girl, before she gets you killed.

Hurling the chair across the room, he lunged forward, curling his fingers under the table's lip, and flipped it onto its side. He then proceeded to kick it over and over and over again. The flimsy metal groaned, buckling into a deep dent around the toe of his boot. He couldn't remember his father. He'd never tried to. And all he had of his mother was the one recurring dream, where it seemed she was trying to tell him the truth about what had happened to her after all this time. He closed his eyes, straining to remember a face or voice... anything of the man his father was. Delving deep into the back of his mind, to the very start of his childhood, he searched. His old stuffed animal, Bear, had been his one link to his past, and now that too was gone. He'd burned it.

Moments in time blurred together, and despite how he tried to sharpen the lines of his watercolor memory, he couldn't separate them.

"Wolf."

Doubled over, he staggered around, gasping for air. Weasel, REDS's Executive Director of Operations, stood in the mess hall entryway, beady eyes impassive. One of the eldest and most senior members in the organization, Weasel helped oversee REDS's most critical missions.

"Wolf," Weasel repeated. "We need you in this meeting."

"What?" Wolf straightened, wiping away a fresh line of sweat coating his brow. He rotated his bad shoulder, wincing. "What for?"

"Spider requested you join us." Weasel lowered his chin, gazing at him down his crooked nose. His face remained blank, making it impossible for Wolf to tell whether he agreed with the decision or not. "Come with me."

Wolf adjusted his jacket, attempting to quiet his ragged breathing by inhaling deeply through his nose. Smoothing back his hair, he followed Weasel down the hall to a heavy steel door. Beyond it, they entered a dim chamber where the committee greeted them with silent stares from around a long rectangular table. Spider sat at the head, his soft smile illuminated under the fluorescent lights. Shadows were stamped in the hollows beneath his eyes, giving him the appearance of a ghoulish phantom.

"Wolf, thank you for joining us. We've felt your absence deeply over the past few weeks." Spider leaned back in his chair and surveyed the Executive Committee.

Tiger sat to the right of him, a seat Wolf had once occupied. Tiger's upper lip curled, the red puckered scars running down the length of his face distorting his sneer. Tiger had been the one to take him and Flynn into REDS's custody after his attack on a downtown electrical substation. It had been during the test phase of Wolf's mission, before they targeted the entire city's electrical grid. He calmed himself with the thought of wrapping his fingers around Tiger's throat and squeezing.

"We've discussed and voted," Spider continued. "We agreed to reconsider your position among us. Contingent, of course, upon your behavior and loyalty."

Wolf still reeled from their life-altering conversation in the stairwell. The lingering shock waves left him unbalanced. Yet the way Spider spoke now, it was as though their earlier conversation never happened.

"My loyalty is to you, Spider," he finally said. "You and REDS."

"Earlier this year I announced you as my successor. Then you embarrassed me. Disappointed me. Defied me in front of the entire organization. However..." He paused. Wolf lowered his eyes, bracing himself. Perspiration stuck the collar of his shirt to his skin. "We wouldn't be here if it weren't for you. I know that. We all know that. You have much to learn. But we also still have much to learn from you."

Wolf raised his gaze. He tried to open his mouth to speak, but his jaw had locked shut. For a brief moment, Spider's empty expression faltered, exposing a glimmer of pain only Wolf could see. But then it was gone, so quickly Wolf wondered if he'd imagined it. His stomach sank. He knew why they'd finally allowed him back into the fold. There had been a moment back in Flynn's room when she had urged Wolf to leave REDS forever.

He's clearly only using you to execute his plans, she had said about Spider.

He'd denied it, of course. Accused her of using him too, which is exactly what she'd been doing—taking advantage of his undeniable attraction to her. But suddenly, it became crystal clear. She'd been right all along. The only reason Spider still hadn't killed him was because he had more to extract from him.

Wolf nodded once. "I won't disappoint you. I'm ready to prove myself. Let me show you what I'm really capable of."

Spider laughed and his white teeth shone. The sound reverberated throughout the room. Tiger shifted in his seat.

"You wouldn't be standing here if I didn't already know what you're capable of." Smirking, Spider tapped the tips of his long fingers together. "I have a new project in mind for you. Something you've never done before. A ransomware I'd like you to develop. It's exactly what we need to win the rest of the country's support." He glanced at Tiger. "But first, we received some information recently that might be of interest to you. We have reason to believe your old *fling* joined a little underground organization."

Flynn. Wolf hadn't heard from her. No surprise there. He hadn't expected to—she did still believe he killed her best friend, after all. She also had no means of contacting him.

"Yes," Spider continued, studying Wolf closely, clearly searching for some sort of emotional response. "A sad rag-tag crew that's been attempting to practice guerilla warfare tactics on us. Apparently, they're referring to themselves as the Allies. Quite symbolic." Spider's smirk melted. "Find her. Find them. You will not rest until you kill every single one of them. If you want to be my successor, then prove it."

He'd hoped Flynn had left the city when she fled her apartment. He'd hoped she'd heeded his warning. He should have known better.

Fucking hell.

"I look forward to it, Spider."

"Good. Tiger has volunteered to assist you. Just to make sure no one is left behind. We detained one of their runners carrying communication over the city line. They haven't talked...at least not yet." Spider grinned in the way he only did when he talked about torture. "In the meantime, allow me to introduce our guest." He nodded toward the back of the room. Two guards flanked a thin man with gouged cheekbones and a sickly gray complexion. Wolf hadn't even noticed them when he first arrived. "This is Dr. Warbler, a nuclear scientist from the Department of Homeland Security's very own FEMA. Krammer connected us. You might've heard me or Hyena mention him, but Dr. Warbler has been a critical asset, passing along information about how to operate the arsenal."

Dr. Warbler dipped his chin in acknowledgement. "It's been an honor."

"He's also agreed to help us during our little chat with the president today," Spider said. "It's time we remind him who has their finger on the trigger."

"How can I help?" Wolf asked.

"We want to record the conversation and air it during tomorrow's pep rally. After we tweak it a bit, of course. You can save it for your ransomware purposes as well. Krammer gave us a heads-up, the president ordered a series of airstrikes throughout the city. Can you believe it? Against his own helpless citizens." Spider stood, walking to a map of Chicago tacked against the wall. Large circles signified REDS strongholds.

"He would risk that?" Weasel asked. "When he knows we could retaliate with his very own nuclear warheads?"

"He's testing us. He'll try to position it as an attempt to flush us out, but how will he be able to defend his motives when he knows we've been occupying public spaces? Hospitals. Schools. Government buildings. All with a huge number of hostages. We knew it would come to this. All we had to do was wait." Spreading his arms wide, Spider faced them. "And who will be there to greet the people of Chicago with open arms when they hear their government has turned against them? Sacrificing them like lambs to the slaughter?"

9

FLYNN

When Flynn jolted awake, Nate still had his arm locked around her. She had dreamt it belonged to Wolf, the crook of his elbow creeping up from her waist to squeeze like a noose around her neck. She turned over, her pulse racing. Every night Wolf haunted her, reminding her she'd let him live. Nate had gotten the perfect opportunity to shoot him, and she'd interfered. She doubted Nate would ever really understand why, and she wasn't sure if she would either, but at the time, it had seemed like showing mercy would allow Wolf to leave the world on his own terms. Killing him would've been letting him win; it would have proven he was right about the innate inability to show empathy toward someone so different from themselves. Maybe her act of mercy would prove to him that compassion will always triumph over hate. Or maybe she would regret it for the rest of her life.

Her digital watch read 5:05 a.m., the most consecutive hours she'd slept in weeks. She hadn't even remembered falling asleep. Struggling into a seated position, she moved slowly so as not to wake Nate. Cold from the concrete floor pierced through her socks. As her weight lifted from the mattress, rusty springs squealed in protest. Wincing, she glanced behind her, but Nate remained sound asleep.

She crept as quietly as she could to the old washroom next door. Built in the 1920s, it once served as an underground bathroom when The Green

Mill had operated as a jazz club. All that remained was a row of urinals lining the wall. Body wipes were the closest they got to showering. Once REDS cut off the fresh water supply, like everything else, it had become too precious a resource to waste on personal hygiene. A week into REDS's takeover, the Allies had tried to send SOS messages to the government transmitted via radio waves. The government responded, promising to smuggle in resources as aid. But REDS had been monitoring their communication and hijacked the supplies. Since then, it had been too risky to communicate with the outside world other than by sending runners with handwritten messages over the city line.

Flynn took off her jacket and began wiping her face, neck, and chest when Kerri shuffled into the dark, musty bathroom yawning. Purple circles ringed her swollen eyes.

"Mornin," she mumbled.

Embarrassed about yesterday's outburst, Flynn concentrated hard on scrubbing her bare forearm. "Morning."

"You know what I miss more than a scaldin' hot shower?" Kerri asked, yanking a wipe from the plastic container. "Coffee. Good coffee. Not that instant mince that tastes like piss."

"Mince?"

"Oh, you know, rubbish."

"Ahhh," Flynn laughed. "Couldn't agree more." Flynn eyed Kerri while she pressed the wet wipe to her face, leaving it there for several long seconds. "Um, Kerri, I want to apologize for storming off on you like that yesterday. I know the pressure we're under, and that, uh, wasn't the time to lose my cool."

Kerri dragged the tissue down the length of her nose and smiled. "No worries. We all have our breaking points, don't we?"

Flynn nodded, rubbing her collarbone. "Yeah. I guess we do."

"If I'm bein' honest, I've been waitin' for you to reach yers. It's like you've been in this daze, and outta nowhere, you came back down to Earth."

Flynn focused on a giant crack in the mirror across from her, doing her best to hold back tears. The glass was so frosted with age she could barely make out her reflection. Probably for the best.

A familiar feeling crept over her. One she couldn't seem to escape—one that felt like an invisible hand reaching up to drag her to the bottom of a lake. Sometimes she fought the feeling, trying to swim up toward the sun shimmering through the water's surface, struggling against heavy weights tied to her ankles. Other times she just let herself sink, the glimmer of light forever out of reach.

I miss you, Cori.

Kerri cleared her throat. "I did really like yer idea about pushing south. Think yer gun seller friend is still there?"

Relieved by the subject change, Flynn exhaled. "I wouldn't really call him a friend, but I think so. Unless he somehow got out. Can't hurt to at least try."

"Alright. Let's get a group together to pay him a visit. Better than sitting on our arses here. We'll see if he can arrange a meeting with some gang leaders in the area. If there are any left."

* * * *

Later that morning, Flynn, Nate, Kerri, Vic, and Antonio headed south. It was a long trek from Lakeview, and the days were getting shorter. They didn't have much time to get there and back. They darted back and forth between neighborhood streets and Lake Shore, avoiding REDS patrols. Low clouds clung to the lake's horizon like a distant, bulbous mountain range. Storefronts on once busy streets stared back at them with vacant expressions. Shadowed mannequins loomed in boutique windows, suddenly menacing in their abandonment.

She used to think fall happened in Chicago overnight, with trees erupting in simultaneous explosions of color, but she now realized she just never noticed the leaves' gradual lightening before, turning yellow one by one. Without the usual distractions of the electric city, it struck Flynn how vivid and clear her senses felt, like someone newly sober seeing the world through clean eyes. For several days after they lost cell phone service, her fingers had itched, tapping her phone screen, searching for text messages or social media notifications or some quick hit of gratification. Now she had no choice but to notice how the air tasted different, how the old ambient sounds of the city had been replaced by silence. Instead of a train's rumble echoing off buildings, only birds' trills punctuated the eerie quiet, singing to each other the season's last songs before retreating south for the winter.

They eventually reached the decrepit barbershop by early afternoon. The same one she'd visited a few months earlier to illegally buy a gun. She'd planned to use it to kill Wolf, to prove to him she had it in her to murder someone as evil as him. But he'd been right about her all along: she hadn't been able to pull the trigger.

Twice, his quiet voice whispered into her ear.

Antonio pounded his fist against the door's rotting wood while Vic stood guard, vigilantly surveying the area. No one answered. Wiggling the knob, he glanced back at them. "Locked. Should we bust in?"

"Not really the best way to win someone over," Kerri muttered.

"Let's try the back," Vic said. He signaled to the group after checking the coast was clear, and they circled around back, skirting down an alley directly behind the shop. Without the loud drone of cars zooming along the nearby highway, their shoes skimming over fallen leaves sounded dangerously pronounced. Flynn ducked beneath a small window covered in plywood and inched toward Mike's tiny porch. The group flanked her, their eyes and guns scanning the perimeter.

Flynn knocked on a cracked storm door. "Mike," she hissed. "Mike. I've been here before. I'm a customer. We're looking to do some business."

A tiny hole appeared in one of the boards. A dark pupil blinked at them once before disappearing.

"Mike." She rapped the glass again. "We're here to talk. Please. Give us a few seconds, that's all."

Mike cracked open the door, peered out at her. The whites of his eyes were all she could make out. "Who the hell are you, and how'd you know my name?"

"I-I came here a few months ago," Flynn stammered. "Bought a gun off you."

He squinted at her for several long seconds until, slowly, recognition crossed his face. "Hm. Yeah, I remember. Don't often see the likes of you 'round here. Lady, what're you doin' back?" He nodded to her entourage, guns still raised. "Looks like your friends got plenty o' heat."

"Long story. Can we come in? I'll explain inside."

"Hell no." Mike lifted his chin in Vic, Antonio, and Nate's direction. "Ain't no one comin' in here with one of those."

Kerri holstered her handgun at her waist and slowly raised her arms, facing her palms in Mike's direction. "Guys, you heard 'em. Stay out here. Keep watch."

Vic shifted, clearly uncomfortable with this order, but didn't object. Mike shook his head, letting out a low whistle before stepping back. Flynn and Kerri edged into the kitchen, filling the cramped space quickly. Mike towered above them, dressed in the same enormous suspenders as when Flynn had seen him last. His reddish beard had grown into what looked like a fluffy bush stuck to his face, and his once corkscrew curls had loosened in tightness with their length.

Mike observed her, chewing on the stub of a wooden toothpick with his two yellowed front teeth. "World's gone to shit since I last saw ya."

Flynn nodded. She couldn't help but wonder if he'd just insinuated that she'd looked better. Well, he wasn't wrong. Her hair had seen better days.

"To say the least."

"You with REDS?" he asked.

"No. Are you?"

"Hell no, I'm not with those crazies."

Flynn smiled and immediately realized how foreign the expression felt. "Good to hear we're on the same side then. You have any guns left?"

He looked Flynn up and down, sizing her up before sighing. "Nah. Those went fast after the power went down."

Kerri swore under her breath. "Do you know where we can get more?"

Mike's attention shifted in her direction. "I might." He shoved his hands deep into his suspender pockets, rocking back and forth on the balls of his feet. "What's it to you?"

"We're part of an underground resistance. We call ourselves the Allies and we want to take REDS down, but we need more manpower and fire-power. Clearly that's not easy to come by at the moment, so we were hoping you would introduce us to any gang networks you might have connections to," Kerri said.

He snorted and shook his head. "I ain't no rat."

Kerri pursed her lips. Flynn could see her patience waning. "It wouldn't be *ratting* them out, mate," Kerri said. "We want to propose a partnership... in light of our current situation."

His eyes bulged. "Lady, these guys don't do partnerships."

"They might now that they don't have any clients or income. Hopefully, it could be mutually beneficial."

"Oh, yeah? Mutually beneficial or beneficial to *you*?" He crossed his arms. "What's it to them?"

"They want their territory back?" Kerri motioned outside to where the men stood waiting for them. "I'm assuming their livelihoods depend on it. We all want REDS gone, even if it's for different reasons. If we join forces, we could make that happen. Unless they plan on sitting around on their arses waiting 'til nothing's left."

Although her tiny form barely reached Mike's bicep, Kerri's brazen stare bore into him. He considered her, sucking on his toothpick nub. "Alright. Let's see what you got to offer. Tomorrow morning. Midway airfield. Between the terminals."

"Tomorrow?" Kerri glanced at Flynn, taken aback. "You can speak with them that fast?"

"Sure can."

"How do we know they'll even agree to meet with us?" Kerri pressed.

"They will."

His easy confidence exposed Mike's influence within the gang network was likely much stronger than Flynn had initially thought. Or, that the gangs were suffering more than he was letting on as a result of REDS's embargo on the city.

"Alright, then." Kerri scratched her head and glanced at Flynn. "We don't have time to make it all the way back to Lakeview before nightfall. Let's head toward Midway now. Camp around there tonight."

Flynn nodded and did her best to squelch the sinking sensation dragging her insides downward. She had no idea what Kerri hoped to offer local gangs in exchange for aid, they barely had more than the clothes on their backs. But at the very least, Kerri was a convincing salesperson, and that counted for something.

Mike pushed open the storm door to let them out. Their time had expired. A breeze drifted through the opening, cooling the kitchen, which had grown warm from their body heat. "Just don' get caught before then."

10

WOLF

Wolf surveyed the enormous crowd gathered before him, his pointer finger resting on the trigger of his AK-47. He stood next to a control panel, nestled in the back corner of a stage, waiting for Spider's signal to play the video they'd recorded yesterday. A giant screen rose behind him.

The grassy green in Millennium Park pavilion had previously served as an expansive picnic space for summer concerts. It was now jammed with people of all ages. REDS had spent the morning driving through streets, summoning people from their homes through loudspeakers, promising rations of food and supplies intercepted from government trucks. Although only a fraction of the city's surviving population had responded, Wolf was impressed with the turnout. They'd raised the bridges stretching over the Chicago River, isolating the downtown Loop like a fortress buffered by its moat. Krammer, along with another group of REDS led by Weasel, hosted a similar rally farther up north, for neighborhoods with residents who could no longer reach Millennium Park.

Spider materialized next to Wolf, watching the mass of bodies multiply. "Not bad."

Wolf tensed and nodded, hyperaware of Spider's closeness. "Not bad at all."

"Only a matter of time before the remainders get desperate. Can't last much longer without food or water."

"Government air strikes will shake 'em out. They'll regret not coming around sooner."

"Yes. Yes, they will." Spider pointed to a group of REDS occupying the small section of tiered seating curved in front of the stage. "Remember, Wolf, redemption for the oppressed," he recited from their manifesto. "These people are here for a reason, even if they don't know it yet. Let's show them, and let's also show them mercy. We need them to join us. We can't expand beyond Chicago alone."

Wolf shook his head, focusing his attention on enormous sculptural metal sheets jutting out from the roof above them, curling upward like billowing ship sails. A canopy of latticed rods stretched outward, exposing large panes of gray sky overhead.

"We've gotten this far," Wolf said.

"We always knew expansion was our end goal. Just like generations before us. Our ancestors didn't think twice when they moved out West. They took what didn't belong to them, because if they didn't, someone else would. The system is fragile, and when it crumbles, people celebrate the chaos—they love it, even if they won't admit it."

"Yeah, well, this *system* doesn't work for anyone but the people in control. The puppeteers. We need a leader to show these sheep how they've been fucked their entire lives," Wolf said.

"We'll show them," Spider said. "Now it's just a matter of whether they'll believe us."

Krammer had spent the past few days sending stories to news outlets all over the country, knowing they would find a way to reach the public. He positioned himself as an on-the-ground government official who refused to leave his constituents behind. He'd planted videos of police fleeing the city, spinning a narrative that the government had abandoned its people. Across various social media accounts, he'd used AI to create fake images of people in Chicago uniting with REDS in comradery, banding together. He'd sent videos of Navy Pier's nuclear arsenal to celebrities, knowing full well it would spread like a forest fire picking up speed with each burst of wind. He posted clips of babies in the hospitals, clutched by desperate mothers. Pictures of hungry children separated from their parents, forgotten by a government that refused to intervene.

Nothing got people going like suffering children. Wolf guessed children suffering in people's own backyards didn't count. It had to be plastered in front of their faces to get them to care. They had to be able to point their fingers in blame at someone other than themselves.

Despite Wolf's initial doubts in Krammer, and as much as he hated to admit it, he was impressed with the man's diabolical creativity. Even he hadn't realized the full potential and virality of social media. All it took was a few strategically planted lies, and the algorithms did the rest. People didn't even fact check news sources anymore. It had been easy—so fucking easy— to create a manufactured reality and convince the public it was truth.

"There are so many unhappy people in this country," Spider said, "so many with nothing to live for. Quick to turn on each other, even quicker to blame others for their unhappiness or their circumstances. It's our job to direct that anger and channel it."

Wolf knew it wouldn't take much to convince the people before him to turn on an entity outside their microscopic frames of reference. "Been there," he mused. "At least, until you found me."

Spider studied him for a moment and grasped his good shoulder. "I've been keeping you at a distance because I thought I'd lost you. Lost you like I lost your father. But I stand by what I said in front of the Executive Committee. We made it here because of *you*."

Something foreign pulled at Wolf's chest at the mention of his father. A man he'd never known because of REDS. So much of his identity had been built on the foundational belief that no one had wanted him—that neither his mother nor his father cared enough to keep him. But it had all been a lie. Everyone who'd ever meant something to Wolf had deceived him, and it was becoming impossible to identify where Spider's web of lies started and ended. He'd thought he was an exception to this man's manipulation, but he was beginning to see he'd become entangled in it without even realizing. A thin film formed on his tongue. A small part of him hated Flynn for being right.

He met Spider's blazing stare. "Salvation for the lost," he recited from their manifesto.

Spider nodded and released his shoulder. "Let's begin, shall we?"

He strode up to the podium to address the crowd. Within seconds, silence settled over the throng of people. Wolf could feel Spider's imminent presence stretching outward to seize them from a distance.

"Welcome, and thank you for joining us." His voice boomed through enormous box speakers, echoing throughout the silent, awaiting city. "We thought it was time to bring everyone together, to move forward and leave behind our old way of life. It was never our intention to cause a rift among us or to intimidate you into submission. You see, our organization believes that destruction comes before creation and sometimes we must start over in order to become greater. We must make sacrifices to find a life better than the one we left behind." He paused, leaning forward in earnest, his brows dipping to convey his sincerity. "Because this...this so-called *system* isn't working for you, it's working for an enormous machine called the United States government. It doesn't care about *you*. You're nothing but a number, and the system's sole purpose is to convince you to keep working, keep funneling your money into their machine, a machine keeping the greediest in power. Which is why we burned it to the ground!" Spider roared. "We did it for each of you." He jabbed a finger in the crowd's direction.

"Despite what you might think, you've never had control over your place in life. Your social status, your education, your class...all determined for you at birth. There's no such thing as equal opportunity. The government has made sure of that." He paused, letting the reality sink in. His lips curled into a wry grin as he opened his arms wide, as if he were embracing the mass of people standing before him. "Until now. Take a look at your state representatives, if that's what you want to call them. Are they representative of this country, of you? Where are they now?" His eyes burned like coal. "You think they serve *you*? *Your* best interests? *No!* That's what they want you to believe. That's what they say to placate you into submission—that's how they control you. They've distracted you with lies, trapped you in circumstances they know you'll never escape. Their laws, policies, and regulations only serve their own agendas. And yet they've convinced you that *we* are the ones brain-washing you." He shook his head and pointed toward the REDS members occupying seats in front of him. "No. No, my friends. We're an open book, and REDS decides its agenda together. Society functions and runs because of *you*, not because of them. They keep order by suppression, but we don't. We built an order on unity and strength. On power. An order that relies on each other. That's why we're the new order."

The seated REDS Enforcers yelled their approval, cupping their hands around their mouths to amplify their voices. They pumped their fists and waved rifles over their heads. Spider began to recite the manifesto, and REDS joined in so their voices merged into a booming chorus. "You are more than the world has allowed you to believe. You are worthy. Among REDS, you serve as an integral part of our purpose. We were once lost, victims of an unjust system. Now, we stand as one, soldiers championing those oppressed by tyranny. We create a binding heart, pulsing fear into society. Destruction must come before creation, and from the ashes of despair, a new order will rise. Together, we will rule. *Redemption for the oppressed. Execution for the unjust. Deliverance for the guilty. Salvation for the lost.*"

Applause through the audience began as a low current, with heads turning to observe those around them. Then it gained traction, exploding into an echoing chorus. Some were nodding, fury etched into their worn faces. Some yelled their outrage at the government's abandonment, at their betrayal. Others looked skeptical, mouths pressed into thin lines of fear.

Wolf did a quick scan, lasering in on a few groups clustered together, shaking their heads while muttering to each other. He pointed to Hyena, patrolling the outskirts of the park, and nodded in that direction. Hyena angled his chin downward, speaking into the walkie-talkie Velcroed to his shoulder. REDS had spotters interspersed throughout the rally on lookout for and ready to act on those who showed signs of opposition to Spider's message. Within minutes, two REDS appeared at the periphery of one such group, shoving them toward a truck with their rifles. Spider had known plenty of people would be unwilling to join them, but it was nothing a little convincing couldn't solve.

Spider stared straight ahead, waiting for people to settle. "Tomorrow," he continued, "the United States Air Force will send in bombers. They want to get rid of us, and they don't care what it takes or who must be sacrificed. It's time you see your government's true colors. They label *us* as the enemy, they label *us* as terrorists, but they're the ones who hid a nuclear arsenal in your backyard, concealed and protected by your innocence."

Spider paused, and Wolf held his breath so he wouldn't miss a single word. Judging by the deafening silence, so did the crowd. Like a venomous snake, Spider had lured in his target right before striking. People glanced at each other in shock, their mouths moving wordlessly. Wolf could almost read their minds from here—searching for some rebuttal, denying it, saying how none of it could be true.

"Your government has never cared about you, but we do. Come, join us. We have set up shelters throughout the city for refuge. We will provide food, water, and most importantly, safety. Step forward if you're willing to rebuild this country to serve everyone and not just the wealthy who pay to stay in power." Spider waited, watching, a preacher on his pulpit. This was the grand finale, the perfect opportunity for REDS to separate the chaff from the seed. At first, nothing. Then, like a wave tumbling forward, a little more than half the crowd took a step forward, visibly separating themselves. Spider nodded in acknowledgment. "To those who responded, we will protect you, we will shelter you, and we will help you win your lives back."

As cheers erupted, prompted by REDS, Spider left the podium to meet Wolf by the control panel. "Let's convince them," Spider said.

Wolf pressed a few buttons, and the tape began to play, magnified on a giant projector screen that stretched several stories high. The mass of upturned faces watched as the president tried to negotiate surrender on a video conference, threatening to send a nuclear missile straight into the city.

"You would sacrifice your own citizens to save yourself?" Spider's voice from the movie echoed throughout Millennium Park. "You were the one negligent enough to house nuclear weapons so close to civilians."

The government had been tracking REDS by satellite. Wolf knew this because he had already hacked into their system. That and, of course, they had a mole in the FBI funneling them information. This was why REDS had strategically focused on securing civilian strongholds like hospitals and water plants whose destruction would continue to devastate the city's population if they became the targets of airstrikes.

"Freedom has a price," the president responded on tape.

Freedom has a price. The line made Wolf grin every time he heard it. He watched as a different kind of realization dawned on the faces throughout the crowd. Mouths dropped in disbelief. Shock waves felled trees that once stood rooted in the earth. It was as if the president had reached out of the screen and delivered a swift uppercut to their jaws. REDS projected proof before the people—proof that the government saw them as disposable. The system that had sworn to protect them and their rights was an illusion. All REDS had to do was crack open its thin eggshell to prove how easy it was to break that belief. He glanced at Spider, watching a smile spread across his face, and tried to smother his growing unease. It tumbled around his stomach, nauseating him.

And just like that, he thought to himself, *the tables turn.*

11

FLYNN

They never would have made it on foot to Chicago's Midway airport before nightfall, so their group decided to take the risk and hotwire an old van they found abandoned on the street. Kerri, Nate, Flynn, and Antonio hid in the back while Vic drove. He wore a crimson mask to disguise himself in case REDS spotted them from a distance.

Flynn lay on the hatch floor, its vibrations pulsing through her body. She stared up at the ceiling, remembering the last time she'd found herself blindfolded in the back of a van. Wolf had taken her hostage after the Green Line concert, and she'd been terrified.

How can it be possible that was only six...seven months ago? she thought.

Images of bodies falling, people screaming, and explosions filled her mind. Her throat began to close at the memories. With every jostle and bump, she could almost feel the pain of her captors' fists beating her shoot through her body. Flynn shut her eyes, swallowing hard, and inhaled sharply through her nose. She held her breath, wishing they could keep driving— driving until Chicago was nothing more than a tiny skyline in their rearview mirror—and never come back.

How long do I have to live like this? she asked herself for what seemed like the hundredth time.

She counted to twenty before her heart rate slowed and she felt composed enough to finally reopen her eyes. The overhead window revealed a gray sky, its borders embroidered with staggered rooflines of tall apartment complexes, passing by like shadows of a former life. Occasionally, the sun shoveled through thick cloud cover, basking half the passengers in late afternoon light. In rare moments like this, when she had a chance to think, she felt suspended in time. Life had tipped upside down, leaving her with a distorted view of the reality she once knew. It was almost as if she was flying in an airplane, looking down on rows of houses and streets that appeared, from this aerial perspective, to be perfectly symmetrical. Except once you zoomed in closer, neighborhood flaws presented themselves. Dirty streets, cracked sidewalks, and roads pocked with potholes—the perfect symmetry nothing but a cruel illusion.

The engine puttered and coughed, jerking Flynn from her reverie. She turned on her side to face Nate, her heart accelerating again. Their eyes locked, and for a second Flynn hardly recognized him. The past months had made him a new person. Once sarcastic, upstanding, and kind, now ready to kill at a moment's notice. He'd become what was necessary in this new, fucked up world. He'd adapted so quickly in ways she still couldn't. How had they gotten to this place? It had all happened so fast.

Oh, right, she thought with a strong kick to the gut, *because of me.* She averted her gaze, as if he were a mirror of guilt staring back at her.

The vehicle slowed, and Vic's cursing in the front seat rose above screeching brakes. Nate squatted in a crouch, facing the tailgate, his knuckles white as he gripped his rifle. Kerri shot to her feet, half bent to avoid whacking her head on the low ceiling. She aimed her handgun above Nate, arms steady and expression focused, ready for whatever awaited them. Flynn's stomach contracted. She had no weapon to reach for. A few weeks ago, Nate had tried to convince her to learn how to shoot a gun. While the weight of cold metal in her hand had made her gag, it simultaneously made her want to shoot everything in sight. The power of such a small, seemingly innocuous item infuriated her. How could a simple piece of carbon steel transform someone weak into a dealer of death by the pull of a trigger?

The cab door slammed, and Vic banged his fist on the side of the van. "Outta gas, folks, we walk from here," he growled. The tension in the cramped cargo space eased like a giant sigh. Kerri lowered her handgun, shaking her head. Vic threw open the tailgate. "Thought we mighta been able to get another mile outta her. Guess not."

"Bloody hell, Vic, you scared the living bejeezus out of us," Kerri muttered. "Thought a patrol had pulled us over."

Vic yanked off his mask and readjusted his bandana. "Doubt REDS woulda done us the decency of pulling us over."

They hopped out onto a deserted street, blinking in the fading light. In order to avoid the highway and REDS patrols, they'd taken a back route through old abandoned neighborhoods. On either side of them, chain-link fences bordered empty lots, overgrown with shrubs and drizzled with rubber tires and gravel. Fallen telephone poles and wires lay haphazardly in front yards, covered in swirling graffiti.

"Let's call it for the night," Kerri said. "We'll continue in the morning. Been a long day."

Flynn surveyed the surrounding battered homes, silent and empty, still eerily watching their every move. Plywood boards covered cracked windows, a weak attempt to deter looters. A chill shuddered down her spine.

"I grew up around here," Antonio said. "We can go to my granny's. My parents took her outta the city before REDS blocked off I-90. It's only a few blocks away."

Kerri nodded, glancing around for any sign of REDS. "Let's move."

Antonio took the lead, and Flynn followed closely behind. What she would give to be with her parents and sister again. A deep ache threatened to swallow her whole. She hadn't spoken to them in weeks, since the electrical grid had collapsed, rendering cell towers defunct. Once she and Nate joined the Allies, the first thing she'd done was try to send them a message via a runner, but she had no way of knowing if it reached them.

"Do you miss them?" Flynn asked Antonio. "Your parents?"

Antonio gazed fondly around the neighborhood. "Yeah. But I'm glad they got out. Probably at my auntie's now. Drinking bourbon on her front porch."

"Wish that was me."

"They tried to get me to go with them, but I thought they were bein' crazy jumpin' ship so fast. I didn't think there was any way the power would be down more than a few days."

"Guess the joke's on you, my friend," Flynn said.

A light drizzle began to fall, breathing a cool mist over them. Flynn blinked the spray out of her eyes and breathed its fresh smell. Rain always reminded her of renewal, washing away the grimy sludge of the city. Maybe it would have the same effect on her now.

Antonio side-eyed her. "Don't think I've seen you smile before."

Flynn didn't realize a grin had spread across her face. Her fingers traveled to her lips. "Hm. It's been a long time."

"Wanna talk about it?"

"I don't know if I'll ever be ready to talk about it." Her grin melted away, the muscles around her mouth settling back into their habitual grimace.

"You know, I can never tell if you're sad or angry."

"I can't either." Lately, her emotions tornadoed through her with such thunderous force she couldn't distinguish what was what.

After several seconds, Antonio said quietly, "I know that feeling."

"You do?"

"Oh, yeah. Pretty much sums up a black man's—actually, any black person's—existence in this country."

Flynn nearly stopped in her tracks. She'd been so absorbed in her own grief, she forgot others carried their own hardships, including many they'd had to endure far longer than she had felt the burden of hers. She'd been enslaved by REDS for a few months; she couldn't imagine experiencing oppression for a lifetime. "How do you live with it?" she asked, her throat constricting in a way she'd become accustomed to.

"You just do." Antonio took off his square glasses and wiped the lenses free of rain. "You learn to hold your head up and let it live there, alongside all your other feelings."

Her shoulders sagged. No matter what, she couldn't escape the pain. "Not really what I wanted to hear."

"The more you try to ignore it, the more you try to smother it, the more it grows"—he stretched his arms wide—"the more space it takes up inside you." He shook his head. "You've gotta sit with it. Talk to it. Form a different relationship with it."

"But racism isn't your fault. What if...what if what you're carrying *is* your fault?" Flynn asked as they came to a stop before a small brick home. "How do you ever learn to forgive yourself?"

He looked at her, brows squeezed together, but before he could answer, the group circled around them.

"This is it," he said, "my granny's."

Kerri holstered her handgun. "Alright, let's scope it out."

A snap hook tethered to a flagpole on the lawn clanged with every gust of wind. It grated on Flynn's nerves, as if an alarm had signaled their arrival to the entire neighborhood. Nate took an axe from his backpack and used its flat blade to pry back the boards nailed over the door. The wood's creaks and groans sounded like shrill shrieks tearing through the silence. Vic, Kerri, and Antonio covered him, scanning the area for any sign of movement. Flynn held her breath and realized again how useless she felt without a weapon. A weak link in this new world where guns were now part of their existence. When they got back to camp, she'd have to make do with something. Someone, maybe even Nate, could get hurt or killed because of her reluctance to *deal* with her repulsion. Antonio stepped in front of her, as if sensing her vulnerability.

"You sure your granny won't mind us busting into her home like this?" she asked.

Squinting through his scope, Antonio smirked. "Are you kidding? She'd be so stoked. She'd think we're pretty much running a modern-day Underground Railroad."

When they finally cleared the entry, they crept inside. A rancid smell immediately flooded Flynn's nostrils. As if their own stink wasn't bad enough. Vic bent over and picked up a dead mouse, flinging it out the front door.

"Mooches are always first to starve," he mumbled.

They spread out, checking each room for inhabitants. Flynn stopped on the narrow staircase, covered in worn red carpet, and took in the rows of pictures lining the ascent to the second floor. Photographs of an old life, one that already seemed like a century ago, smiled back at her—young Antonio with his cousins at the pool, Antonio with a beaming couple who looked to be his parents at his college graduation, family gathered together at a barbeque. She wanted to step into the frames, to become a part of those moments frozen in time, moments that felt like another lifetime.

Once they had scoured the premises, they settled into the small living room while Kerri stepped onto the back porch to radio camp. They had to assume all networks were monitored, so they talked primarily in code and often rotated who spoke.

The rest of the group sat in silence, eating a light dinner from passed around cans of whatever Antonio's granny had left in her pantry. Flynn shoveled green beans, corn, and baked beans into her mouth, trying to eat as fast as she could to avoid the gritty, salty flavor that lingered on her tongue after she swallowed. They had two canteens of water to share, which did little to quench their aching thirst that only intensified with each bite of food. Flynn had never been a salad kind of girl, but at this point, she would give anything for a bowl of fresh vegetables.

A loud bang shattered the silence as the swinging porch door slammed closed.

Vic and Nate leapt for their weapons.

"Skin the hide off a horse's arse," Kerri swore as she stormed back inside.

"Jesus, Kerri," Vic grumbled. "Give us a warning, would ya?"

Kerri ignored him, pacing up and down the length of the room in only three strides. "One of our runners is still unreported for, and worse, REDS held two rallies today. One downtown, one in Lincoln Park."

An acrid taste pooled in Flynn's mouth, mingling with the food's aluminum tang.

"A rally?" Nate unwound a fraction, setting his rifle back at his feet. "What for?"

"To recruit supporters. Apparently, REDS showed a video of the president threatening to send in military bombers. They made it seem like the government is cutting off Chicago like dead skin...like, like the government is refusing to send in supplies and resources to help."

"There's no way people believed that," Nate scoffed.

"Of course, they believed it!" Kerri snapped. "People are desperate, they'll believe anything."

"This is exactly what they knew would happen," Flynn said. She blinked, certain her expression mirrored the surprise of everyone in the room. Clearly they were still unaccustomed to hearing her speak.

"Knew what would happen?" Antonio asked. He watched her so intently she knew he understood there was a lot more to her than she'd revealed.

"That once they destroyed the system, people would follow them." Flynn collapsed back into the lumpy couch, wishing she could disappear into the folds of its brown velvety fabric. "Follow them like sheep. And then they could use those people to rebuild a new system...one they controlled."

The thin lines on Kerri's brow deepened. "And you know this how?"

"Because I helped them do it—" Flynn's voice cracked. She closed her eyes. Swallowing hard, she cleared her throat and shoved the words out. "I helped destroy the system."

Silence pulsed through the room. Nate sagged against a wall and looked at the ground, avoiding her desperate stare. She was on her own.

"You helped them?" Kerri repeated. She looked back and forth between Nate and Flynn as if something had finally clicked into place. "You helped... REDS?"

"I was the REDS hostage who survived their attack at the Green Line concert." Flynn focused on her hands, clenched into tight fists in her lap. *Keep talking*, she told herself. *No matter what, just keep going.* "They tortured me. Threatened to kill my family, kill my best friends, unless I helped them. So, I did. They forced me to hire one of them into Magnetic, and he implemented some sort of virus that compromised the company's entire network." She looked up and met each person's gaze. Her throat had turned so dry each inhale burned its walls. "There's nothing I can do to take it back. I stayed quiet for too long. That silence almost got Nate killed, and it killed my best friend. It's killed hundreds of innocent people."

"You knew about this?" Kerri said to Nate. "And you kept this intel from us?"

Nate folded his arms across his chest, a guarded expression on his face. "It wasn't mine to tell."

Flynn wasn't surprised by Nate's response. He'd done everything in his power to reach her while she was under REDS's control. But each time she'd stepped a toe out of line, Wolf had tightened his lasso. She'd lied to Nate over and over again. If their roles were reversed, would she be able to forgive him?

Kerri sighed loudly, running a hand through her cropped hair. The ruffled ends remained upright like a woodpecker's red plume. "Frankly, I don't give a crap *who* should've been the one to tell me. It's mission-critical information."

Nate stayed silent, continuing to stare at the floor. Even after everything she'd put him through, he was still protecting her. The realization spread, warming her entire body like a hot drink.

"It's not your fault, you know," Antonio finally said, breaking the awkward silence. A sad smile tugged at his lips. "They would've killed all those people with or without you. You just did what you had to do to stay alive and protect the people you love. Anyone would've done the same. They're lying if they say otherwise."

Tears sprang to Flynn's eyes, a waterfall of relief pouring over her. Nate had pretty much told her the same thing only a few days ago, but it felt different to hear it from someone else who didn't really know her. For the first time, she thought of Cori and the sting felt more like longing rather than a syringe of venom plunged straight into her heart.

"What kind of new system do they want to build?" Kerri asked. "Like, what's their end goal here? Fascism?"

Flynn shrugged. "Power. They believed people are selfish and would turn against each other, given the chance. All they had to do was breed distrust. Give the illusion of handing power back to the people but continue to hold it all for themselves. Put a dictator in place, but have everyday people do the work for them." She tangled her fingers in her matted hair, overwhelmed with sudden, deep sadness. "I never thought it was possible. I mean, of course REDS is evil, but I never believed people would so easily fall right into their trap."

Wolf had been right. She could almost see his smug sneer spreading across his face. The thought revolted her.

"What do you think is next?" Vic rubbed a finger over his chin. "The rest of the country?"

"There's one more thing," Kerri interrupted. They watched her expectantly when she didn't complete her thought. She wiped a hand down the length of her face. "Apparently during the rally REDS showed a video of the president *confirming* REDS has access to a nuclear arsenal under Lake Michigan...right off Navy Pier."

"Wait a minute," Antonio said, "that wasn't propaganda? Or some bull-shit rumor?"

"I dunno," Kerri said, biting her lip.

"So, in other words, we're sitting on a literal time bomb right this very second?" Nate pressed.

Kerri shrugged, doubt furrowing her brow.

"Holy shit." Antonio pulled his knees to his chest.

They sat in silence, allowing the possibility to sink in. Despite Flynn's best attempts to smother it, a kernel of terror sprouted in the pit of her stomach, growing until it felt as though it were strangling her from the inside. How could the government be so negligent and irresponsible? To endanger the city like that?

Kerri glanced at Flynn. "Did you know about this?"

Flynn's mouth dropped open. "The nuclear arsenal? No. No, of course not. I just thought Chicago was their target because of its weak electrical grid."

How had Wolf not mentioned nuclear missiles? Had he known? Is this why he was so convinced REDS would prevail? One thing she did know without a shadow of a doubt: REDS was a sophisticated military organization. The fact that their influence had spread to the degree it had and gone undetected for so long was undeniable evidence of their power, and frankly, their brilliance. She should've known. She should've heeded Wolf's warnings and not underestimated them.

"I wouldn't put it past them to send a nuke straight to Washington," Flynn said. "They won't stop until they've gained complete control. Chicago is just the beginning."

12

FLYNN

An hour before sunrise, the group packed up and headed toward Midway. Cloaked in darkness, they made their way south, skirting through alleys the last mile. They moved carefully, staying close together, unable to use flashlights. Flynn had never seen the streets of Chicago pitch black. No streetlamps, no vehicle headlights, no skyscrapers stretching into the sky like bespeckled beacons. Instead, stars twinkled above them, and she marveled at their visibility without light pollution to snuff them out. A smoky moon cast them in occasional shadows as they jogged, the *swish, swish, swish* of their pants filling the silent void encasing them. Her hair follicles stood on end, thousands of tiny radars searching for life.

Flynn could make out Nate's outline in front of her, his posture tense and alert. Without the burden of their secret leeching every ounce of her strength, uninhibited energy shot through her. Dwelling on the past had gotten her nowhere. Wolf didn't control her anymore, and no one would again. The release was equally liberating and exhilarating. She quickened her pace until she matched Nate's stride. "Do you think it's true?" Flynn whispered to him. "Do you think Chicago has been sitting on a bunch of nukes this whole time?"

His head turned in her direction, but she couldn't make out his expression. "Can't say I'd be shocked, to be honest."

"Nuclear missiles, Nate? Under arguably the biggest tourist attraction in the Midwest? That's a different level of fuckery."

"Yeah." Nate rubbed his eyes. "It's not a good look, to put it mildly."

"Uh, I'll say," she muttered. "And we have no idea how or if the government is spinning this to the rest of the country."

Nate didn't reply, but his back straightened into a rigid line. "If this gets out...if it's gotten out," his lips barely moved, "it could be what tips this country in REDS's favor. It could be the start of a civil war."

"I can't even let my mind go there." Flynn's stomach clenched. "The country's eyes are on us, and we have no idea what's happening. It's like we're trapped in a snow globe or something."

"Crazy how quickly you lose sense of time," he said.

Kerri snapped around. "Shh!"

They both fell silent, watching as Kerri moved ahead, using sign language to direct Vic and Antonio to spread out. Walking next to Nate felt so familiar, like it had on their stroll around Wrigley Field right before she'd kissed him for the first time. She missed him so much—missed their closeness. Wolf had wedged himself between them, an invisible and immovable barrier. Without thinking, she reached out, searching for his hand. His arm jerked in surprise when she touched him, but after a moment his fingers found hers, wrapping around them and squeezing.

"I'm sorry for lying to you," she whispered, more quietly this time. "I don't think I've told you that yet—how I'm truly sorry. You don't need to accept my apology, and I understand if you never forgive me, but it's important for me to say it."

Nate didn't respond for what seemed like an eternity. "It's not that simple, Flynn," he finally said. "It's like I told you the other night, I don't doubt your intentions behind why you did what you did. But I'm confused...conflicted, I guess. Every time I see those masks, I think about the little boys from the concert. The one I couldn't save." He paused, his hushed voice tight. "So, when I had a chance to kill one of those...those demonic bastards in your apartment, and you stopped me...that I couldn't understand."

Flynn wished she could see his face. Instead, she focused on his calloused palm pressed against her own. When she'd woken that morning, something within her had changed. New seeds had been planted overnight, but these seeds crackled with rage so hot they burned in the pit of her stomach. Like embers flaring to life, the kindling sparked and her anger grew.

Is this what revenge feels like? she wondered.

"I can't explain it," she said. "I just knew if you or I killed him, it would almost be like letting him win. Like it would reduce us to nothing more than the hate that's consumed him. We're not like him, Nate, we're not murderers. It doesn't come easily to us. But I can't say that I don't regret that decision now." Flynn told herself that given the chance to kill Wolf again, she would take it. She'd *finally* be ready this time. Something had stopped her before. Mainly, how much of herself she'd seen in him. That realization had haunted her, and it had an abusive, cyclical effect leading to the same outcome every time—self-loathing. Killing him had to be the only outlet to channel her seething hate, the only option to ending the cycle. "Now, I know better."

"I know why you did it."

"Why I did what?" she asked.

"Why you tried to take on a psychopathic terrorist all on your own."

"Oh, and why's that?"

"You're a protector." Their eyes met, and her heart stuttered. He saw her so differently than she saw herself. Was it the real version of her or the version he wanted her to be? "It's who you are. It's why you carried that burden on your own for so long. You really believed you could change him and stop it."

Flynn considered this. "I don't let many people in. Sometimes I think that's because when I love, I love hard. With everything I have. But it also took me a while to grasp what I was up against. I'm familiar with hate." She paused for a moment, reflecting on the fresh hate building within her—its tight control, its recklessness. "I mean, I'm Jewish. My synagogue's been vandalized, my house egged. And I thought I knew fear. But this is something I've never experienced before... It's evil."

Nate's fingers tightened around hers. "Now we know. Now we're prepared to fight it."

"Speaking of which, I've been thinking. I can't go out on missions without a weapon again. It's too dangerous. Plus, it puts everyone else at risk."

The sun had begun to rise, diffusing tendrils of electric color across the sky. Dim light spread like a glass of spilled water, creeping outward to engulf them. She could finally make out Nate's face but still found herself taken aback by his haggard appearance. Shadows painted his profile a ghostly shade and sank into the gaunt hollows under his eyes and cheekbones. Patchy scruff ran down the length of his neck. She wondered if her appearance had the same effect on him.

He released her hand and reached into his backpack, withdrawing the axe he'd used to break down Antonio's granny's door. "What about this?"

"An axe?"

"Yeah. Remember that team outing we did last year? At Bad Axe Throwing, in the West Loop?" Kerri glanced backward and gave them another withering glare. Nate dropped his voice even lower so Flynn had to practically rest her chin on his shoulder to hear him. "You had the skills, from what I remember. Shouldn't be much different."

She grasped the smooth wooden handle, balancing its top-heavy weight in her grip. Her chest tightened, but holding this weapon didn't have the same nauseating effect as handling a gun. "I'm supposed to attack someone with an axe?" At that moment, the bizarreness of the statement made her want to both laugh and cry simultaneously. To think she would ever find herself longing for her old, boring desk job at Magnetic.

"Not to attack, to protect yourself." His eyes skated back and forth, finger resting on his rifle's trigger. "I never *want* to use my gun, but whenever I pick it up, I remind myself what's at stake, what we're fighting for."

Flynn nodded, hardening her resolve. This is what their new world called for, and she had to adapt in order to survive. "It's better than nothing."

Midway's multistory parking garage loomed ahead of them as they reached a strip mall. Clinging to its perimeter, they moved with caution, their feet crunching over shattered glass piled in front of smashed storefront windows like mounds of crystalized snow. As Flynn inched past, she peered through the gaping holes, ringed with jagged icy teeth. Her heart pummeled her chest. At any moment she half expected someone or something to leap out at them from within the store's depths.

Kerri paused beneath an overhang, holding up a fist. They halted their progress without a word. Pressing up against the doorway of a pillaged vitamin store, they crouched low, retreating into the shadows.

"Alright, let's figure out a game plan." Kerri's breath extended before her in a small cloud. Despite the early morning chill, a sweaty sheen glossed her forehead beneath her black wool hat. "Mike said to meet on the airfield between two terminals. If we're gonna avoid getting trapped in an enclosed space, we better not enter through the airport. Let's go around front and cut through the fence."

Vic's brow dropped low over his eyes. "We won't have any cover."

Kerri mashed her chapped lips together. "True... But we'll have a full visual on our surroundings so we can avoid an ambush."

"Which will also make us prime targets for snipers," said Nate.

"It's a risk, but I'd rather have a clear escape route." Kerri's tone made it clear her decision was made.

"I'll hang back by the fence and keep a lookout," said Antonio.

"Good call," Vic said. "You're the best shot. Give us cover."

"Everyone aligned?" Kerri looked around, awaiting each of their nods. "Right, well then, as you Americans say, let's get this show on the road."

13

FLYNN

They diverted around an expansive parking lot, through another neighborhood, and across an empty street until they came to a chain-link fence surrounding the airfield. Standing at least twelve feet high and topped with swirls of barbed wire, the fence towered above them. Vic extracted a pair of wire cutters from his pack and, with several sharp pings, clipped a small opening in the fence. Flynn held her breath, surveying the wide-open space that awaited them. Other than an occasional abandoned luggage truck, tarp flaps snapping with each gust, there was no cover.

"Alright," Kerri whispered. "Antonio, you're from these parts, any idea what we might be walking into here?"

Antonio shook his head. "Not really. Me and my crew tried to stay far away from street gangs. There were kids in my high school who'd get dragged into that mess and it caused nothin' but trouble."

"Were there gangs most known for local violence? Any that came up often on local news?"

"Hmm. I mean, it's been a while since my high school days, but I think there were two 'round here that got talked about most. Skulls and Bloods. The Bloods were kinda flashy from what I remember, always tryin' to stir shit up. But Skulls…man, you never wanted to see Skulls around. They were more conspicuous, probably didn't have to prove their power or influence because they had bigger fish to fry. A lot more secretive too."

Kerri considered this. "Interesting. Well, if anything goes down, don't come after us. You go straight back to camp."

"Yes, ma'am."

Antonio shoved through the metal hole and held it open as each of them squeezed onto the airfield.

Wind whipped across the flat airfield, yanking at their clothes and hair. Strips of runway stretched as far as the eye could see, crisscrossing through patchworks of now overgrown grass, yellowing in the fall months. They set out at a jog, heading toward the back of the airport, where two terminals extended outward like the prongs of a giant U. As their boots pounded across slabs of thick concrete, Flynn grew winded, surprised at the deceptive distance. Malnourishment and dehydration didn't help either.

Almost there, she told herself. *Almost there. No looking back. Only forward. Forward. Forward. Forward.* She sang the words in her head, matching the mantra to each step to distract her from the dread that any second a bullet could whiz straight between her shoulder blades. Vic and Nate flanked her, their breaths releasing in sharp huffs. They swiveled every few feet, swinging the heads of their rifles in different directions, searching for an enemy none of them could see. Flynn kept her gaze locked on their destination, her axe swinging awkwardly in her double-fisted grip, useless at a time like this.

As they drew closer to the terminal buildings, they slowed and backed up to each other, forming a small circle with their weapons raised to scan the surrounding area. Haphazard jet bridges splayed out from terminal gates, some still connected, their trunks extended to meet the mouths of empty planes. Others stood askew, collapsed like expressed accordions. Vic waved them under the cover of a plane wing, with their backs to the airport. Flynn craned her neck, marveling at the enormous aircraft's sleek underbelly. It sat in silence, as though it were in a deep sleep.

Suddenly, Flynn snapped back to attention and squinted into the distance, her heart stuttering when a tiny vehicle appeared on the horizon, glinting in the morning sun. Its hum shook the stillness. Kerri, Vic, and Nate aimed their rifles, while Flynn widened her stance, squeezing her axe so tightly the blood rushed out of her fingers. *What the hell am I supposed to do with this thing?* she thought, all moisture in her mouth evaporating.

The car sped toward them at full speed, sending small vibrations through the concrete all the way to their feet. Flynn's legs trembled, absorbing the energy like roots of a tree. As it drew closer, she could make out three people crouched in the bed of a pickup truck, all dressed in black uniforms streaked with white.

Vic pulled back his AK-47's charging handle. "What the fuck is going on here?"

"Did we get set up?" Nate asked.

Kerri wrapped both hands around her gun, her arms steady. "Nobody shoot unless I give the order."

Ten yards out, the driver slammed on the brakes, leaving skid marks and a contrail of burned rubber in his wake. With the vehicle still in motion, two people hopped out of the truck bed, landing lightly on their feet. A third stood, pointing his own rifle in their direction. Goosebumps prickled up Flynn's arms. The gang members all wore full black body armor with bones emblazoned on the outside. Masks painted to depict skulls covered their heads, concealing their faces except for tiny eye holes in the sockets. In Flynn's old life, the group's effect would've been Halloween-ish. But here, the result was foreboding.

The passenger door swung open with a shrill squawk and Mike emerged, his weight tipping the entire cab in his direction as he stepped down. "Looks like ya'll made it," he called out. He sauntered toward them, oblivious to the strangeness of his costumed companions.

"Don't come any closer." Kerri aimed her gun directly at his chest.

Sucking on a new toothpick stub, a slow grin spread across Mike's face. "You wanna work with the best or not?"

Flynn and Nate exchanged glances. Her empty stomach twisted.

"These guys don't look like any gang I've ever seen," Nate muttered through one side of his mouth.

"If ya'll knew anything about anything, you'd know Skulls are legend 'round here. But you don't know shit about the real world, being from your uppity neighborhoods way up north." With a massive paw, he waved forward two skeletons waiting by the pickup truck. "Skulls got more territory than any other gang in these here hoods. Got cells all over the country, matter o' fact. Got the most manpower an' the most firepower, which last I heard"—he pointed his toothpick at them, smirking—"you need real bad."

Swallowing hard, Flynn leveled her chin. Maybe if she appeared confident, she could hide her unease as two skeletons walked toward them, rifles slung casually over their shoulders. One towered over the other, his broad shoulders and thick arms swaying with his long gait. The other had a thin, wiry build, limbs swimming in the bodysuit.

Mike pointed to the large skeleton first. "This here is Nymph." He swiped toward the petite one. "And this is his partner, Tawny. They run shit 'round here."

Tawny removed her mask, releasing a mop of cropped smoky-purple hair, its shade so light it almost appeared gray. Tilting her head, she observed them, her lip curling to reveal a row of crooked teeth. Nymph didn't move.

"Aw, come on, Nymph. You can take off your mask," Tawny drawled. An invisible halo of self-assurance radiated from her relaxed posture. "These guys ain't gonna do nothin.'"

Nymph waited several seconds before uncrossing his arms to remove his mask, shaking free spiky red hair. He remained silent, his steely glare ice cold.

"Which of you's the leader of this..." Tawny gestured a limp hand in their direction. "I mean, I don't even know what to call you lot. Looks like you're falling apart at the seams."

Kerri lowered her rifle. "That would be me. And, if you haven't noticed, a bunch of terrorists have taken over our city. We've been a bit preoccupied with salvaging what's left of it."

"And how's that goin' for ya?" Tawny's lip curled even higher. "This city hasn't done shit for us. We don't owe it nothing."

Kerri squinted, the sun a bright orb climbing higher in the sky. "Then why did you agree to meet with us?"

"Money." Tawny shrugged, her gun rattling. "Why else?"

"I don't know what Mike told you, but we have no money."

Rolling her eyes, Tawny snorted. "Clearly." She shuffled her feet, an almost bored expression on her face. "But REDS does."

"Maybe," Kerri said. "But we don't have the people or firepower to help you take it from them. That's why we're here."

Tawny let out a loud cackle, shaking her head. "Guess college education don't get you much these days." Running a pointed tongue over her lips, she nudged Nymph with an elbow. "Tell 'em."

Nymph blinked, his blue eyes watering in the wind, and scrunched his nose in disgust. Flynn wondered whether he'd been dragged here against his will. "REDS took over Chicago's major banks, the ones with the biggest cash reserves." His tone carried a current of disdain, confirming Flynn's suspicion he thought they were a waste of his time. "They couldn't maintain strong-holds at each one, so they transported and consolidated all the cash into one location—the one with the biggest safe. Problem is, it's in the Loop, and we all know REDS raised the bridges over the Chicago River."

"Again, how does that involve us?" Kerri asked. "I wish we could, but I don't see how we can help you solve that problem. Trying to cross the river would be suicide. REDS would pick us off one by one."

"Yeah, no shit," Nymph scoffed. "But when Mike told us about your little resistance, we did some digging. Found out where you set up headquarters has underground tunnels the mob dug to transport dirty money and booze. I thought it'd be simpler to just take you guys out and move ourselves in. 'Til Tawny convinced me that could backfire and expose us. So...here we are."

Kerri stiffened. "How'd you know where we're headquartered?"

"REDS aren't the only ones with spies. We've got our own posts through-out the city," he said.

Kerri's mouth drew into a thin line of confusion. She hesitated. "We have access to tunnels, but none that go under the river and into the Loop."

"Ya sure about that?" Tawny interjected.

Kerri glanced at Vic, who knew the tunnels like the back of his hand. Vic chewed a piece of gum he'd stuffed into his mouth while considering Tawny and Nymph. "Our tunnels stop at The Old Post Office. The one by the river they use for fancy parties now. That's as far as we've gone."

Tawny's eyes narrowed. "I dunno. Maybe you should check your source."

"Vic, a word please," Kerri said, her voice sharp. Kerri and Vic huddled together, while Flynn and Nate kept watch. Thankfully they were still close enough to hear their murmurs. "What in the bloody hell is this nut job talking about?"

Vic scuffed a boot on the ground, his jaw chomping and snapping his gum. "There's rumored to be another tunnel in the post office that goes under the Chicago River. Kinda like the Holland Tunnel in New York. The one that goes under the Hudson River."

"You never thought to mention that little detail?" Kerri asked.

He shrugged. "Never mattered. We've been trying to avoid REDS, not jump right into their laps. Besides, do *you* wanna be the one who tests a non-functioning tunnel that goes under water and hasn't been used in decades?"

"Where does the tunnel go?" Kerri asked.

"Can't be sure." Vic shrugged. "Based on some of the old maps I came across, could go all the way to Willis Tower."

"So, you want our help to get you across the river and into the Loop so you can steal the money?" Nate jumped in.

Tawny looked Nate up and down, eyes scanning him like a rising elevator. "That's right, pretty boy. Get in, get out. Stay as incognito as possible."

"No," Nate said. Flynn stared at him. "That could point them right back to us and where we're located."

"Not if we blow the bank up after." Nymph's voice carried no inflections.

"Ba-da-bing, ba-da-BOOM." Tawny threw her arms into the air, snorting at her own snark. "Destroy the evidence of anyone involved and kill some of these REDS fuckers while we're at it."

"Doesn't sound very inconspicuous," Nate snarled.

Tawny swatted her hand at them. "Ahhh, we're just kiddin'. Come on now, can't ya'll take a joke? No way we're blowin' up something that big and drawin' even more attention to ourselves. Once we're in the Loop, REDS will have no idea how we got there."

They stared at Tawny and Nymph in silence. Nymph had barely even blinked, let alone shown a glimmer of a smile.

"What's in it for us then?" Kerri asked, rejoining them.

"This fight with REDS...it ain't our fight. But we've had ways of smuggling guns into Chicago for a long time. We'll give you a third of our current arms stock. Got real low after the world went to shit," Tawny said.

Mike looped his thumbs in his suspenders and stretched them outward. He spat his toothpick to the side. "Hmm. Lemme think 'bout that one. That's 'bout 300 guns and 1,000 magazines to start. Give or take. Should get y'all to 'bout 30,000 rounds."

Hope flickered inside Flynn's chest. Three hundred guns? They'd been struggling to squabble together a meager fifty. This could be the turning point they desperately needed.

"What about the manpower?" Nate asked.

"*If* we get the money, you get me and Nymph."

One of Nate's brows shot upward. "Two of you? That's it?"

Mike and Tawny chortled. For the first time, a wide grin stretched across Nymph's face.

"Oh, honey," Tawny drawled, "you got no idea who you're workin' with."

14

WOLF

Wolf raised his face to the morning sunshine, breathing in the brittle air. He hated summer and the throngs of people it beckoned outside. Few were willing to brave the harsh cold of a Chicago winter. He'd once read about a Dutch extreme athlete who'd trained himself to withstand arctic temperatures by controlling his own body heat. A year or two ago, Wolf had begun to experiment with it himself, plunging into Lake Michigan in the middle of December. He'd repeated the torture, discovering another way to condition his mind to endure the bleakest environments.

"Daydreamin' about that bitch again?"

Tiger's voice snapped Wolf back to the train tracks, elevated over the deserted South Loop. They'd received a tip-off that a group of Allies had been spotted heading southwest toward Midway. They'd decided to head there on foot, and Chicago's orange line train was a straight shot to the airport. Driving drew too much attention, alerting those in the surrounding areas wherever they went.

"We're wastin' time tracking down a bunch of fucking pests," Tiger continued, as if this had been Wolf's idea. For the fifth time that morning, Wolf fought the urge to sock Tiger in his smug face. Clearly Spider still didn't trust Wolf to track down the Allies on his own.

"Tiger, shut the fuck up and keep moving," Piranha snapped. His bulging eyes surveyed their surroundings, thick lips protruding over a severe overbite.

Although the raised tracks provided a decent vantage point, they kept their masks off to remain as inconspicuous as possible.

Tiger inhaled loudly through his nose and then hocked a loogie, sending it arching through the air to land uncomfortably close to Piranha's shoe. "Why? We run shit 'round here now. Don't got to worry about nobody."

"We started as an underground organization too, remember? Look what happened when people underestimated us," said Piranha.

That finally shut Tiger up. Wolf stared at the back of his buzzed head. Stripes zig-zagged over his scalp, like carefully plotted farm rows, exposing his pale skin. He often found resisting the urge to kill someone was harder than the act of doing it. He cracked his neck, tension squeezing his back muscles. He'd finally been able to lose the sling around his bad shoulder, but that side still felt noticeably weaker.

Tiger began to hum loudly, scuffing his boots along slats of rotted wood, slick with early morning dew.

Cocky son of a bitch, Wolf thought.

Although he couldn't argue against Spider's doubts, forcing this prick on him as a chaperone had been a gut punch. Yes, Wolf hadn't been able to kill Flynn, or even her best friend, for that matter. Nonetheless, it bothered him that Spider didn't trust him to get the job done on his own. Ever since Spider told him about his father, a thread of suspicion had wound its way around Wolf's insides, like a boa constrictor wrapping itself around its prey before crushing it to death. Everyone was expendable to Spider. He knew that. Wolf had just never considered himself within that grouping too. Was Spider only using Wolf to do his dirty work? Once he killed Flynn and her companions, would Spider then do him in? The questions appeared out of thin air, swirling around his brain.

"You know, I don't mind huntin' 'em down," Tiger piped up again, "but I do mind having to babysit *you* to make sure shit gets done around here."

"You're lucky to be working with me, and even luckier I haven't killed you yet," Wolf said. "We all know how desperate you are to climb the ranks, even if it means riding the coattails of everyone around you."

"Whatever," Tiger growled. "That's the biggest load of bullshit. At least

I'm climbin' ranks and not falling down 'em like you. What happened to the 'brilliant' Wolf?" He air quoted, his mouth puckering into a sour expression. "You showed your true colors the second that bitch came along. Guess it only takes a rack of tits."

Humiliation welled inside him, as hot as bubbling lava. When Wolf saved Flynn in front of the entire organization, he'd revealed his weakness, laying it bare for everyone to witness.

"You don't know what you're fucking talking about," Wolf said.

"Damn right I don't. I'd never let some bitch stop me from doin' what needs to be done."

Piranha shoved Tiger forward. "Pick up the damn pace. And I'd watch it if I were you. You've got no idea who you're fucking with." Piranha and Wolf had known each other a long time. They'd been in the same initiate class and had spent the past ten or so years witnessing each other's growth.

"What? I've already done what this pussy can't seem to grow the balls to do."

"Oh yeah, and what's that?" Wolf sneered. "Take down Chicago's electrical grid and gain control of a nuclear reserve? Didn't think so. A dumb shit like you can't even read."

Tiger turned around so Wolf could stare right into his ugly face. "Nah. Better. I killed that little bitch."

15

WOLF

Wolf stopped in his tracks, Tiger's words yanking him like a dog on its leash. *No,* he told himself. *It can't be true. Flynn can't be dead.*

"Yup," Tiger continued, walking backward, as if Wolf had said the words out loud. "'Bout a week or two ago. Recognized her right away trying to break into a pharmacy. Not quite as hot as I remember, but it's been a tough few months—"

"Ignore him, Wolf," Piranha interrupted.

"Thought 'bout shootin' her on the spot." Tiger stumbled over a metal rail, but quickly regained his composure. "Then I realized that'd be too quick. I wanted to see the look on her face when she died."

Lightning-hot rage struck Wolf, sending a fiery trail sizzling through his core. But some other emotion sprinted alongside it, winding him and moving too quickly to place.

Fear. It was fear.

"You're a fucking liar." It took every ounce of self-control to keep his voice steady.

"Nope. Hadn't had a good fuck in a while either."

Wolf lunged at Tiger, moving so fast he didn't have time to react. Wolf threw Tiger onto the tracks, a yell barely escaping the smaller man's lungs before Wolf stomped his boot onto his chest. Tiger sucked for air, gasping and flailing like a fish wrenched from water. Crouching down until they were eye level with each other, Wolf wrapped both hands around Tiger's throat.

"Let's try again, shall we? I have no problem killing you."

"S-S-Spider would—" Tiger tried to sputter.

"Spider would never know." Wolf squeezed tighter, his fingers pressing into the ridges of Tiger's esophagus. "Did you or did you not kill her?"

"Y-y-you. Are. W-weak," Tiger gasped.

Wolf pulled Tiger up by his neck before slamming him back onto the train tracks. Tiger's eyes swelled. "What did you do with her?" Wolf yelled. He could no longer see Tiger's face. A black hole had opened and swallowed him whole.

Piranha grabbed Wolf around the waist. "Wolf! Let go of him! Let go!" he yelled, hoisting him off Tiger.

The world came back into focus. Wolf released his grip, knuckles cramping from their tight hold. Tiger rolled onto his stomach, spluttering and heaving.

Piranha shook him. "Come on, Wolf. Don't let his shit get to you. He's just trying to rile you up. You made it way too easy."

Wolf yanked his arm away, rubbing his tender shoulder while trying to even his own breathing. The terror that had hijacked his body subsided, but his limbs still shook from lingering adrenaline. Wiping his face, he took off without looking back, not caring whether Piranha or Tiger followed. They were only a mile from Midway. They could catch up.

He's lying, Wolf told himself over and over, but the thought wouldn't stick no matter how many times he recited it. *She can't be dead.*

He hadn't allowed himself to think about Flynn over the past few weeks. Every time she flashed into his mind, it shocked him, a jolt of electricity stinging every nerve. His memories of her refused to disappear, and he didn't know what to do with them. He wanted to shove them into a box and burn them, like he'd done with his childhood stuffed animal, Bear, eliminating any trace she'd ever existed. But each time, she rose from his memory's ashes, a ghost haunting the deepest corners of his mind. Even now, he could see her. Her steel-gray eyes, alive and angry. The deep crease between her brows when she concentrated intently. The perfect Cupid's bow of her lips.

She can't be dead. It's not possible.

He shook his head, focusing instead on the anger swelling inside him with each step. After all he'd done, after all he'd given to Spider, this was how he repaid him? Tethering him to Tiger. No. Fuck that. Any chance of a meaningful relationship with someone had been stolen from him because of REDS. First Beta, then Flynn, even his father. He'd never realized it until now, until Spider had cast him aside so easily. Now, he was more alone than before.

The slap of boots against wood alerted him to Piranha and Tiger catching up, but Wolf kept walking. The above-ground tracks gradually leveled with a highway running alongside them. He wished Piranha would've let him kill Tiger and be done with it. Tension zinged through the air as they trucked along in silence until a voice crackled from the radio attached to Wolf's shoulder.

"W, T, P. Incoming targets. Heading back north. Half mile from intended destination."

Piranha raised his binoculars, flicking the focusing thumbwheel while doing a quick scan. As he angled west, he froze. "There." He pointed to a street bridging over the abandoned highway. He handed Wolf his binoculars. "Five of them."

Wolf peered through the lens and a miniature group appeared, heading in the direction from which they just came. Even in this condensed view, they looked disheveled and worn. Three men. Two women. Suddenly, his heart catapulted in his chest. He pressed the eyepiece against his eyes so hard the plastic cut into his skin. One of the women's gaits looked familiar, her shoulders slightly rounded, as if withdrawn into herself.

No. It can't be. Flynn?

Her thick, dark hair didn't have its same luster, probably dulled from dirt and grime. Right at that moment she turned to talk to the man behind her, her face splitting into a wide grin. Wolf almost dropped the binoculars, a spell of dizziness stabbing his head.

It is her.

Tiger shouldered his rifle, squinting through his scope to aim in the group's direction.

Piranha reached for his radio to respond to camp. "Tiger, don't do anything until one of us gives the command."

Without warning, Tiger fired, narrowly missing one of the larger men.

Grabbing Tiger's upper handguard, Wolf twisted the rifle from his grip, kneeing him in the stomach. "You dumb fuck! What the hell are you doing? You gave away our position!"

A bullet whizzed by Wolf's ear. They flung themselves to the ground, flattening against the track.

PAT. PAT. PAT. PAT.

More shots skimmed overhead, pinning them in place.

"You blew it, Tiger. Wait 'til Spider hears about this one," Piranha growled, his cheek pressed into rocks jutting between the wooden slats.

"Someone's gotta get shit done around here." Tiger snatched his gun from Wolf and leapt to his feet. Wolf lunged, but Tiger dodged him, sprinting down the tracks toward a highway off-ramp, which sloped up to where the Allies took cover behind a raised concrete guardrail.

Wolf scrambled after him, a shot drilling into the gravel just next to his right boot.

"Shit," he cursed beneath his breath. He had on a bulletproof vest, but that would do little to protect his other limbs, and the last thing he needed was another hurt arm.

Machine-gun fire rained down like hail. Wolf accelerated to full speed. At the highway divider, he dove to the ground, pressing his back against it. The Allies clearly weren't well trained, or else he'd be dead. Now, about ten yards out, he could hear them shouting to each other.

"GO. GO. GO. We'll cover."

Wolf swiveled around, pulling back his charging handle. He sprung up, releasing a round straight at the overpass.

RATTA-TAT-TAT-TAT.

Dust plumed into the air as bullets sank into concrete. Tiger had just reached the off-ramp when a bullet hit him square in the chest. His vest likely blocked any major damage, but the impact blew him backward. For a few seconds Tiger didn't move, and the shots subsided as the Allies made a run for it. Wolf turned and headed north along the highway, back toward the city. He would intercept them at the next off-ramp.

Without warning, three F-22 bombers appeared overhead, the roar of their engines filling the sky for several seconds before their stout gray bodies caught up to the speed of sound. One broke off from the rest, circling back in their direction. Staggering to a stop, Wolf turned and retreated to the cover of the overpass. As it flew over Midway, it released a bomb straight into the center of its airfield, probably targeting its control tower. An explosion shook the ground like a mini earthquake, knocking Wolf to his knees.

Tiger had disappeared, but Piranha raced toward Wolf, eyes wide, mouth set in focused determination. The plane overtook him, heading back toward the city, releasing a trail of missiles in its wake—tiny black pinpricks hovering against a bright blue sky, suspended until they were overwhelmed by gravity's pull. Within seconds they pummeled toward earth, erupting on contact along the highway's intersection points.

Wolf clamped his hands over his ears. "Come on, FASTER, P!" he tried to scream, but a timed orchestra of booms swallowed his voice.

Ten yards out, an explosion engulfed Piranha in flames, throwing Wolf onto his back. Gasping, ears ringing, he rolled over, pushing himself up onto his knees. He watched helplessly as Piranha flailed and writhed within a fiery furnace. An intense heat wave forced him to his feet, his eyes watering. Choking and coughing, he ran. Black smoke curled from melting asphalt, chasing him.

"Base camp, this is Wolf," he heaved into his radio. "Air—airstrikes heading inland. Toward the city. P down. T unaccounted for."

A crackling voice responded, but Wolf's ears still rang too loudly to hear what it said. A wall of fire roared before him, blocking the road into the city. He knew transportation routes would be a target for the government airstrikes in an attempt to cut off REDS's access to outside supplies. It's why they'd stockpiled so much up front.

A plane circled back around, its jet engine vibrating and grinding air, breaking through the sound barrier as its thin nose pierced the sky. It dropped another round of missiles a few hundred yards away, aiming for another major highway artery. Wolf braced himself, covering his ears again as more explosions ripped through space. Flames expanded outward in every direction, forming an even larger ring of fire.

Flynn. She was directly in the line of fire. His stomach somersaulted. Without thinking, he yanked his radio off his shoulder and tossed it into the flames before taking off, weaving his way past Piranha's burnt corpse and up the on-ramp.

16

FLYNN

For the first time in weeks, Flynn's feet felt lighter as they made their way back toward Lakeview. With Midway behind them, hope fizzled inside her like carbonation rising to the top of a fresh-poured beer. *Maybe we can figure a way out of this,* Flynn thought to herself. Since joining the Allies, she hadn't allowed herself to manifest any sort of optimism, but with Skulls' promise of help, a glimmer of light appeared at the end of a long tunnel for the first time. It only took a few seconds for that spark to extinguish when a bullet whizzed by Flynn's head, its tiny, aerodynamic shell puncturing the air.

"Down!" Vic yelled, dropping into a crouch.

Diving to the ground, they scrambled to the guardrail of an overpass they were in the midst of crossing, taking cover behind its thick concrete.

"Shit," Kerri spat. Amid the elation of their small win, they'd let their guard slip, exposing them like a flock of fat turkeys in hunting season.

Vic and Antonio kneeled, peering over the edge for several seconds to aim in the general direction from which the bullet came.

"Can't tell how many there are," Antonio muttered, doing his best to survey the area.

"There." Vic pointed. "Coming right at us. Another behind him." He held the trigger, discharging bursts of ammunition.

RAT-TAT-TAT-TAT-TAT.

Lagging several paces behind, Flynn's brain struggled to catch up, overwhelmed by noise and a surge of adrenaline.

"GO. GO. GO." Vic ordered. "We'll cover. Head toward camp. Meet us there."

Nate grabbed her arm, but before they could take off, three tiny jets appeared in her peripheral vision. They rocketed overhead, their astounding speed only outpaced by their engines' ear-splitting shriek. Black dots scattered behind them, like seeds floating in the breeze.

"What...?" Nate's question trailed off. "Take cover!"

Nate threw himself on top of her as the first bomb exploded a hundred yards behind them.

Dragging Flynn to her feet, Nate pulled Kerri up along with them. "Move, move, move!" he screamed, shoving them forward right as the second explosion shook the pavement beneath them.

Flynn took off toward the exit ramp leading to the main highway. *Keep running. Just keep running,* she told herself. *Don't look back.*

One step. *BOOM*. Another step. *BOOM*. A third step. *BOOM*.

The missiles chased them, dropping closer and closer. She didn't know where to go. The road stretched before her, offering nowhere to hide. She pumped her arms, but her legs moved in slow motion, hardly gaining any ground. The next missile overtook them, its blast obliterating the road in front of them. Nate shoved her to the side, right as the force flung her backward. She went skidding across the pavement, and a piece of debris smacked her in the head. Flynn pushed herself to her knees, the world spinning.

"Nate!" she screamed, expanding her lungs as wide as she could. "Nate, where are you?!"

What if he's dead? she thought, her heart freezing into stone.

She crawled through the furnace blindly, blood gushing down her forehead and into her eyes. She couldn't see. She couldn't breathe. The hot asphalt scorched her palms. If she stayed in one place for a second too long, her skin might melt off her body. She was trapped. A ring of fire closing in, ready to devour her.

"Flynn?" A voice called her name. It sounded so far away. "Flynn!"

"Nate?!"

"Flynn?!" The voice was closer this time.

Claustrophobia overwhelmed her as thick, black smoke stung her eyes. Suddenly, an arm wrapped around her, half guiding her, half carrying her away from encroaching flames. She blinked back tears and blood as they staggered along. The body guiding her was hard…unnaturally hard. Not like Nate's more moldable form.

It felt familiar.

Wolf? No. It can't be.

Every way they turned, a wall of heat pushed them back. Disoriented, they headed in a different direction, finally bursting through a hazy screen. Flynn's hips collided with a barrier, pitching her forward. She groped the obstacle, her slick fingertips sliding across smooth metal. A guardrail. Droplets of her blood splattered its surface, smearing like paint as two hands helped her swing a leg over the barricade. They stumbled down a steep incline, slipping on damp grass into a neighborhood bordering the highway. Flynn fell to her knees, coughing so hard she couldn't stop. Heaves wracked her body, incapacitating her.

"Come on, just a little farther. Up here."

That voice.

NO, something inside her screamed.

Flynn's stomach clenched so tightly that had any food remained in her stomach, it would have emptied onto the street. There was no denying that silky smooth voice. It pierced through her, splintering her into a thousand unrecognizable pieces. She closed her eyes, counting to three before forcing herself to look up. Wolf stood over her, his entire face coated in black soot. Sweat streamed down his forehead, cheeks, and neck. She couldn't move, her limbs paralyzed, and without hesitation Wolf bent over to help her up.

"Get away from me!" Flynn shoved him with what little strength she had left. It hardly had the intended effect. Wolf barely moved, and she fell backward onto her ass.

"Flynn, we have to keep moving. They'll be back."

She wrapped her arms around her shins, withdrawing into herself. *How can this have happened?* she asked herself. How had they found each other? Again?

Her brain refused to function, retreating into temporary shutdown mode. She began to shake uncontrollably. Wolf grabbed her shoulders, his ocean-green eyes peering into hers. They were so deep, so clear, and once again she was overcome by an eerie sensation she could fall straight into them. She didn't think she'd ever see them again. "Focus on my voice," he said. "You're in shock."

She leaned over and dry heaved, but all that came up her throat was bile. She spit it out, its taste burning the roof of her mouth. Wiping her lips with the back of a trembling hand, she struggled to catch her breath. What twisted, fucked up version of fate kept bringing them back together?

"Leave me or kill me," she finally managed.

Without another word Wolf scooped her up, thew her over his shoulder, and took off. If she had the energy she would've kicked, she would've twisted, she would've pounded his back until her fists went numb. But her arms were unresponsive, overcome with seismic tremors. Instead, she lay her cheek against his back and closed her eyes, focusing on the trickle of blood sliding down her temple and onto his shirt.

17

FLYNN

Wolf ran a short distance, launched up a small flight of steps, then finally placed Flynn on her feet in front of what looked like an abandoned elementary school. An overgrown playground sat outside the entrance behind a rusted chain-link fence, waiting forlornly for students to return. Ripping open his rucksack, he withdrew what looked like a miniature sledgehammer. He slammed it against the lock linking a long chain that snaked around the two door handles to the school's main entrance. Flynn's knees buckled. She leaned against the brick, watching as the lock broke apart.

Kicking open the metal door, Wolf slung her arm around his neck and helped her inside. The door slammed shut behind them with a loud bang that reverberated down the narrow hallway. Wolf's boots screeched on the linoleum as they shuffled past a row of miniature lockers. He fumbled into a small classroom, sitting her gently on the floor. He yanked off his jacket and wrapped it around her. Her body shuddered as if hundreds of electric shocks were jolting through her limbs. He held her tightly, rubbing her arms. She wanted to resist his touch, she wanted to resist his closeness, but it only made the shaking worse.

"Take a deep breath. Breathe with me. In through your nose, out through your mouth."

Closing her eyes, she pretended the person holding her wasn't Wolf.

She pretended it was her father, rocking her back and forth, his thick voice whispering into her ear. Little by little she allowed herself to relax into his body, to sink into its warmth. She focused on matching her breath with his.

In and out. In and out. In and out.

It took several long minutes before the tremors subsided and Wolf's vigorous rubbing brought feeling back into her limbs. Settling back into reality, she allowed new thoughts to begin circling through her brain. She couldn't believe it. Wolf had saved her.

Again.

Equal parts guilt and revulsion washed over her. Flynn pulled away, clenching his jacket around her shoulders.

He reached toward her. "Let me see your head."

She flinched, cringing back from his touch. "I'll be fine."

"You're still bleeding. Badly. You need stitches."

"Don't. Touch. Me." She could barely squeeze the words through gritted teeth.

Wolf opened his rucksack again, this time withdrawing a small first aid kit. "You know what, Flynn, I'm trying to help you. Be as angry as you want after I stitch you up."

Flynn stood, dropping his jacket, but regretted it as soon as she did. She stumbled forward, catching herself right as she fell into a wall. Lightheaded and woozy, she sank back to the floor.

Shaking his head, Wolf sighed. "Here's a thought, how 'bout you save yourself the effort and listen to me the first time? Every once in a while, I might know what I'm talking about."

"Here's a thought, go to hell," she spat.

Gripping her chin, his touch firm but gentle, he concentrated on her forehead as a small smile played at his lips. Her breath caught. She had dreamt about that smile, even though she would never admit it to herself.

Even though she hated herself for it.

"You'd like that, wouldn't you?" he said softly. Using an antiseptic wipe, he cleaned the cut, wiping away the blood, before ripping open a small package with a needle and sutures. "This is going to sting but try not to move."

Sharp pain sliced into her forehead as he slipped the sutures through her skin. She inhaled through her nose, holding her breath in the back of her throat. Tears sprang to her eyes, but she sank into the pain, allowing it to serve as punishment for the guilt wringing her insides. Gritting her jaw, she focused on his green irises. They weren't filled with their usual anger or hate, and she couldn't help but notice his concentration carried an unusual, almost trancelike intensity.

When he finished, he spread a thick slab of cream over her newly sewn stitches and secured a bandage. "Done."

Slowly, Flynn reached out to touch his face, mesmerized. Every feature appeared frozen in place, set in rigid defiance and affixed there, probably from resting in the same bitter expression for so long. His eyes finally met hers, and they sat there staring at each other for a long time.

"Why?" she whispered. "Why did you kill her?"

A wave of fury she'd never experienced before overwhelmed her so quickly it took her by surprise. It doused her, pummeling her from the inside out, and she couldn't contain it. Snatching a pair of scissors from the first aid kit, she shoved their pointed tip against his throat. Her blood flecked his soot-streaked skin like a scattering of freckles.

"Is this what she looked like?" Flynn screamed, her vocal cords raw, as if her anger had stripped them bare. "Is this what Cori looked like before you killed her? Or is that why you stabbed her in the back...so you couldn't see her face?"

The silence that followed seemed to last forever. "I didn't kill her," Wolf finally said, "but I didn't save her either."

Flynn froze. She pressed the scissors against his jugular, harder this time. "What do you mean you didn't kill her? You were there...in our apartment."

"Spider did it." He spoke slowly to protect his neck from the blade. "I...I couldn't. So, he did."

"You're lying," Flynn spat. Her fingers began to tremble, and a drop of blood skated down the length of Wolf's neck. The bright color made her head swim. It was the same color as Cori's. The same color as Nate's. The same as hers. The same color blood flowed through all their veins.

"Why would I lie? I have nothing to hide from you."

"You're lying!" Flynn screamed. She jammed the scissors as hard as she could into the shag carpet. She yanked them out, their point snagging on a loose thread, and stabbed another hole, again and again and again.

After several seconds, Wolf cupped a palm around her cheek. She hated him, but its warmth was an anchor, grounding her, guiding her back down from the swirling cyclone that had ripped her from Earth.

"I couldn't stop him," he said.

Letting go of the scissors, Flynn shoved his hand away and then sat back on her heels. "You blew up Chicago's entire fucking electrical grid. You could have figured out a way to stop him."

Struggling to her feet, she weaved between rows of tiny desks, marching to the opposite side of the room.

"You know better than anyone it's not that simple. The choice is never that simple," he said. "He would have killed you."

She spun around. "I wish he had! I threw you a lifeline. You could've left REDS."

"And done what? Run away with you? They would've found me and killed us both. I'm trapped, Flynn. Trapped. This is the only way to survive."

He hadn't been able to kill Cori? She tried to grapple with this new understanding, so different from the version of events she'd spent the last few weeks replaying in her head. It had been Spider who killed her best friend, who wanted her dead, who'd turned Wolf into this monster. Still, fury blasted through her.

"I wish they'd killed us both. Look at what you've done." Flynn waved her arm toward the empty classroom. Bookshelves barren, chairs flipped upside down on top of desks, saluting their former lives. Nothing remained except for several whiteboard markers and alphabet posters tacked on the walls. "*You* destroyed an entire city." She jabbed her finger at him, venom dripping from her voice. "*You* did this."

"Yeah, well, I told you I couldn't change. I told you this would happen. Unlike *you*, I've been honest this entire time."

Her forehead began to throb. Intense thirst pierced her throat. "The people you've killed, all the blood you've spilled...that's on your hands, not mine." Even as she said it, she knew it wasn't true. Her condemnation was for her own assurance.

"I've never had a problem living with blood on my hands."

"Then why do you keep saving me?" she yelled. "I never asked you to save me. Everything I did, I did to save Cori, and you still took her from me. Why won't you just leave me to die?" He didn't answer, his face hardening back into the same cold shell she knew so well. Flynn grabbed the first small chair she could reach and hurled it at him. It collided with another desk, metal legs clanging against plywood. Wolf didn't even blink. "The Green Line concert. Your attack on the Loop. Your crazy, fucked up REDS lair. Here. Now."

"Maybe it's the same reason you can never seem to kill me. Maybe it's because we're the only people in the world who see each other for who we really are."

Flynn narrowed her eyes, trying to calm her erratic breathing. A memory of them laying in bed together flashed through her mind. His skin resting against hers. The scars on his body. "I thought—" Her voice cracked, soot and smoke clogging her throat. "I thought you cared about me."

Wolf's brows shot upward. "I thought the same."

"Guess we both lied to each other then. To get what we wanted. Maybe you're right, maybe we are the same."

Wolf didn't respond. He reached into his bag, retrieving a large canteen, and shook it, enticing her back over with its delicious sloshing sound. Hesitating, she relented, her fingers clenched into fists so tightly her palms pulsed. Snatching the bottle, she slid down the wall so they sat shoulder to shoulder. Precious droplets dripped down her chin as she drank, her thirst intensifying after her first sip. Even after everything, something about his presence enveloped her, shielding her from the outside world. She returned the bottle, and he took a swig, giving her a long look.

"What?" she asked, self-conscious. She hadn't been able to recognize herself in the strip mall's cracked window glass; now she could add singed hair and eyebrows to her bedraggled appearance.

"Nothing," he said.

"No, spit it out."

He lowered his gaze, but not before a flash of pain darkened his face. "I do care," he said quietly. "I know now I'll always care."

18

WOLF

Wolf woke with a sharp twitch, the shadow of his dream stamped on the forefront of his vision. It had been of his mother again, a rarity that only seemed to occur when Flynn was around. Wolf wondered if maybe it was because, at some subconscious level, Flynn made him feel safe. His mother's pale face and round, green eyes had stared back at him, vivid for several seconds, before fading away, an orb of light swallowed by thick fog. Except this dream felt different. It left a lingering sensation, like a burn continues to singe the skin. It had been the first dream of his mother since he'd learned she hadn't abandoned him by choice, but because she'd been forced to in order to save him. Suddenly unable to sit still, he pushed himself to a seated position. Several feet away, Flynn lay curled on the ground, her back to him. Drawing his knees to his chest, he dropped his forehead onto his crossed arms.

Eliminating emotion had always been a core principle of REDS. Wolf had spent almost a decade attempting to carve that capacity for feeling out of himself, but right when he believed he'd succeeded, Flynn proved he never could. He would never kill her. He'd already lost too much at the expense of REDS, and now the heavy realization struck him that he was gaining less and less in return.

As if she could feel his gaze boring into her back, Flynn stirred. Coughing, she turned over, mouth squeezing into a grimace when she saw he was awake.

"Can't sleep?" she asked, voice hoarse.

Leaning his head against the wall behind him, he sighed a deep exhale. "No."

She groaned, flipping onto her back. "My mouth still tastes like smoke." She glanced at him. "You know, I never fully realized how many things I took for granted until you ruined this city. My bed, for one, although who would've thought I'd get used to sleeping on the floor. Hot water. Hot coffee. Hot food. Family. Friends." She ticked them off on her fingers. "I miss the mundane boringness of my old life."

"How nice you've been able to enjoy the fine things in life for so long."

"Mm...don't know that I'd consider what I just listed as *fine things*."

"Spoken from someone with privilege."

Flynn sat up, crossing her legs. "Ah, how could I forget. You're the person who always has to be worse off than everyone around him."

Wolf's lip instinctively tugged into a small smile. "Guess I can't help myself."

He glanced at her, and she returned the small smile.

"I remember when I was younger going grocery shopping with some of my foster families. Half the time they'd use the money they got from the government to buy booze, or cigarettes, or whatever they could buy in bulk... Chips and canned fruit or canned green beans." Wolf shuddered. "I still remember the rows and rows of color in the fruit and vegetable aisle. The red strawberries, or the blue blueberry cartons...all the different kinds of apples. Fresh. The kind that's crisp and doesn't leave this weird taste in your mouth after you're done eating it like all that other processed shit does. I never really had a birthday to celebrate, but on holidays that's all I would ask for...fresh fruit."

"Did you ever get it?" Flynn asked.

Wolf looked at her, almost forgetting she was there, before shaking his head. "Never got it, so I'd steal it from other kids' lunch boxes. One of the very first lessons I learned was if I wanted something, I had to take it for myself."

Flynn pursed her lips, her brows creasing together. She nodded. "Don't blame you. After living off canned food the last few weeks, I was just thinking yesterday how nice a salad sounded."

They were silent for several long minutes. "You're right, you know," Flynn finally said.

"Excuse me? Did you just admit that I might actually be right about something?"

She shoved his shoulder, which did more to off-balance her than him. "Shut up. I mean, you're right about how there's a lot I don't know or see about my own privilege. And there was so much I didn't know about hardship or pain either..." Flynn stared at him unseeingly, lost in some memory. A cloud of sadness settled over her face, dimming her eyes. A pang sliced through Wolf's chest, sinking deep into his sternum.

"Hardship and pain," he repeated, his lips pulling into a wry smile. "Two of my closest friends."

She studied him. "Something's happened. You're different somehow. You've changed."

Wolf looked at his hands, stained red with Flynn's dried blood. He couldn't deny it, but he also couldn't articulate how this might be true. Several weeks ago, when Flynn had asked him while they lay together in her bed whether he wanted to change, he hadn't known how. But this shift wasn't intentional. It happened after he'd learned his entire identity was a lie. For a brief moment, he debated telling Flynn everything—about Spider and his father. Torn, he hesitated. Saying it aloud would cement in place a new reality he could never retreat from.

"Maybe," he said.

"Maybe? What happened?" She waited in silence for him to divulge more. When he didn't respond, she sighed, closing her eyes for several seconds. "Fine. Well, what now then?" she asked. "Are you going to hold me hostage again? Ransom? What do you want with me this time?"

"No." He met her gaze. "I'm not."

Taken aback, Flynn raised her brows. "You're not...?"

"No. I'm not. I'll help you get back to your camp."

"Oh, I see. You want to know where our camp is."

He sighed. "I'll take you as far as you like and drop you off, how's that?"

Flynn lay back down, resting her head on her forearm, scanning his face like a lost traveler trying to read a map. "Right when I think I'm beginning to understand you, right when I think I have you figured out, you prove me wrong. I can't pin you down."

His lips twitched. "Join the club."

19

WOLF

Flynn woke Wolf an hour or two later. He hadn't realized he'd fallen back asleep, until firm pressure on his arm roused him with a start. His eyes snapped open, focusing on the white bandage across her forehead.

She held out a granola bar. "Morning, sunshine. Time to get moving." In her other hand she clutched an axe.

Rubbing his face, he took the bar, ravenous. He took his time chewing, going back and forth between repacking his bag and reloading his rifle. Flynn fidgeted by his side, clearly anxious to leave.

"Will you relax? What's the rush?"

"I want to make sure the others in my group are okay," she said. "They could've been hurt or killed in the explosions. I have no way of getting ahold of them."

"You mean that prick who shot me?"

She glared at him. "If you're talking about Nate, let's not forget who almost beat him to death."

He scoffed, then pointed to her bandage. "He asked for it. Let me check your stitches first."

Her fingers flitted to her head, as if she'd forgotten the sutures were there. She rubbed the bandage gingerly. "I'm fine. And he didn't *ask* for it, he kissed me. If I didn't know any better, I would say you're jealous."

"You won't be fine if it gets infected and you don't have antibiotics," Wolf said, ignoring her very accurate observation.

She sighed, kneeling before him. "Fine, but can we hurry it along?"

Carefully holding her chin, he peeled back the medical tape, examining his handiwork. He had to admit, he'd done a pretty decent job, given the circumstance. She kept her eyes lowered, staring at the ground to avoid meeting his gaze. With an unexpected jab to the gut, he realized how much he'd missed her—how, for the first time in weeks, he no longer felt alone. Using a cotton ball, he dabbed more antiseptic over the even row of stitches before spreading on another layer of cream and applying a fresh pad.

"You'll need to keep this clean." He passed her a few more gauze pads from the first aid kit. "Change your bandage every morning."

She took the pads, finally lifting her eyes to meet his. "Thank you," she said softly.

Insides squirming, he stood, shouldering his bag and rifle. "You stopped Nate from shooting me to death in your apartment. Let's consider ourselves even."

Rising to her feet, Flynn nodded. "Good. Even."

When they stepped outside, the smell of burning asphalt stung his nostrils. Interspersed threads of smoke wafted in the distance, spiraling into the lightening sky. The fresh early morning air had diluted the billowing columns of thick, black smog to a hazy gray.

"I'll follow your lead," he said.

Flynn's mouth angled into a smirk. "There's a first."

As they headed east, weaving through neighborhood back alleys, he nodded toward the axe in her hand. "So, that's your weapon of choice, huh?"

"Yup. Can't say I really know how to use it, to be completely honest."

"And how's that supposed to protect you when rounds of bullets are flying at your head?"

"Haven't quite figured that one out either, but it's better than a gun."

Wolf extended an open palm. "May I?"

Flynn handed him the axe. "Be my guest."

Wolf pointed to a utility pole about twenty feet away. Arching the axe backward so the blade almost rested by his cheek, he flung it forward, releasing it like a boomerang. It spun around and around, sinking squarely into the soft wood with a satisfying *THUNK*.

Flynn crossed her arms over her chest, lower lip pushed outward. "Shocking. Just one more thing you're good at."

Wolf retrieved the axe, twirling it around his fingers and examining the blade. "Not bad. Blade is nice and narrow, better for throwing than a wood axe. Where'd you get this?"

She snatched it from him. "Nate gave it to me."

Anger skewered through his ribcage. "So, you're still seeing him?" He tried to keep his voice even, noncommittal.

"What do you mean '*seeing*'? He's one of my best friends."

He scowled. "Yeah, okay."

"Say or think whatever you want to, I don't care. You don't control me anymore, and you never will again. No one will."

The same fire he'd loved provoking reignited in Flynn's steel-gray eyes, but her voice was light and her expression was different. She seemed resolved instead of defiant or angry. Even her posture held more assurance. He knew firsthand, pain has a way of exposing its victim, cracking them open right down to their core. One either takes strength from it, or they let it consume their every waking moment. She was clearly channeling it—using it as a generator of power.

"Don't be so sure," he said. "Everyone will be under REDS's control soon enough."

She rotated the axe's wooden handle in her hands. "I'm so sick of it. Sick of men like you...like REDS...who need to control others to make themselves feel worthy. Who need to belittle...and, and terrorize, and kill in order to get a high off power."

"Take a look at the people who are at the top of the food chain, Flynn. You get there by taking no prisoners. You don't get there by playing nice and making friends with everyone."

"I'm not talking about making friends with everyone. I get being ruthless is part of life and being successful. I'm talking about this method of tactical warfare. This way of getting to the top and staying on top. I'm talking about your fucking hypocrisy and how you can talk about privilege when *you* of all people know what it feels like to be stuck on the bottom rung of society's rigged ladder." She jabbed a finger at him, which he swatted away. "I'm allowed to wish the world doesn't have to operate this way. Maybe, just maybe, instead of spending all our energy on keeping people at the bottom, we can finally recognize that privilege isn't finite and we can bring others up the ladder alongside us. We don't always need to keep others down in order to stay at the top. At least I'm able to admit what I've lost through all this has opened my eyes to my own privilege."

Wolf rubbed the back of his neck. *And she thinks I've changed?* he thought.

"No. I'm done," she continued. "I'm done with men like you...with people like *you* who've only ever made me feel powerless." Her mouth stretched into a grimace. "Because now I've seen firsthand, life is too short to waste it on something as insignificant as you and your fucking ego."

She turned on her heel, storming away without a second glance. Wolf let out a long breath. "You've got to be kidding me," he muttered, setting off at a jog to catch up with her. He still towered over her, but she seemed taller. "Are you done?"

She continued staring straight ahead, profile rigid. "I don't know. Haven't decided yet."

"Well, at this rate, you'll never learn how to use that thing." He nodded toward the axe.

"Seems a little twisted, doesn't it? You're going to teach me how to throw a weapon I'll use to kill your friends?"

A laugh bubbled in Wolf's chest. "Yeah. We'll see about that."

Using one arm, Flynn swung the axe behind her head like she was getting ready to throw a baseball.

"Whoa, whoa, whoa." Wolf grabbed her wrist. "Hold on there before you lose a toe. Stop walking. Minimize movement. Start with both hands on the handle first."

Rolling her eyes, Flynn planted her feet and wrapped all ten fingers around the handle.

"Relax your grip," he instructed.

Flynn let out an exasperated huff. "Would you just let me give it a try?"

"Fine."

She snapped her forearms and watched as the axe spun straight into asphalt, its blade striking a spark.

"Over rotated."

Dropping her chin to her chest, she glanced at him, daring him to comment further. "Okay, I never said I didn't need practice."

"A lot of practice." He went to retrieve it, holding it out as a peace offering. "May I?"

Flynn nodded, wrapping both hands around the axe's handle. Standing behind her, he reached forward, pulling her arms back, until her triceps were parallel with the ground but her forearms were cocked at a 45-degree angle. He could feel her body tense at his touch and an uncharacteristic urge to hold her overwhelmed him. "Square up and point your elbows toward the target. Don't move your shoulders. Release right in front of you. It doesn't require much force. Remember, less movement, more precision."

She released the axe, arms straightening into a line. It spun, sending a slight whoosh through the silence, before wedging itself squarely into the wooden utility pole.

Flynn glanced back at him and grinned.

"Not bad," he said, tilting his head to the side.

"I get it now." Flynn stepped away without turning back. "It's a feeling you get, right before letting go."

20

FLYNN

Now that the shock of seeing Wolf again had worn off, Flynn felt more at ease around him than she ever had before. It was as if, for the first time, she could be present in their interactions without having to simultaneously choreograph a dance in her head. No more complicated steps. No more games. Except a new discomfort had replaced it. Coarse and itchy, like wool brushing against raw skin, it refused to go unacknowledged. Wolf hadn't killed Cori. No, he hadn't saved her, but he hadn't been able to kill her. And for a person as vicious and merciless as Wolf, that meant something.

It also meant the target she'd spent the past few weeks narrowing in on had been the wrong one.

"Spider." Flynn said his name out loud, tasted its sourness on her tongue.

Wolf stopped walking, his brows stretching as high up his forehead as they could reach. The color of his face turned sallow at the mention of his name. She might as well have kneed Wolf in the balls.

"What about him?"

Flynn surveyed their surroundings. They'd spent the past two hours avoiding the main roads. It seemed as if the government attack had been primarily isolated to highways and perhaps some key targets downtown, so they stuck to a longer, more jagged route by cutting north. Neighborhoods blended into each other, and like an ascending staircase, buildings gradually grew taller and closer together as they trekked closer to downtown. They stood before an abandoned construction site. A towering sign planted out front advertised fancy features of the new high-rise apartment complex. LUXURY KITCHEN, THREE BEDROOM UNITS, ROOFTOP DECK WITH POOL. The incomplete structure gaped open, exposing its guts amid scaffolding and dumpsters stuffed with debris. There'd been no sign of REDS Enforcers patrolling, likely due to the threat of more bombings.

"He was the one who killed Cori then?"

Wolf's jaw tensed. He nodded once and resumed walking.

Flynn jogged to catch up with him, grabbing his arm and spinning him to face her. She wasn't scared anymore. She didn't care what he did to her, and with that came a gush of recklessness.

"This is the same asshole who almost killed me? Twice, I might add. The same asshole who threatened to kill *you*."

Wolf dropped his gaze. Even the mention of Spider made him cower in a way she'd never seen, like she was suddenly the abuser and he was the victim.

Taken aback, guilt torqued her stomach into a tight knot. Without warning she was back in her old bed again, Wolf hovering over her, long scars slicing his abdomen into a checkerboard. No matter how she tried, she couldn't push the memory from her brain. Her first instinct was to wrap her arms around him, to pull him close. Nate had been right—she felt an inexplicable desire to protect him. She squeezed his bicep, searching his eyes.

"What's going on? What does he have on you?" she asked.

Stepping away from her, the muscles around Wolf's neck tightened. "Spider is..." His voice trailed off. He cleared his throat. "Spider is the only father I've known."

He spoke with reverence and the kind of conviction her rabbi had projected during services that made her wonder about faith's power over the mind.

"But he's not your father." Flynn said the words slowly, like she might to someone standing on a cliff's edge.

"I know." Wolf sighed, finally meeting her gaze. "I know he's not, because he killed my real father."

Flynn's mouth dropped open. Her axe slid from her grip with a loud clunk. "What?" Unable to hide her disbelief, she shook her head, as if she could fling his confession out of her ears.

His face contorted. "I never knew. I mean, obviously. Spider's been punishing me ever since I couldn't kill Cori. I think he told me as a last-ditch effort...thought it might knock some sense into me."

"Why would *that* knock sense into you?"

"Because my father started REDS. But he tried to leave after he met my mom and she had me."

Flynn pressed a knuckle to her mouth and bit down. Rubbing the knobby bone back and forth, feeling it snag against her chapped lips. She couldn't summon any words.

"When REDS found out...about her and, and...about me, they killed him. He and Spider were best friends, so when Spider heard what they were going to do, he tipped my father off. Must've given my mom time to leave me at some fire station and run."

Stooping to pick up her axe, she exhaled, the air whistling through her teeth. She rose slowly, her back and hips aching, suddenly feeling a hundred years old. "What happened to her?"

Wolf's eyes shuttered like they did when he withdrew into himself. Silence stretched between them for almost a full minute before he responded. "I don't know."

"Do you know her name?"

"I don't even know *my* real name. Just the name the state gave me."

Flynn ran a hand through her hair, but her fingers got stuck in a matted clump. She still had trouble wrapping her head around the fact that a young man existed before Wolf came to be—that he'd had a whole, lonely life that prepared him to step into this role as a killer.

"So, Spider kept all this from you...and only told you because he thought you'd leave REDS to be with me, just like your father did with your mother?"

Shifting his weight between his feet, Wolf shrugged. Flynn's breath caught as the weight of this revelation sank through her skin and into her bones.

"But...but you didn't leave. You stayed. You chose REDS."

Wolf turned his back to her and crossed the narrow alley. They'd been looking for a car to jump, but had yet to come across a viable option. All the ones they'd found had already been siphoned for gas, broken into, or had missing tires. He stooped over to examine a beat-up sedan.

"I chose you, Flynn, when I didn't kill you or Cori. Spider knows that. Why do you think I'm here?"

Flynn tried to steady herself. It was as if she were on a boat, pitching up and down over enormous waves. She wanted to grab on to something, but had nothing to hold except her axe's smooth handle. The sensation felt eerily familiar. It'd been a constant companion since meeting Wolf again. Their entire reunion had been volatile, a rising tide threatening to submerge her and drag her out to sea.

She followed him, tripping over a pipe strewn in the middle of the road. "I don't...I don't understand. I told you to leave. I *asked* you to leave. You didn't choose me. If you had, we wouldn't be here. You're just angry with him. And you're angry with yourself for not being strong enough to kill me. You're only here because he's abandoned you and you're alone."

Spinning around, he strode toward her, his face a mask of stone. Flynn's heart plummeted. She gripped her axe in both hands, but he snatched it from her grip and threw it to the side. As if she were weightless, he picked her up, catching her completely by surprise.

"Wha—" Before she could finish her question he kissed her, crushing her body into his, forming her to him like a piece of clay. Flynn closed her eyes, resistant at first until a spark snapped to life inside her. She felt alive—alive for the first time since Cori died. She couldn't think, and she didn't care. She let it wash over her. Locking her fingers around his neck, she wrapped her legs around him and kissed back. He tasted both foreign and familiar, sweat from his upper lip catching on her own.

It's happening again, a voice warned her.

Just like that she was back at the water's edge, mesmerized by the waves and their rhythmic pull.

One more time, she thought, kissing him harder, not wanting it to stop.

Even as Wolf lowered her back to the ground, she couldn't pry her fingers apart. Foreheads pressed together, their warm breath merged into one cloud. Tears slid down her cheeks, releasing weeks of pent-up emotion. Each one seemed to signify something different.

"I'm here," he said, "because that's all I've wanted to do since seeing you again."

What would Cori think of her right now? Would she be cheering her on, or rolling her eyes like she used to when something disgusted her?

This time, Flynn pulled away, disentangling herself from him. She pressed her palms onto the car's rusty hood, leaving damp rings on the cool metal. Right when she thought she had the upper hand, he landed his knockout punch. He'd surprised her, and she hadn't been ready for it.

"Wolf, no amount of chemistry or attraction, or, or whatever it is that's going on between us can make up for what you've done. I can't...I can't reconcile that."

"I'm not asking you to."

Flynn whirled around. "Then what do you want from this other than to clearly fuck with my head? It's like you love the control you have over me or something. It's just another way for you to have power."

Wolf exhaled forcefully through his nose. "I'm not trying to fuck with your head."

"That part of you—that part that seeks out power—REDS has branded that so deep into your psyche you can't feel complete or worthwhile or satisfied without it."

"This," Wolf gestured between them, "isn't about that."

"Then what is it about? You're not going to leave REDS, so what's your end goal?"

He considered her, his bottom lip pressing upward at the same time his brows deepened. "Alright." He slung his rifle over his shoulder. "What do I need to do?"

"What do you mean?"

"How do I prove myself?"

"Prove yourself?" Flynn asked, her voice hollow. "I thought you said you couldn't change."

Her brain moved at an inchworm's pace, struggling to catch up after what had unfolded between them over the past twenty-four hours. She still couldn't comprehend how far off it was from the scenario she'd spent weeks playing over and over in her mind—the one in which she killed him.

"I've never put limitations on myself before." A small smile lit his face with an unnatural glow. "Why start now?"

21

WOLF

An hour later, Wolf gave up on trying to get the shitty old Volvo to start. They made a few more attempts, breaking into decrepit garages that were detached from their assigned walk-up buildings. Each one yielded jack shit. He'd almost given up on the idea of driving altogether when they came to a squat shed with a sunken roof. Taking the butt of his rifle, he jammed it against a lock screwed into the bottom of the door. It popped off. He bent over and then yanked upward, the metal protesting with a long, sharp screech. A rusty motorcycle greeted them. Wolf beamed.

"Bingo."

Flynn scrunched her nose. "No. No way."

He lifted a leg over the seat. Straddling the bike, he gripped the handlebars. "It's ancient, but it'll do. We'll be able to stick to back roads since all the main highways are blown."

"You can't be serious. We might as well put a flashing red siren on our heads."

"You forget your escort is an insider. I know where all our outposts are, our scouts' radius, and most importantly, where our snipers are. We won't take it far, just to get us closer to the lake," he said.

She wrapped her arms around her now bony frame. "We'll be sitting ducks. Plus, there's no way that thing still runs."

Wolf looked around. Two helmets beckoned from a dusty shelf, their dull outer casings scratched and worn. Each had a visor that would cover their faces. "Not if we wear these."

Flynn picked one up with two fingers and sniffed its worn padding. "Ugh. How many heads have sweat in this thing?"

"And when was the last time you showered?" She glared at him, her neck turning a splotchy red. "It's going to get dark soon. It's either this, or another night with me."

That did the trick. She tossed a helmet at him—a little too hard—and gathered what she could of her unruly hair, tucking it into her jacket. She shot him another look before gingerly maneuvering the helmet over her bandage and shimmying it down onto her head. Awkwardly, like a dog raising its leg to piss on a hydrant, she clambered onto the bike, settling herself behind him.

Wolf flicked the key already waiting in the ignition and kicked down on the starter, awakening the engine with a deep, spluttering roar. Flynn clutched him, hugging his midsection. A grin stretched across his face, and for the first time since he could remember, he wanted to laugh.

Fumes engulfed them as Wolf squeezed the clutch, stepping down on the shifter to first gear, and the motorcycle peeled out of the garage, accelerating so fast it reared up onto its back wheel. Flynn's muffled screech pierced his ear, rising several octaves above the booming engine. Wolf bowed over the handlebars as they zipped down back streets and alleys, Flynn practically Velcroed to him like a backpack. Wind whipped their clothes around their limbs. A buoyancy rose within him, along with a sensation that his heart might get yanked from his chest. For a brief instant it felt as if he'd departed his body. He knew the exhilaration would be fleeting, but maybe if he kept going, he could outpace his thoughts waiting to descend the second he slowed enough for them to catch him.

Wolf backtracked slightly and headed west. He couldn't go straight toward the lake, since that would take them right through the South Loop and into the thick of REDS territory. They'd have to head north first before cutting back east. He knew the area well after weeks of patrolling and rounding people up. They'd done what they could to keep people in the city, but many had fled. Others had flocked to community stations REDS had set up for people to congregate—hospitals, schools, convention centers. They'd done this strategically throughout the city, not to serve as refugee centers—which is how REDS had presented them, of course—but to protect them against what had just transpired: government counterattacks. He knew Spider must be thrilled. A government attack against its citizens played into his propaganda perfectly.

As they drew closer to the lake, smoky clouds sank downward to meet a thin yellow strip of sky hovering over the water's horizon, separating the two gray planes. Wolf rocketed the final stretch back west, entering Lakeview's residential neighborhood. Shifting gears, he veered off the street and onto a walking path, slowing to a stop as it dipped beneath Lake Shore Drive, now devoid of cars. Resounding quiet replaced the motorcycle's vibrating drum. The path continued on toward a harbor, and a small waterway ran beside them, guiding boats out to the lake. Water lapped the concrete storm wall, its monotone color changing moods to match the dull fall weather.

Flynn swung a leg over the seat, sitting sidesaddle before sliding down to safe ground. She flexed her hands.

"Hold on tight enough?" he asked.

She yanked the helmet over her chin, shaking her head free. Wincing, she touched her bandage. "Did you really need to go that fast the entire way? You couldn't have gone just a tad slower?"

Wolf dismounted and swiped down on the motorcycle's kickstand with the heel of his boot. Dragging his helmet from his head, he allowed the fresh air to caress his face. "Where's the fun in that? You don't ride a motorcycle to go slow."

"I thought the word 'fun' wasn't in your vocabulary."

"It's used sparingly and reserved only for certain activities."

"Yeah, I'll bet. Twisted and disturbing ones like, say, murdering people, blowing up cities and stadiums, oh, and let's throw in decimating Chicago's electrical grid too." She gave him a huge, mock smile. "So, what's next?" She waved an arm toward the columns of smoke spiraling from the heart of the city. "What does REDS want from all of this, Wolf?"

He ignored her condescending tone, but irritation swirled in his chest. He hugged his helmet to his chest. "What do you think? Use your head, Flynn. Power. More of it."

"What does that entail? Taking over the entire country?"

"Essentially, yes."

Flynn drew her shoulders back, the way she always did when preparing for a fight. "Is it true what your leaders have said? That you've hijacked an entire nuclear arsenal?"

Wolf dropped his helmet to the ground and shifted his weight forward to rest his forearms on the motorcycle's seat. "Yes, it's true."

Flynn shook her head. "I don't understand. REDS robbed you of a mother...of a father."

"They also gave me a life when no one else gave a shit."

"No, that's bullshit and you know it. They robbed you of an entire life you *could've* had. And even after all their lies, all of their betrayal, you're still going along with their plan? With *your* plan? Do you really think they still care about you?"

Again, Tiger's ugly face flashed through Wolf's mind. Spider had saddled him with that sack of shit. Something squirmed in his gut. Had Spider told Tiger to finish him off? Great. The last thing he needed was a healthy dose of paranoia.

Flynn turned to stare beyond the mouth of the tunnel toward the lake. "You can't have this both ways, Wolf. You can't keep coming to my rescue only to throw me back into the fire again and again."

Wolf now knew beyond doubt he felt connected to Flynn in some way he could never explain. Amid the chaos, amid the confusion, she was the only person who made sense. She was the only person who gave him a glimpse of a life beyond REDS—of the possibility of ever experiencing a glimmer of happiness. But that feeling seemed so foreign and distant and unreal as it hovered just beyond his reach. Almost as if he was doomed to never fully experience it, to never know true happiness.

"I know," he said, rubbing a hand down the length of his face and straightening. "I just need to figure out what's next...what my next move should be."

Flynn didn't respond for several minutes. She gazed out over the water, eyes stern, mouth drawn. He never knew what she was thinking.

"I know what's next," she finally said. "I know how you can prove yourself."

Oh, boy, this'll be good, he thought.

"How?"

She looked back at him, her chin resting on her shoulder. Shadows from the overhang covered the upper half of her face. "Spy."

Wolf's skin prickled. "What?"

"You said it yourself, you know where the outposts are, the scouts, everything. This could be your chance to escape… Leave them. Take them down."

"I can't."

"Why?"

"If anyone found out, they'd kill me without thinking twice."

"They'll kill you no matter what. It's just a question of whether they can get more out of you first."

Complete betrayal.

The thought punctured him, like a tack pricking a balloon with an ear-cracking *pop*. There would be no coming back from it. If he passed information to the Allies, it would be the end of it all—his entire existence.

Then what? a small voice asked.

"It's not that simple," he said. "You're essentially asking me to undo everything I am."

"You'll never know if you can unless you try."

Flynn reached a hand toward him. Her fingers were delicate—slender—an invitation. Was he ready to give everything up for her? His brain said no, but he stepped forward, his body responding for him. He took her hand, his palm absorbing her icy fingers, encasing them in his warm grip. Could she do the same for him? Could she melt away an entire decade—no, an entire lifetime—of rage that had calcified into who he was today? Could he even trust her to try?

He closed his eyes, his throat tightening. "I'm not normal like you, Flynn. I'm…I'm empty. All I have are these wild urges to kill people. I can't control them."

He opened his eyes, afraid of what he might see. She wore a wary expression, one of knowing. "You're killing the wrong people."

She wrapped her arms around him and rested her head against his shoulder. Slowly, he returned the embrace, marveling at the slightness of her shoulders, at the imprint of her spine. He couldn't let her go, not again.

"I'll think about it."

22

FLYNN

There was no other way to beat REDS. Except this time, she wasn't manipulating Wolf. The Allies needed him, but he also needed her. He couldn't untangle himself from REDS without her, and regardless of her convoluted feelings, she could make this compromise to serve both parties. One thing Flynn now understood about trauma after experiencing it firsthand was it manifested in different ways. It had settled in both of them, different forms of the same vicious beast. They carried it with them, a burden they both shared. She never could've known it would be such a fucked cycle, and she had no idea how to stop it or whether she even could.

"How will I find you again?" Wolf asked, his voice muffled in her hair.

She pulled away from his embrace. He released her slowly. Each time she touched him she wanted more. She never wanted it to end, and the thought both made her heart stop and caused her stomach to flip at the same time. It terrified her. Did that make her a monster too?

"Come with me," she said. "I'll show you where we can meet next. Let's say in two days? At five o'clock. I'll present the idea to the Allies, and you think it over."

"And if they don't agree?"

Flynn bit her lip, anticipating Nate's unfavorable response to her idea. It was very likely the group would be against it, but they were desperate, and Wolf didn't know the extent. With both Skulls and Wolf behind them, the winds might finally turn in their favor. "I don't think they'll be able to pass up the intel. The question is whether they'll trust you to deliver accurate information."

"They'll have to take their chances," Wolf said, hinting he was more aware of their desperation than she'd suspected.

"Let's practice." Flynn turned to face him, walking backward out of the tunnel. As daylight dissolved and darkness enveloped them, she felt safer walking in the open. "How do you plan on influencing the entire country to become your subjects? How do you plan to rule—a dictatorship?"

Wolf locked his eyes onto hers. She could see him weighing all his options, the scale in his head sliding back and forth as he considered his future. He opened his mouth, then closed it, his jaw clenched against the words. Flynn decided in this instance patience would behoove her. If she pushed too hard, she might spook him. She turned back around, leading him to a small cluster of benches overlooking the water. They were a few blocks away from one of their outposts that had an access point to the underground tunnels beneath the city. This one was an unassuming bodega with boarded up windows that had done little to deter looters.

"Here," she said. "This will be our spot."

"How do I know you won't try to kill me again once I tell you everything?"

"Guess you'll have to take your chances," Flynn said, one corner of her mouth lifting upward.

Wolf stepped toward her, reaching for her again. His palm cupped her cheek and he rested his forehead against hers. She knew if he were to do this, if he were to help them, she would be his one lifeline—the single person who could possibly strip back all the layers of brainwashing. What would they find? Who was Wolf without REDS? She knew he didn't know, and that was what scared him. Flynn covered his hand with her own, her heart rate accelerating. She suddenly realized they had no idea what awaited Wolf once he returned to REDS. Ice cold fear breathed goosebumps up the back of her neck.

Does this mean I care about him? she wondered. *How did I come to care about him so quickly?* Had she ever really stopped? Had it been hidden beneath all the other emotions that had buried her since Cori's death?

"I'm worried about you," she whispered.

"Why? Didn't you just try to stab me with scissors?"

"I don't trust them...any of them."

"I know what I'm doing," he said. "Trust *me*."

"But I don't trust you. I don't trust any of this." She forced herself to look into his startling green eyes, their color so brilliant she could never forget them. For the first time she allowed herself to fully appreciate how handsome he was, to savor it.

"Neither do I," he said. "Too much has happened between us. But what's the alternative? Do we start over? Is that even possible?"

Flynn pulled back, retreating from him. "Maybe. But only after what I promised myself I'd do."

He raised a brow. "What's that?"

"Avenge Cori's death," she said simply. "Now that I know you didn't kill her, maybe I'll be able to see you differently... But I'll only really know after I kill Spider." Wolf let out a barking laugh. Flynn gave him a shove. "What's so funny about that?"

"I'm sorry, but didn't you threaten to kill me multiple times?"

"Maybe. But that was different."

"How is it different?"

"Because I got to know you," she said, her heart lifting into the base of her throat. "I saw you for who you really are behind that mask. Spider is evil."

"You thought I was evil too. Probably still do, for all I know."

"Yeah, well..." Flynn faltered, unable to articulate how, even after everything, a small part of her wondered who Wolf could be if all the things that made him so effective at driving REDS's mission forward—his intelligence, his determination, his conviction—were applied to doing good. "Maybe you've changed me. Maybe Cori's death changed me. Maybe when you spared me at the Green Line concert and spoke to me in that cell for the first time, I knew there was something more to you. But I hate him. I hate him for what he made you into. He brutalized you. He turned you into this...this killing machine to do his dirty work and whatever else *he* wants."

"What did he make me into, Flynn? A monster?" His guard returned. "You make it sound like I haven't been acting on my own accord."

"You've been brainwashed. How can you not see that?"

Wolf turned away. A gust of wind ruffled his hair that had grown out over the weeks. "We wind up in the same place, don't we? Every time. Look at what we've done to each other. You think you're insane for believing that I, this...monster, could ever change or at the very least could be a functioning member of society. And a year ago I would've thought you're insane too. But now..." He paused, unable to finish. "Now, I'm questioning everything. Who I am. What I've done. Who I could be. I never thought it was possible for me to waver. But look at what you've done to me."

Flynn's voice evaporated. Everything around them vanished into thin air. All she could see was him, standing before her. Wolf had never been vulnerable like this. The closest he'd ever gotten to revealing anything was in her bed after his attack on the Loop.

"My training—my *indoctrination*, as you keep calling it—centered around not feeling. Extinguishing our pasts and our former selves." His eyes met hers. "Eliminating anything or anyone we might want. I don't know what I want to come from this." He gestured toward the smoldering city. "I don't know who I am without REDS, but I do know I want you."

Flynn stared, unable to form a response. All she could think about was the fact that he'd killed people. So many people. She could never forgive that. And yet here he was putting everything on the line. Time after time, whether he'd done it purposefully or even subconsciously, he'd put everything on the line for her. At the stadium, when she was a hostage, at the train station, and again at the whim of Spider. She wanted to run from him, she wanted to escape him forever, but she knew even if she did, she could never deny the truth: a part of her wanted him too.

She swallowed hard. "I don't...I don't know what I want either. I just know I can't lose you."

23

WOLF

Wolf shoved open the heavy door so hard it slammed against the wall with an ear-cracking bang. Spider stood at the head of a long conference table, surrounded by wheeled chairs. He didn't acknowledge Wolf's dramatic entry, remaining bent over, eyes glued to a report. Krammer's, Weasel's, and Tiger's heads snapped up, looking back and forth between them, shifting in the three chairs they occupied.

"Ah, Wolf, you're back. We've been waiting," Spider said.

Wolf stormed into the windowless room, trying to wrangle his thrashing rage. Spider's calm demeanor only fueled the fire building inside him. Each exhale burned his nostrils. Everything in him screamed to smash Tiger's face in, but a small sliver of smugness squeezed through his fury at the sight of Tiger's swollen eyes and bruised nose from their exchange on the train tracks.

"Would've made it back sooner had this fucking prick not compromised me and left Piranha to die," he said.

"Tiger already filled me in." Spider sounded bored. "Spare yourself."

"So, he told you that because of him, P is dead?"

"He told me he did what you couldn't do...again."

"What *I* couldn't do?" Wolf pointed to his chest. "He exposed us!" He jabbed his finger at Tiger. "And then left us to be burned alive. Unless that was your plan all along, Spider?"

Spider finally glanced up at him, brows raised. "If I wanted to kill you, I would hardly need to plan a covert way to do it. The girl was with them. She was alive. *You* should've been the one to shoot first. *You* were supposed to find them and take them out before they become more than a splinter in my ass." His eyes blazed beneath his hooded stare. Tiger's lips lifted into a smile.

"Tiger revealed our position before we had the opportunity to organize our attack. I wasn't going to be reckless. And because of him, we missed our chance." As he said it, Wolf realized Tiger had always planned to be the one to shoot first—to take credit for doing what Wolf had never been able to do: kill Flynn.

Wolf wanted to ask Spider whether he cared if he'd made it back or not. But he refused to ask—and besides, he already knew the answer. It twisted like a rusty screw tightening in its hole. He would never be able to redeem himself in Spider's eyes.

The corner of Spider's mouth twitched. "Tiger told me he did the job. He took them all out."

"He did, did he?" Wolf stared at Tiger. Tiger's gaze lasered onto his hands clasped in front him. "That's not quite how it happened. Thankfully, the bombings finished the job *he* couldn't."

It took Wolf a beat to realize that he'd lied. It had fallen off his tongue and now lingered there, hanging awkwardly in the room. Yes, Tiger had given him an easy lay-up, but he'd done it without thought to protect Flynn.

"Whatever, Wolf," Tiger sneered. "You just can't admit that once again you were too big of a pussy to pull the trigger."

Grinding his teeth together, Wolf advanced toward him. "You better watch your fucking back. I'll beat your ass. Again." Tiger's eyes flared, the puckered scars running down the length of his face stretching upward, and Weasel stood, stepping between them. "Don't try to make *me* seem like I'm the liar. You're the one who fucked us. Because you can't follow orders and don't know what the fuck you're doing, P didn't make it!"

"Enough." Spider cut in before Tiger could respond, leveling Wolf with a glare. "In case you don't remember, we've lost our own at your hand too." Tiger leaned back in his chair, linking his hands behind his head with a satisfied smirk. "Let's move on, shall we? Krammer was just about to brief us about the impact of the government bombings. We told the city it was coming, we told them to expect it—many didn't believe us, of course. So, we took videos of people we kept safe and moved to bomb shelters, and then took videos of people who didn't think to listen to us and where that left them." A crooked smile stretched across his face, brightening his entire demeanor, an expression he reserved only for mass destruction.

Krammer also grinned, his shoulders relaxing at Spider's glee. "Yes, yes," he chuckled. "My team made sure those videos went viral. It was the catalyst we needed. People are losing their damn minds! I don't think anyone thought the government would actually bomb their own people."

"How is the president responding to the pressure?" Weasel asked.

"He threatened a ground invasion. Promised to send the National Guard into Chicago. We told him if that happens, we'd send a nuke straight to Washington—"

"Krammer and I devised a little plan to drag this out a bit," Spider interrupted. "We have a small window of time to take advantage of the heightened emotions. We thought, why not give American citizens outside Chicago a chance to be involved? Spread distrust further."

"How?" Weasel asked.

"We call on the states to sacrifice their senators," Spider said. "Our government calls themselves the voice of the people. We need to show this country it's because of those spineless slugs that the system is broken. Show people how little they're needed. Show them they knew about the attack and did nothing. Show them these assholes don't represent them, but we do."

Weasel and Wolf exchanged knowing glances. It took several more seconds for Spider's real intention to click for Tiger. "Ohhh, and if a state doesn't, they get nuked?" he asked.

"Precisely," Krammer said. "It shouldn't be hard once we target the right people. Primarily people in rural areas. Podunk towns. If we get 'em in big enough numbers, they can overtake cities. And what better way to get 'em to band together?"

"Which is where you come in, Wolf," said Spider.

Wolf glanced up. "What do you need me to do?"

"The ransomware we discussed."

Wolf froze. His stomach plummeted. He'd completely forgotten.

"Your readmittance back onto the Executive Committee was contingent on developing this ransomware. It will allow us to extend our control beyond Chicago and open the doors for REDS cells in other states."

"What type of ransomware?" Weasel asked.

Spider narrowed his eyes, an icy cloud passing over his disposition. "One that takes over computers, phones, and smart TVs. We use it to frame the government and demand people show their support to REDS by killing their senators...or face the consequences."

For the first time, Wolf hesitated, searching for a response.

"Hmmm." Weasel drummed his fingers against his chin. "Make it seem as if the government is applying censorship? Violating the first amendment by limiting people's exposure to what's happening throughout the country?"

"Precisely," Spider said.

Tiger furrowed his brow. "I'm, uh, I don't get it..."

Wolf snorted and shook his head. "That's because you're a dipshit. I dunno, I've never created a ransomware, I have no idea how long it'll take."

"Everyone out," Spider ordered. "Except for you, Wolf."

Tiger and Krammer exited the room without question. Weasel gave Wolf a brief pat on the shoulder as he walked by. "Pretty brilliant, if I do say so myself," Weasel muttered under his breath.

Wolf sank into a chair knowing full well a lecture awaited him.

"I can't figure you out, Wolf. What the fuck has gotten into you? We allowed you back into EC meetings, which you seemed to so desperately want. Now you're pulling back. Again! You do realize you're on thin ice? Tiger is vying to be my successor—to lead REDS instead of you. You're choosing *now* to backpedal on everything we've worked toward together for years? When we're so close...when this country is practically ours for the taking!"

"I thought I meant something to you." Wolf cringed inwardly, his boldness surprising even himself. "I'm not sure why I allowed myself to believe that. I know it's against who we are and what we stand for."

Spider didn't respond. He straightened, his body rigid, almost as if he were summoning a shield against Wolf's emotions. Despite everything Wolf tried, despite how hard he'd worked to sever all attachments to the outside world, he now understood and accepted, he couldn't. Not just with Flynn, but Spider too. A wave of relief washed over him. It had been easy to disguise his longing for Spider's approval as obedience or a shared vision honoring their mission—a lie he'd told himself over and over again until he believed it. Resisting emotion and connection had drained him of everything, and to finally release himself from that requirement was liberating.

"If Tiger succeeds you," Wolf continued, "it would be the end of REDS."

Something in Spider snapped. He stalked toward Wolf, closing the distance between them in three strides. Wolf could practically see the salvia dripping from his mouth, a predator anticipating the kill. His hand shot out, fingers wrapping around the tender part of Wolf's neck just below his chin. He tilted Wolf's head up to meet his gaze. Wolf's nails dug into the armrest as Spider's grip tightened, his nostrils flaring.

"If that's true, it's you who is to blame. We both know you were supposed to be my successor. *You* were supposed to lead REDS, just like your father. You're a fucking disgrace. You disappointed me. I'll never forgive you for that."

Wolf stared into Spider's eyes, allowing the realization to settle over him that his leader and mentor was no longer either of those things. He'd been used again. Spider's loyalty had already shifted to Tiger. Even if he did create the ransomware, Spider would find another reason why Wolf was no longer worthy. He would hold it over his head, using it as a way to continue manipulating him. He was no one's puppet.

"If I find out that bitch is still alive, I will rip your heart out and feast on it for dinner," Spider growled, baring his teeth as he squeezed one last time before shoving Wolf away from him.

Wolf broke the heavy silence between them. "I'll start developing it. Should be complete in the next week or two."

"It better be."

24

FLYNN

When Flynn slipped through the door of the tiny bodega market, a tiny bell jingled merrily overhead. Two Allies soldiers materialized from behind a shelf, greeting her with raised rifles. Flynn dropped her axe, holding up her hands. Recognition flickered across one of the guard's faces.

"Flynn?"

Flynn nodded, stooping to pick up her weapon.

The guards relaxed, lowering their rifles. One reached for her radio. "Bat has entered the cave, I repeat bat has re-entered the cave. Over."

Assuming REDS were listening on the airway, the Allies had code named this entrance to their underground tunnel network "the cave."

Another voice replied, one that wouldn't expose Kerri. "Copy. On our way."

The soldier nodded at Flynn. "Head on down. They've had search parties out looking for you."

Flynn wove her way through ransacked shelves that had been tipped over like a stack of fallen dominos. The woman's walkie-talkie chirped as she whispered into the speaker. Flynn entered a supply closet and sidestepped down a narrow staircase, the steps bending precariously under her weight. She'd barely reached the bottom when Nate's voice echoed down the cramped corridor.

"FLYNN."

She turned to see him sprinting toward her with a grin that lit up his entire face. It glowed through the dimness. She couldn't remember the last time she'd seen him genuinely smile. She returned the expression instinctively, the muscles in her shoulders loosening, her body responding to the comfort of being back in his presence. His steps resounded off the walls and before she could take a step toward him, he swept her into his arms. Lifting her off her feet, he buried his head in the crook of her neck, holding her tightly. He swayed back and forth, his wiry scruff scratching her tender skin.

When he finally lowered her back to the ground, he didn't release her, and she didn't want him to. His breath steamed her cheek.

"We thought... We weren't sure what happened to you after we lost you in the explosions. We tried to go back for you, but we couldn't find you anywhere, and—and all the smoke... You were just gone..." His voiced cracked and then trailed off. His hand traveled to the back of her head. He pulled away and gently brushed her hair from her face, examining her bandage.

"I know. It was chaos. First REDS, then the bombs. It all happened so fast." Flynn's chest tightened. She'd been dreading this conversation with everything she had. Nate would lose his mind when he heard she'd been with Wolf. She wouldn't be able to convince him they needed Wolf to be successful—to win—but maybe she could convince Kerri. "There's—there's been a development. I need to speak with Kerri right away."

He raised his eyebrows. "A development?"

Flynn opened her mouth to elaborate, but no sound emerged.

Nate tilted his head. "Alright, well, she wants to see you anyway. She's been coordinating search parties for you. It's been risky, REDS Enforcers are everywhere since the bombings." He grabbed her hand, gluing her to him. Kissing the top of her forehead, his lips lingered. "Let's try to stick together from now on."

"Agreed." She extracted her hand from his so she could wrap an arm around his waist, pressing close to him. She tried to ignore the guilt bubbling up from the depths of her stomach, Wolf's kiss fresh in her memory. They walked side by side, their steps matching each other's. She would do anything to stay in this moment with Nate, to not have Wolf come between them again. "Has she thought anymore about Skulls and the bank robbery?"

"I think she's trying to weigh the pros and cons, but she's also been pre-occupied with finding you. We just don't know if we have the manpower we need for it to be successful, even with Nymph and Tawny on our side." Nate escorted Flynn to a small closet-like room off the control center where Kerri was deep in conversation with Vic and Antonio. Antonio saw her first and threw his arms up in the air.

"Flynn!" he yelled, his voice carrying in the compact space. "Girl, where've you been? You sure know how to keep us on our toes."

Kerri turned and grinned. She shook her head, grasping Flynn's shoulder when they reached her. "Praise the sweet lord, we needed this win." She squinted at the bandage right beneath her hairline. "Glad to see you're in one piece. Do you need someone to look at that?"

"I think it's okay. I've already been stitched up, I just need to change the bandage at some point."

Kerri pushed her bottom lip out. "And you stitched yourself up, did you?"

Flynn sighed. *Here we go.*

"I had some help, which is what I wanted to talk to you about." Flynn took a deep breath, squeezing Nate's side.

"Help from who?" Antonio pressed when she couldn't bring herself to elaborate.

"From one of them...from REDS."

Shocked silence enveloped them. Nate stepped away from her, and Flynn watched as his expression transformed from relief to fury. His complexion turned deep red. "Flynn, tell me you're not serious."

She swallowed hard, searching for some explanation that he might understand.

"What the fuck? You *are* serious."

Tears filled Flynn's eyes. She could feel the betrayal leeching from Nate's body as strongly as if she'd stabbed him with a knife. "Nate, come on, let me explain. He got me out of the explosion. He and two other soldiers were the ones who attacked us on the overpass. But after those jets started bombing the city, he f-found me and pulled me from the fire... He saved me, I guess."

"He?" Kerri butted in. "Who's he?"

Nate ignored her, linking his fingers behind his head. She could see him trying to keep his breathing even and measured. "I should've killed him," he muttered. "I never should've let him go. That motherfucker should be dead."

"Well, it's a good thing you didn't, because then *I* might be dead. He could be the answer to some of our problems."

"I'm sorry, what? We're in this shitstorm because of him!"

"I asked him to spy for us," Flynn blurted. "To provide intel for us on their outposts and positions. He already confirmed they have control of the nuclear arsenal, and there's no way we can launch a successful attack against REDS without an insider, especially at one of their most heavily guarded sites. He could be the one who helps us get Skulls on our side."

"Flynn, are you crazy? You should know by now, you can't trust him."

"Enough!" Kerri bellowed. "Flynn, who are you referring to? If you gave this guy any sort of information about us, we could be compromised."

"The psychopath who took her hostage," Nate said, jabbing toward Flynn. "The one who blackmailed her into helping him infiltrate Magnetic and then took down the electrical grid."

Flynn shot Nate a glare. "His name is Wolf. And it's...complicated. Besides, circumstances have changed. He's more inclined to join us now."

"Join us?" Nate asked, aghast. "This guy is responsible for killing hundreds of people."

Flynn resisted the urge to cringe, the urge to defend Wolf for the indefensible. "I'm not saying that what he did isn't the worst act possible, or that it will ever be forgivable. I'm just saying, maybe this is the break we need."

"And some people never change. Kerri's right, what did you tell him? Are we compromised?"

Flynn's heartbeat spiked. She tried to calm it, reminding herself how appalling her suggestion must sound to an outsider. "I told him nothing. Nothing, okay?"

Antonio stepped between them, attempting to de-escalate the crackling tension. "Alright, alright. Clearly there is still a lot here we don't know, but I gotta side with Nate on this one. No way we can trust one of them, even if he did save you, Flynn. There are too many unknown variables."

"Look, I didn't promise Wolf anything. I told him I'd propose it to the group while he thought it over and he could give me an answer in two days. Kerri, you can come with me to meet him. You or Vic, whoever, and you can make the final call yourself. He knows their end goal, he knows the intricacies of the organization, he knows their weak spots. He has all the answers we've been looking for."

"So, he hasn't even agreed to this?" Kerri asked.

Flynn's legs trembled. She shook her head.

Kerri, Vic, and Antonio exchanged glances while Nate snorted like an enraged bull, his hands clenched into fists. Flynn worried he might swing a punch into the wall.

"I dunno, Flynn," Kerri said, blowing air from puffed cheeks. "We're going to need more background here, specifically why he'd be willing to consider this arrangement and what circumstances have changed. What's in it for him?"

Flynn met Nate's fiery gaze, then turned back to answer Kerri. "We give him protection from REDS. If they find out he helped us, they'll kill him. He would need to become one of us."

Nate's mouth dropped open. "You cannot be serious."

"Why would he be willing to throw everything with REDS away?" Antonio asked.

"Let's just say he's on the outs with their leader and has realized he's disposable. Look, I get how crazy this sounds. I get how hard it is to wrap your heads around this possibility. Trust me, I was in the same mindset yesterday. But how are we going to pull off this bank heist without an insider? We know nothing about what we're walking into and have no way of scouting it out. Things are getting worse, especially now that we know for certain REDS is in possession of nuclear weapons."

Kerri sighed and shook her head, rubbing the back of her neck. "We need to think about it, and now that you're back, Flynn, we need to sit down and you need to tell me everything. No more secrets."

"What's there to think about?" Nate interjected. "This piece of shit almost single-handedly brought down the entire city of Chicago. And now *you*—" He jabbed his finger at Flynn again, so hard she flinched backward. "You're actually considering bringing him into our organization and risking everything we've created here? At this rate, *we*"—he gestured around wildly—"are our only hope for saving this city and getting everyone out of this fucking mess!" Nate shoved past Vic, heading for the control center.

"Nate, wait!" Flynn lunged for him, grabbing his arm, but he tore it from her grip and stormed off. Flynn's heart sank. Right when she and Nate finally were back on solid ground, the rug had been pulled out from underneath them again.

"Okay, fill us in on this Wolf guy. Clearly there is a lot of history," Antonio said.

"It's..." Flynn searched for words to explain her and Wolf's complicated and toxic relationship. "I honestly don't know where to begin."

"I need to speak with Flynn alone first," Kerri said. "Now."

Vic and Antonio exchanged glances and left, mumbling quietly to each other.

"Alright, out with it. Antonio's right. There's a lot I'm not understanding. If this—this Wolf character is responsible for Chicago's downfall and now he's willing to turn his back on REDS, I need to know why. What's the catch?"

"I am," Flynn replied so quietly Kerri had to lean forward to hear her. "I'm the catch."

Kerri sucked in air so sharply it whistled through her teeth. "Oh, boy. Come on, Flynn, Nate's right. We can't compromise what we have for a damn love triangle. Too much is at stake."

"A love triangle? Who said anything about that?"

"What else do you wanna call this then? Nate clearly loves you. This bloody terrorist must feel something for you if he's willing to throw away his entire history with REDS for *you*."

Flynn's tongue went dry. Her lungs squeezed in her chest. Love. The word terrified her. It sounded so extreme. So finite.

So inescapable.

Flynn stared at Kerri in a shocked stupor. Kerri raised her brows. "Oh, come on, you can't see that? Nate hasn't slept since you went missing."

A fresh deluge of guilt washed down the length of her body and seeped through her skin. She felt nauseous. "I don't—I don't…I don't have the capacity to love anyone right now, let alone think about it."

"That may be so, but it doesn't exempt you from being right smack in the center of this. And love is fickle, it's cruel, and it's fleeting, and fragile." Kerri flung an arm toward the door Nate stormed through. "Clearly it's jealous."

"Kerri, I'm not here to play mind games or mess with people's hearts." A zap of annoyance shot through her; she suddenly felt impatient at having to entertain any discussion about love. "I'm here to help figure out how to get out of this shitstorm, and Nate's right, the Allies are our only shot. But you and I both know we're at a huge and dangerous disadvantage. Our situation is becoming more precarious every day. And now we have Skulls to deal with. If you have a better idea that can bring us closer to finally getting a shot at REDS without involving him, I'm all ears. I don't know how to navigate this either! I didn't ask for this stupid, petty bullshit. I just know we're desperate."

Kerri's stoic façade slipped, and for a brief moment Flynn saw fear in her dark green eyes. "Alright," Kerri conceded. "But there will be a trial period. We bring him here, blindfolded and cuffed, and he stays in a cell while we interview him. Then we'll make the decision. Those are the conditions."

Flynn exhaled, but as soon as the landslide of relief passed through her, sheer panic settled in its aftermath. Could she trust Wolf enough to bring him within their ranks? If this went south, it was all on her. Again. She would be the only person to blame. What if Wolf was simply using her, like he had to infiltrate Magnetic?

No, she told herself.

Wolf had never been one to hide his intentions. He'd always been forthright about what he wanted from her. She had been the one who tried to deceive him in order to stop him.

"Agreed."

"You going to break it to Nate?"

Flynn groaned. "Can't you?"

"Absolutely not. I'm not touching that with a ten-foot pole. This one is on you."

25

FLYNN

Flynn found Nate sitting on the cot in their closet room. His elbows rested on his knees, both hands buried deep into the tangled roots of his hair. She leaned against the door, observing him. She took a deep breath and held it behind clenched teeth until her lungs burned. How could she explain to him that suddenly the tables had turned and Wolf was their only shot at staying alive?

"Nate," she tried to whisper, but instead it came out as a croak.

Nate kept his gaze glued to the floor. His foot tapped against the concrete, agitated. Clearly his feelings hadn't settled. "I can't believe you. I can't believe you're entertaining bringing that asshole into our fold."

Flynn's shoulders sagged. "Nate, will you just hear me out? Please."

He angled his head toward her, his glare freezing her in place and forming an icy barrier between them. His hazel green eyes had never looked so cold.

"I hate him," he whispered. "I hate everything he's done to you—everything he stands for."

"I know," Flynn said. "I know, because I hated him too. I told myself I'd kill him if I ever saw him again. But something's different this time. I can't explain how, because I know him—"

"You *know* him?"

Flynn crossed the room and sat next to Nate. He shifted his body to avoid touching her. "Yes. I mean, I dunno... Better than anyone else, I guess." She could hear her voice rising despite how she tried to keep it level. "It's almost like—" Flynn kept stumbling over her words, her throat so dry she couldn't swallow. "It's almost like he's finally seeing this isn't how he wants the world to be. That the part he's played in it is all wrong."

"It's a little late for that, don't ya think? I don't understand how you can defend him," Nate roared. He shot off the bed, and Flynn knew if there'd been something within his grasp, he would have thrown it. "Somehow...after everything, after him ruining your life, you're still defending him."

Flynn stood and grabbed his arm, forcing him to look at her. His shoulders rose and fell as he tried to steady his breathing. "I'll never be able to defend him, and I'll never defend what he's done. Not ever. But I *have* weighed the risk and the reward of involving him in our plan. I've also tried to play out a bank theft scenario without him, and in every case, it resulted in all of us dead. Why else would Skulls agree to work with a group like us? Because it's no skin off their back if we die. If they get the money, great, but if not, they don't care. We're the ones who would lose everything. They don't give a shit about us."

Nate's jaw was so tight he could barely open his mouth. "You keep trying to fix him. You keep thinking he's going to change. But he won't. You can't fix everyone. Sometimes, people are just broken."

"Yeah, well, who's going to then? How will things ever get better if we don't try...if we stop believing they can be?"

"He's going to use you and take from you until there's nothing left," Nate said.

"No one's taking anything from me anymore. Not after Cori."

Nate looked at her. "*He* killed Cori."

"He didn't. His leader did."

"And you believe that?"

"Yeah, I do. He's not the type who would ever deny something like that," Flynn said.

"He might if it would get to you. Regardless, what does it matter if it's him or his boss?"

"None of this has to do with me!" Flynn yelled. Silence stretched between them. "It has to do with stopping REDS."

"Oh, please, it has everything to do with you. You know he has feelings for you."

"Nate," she sighed. "I know you think that this makes me weak. I know you think I'm overplaying my hand here. I know you think because I'm choosing not to kill him, I'm not strong enough to. But I am. I'm just redirecting my anger at the right target. Not all power has to come in the form of compounding pain on top of pain—destruction on top of more destruction. Where does it ever leave us? In a wasteland of more anger. Maybe it's time to try something different this time."

Men always thought they knew best. They were such simple creatures, thinking there was only one way of doing things. That if you eliminate the person, it eliminates the problem. But it lives on and regrows, poking its angry head back through the soil like a weed. Men underestimated women and their emotions. Their empathy. They never saw it as a strength, only as a weakness.

"How could you ever forgive him?"

Flynn released his arm. "Again, I haven't forgiven him. This doesn't have to do with forgiveness. What would that achieve anyway? It wouldn't fix any of what he's done in the past. It sure as hell won't solve our problems now. I don't know if I'll ever be able to forgive him... But the world moves on, and so I'm going to move forward with it. I don't know what the future holds, I just want a future."

Nate rubbed a hand down the length of his face, but none of his muscles loosened. "Flynn, I'm not going to miss my shot again."

"Yeah, well, neither am I. Except this time I'll make sure I'm aiming at the right person." It struck Flynn for the first time that, maybe, that was why she'd never been able to kill Wolf—because she'd known deep in her gut he wasn't the right target. That maybe, because he had saved her, there had to be something, however small, resting in his heart waiting to be discovered.

Flynn put her hands on both sides of Nate's face and guided his eyes toward hers until they met. "I won't ever let him come between us. Not again."

Nate stared at her, and for a brief moment, the world froze. It stopped spinning on its axis. Then he reached up and lowered her hands, letting them linger in his for a brief moment before letting go. As he walked past her to leave the room, she caught his whisper:

"You already have."

26

WOLF

Wolf waited at Flynn's designated meeting spot in the tree's shadow, its branches now mostly shed of leaves. Two benches beckoned, nestled under its cover, but rather than sitting, Wolf remained vigilant. He braced himself against the cutting gusts of wind, his eyes watering from the chill. He loved how clean and thin the air tasted as it collided against his face.

I can't believe I'm actually here, he thought. He tried not to let the emotions of the decision overwhelm him, but they waited at the periphery, threatening to pounce at any second. Instead, he focused on his roaring anger, allowing it to smother everything else.

The ransomware.

Spider dangling Tiger as REDS's new leader over his head.

The sting of Spider's rejection.

Spider knew how detrimental Tiger would be to REDS as their leader, and the fact that he'd used it as a threat to manipulate Wolf had him reeling. His anger flared again. He would rather throw himself into the lake's dark waters than report to Tiger. Spider had moved on from him so easily, without a second's hesitation, all with the goal of showing Wolf how he was disposable.

Replaceable.

He'd always been an outcast, but it had been on his own terms. This felt different. It was abandonment. Betrayal. He'd trusted Spider as a leader and, although he struggled to admit it to himself, as a father figure too. Now, he had no one to turn to except Flynn while he grappled with the loss of the persona he'd spent over a decade creating. It was almost as if he'd been building a mold to pour himself into only to find that he no longer fit.

Wolf stared out at a tiny lighthouse floating in the great expanse of the lake and closed his eyes. Little by little, these past few weeks had peeled back layers he didn't know had existed, and he was still discovering what was beneath each one. Months ago, when he and Flynn had been on a boat ride, she'd pointed out how other people had defined who he was his entire life. He was beginning to realize she was right. He had no idea who he really was. Then, something had sparked when he saw Flynn again. Something undeniable and true. Each time he kissed her, he caught a glimpse of it... Was it hope? Is this what hope felt like, heavy but also unbelievably light? He wouldn't know.

"Hands where we can see them," a warning voice broke him from his reverie.

He opened his eyes and exhaled before slowly raising his hands and placing them behind his head.

"Turn around," the voice commanded.

Wolf turned. Two men approached him, guns raised. Flynn stood behind them, next to a small woman with dark red hair.

His eyes met Flynn's, and in that instant, he knew he'd made the right decision. He would do anything they asked him to. He wanted her. REDS had always dictated what he should want. He'd built his life around their decrees. But then he met her, and now he finally understood what it really meant to want something. Maybe that's why he'd never been able to kill her. He'd denied himself of her for so long, but what if he finally relented? What would happen? The thought terrified him, but he couldn't go back to the way things were.

Would she ever be able to accept him?

Flynn's face remained unreadable as she took him in. Her steely gray eyes seemed cloudy, like the murky water behind him. He would have to prove himself to her, and it started here.

"We're going to assume by you showing up here today you're agreeing to come with us?" the redhead asked. Her strong Scottish accent took him by surprise. Wolf lowered his chin in confirmation. "Alright, well, hand over your weapons."

Wolf hesitated, then offered his rifle, handgun, and knife.

"Blindfold and cuff him," the woman ordered.

One of the guards cuffed his hands behind his back and placed a piece of cloth securely around his head.

They walked in silence for several long minutes until a door creaked open and the ground beneath him changed from hard concrete to a more pliable surface. The sound of their footsteps became more pronounced as they shuffled into an enclosed area. Hard objects, likely furniture or shelves based on their comparable height to him, brushed against his arms and shoulders as they maneuvered him through the space. A loud creak squawked; at the same time, one of the men released a grunt.

"Steps. Watch your feet."

Rough hands pushed his head down as he fumbled forward, hesitating before dipping a foot to meet the first wobbly step. He couldn't help but think of when REDS had blindfolded him right before initiation, also leading him to an unknown fate. He'd grown up since then.

Light through the blindfold dimmed as they descended farther underground and the air turned stale and stuffy. His shoulders tensed, an automatic response to being in an unfamiliar place. He resisted the instinct to strain against his cuffs.

They walked for several more minutes, past an area where a large number of voices carried. A booming laugh was met with others, and Wolf noticed how jarring it sounded. Laughter. People were capable of laugher even as the city crumbled around them? They continued on until the voices faded and silence, except the scuff and slap of their boots, enveloped them again.

Once they finally came to a stop, he waited as the jangle and clink of keys unlocked a door. Hands pushed him forward and someone turned him by the shoulders before forcing him to sit.

"Wow, can't believe he actually showed," a man commented. The voice was distantly familiar.

Someone yanked the blindfold off his head. He blinked, eyes adjusting to the dim room. A lantern was the only source of light. The two guards left, keeping him cuffed, but the small space felt claustrophobic due to the cluster of people crammed around him. Heat from their bodies pressed in on him, and Wolf fought the instinctual urge to fight, to attack and kill them. That's what he'd been trained to do—kill without thought. It had always been easy in the sense that he'd never thought much about it. He'd never felt remorse because he'd never cared about the person.

He'd never cared about anyone.

A tall man stood before Wolf. It took a second for him to recognize Nate's glaring face, hate etched into every line of his features. Nate took a switchblade from his pocket and flicked it open, holding the blade's tip within a centimeter of Wolf's nose.

"Try anything or fuck us over, and I'll pluck your eyes out."

Wolf sneered up at him. He loathed being in the subordinate position. "I'd love to see you try."

The redheaded woman grabbed Nate's arm and pulled him back. "Nate, that's enough."

Wolf counted seven people surrounding him. He searched for Flynn, locating her in the back next to a man with a short afro and square glasses. She had her arms crossed over her chest, and he could tell by how her hands clutched either bicep she was anxious.

"Welcome to our camp. As you might know by now, we call ourselves the Allies. My name is Kerri, and the goal of our meeting today is to determine if we can trust you enough to work with us. So, before we begin, we'd like to understand what you want out of this...so-called partnership. In other words, what are your conditions?"

Wolf swallowed. He looked down at his lap. "I only have one. I want immunity."

"Well, we can't guarantee that, but we can agree to a trial."

Wolf glanced up. Even when sitting, Kerri wasn't much taller than him. The woman had pixie-like features—a small, upturned nose and vaguely pointed ears. "Seems like a waste of everyone's time. We know what a trial would determine. I'm not going to argue for my innocence. We all know I'm guilty."

Kerri didn't say anything. Her lower jaw shifted back and forth as she considered him.

"I can't offer up much more than my life. I'm here, aren't I? I showed up. You realize if REDS knew I was here, they'd execute me on the spot?"

Another woman with smoky hair studied him. He couldn't tell its color in the dark light, but she wore what looked like a full black bodysuit with skeleton bones painted along her limbs and rib cage. "He's a rat," she spat. "How do we know we can trust him?"

Kerri eyed her, annoyed. "Tawny, this is my team, so I'll make the final call. Unlike *you*, I care about whether we make it out of this alive. That is, unless you have some secret stash of intel you've been withholding."

"Yeah, well, this plan determines whether *we* get our cash or not—"

"This is a waste of time if we're going to spend the next hour going in circles deciding whether to believe me or not," Wolf said. "Why the fuck did you guys agree to meet me and take me here if you're not going to believe me? I know it's because I'm your only chance. I know you don't have any other option, or else we wouldn't be here, so let's cut the bullshit and move on."

No one responded.

"Who's in charge here?" Wolf asked.

"I am," both women said at the same time. Kerri glared at the one she called Tawny.

Wolf rolled his eyes. "You've gotta be fucking kidding me. Well, this explains a lot. I'm not saying anything with all these people here. I'm not gonna talk unless everyone's out except the person in charge, whoever the fuck that is, and Flynn."

"Uh-uh." Nate shook his head. "Nice try. We're not letting a psychopathic terrorist call the fucking shots."

"Uh, yeah, you are, because you don't have a choice."

"Alright, out! Out! Everybody, get out," Kerri yelled. "I can't hear myself think with everyone shouting their bloody two cents." The group started filtering out of the room. "Not you, Flynn," she barked as Flynn inched toward the door. "You heard him. You stay."

Nate and the other woman lingered. "Tawny, you heard him. You're not in charge here, I am."

"While I'm relieved to say I don't associate with your whatever-the-fuck-you-want-to-call-it crew, I'm in charge of Skulls, Kerri, so no, I stay."

"You're trusting this *crew* to get you your money."

"Trust is a loose term."

"Alright, both of you stay, I don't give a shit, but get him out of here." Wolf inclined his chin toward Nate.

"Nate, you heard him, out," Kerri ordered.

Nate's fingers curled into two fists, and Wolf wondered if he was going to slam one of them into his face. He shoved past Flynn, storming out of the room. Wolf allowed himself a brief moment of smugness.

"That looked icy," he said to Flynn.

Her mouth pulled into a hard line and she crossed her arms over her chest again, withdrawing into herself. "Yeah, he's not your biggest fan."

"I'd say that's an understatement."

She raised her eyebrows. "Can't imagine why. Maybe it's the hundreds of people you've murdered."

For the first time, Wolf cringed internally from the sting of her words, like a slap she'd landed on his cheek. How could he have thought it would be so easy for Flynn to consider starting over with him? He wondered if it would ever be possible for her to move past his history. He doubted it. No one would ever understand—could ever really understand—why he'd done what he did. How, in his mind, that had been his only option. How he'd never been able to see beyond that moment in time. How REDS had been his only hope at a future and a livelihood. He would never be able to explain that to her, let alone anyone else. The only people who would be able to understand it were dead.

"Look, I'm sure Flynn has filled you in enough to know I'm not in good standing with REDS. But I'm not funneling them information about your group. In complete transparency, REDS doesn't consider you much of a threat. They have bigger fish to fry right now than to concern themselves with your group."

"Then why did you attack us several days ago?" Kerri asked.

"That was my comrade...or should I say, associate. He's a piece of shit. We were on a mission to find you because my leader got intel Flynn was with you. They wanted me to prove my allegiance to REDS by killing her."

Kerri looked over her shoulder at Flynn. "Hm, you left out that tiny detail."

Flynn's face had turned ghostly pale, even in the shadowy room. "In all honesty, I didn't know."

"The good news is they think she died in the government bombings," Wolf said, meeting Flynn's gaze. He still couldn't read her expression. "They think you all did."

"So, you lied to your leader to protect her?" Kerri interpreted back to him, while pointing to Flynn.

"Yes. And if I'm going to keep talking, I'm going to need guaranteed immunity," Wolf said. "From both your groups. We all know I'll be a walking target wherever I go, so I'll need some sort of protection."

Kerri's eyes flicked back and forth between Flynn and Wolf. "Okay, granted," Kerri relented. "On the one condition that this mission is a success."

Tawny nodded. "Agreed."

"Done," said Wolf. "If it's not, we'll all be dead anyway. Okay, moving on, tell me more about this mission." He looked between Kerri and Tawny. "Clearly you two are at odds. And this is a pretty unlikely pairing. I'm familiar with Skulls, we have a few members who joined our ranks after leaving them. Bought quite a few guns off them in the past too. But I can't figure out what would've brought you two together."

"We needed more gunpower and manpower to take on REDS," Kerri said. "So, we sought out help."

"What's in it for you?" Wolf asked Tawny. "Skulls doesn't seem like a gang who would offer their services *pro bono*."

Tawny ran a pointed tongue over her top teeth. "Moola. We wanna rob REDS. The ultimate bank heist."

Wolf's mouth dropped open before he broke out in laughter. "I'm sorry, what? You plan on using the Allies to help you steal money from REDS? No offense," Wolf offered to Kerri, "but what're you thinking? Do you even have a plan of attack?"

One of Kerri's eyes twitched in annoyance. "We have a means of accessing the bank where REDS is holding their money."

"And that is…?"

Kerri hesitated, clearly still weighing what to disclose and what to hold close to her chest. "One that would allow us to get in and get out as quickly and discreetly as possible. With the least number of causalities."

"And how do you expect to do that?"

Kerri shifted her weight. "Tunnels."

Wolf had to admit he hadn't been expecting that one. "You have access to tunnels that go under the Chicago River?"

Both Kerri and Tawny nodded.

"It's risky," he said. "You could compromise your position. Probably not worth it… You could lead them right back to you."

"That was my concern as well," Kerri admitted. "But, as you concluded, we're desperate, and the tunnel is the only way to get us into the Loop with the bridges all raised. If we take any other route, we're sitting ducks. Literally. Our number-one priority is to never reveal our location to REDS."

"Why do you want this cash? Is it really worth it?" Wolf asked Tawny.

"The entire country is moving on outside of Chicago, and it's only a matter of time until we move on too. With or without REDS. Money ain't goin' nowhere. Period. And when the world gives you lemons, make lemonade, baby. This cash could secure our position for decades."

"You do realize, after REDS consolidated all the money to one location, they ensured it's heavily guarded. Have you ever run an operation like this before? Of any kind?"

Kerri hesitated before shaking her head. "This is why we need you to take out REDS's guards and systems."

Tawny glanced at Kerri, nodded, and then shrugged. "I mean, Skulls has, but never against another militia-like organization."

"How many of you will there be?" Wolf asked.

"From Skulls, just me and my partner, Nymph. He was the big guy with the beard and spiky red hair."

"Haven't decided yet," Kerri admitted.

"How do you plan on opening the vault?"

"Torches," Tawny said.

"The door is four feet thick. You know how long that would take? Why do you think they chose this vault?"

Tawny placed her hands on her hips. "I dunno, got any ideas, buddy? We've got some grenades that should do the trick. Should weaken the steel."

Wolf had been doing his best to hide his disdain, but now his impatience was officially boiling over. "What are you, a bank robber from the fucking '50s? If torches and grenades are all you've got, you're shit out of luck. Torching that door would take forever. And you can kiss your cash goodbye if you use grenades."

"Alright then, Mr. fucking Genius, what's your plan then?"

Wolf's lips lifted into a half smile. He couldn't resist playing with them a bit. "We hack the lock."

Kerri's brow furrowed. "Hack it?"

"The vault in the Chicago Board of Trade has been inoperable for almost eighty years. REDS had to make some upgrades when we took over to ensure it was functional."

"You can do that even if there's no WiFi or shit?" Tawny challenged.

"I can hack the government, but you don't think I can hack some wonky lock combination?"

Tawny scratched the back of her head. "Guess safecracking really ain't what it used to be."

Wolf sat back in his seat. "Welcome to the digital age."

27

FLYNN

Flynn watched Wolf from the back of the room, her heart wedged in her throat. Her credibility, their lives, everything was at stake with his very presence. But she knew they could never get this done without him. He was there because of her, and that knowledge tugged her in a million different directions. A tiny part of her was grateful. Another part felt as if two shackles had been slapped around her ankles, attached to a ball and chain for her alone to drag behind her.

Kerri stepped in front of Tawny, shooting her another annoyed glare. The two of them had been vying for control over the bank heist and, in the process, continued to butt heads. Both held two completely different priorities. Kerri wanted her people alive. Tawny wanted the money. "Look, we know this situation is less than ideal and you understandably have your doubts, but as you clearly are aware, Skulls is one of the largest illegal arms smugglers in the Midwest, and we need all the firepower we can get to go up against REDS."

Wolf sighed. "It's going to take more than guns to take down REDS. Despite what the media has led people to believe, it's an extremely sophisticated organization that has been planning this takeover for years."

"That was my next point of discussion." Kerri paused, her eyes narrowing as she scrutinized Wolf's face, studying it like one might a difficult text they were trying to pick apart. "Another reason I wanted to meet today was to discuss your involvement with us after the robbery."

Flynn bit the inside of her cheek. Admittedly, she had been shortsighted in her thinking about partnering with Wolf for this mission. She hadn't put much thought into the long-term advantages of his insider knowledge.

He raised his eyebrows. "Meaning what, exactly?"

"I'm assuming you've been in communication with the government. Whether it be through spies, representatives, or directly with the president. As you just said, even with the additional firepower and Skulls' help, we both know the Allies can't take on REDS by ourselves. Especially with your access to nuclear weapons. We're going to need more help."

Wolf's eyes met Flynn's and even through the dimness of the room their clear green sent a shock through her. "*If* I decide to do this, I won't have a choice but to continue my involvement until there is some resolution. There's no going back. Spider knows I'm the only one who could ever hack into the vault lock. And the second I do, alarms will go off. He'll know it was me."

Quiet settled over them. "Who's Spider?" Kerri asked.

Wolf swallowed and dropped his gaze back to the floor. Flynn watched as his expression shuttered closed at the mention of Spider's name. "REDS's leader."

Kerri glanced over at Flynn. "How can we trust you won't go running back to REDS and tell him about our plan?"

"You can't really, I guess. Just trust your gut. I think you know this is your only option if you want to keep your group alive and intact. Besides, like I said, you aren't a threat to him." He finally met Kerri's intense stare. "You should keep it that way as long as you can, because this heist is going to open up a whole new world of problems for you. You prepared for that?"

"We are," Kerri said quietly. "Like you said, this is our only option."

Tawny clapped her hands together, making Flynn jump. "Well, now that it's settled, what're you thinkin' in terms of timing?"

"I'm assuming most of your team is very green. In an ideal world, minimum of three weeks. To prepare, scout, and practice. And even then none of you would be ready. But we don't have three weeks. We have maybe a week and a half at most."

"Alright, look, this ain't *my* first rodeo," Tawny said.

Wolf shook his head. "REDS isn't your everyday gang shoot-up. They're not even like the CPD. Even if you can point and shoot a gun, it's going to take a lot more than that. I don't know how many more times I need to remind you, but it's critical for your survival to remember that REDS is a professionally trained organization."

Silence reverberated between them. Tawny shot a look at Flynn. "I still got no clue how you wound up in the middle of all this. You sure as hell don't look the terrorist type."

Flynn's lips tugged upward. "Guess that's what makes me such an effective double agent."

"When do we meet next to nail down the plan?" Kerri asked, keeping them on track.

"Best time for me is at night. When I'm on patrol. I'm usually the night shift and get off at 5 a.m. We can decide different places for us to meet to avoid wasting time coming back here and to avoid getting tailed. It's all risky, so the fewer times we meet, the better."

Kerri nodded. "Agreed. Next meeting two days from now sound like a good place to start?"

"Yes. Oz Park by the statue, 10 p.m. That area tends to have the least number of patrols since it's been cleared out and all the people rounded up. And it's harder for REDS to access since the bridges have been raised."

Kerri pointed to Flynn and Tawny. "Alright, any last thoughts? Anything you'd like to add?"

"I'd like to speak with Wolf alone for a minute, if you're okay with that," Flynn said.

Kerri hesitated, then nodded. "Okay. But make it quick. We'll wait outside to escort him back to the lake."

When the door closed behind Tawny, Flynn approached Wolf. It was strange to stand over him when he always towered over her.

"Wolf, I know how much you're risking to do this and be here. But I want you to come to this decision on your own and for your own future, not because of me," Flynn said.

"You need me," Wolf said simply. "You all do if you want to a pull off a stunt like this. None of you have any sort of training and yet you thought you could waltz in and steal a shitload of cash from right under REDS's nose? It's a fucking suicide mission, Flynn."

Flynn hated that he was right—how he always seemed to be right. He always had the upper hand and always seemed one step ahead. He was too fucking smart, and worst of all, he knew it. "That may be true, but making this leap is only going to work long term if it's what *you* want. If you're doing this to hang it over my head or add it to your growing list of ways that you've 'saved me,'"—she air quoted—"then don't. That's all I'm saying."

"That's not why I'm doing this."

"Then why? Out of the goodness of your heart? Since you have so much of that."

Wolf blinked, taken aback. "I still don't really know why," he said quietly. "But this is the only way I can figure that out while also figuring out what I actually want."

It took several seconds for Flynn to realize she'd stopped breathing. Tension radiated between them. They still couldn't trust each other. How could they when neither of them fully understood his motives? Her head spun, propelled by a wave of intense anxiety. Flynn turned on her heel and walked to the door. She knocked loudly three times. "He's ready to go."

The guards went back in and replaced his blindfold before leading him out.

"Oz Park, 10 p.m.," Kerri said to Wolf. "Two days. We'll kick everything off and finalize a plan."

"See you then," Wolf said.

Flynn swallowed the knot in her throat, trying to find the right words to say goodbye. She wished she could thank him, but she couldn't ignore the well of resentment filling her chest. Once again, she was in his debt.

"See you," she managed.

The muscles around Wolf's mouth tightened, as if he wanted to say something, but before he could, the guards led him away. Flynn watched their retreating backs, guilt tugging at her. They were putting everything on the line for this mission. There would be no turning back. Should she have thanked him instead of immediately questioning his motives? Still unsure about where they stood, but knowing it was with shaky footing on unstable ground, Flynn took a deep breath. She couldn't control Wolf or the outcome of this heist any more than she could control the weather. No point in looking back when the future required their full attention.

"You were right." Kerri put a hand on Flynn's shoulder, startling her from her spiraling thoughts. "If this is going to work, if we're going to have any sort of shot, we need him. I kept trying to think of a way we could benefit from this plan other than guns and ammunition. He's our answer. He's the only way we can win this whole thing."

Flynn nodded, relieved Kerri also understood this. "I just wish Nate could see that."

Kerri's eyes creased with sympathy. "He won't. Not when it involves you."

28

WOLF

Wolf gripped the steering wheel to the Humvee and winced. Pain shot up his arm, triggered by muscles wound so tightly around his joints they might as well be a python suffocating any hope for normal movement. He still hadn't fully recovered from Nate's bullet to his shoulder but had no time to properly rehab it. He rolled his head, massaging the twinging knot in his neck.

From the passenger seat, Tiger's tobacco chomping resounded in Wolf's right ear, interrupted only by guttural throat clearing when Tiger would roll down the window to hock a loogie onto the empty sidewalk.

Wolf ground his teeth so hard he could hear the pop of his jaw. He eyed Tiger's greasy skin and pit-stained shirt underneath his military vest. The man repulsed Wolf on every level. "No wonder your breath smells so fucking rancid all the time."

Tiger beamed, specks of chaw flecked over his yellow teeth. He dug his tongue into his bulging lower lip. "Too white collar for some dip, eh, Wolf?"

"Not while I'm on patrol."

Wolf didn't like anything that altered his senses. Especially when he couldn't rely on Tiger as a partner.

Tiger snorted, shaking his head. "Always such a goody two-shoes. Well, at least until it came to that bitch. Too bad she's dead now."

As a form of punishment and likely suspicion, Spider doubled Wolf's patrol duty and saddled him with Tiger during both the afternoon and evening routes. This could complicate things. He was supposed to meet with the Allies in Oz Park the next day. Thankfully, much as it offended Wolf's intellect, Tiger couldn't be any dumber. It shouldn't be hard to ditch him somehow. If only he could squash him altogether. Smash his face into the windshield. Curb stomp his skull. Wolf's adrenaline spiked, his pulse jackrabbiting at the delicious thought of wrapping his fingers around Tiger's throat.

Everything would be so blissfully quiet.

Another loogie hocked out the window startled Wolf from his peaceful daydream of murdering Tiger. He inhaled deeply through his mouth to avoid Tiger's stench, holding his breath in the back of his throat and counting to three before releasing it slowly. He rolled down his own window as a respite from the nauseating mix of tobacco and B.O. lingering between them.

They whizzed past abandoned bus stops, jumped into a bus lane, and turned onto Michigan. The famous avenue usually bustled with constant activity, a buzz that had once made Wolf's head swim. He'd used to avoid this area at all costs due to the teeming masses of tourists clogging the sidewalks like a cholesterol-filled artery. Now, battered buildings loomed above them—crippled giants REDS had bent into submission. Smoke and ash from the military bombings still hung over the area, blocking the afternoon sun, a cloud that wouldn't dissipate. They continued driving south past Millennium Park, where REDS had held their rally, and the Art Institute of Chicago. At the foot of the grand steps leading up to the museum entrance, two giant lions stood on concrete blocks, their expressions haughty and regal despite their altered surroundings, this new desolate wasteland.

Wolf suddenly slowed.

A huge makeshift fence had been erected. Plywood hid whatever occupied the area and barbed wire decked the top, coiled and glinting like sparkly tinsel.

When did this happen? Wolf thought to himself.

True, he hadn't patrolled this far south since he'd come back from Midway. He and Flynn had bypassed this area completely on their roundabout route back toward Lakeview. He glanced at Tiger, suspicious of the smug expression cleaving his face.

"You gonna tell me what's going on here?"

"What, you don't know?" Tiger's tone was sly and slippery.

"Obviously not, shithead. Why do you think I'm asking?"

"Guess you really aren't in Spider's circle anymore." Tiger beamed. He wasn't even trying to hide his glee.

Rage boiled in Wolf's stomach.

He jerked the steering wheel, guiding the truck up and over the sidewalk. He drove alongside the fence, which ran the length of the city block, around what was likely a good chunk of Grant Park. One of the city's largest and most prominent parks, Grant Park was over 300 acres and ran parallel with Lake Michigan.

"Remember that giant music festival they used to have here? What was it called?" Tiger thought for several long seconds, then snapped his fingers. "Lollapalooza! That's it! Can't believe people actually paid money to go to that bullshit. Probably just a bunch of dudes wanting to see slutty girls running around with no clothes on. Not like the music was good or anything."

Wolf side-eyed him. "Nah. I never wasted my time on that shit."

He wasn't quite sure why he lied to Tiger. Maybe because admitting the truth would have sounded too pathetic. He remembered in between summer classes at community college watching gaggles of teen girls with glitter tattoos curved around their eyes and collarbones. They'd barely looked old enough to get into R-rated movies, yet there they were, without a care in the world other than to get drunk and watch a band scream at them. The injustice of their carefree lives had enraged him, and it's ultimately what inspired his idea for REDS's attack on the Green Line concert at Soldier Field.

Tiger grabbed the passenger handle while the truck bumped over uneven ground. Wolf finally slammed his foot on the brake, shifted the vehicle into park, and turned off the engine. Silence settled around them in the absence of its reverberating roar.

Wolf pointed toward the passenger door, his knuckles inches from Tiger's nose. "Get the fuck out."

Tiger tried to maintain his composure, but Wolf didn't miss the flash of panic in his shifty eyes. He stumbled out of the truck as Wolf leapt down from his seat, slamming the door behind him.

"I'll only ask nicely one more time... What. The. Fuck is going on here?" Wolf thrust his thumb toward the fence.

"Ask Spider."

"I'm asking *you*."

Tiger shot a wad at Wolf's feet.

Wolf leveled his rifle at him. "I'll give you until the count of three. Then I blast your head off."

"You—you would never. S-Spider would kill you."

Wolf shrugged. "I'd say it's worth it to see your brains on the ground."

The color leeched from Tiger's face, still slightly swollen and bruised from repeatedly colliding with Wolf's fists a few days ago. The thought of killing him prompted a fizz of joy to rise through Wolf's body, warming his fingers.

"One." His grip relaxed around the trigger. *Slight pressure. Release.* "Two. Th—"

"Alright!" Tiger threw up his hands. Even from several feet away Wolf could see dirt caked under his long fingernails.

Wolf grinned.

Pussy.

"Show me." Wolf lowered his gun, albeit reluctantly. "Get back in the Humvee. Asshole."

They got back in the truck and as it lurched forward Tiger directed Wolf to the end of the block before he had them turn and head toward the lake. They continued to run parallel with the fence. Stretching about 50 feet high, with pieces of the plywood anchored haphazardly on top of each other, it looked almost like a temporary construction barrier.

"How did you guys get this up so fast?" Wolf asked. "And why the fuck did you use raw plywood? That thing will flop like a fish the second it rains or snows."

"Yeah, well, it ain't supposed to last long. It's a shit job," Tiger admitted, hunched in his seat. "Had to throw it together after the bombings. Shifts worked on it pretty much round the clock 'til it was done."

Wolf glanced at him, unnerved. What else did REDS have in the works that he didn't know about?

How could Spider keep something this big from me?

"Did the EC sign off on this?"

Tiger smirked. "Sure did."

So, they'd all known about this except him? "Fuck your shit-eating grin, you little troll."

"Stop here." Tiger gestured up ahead where two armed REDS guards stood in front of metal grated gates. Tiger rolled down his window and stuck his head out.

"Eh! Let us through."

One of the guards recognized him and unlocked the giant bolt across the gate. It took two of them to push it open.

Wolf rolled past into the giant enclosed space.

His nose instinctively scrunched as a strong raw sewage stench wafted through the open window.

"Fucking disgusting," Tiger muttered, jamming the window's close button.

Wolf shifted the Humvee into park, stopped dead by the sight before him. Repulsion stirred inside him, awakening and spreading until it reached every corner of his insides. Stretching as far as the eye could see, people sat, stood, or lay huddled next to fire pits burning in large metal trashcans. Humans. Prisoners.

"Aren't these our hostages?" Wolf asked.

"Spider decided they'd served their purpose. After the government bombings, we don't need 'em to protect our strongholds no more. They were takin' up too many resources, so we threw 'em all in here."

Wolf didn't quite understand his visceral reaction to the sea of people. He saw no tents, no aid, no sign of clean water or food. A big part of him had always believed he was working toward building a new world. But this new world wasn't better than the one they'd left behind.

Wolf exited the truck and Tiger followed, pinching his nose.

"Man," Tiger groaned, "smells like actual shit in here."

Wolf's eyes stung and he held his breath against the overpowering barrage to his senses. Every twenty feet or so REDS soldiers patrolled, wearing bulletproof vests over thick jackets and carrying automatic rifles. They each had crimson neck and face masks pulled up over their noses, making them easy to spot among the endless bleak gray. As Wolf surveyed the scene, his eyes caught the wary gaze of a little girl watching him, fear plastered on her tiny pale face. Matted brown curls sat askew on her head. She shrunk back into the cover of her mother's arms. Wolf tried to swallow, but it was as if his body would no longer respond to his brain. His fingers tingled. The mother squeezed her little girl tightly, burying her nose into the mop of curls before laying her cheek upon her head. Wolf did a double take, his heart stuttering to a stop.

She had clear, emerald-green eyes.

He blinked several times, but by the time his head cleared, the mother had turned away from him to lay on the ground, her body tucked around her daughter.

For a brief moment he could've sworn he saw his own mother.

He only had one faint memory of her. Like the little girl, he'd been wrapped in her arms as she carried him out of their apartment, enveloped in the smell of lilacs drifting from her hair. He always wondered why she'd let him go—why she'd left him. Now he knew she'd been trying to protect him.

To save him.

What would his life have looked like if she'd been able to keep him? What could his future have been if REDS hadn't stolen it from him and twisted his fate into an endless pattern of loneliness and abandonment?

"Alright, happy now? Can we get the fuck outta here?"

"Spider said we needed to show the hostages mercy to unite them under our cause."

Tiger cackled. "Mercy? When has Spider ever shown mercy? He don't know the meanin' of that word."

The knot in Wolf's stomach cinched tighter. Spider had been lying to him all along—telling him exactly what he thought Wolf wanted and needed to hear in order to comply with his order to create a ransomware. "What's going to happen to them?" Wolf asked, his voice hoarser than he expected. "It's getting colder. These people will freeze to death."

"Who gives a shit?" Tiger snarled.

"I just thought... What about getting more supporters?" Wolf asked. He cleared his throat, realizing how he sounded to Tiger. He reeled his emotions back in, slamming the lid back on before everything released from Pandora's box. "What about the army we're supposed to create? We need bodies."

Tiger shrugged. "Dunno. I'm sure they'll have a choice."

Wolf thought back to the Green Line concert. To the rifle he'd held in his hands and unloaded without thought. He'd been so confident. He hadn't once questioned himself or his actions.

But now he'd caught a glimpse of what this new world would look like—the new world he'd worked his entire adult life to bring to fruition. It didn't bring the joy or satisfaction he'd anticipated. It felt empty. This wasn't liberation. It was a different form of enslavement.

You're killing the wrong people. Flynn's voice reverberated through his memory.

Tiger watched him, his tar-stained lip curling in disgust. "You really have gone soft."

Wolf couldn't reply. Could it happen that quickly? This shift made no sense. He tried to identify the sensation taking over his whole body. He couldn't put a name on it other than a sharp nudge in his gut. Heat climbed up his neck. His heart screamed to free these people, but his brain fought against it. His conditioning—his years of training—tried to reroute his thoughts back onto their familiar, safe neural pathway.

Who cares about them? What did they ever do for you? a small voice whispered. *You don't have the capacity to experience joy.*

His hands trembled. He clenched them into fists, attempting to trap the shudders and prevent them from vibrating up his arms.

"I see right through you." Tiger advanced toward him slowly. "Spider was right. He's always right. He knew to kick you to the curb the second you came crawling back to REDS after you couldn't kill not one but *two* bitches. He knew you'd never go back to how you used to be, but he had to squeeze everything he could outta you first."

How I used to be. I don't remember how I used to be.

Tiger unsheathed his knife from his belt and slid it under Wolf's chin. "First thing I'm gonna do when I'm REDS's leader is kill you in front of everyone. Show 'em what happens when you're weak. Fucking pathetic."

Wolf's head swam, the overpowering stench of human waste making him want to hurl. The serrated blade pressed against his throat, and in a flash, Wolf was back in the school with Flynn, her first-aid scissors' sharp point against his jugular. Why did it seem like no matter what he did, someone wanted to kill him? Tiger pressed harder and the knife's edge punctured his skin, sending droplets of blood skating down his neck, but he could hardly feel it.

"I'd like to see you try."

"You think I'm fucking with you?"

"No." Wolf grabbed Tiger's wrist. Tiger's reflexes had always been even slower than his brain. "I'm just not afraid of you."

Wolf twisted Tiger's arm. He yelled out in pain, dropping the knife. It hit the trampled-down grass with a thud. Wolf angled Tiger's arm upward, using it as leverage to force him to his knees to prevent it from snapping out of its socket. Tiger whimpered, his face screwed up in pain, shit-colored drool oozing down his chin.

Wolf released him, shoving Tiger to his side using his boot. "And you think I'm pathetic. Find another way back to base. I've got a ransomware to finish."

He'd make Spider his ransomware. It just wouldn't be the one he expected.

PART TWO

* * * *

RISING SUN

29

FLYNN

Two days later Flynn, Kerri, Nate, Vic, and Antonio waited at the base of the Dorothy and Toto statue in Oz Park. Dorothy's head and the basket looped on the crook of her arm had been blown off. Flynn shoved her hands deep into her jacket pockets and squinted into the darkness. She could make out the outline of empty tennis courts and the strange shapes of a looming playground, lonely for shrieks of happy children and pinging tennis balls ricocheting across nets. Another reminder of emptiness and silence stretching around them, pressing in on all sides until her ears rang. She used to crave peaceful quiet, was grateful for it whenever she'd return home to the Indiana suburbs on long weekends, but it was unnatural for a city like Chicago that had always buzzed with life at all hours of the day.

"I don't think I'll ever get used to the city being so silent," Flynn whispered into the darkness.

"Man, I miss TikTok," Antonio muttered. "Bet that shit is blowing up about all that's going down here. It's like we're living in a giant fishbowl. The whole world watchin' us implode."

"Never understood social media," Vic grunted. "People just talking at ya for hours on end. Blah, blah, blah. A buncha people you don't know yappin' and bitchin' and moanin.'"

Flynn smiled. "Never thought of it like that—people talking *at* you."

Kerri ran a hand over the grooves of fur etched into the little dog jumping up on its hind legs to reach Dorothy. "I like the silence," she whispered. "It's an equalizer. You know when you visit another country and speak a different language and immediately feel like an outsider? People could be having a regular conversation about muffins at a coffee counter and you wouldn't know or understand it. For once, I feel like I belong."

"Strange how you can't escape it," Nate said. "For the first time we have to confront it. Sit with it. Listen to what it does to you with nothing to distract you from it."

"Silence is the ultimate master." Wolf materialized in front of them, emerging from the shadows, his black hood shrouding his face. "You can never beat it, but you can be its equal."

Chills skated up Flynn's arms as she remembered the last time Wolf had appeared from nowhere in a park and attacked Nate. Instinctively she moved to Nate's side, wishing she could wrap her arms protectively around him.

They fell quiet, full of nervous anticipation. "Let's move inside somewhere," he said. "We're too exposed out here in the open."

They followed him toward the row of walk-up buildings ringing the perimeter of the park. Flynn stared at his broad shoulders, made bulkier from the military vest strapped around his torso. They barely moved as he walked. There was so much she didn't know about him, and she wondered if she'd ever really get a chance to know. Moving quickly, he chose a building with a black metal entry gate that had been blasted off its hinges, leaving a crater in the low brick wall surrounding the outdoor patio area.

Kerri directed them into the windowless basement unit. An L-shaped couch sat across from a mounted TV. They made themselves comfortable, relaxing into the plush cushions, and finally lit a small lantern on the coffee table, no longer at risk of being seen. Wolf pushed his hood back, shaking his hair free so it flopped across his forehead. A gauze pad on his neck made her heart leap. Something must've happened. Had REDS harmed him?

His eyes landed on hers, and she gave him a small smile. Her stomach squirmed; she still felt guilty about accusing him of helping them for the wrong reasons. Trust wouldn't come easily, and it definitely wouldn't happen overnight, but she was willing to try if this was going to work.

Wolf looked to Kerri to kick off the meeting, giving her a nod to indicate he was ready.

Kerri surveyed the group, resting her gaze on each of them. "As we all know, we're pressed on time. Let's keep our focus and use it wisely. It's critical we establish a plan tonight so we can spend the rest of the week bringing it to life. I know among our group there have been concerns—valid concerns—about bringing Wolf into our midst. Let's put those doubts aside so that we can make this happen. I think we're all in agreement, we need him if we want this to be a success."

Nate's brows dipped. He pressed his lips together.

"If you still have reservations, take it up with me after, but for the sake of not wasting time, let's all agree to move the fuck on."

A murmur of assent rumbled through them.

"Good. Vic has already begun scoping out the tunnel in the Old Post Office building leading underneath the river."

"I've been studying the old plans," Vic interjected. "They seem to indicate that the tunnel leads to the Willis Tower."

"That means our team will own the logistics of getting from point A to point B. First from Lakeview to the post office in the West Loop, then from the Willis Tower to the Chicago Board of Trade where the vault is located. Critical pieces of information we'll need from Wolf are the number of REDS guards we'll be up against and the amount of time we'll have to complete the operation. From there we can talk assignments, but it'll come down to Vic, Antonio, and Nate on our end and Nymph and Tawny from Skulls. We need people with the best shot."

Wolf gave a terse nod. "Once the vault is opened, you'll have four minutes tops to get in, get the cash, and get the fuck outta there. There are five guards there at all times, and what will be important is killing them before they sound the alarm. I can hack into the security cameras beforehand, but that could arise suspicions if I'm detected in the network so we'll need to wait until the last second."

Kerri's front teeth raked over her bottom lip. "I'll make sure Tawny and Nymph are prepared for that."

"We'll need a vehicle ready to go, and we'll head in separate directions," Wolf suggested. "Once the alarms go off, REDS reinforcements will be there by the time we leave. One group will take the cash toward the Willis Tower tunnel. The car will serve as a decoy to lead REDS away from it. If someone falls behind..." He looked around the group clustered together on the couch before continuing. "They stay behind. No exceptions. I'll go in the car without the cash. They'll be most motivated to go after me once they learn I'm involved. I also know where all the checkpoints are and can lead them away from the Willis Tower area. Skulls can either be waiting to pick up the cash at the post office or come back for it another time with the guns and ammunition. Speaking of which, I can drop off gas and ammunition during my next patrol route, but it can't be much or someone will notice it's gone missing."

Kerri rubbed her hands together. "Right. At no time will we return to the Allies base until cars have been ditched and we make it back on foot. Even then, might make sense to designate a spot in the area to try to stick it out for the night."

"Agreed." Wolf leaned forward, resting his forearms on his thighs. "REDS will be on high alert, tearing the city apart to find us...mainly me."

Flynn's whole body tingled from the rush of blood surging to her head. She closed her eyes, stomach woozy, like she'd stood up too fast.

"Be sure to have a backup weapon in case they take any of you alive," Wolf said. "And be prepared to use it on yourself. Trust me, it's better than what awaits you."

30

FLYNN

Silence filled the room as the group processed what Wolf had just said. Flynn glanced at Nate and had to stop herself from reaching for his hand. His eyes stared off in the distance, his jaw set. Instead, she allowed her leg to rest against his, trying to draw strength from him by osmosis. Wolf plowed on as if he hadn't just suggested their imminent deaths.

"As discussed, we keep the group small, nimble and less suspicious. Four, maybe five Allies soldiers. Tawny and Nymph from Skulls. We dress as Skulls to ensure REDS associates us with a gang. We don't want them suspecting the Allies as being capable of an attack like this."

Vic folded his arms across his chest. "Antonio, Nate, Wolf, and myself. Kerri, it's too high-risk of a mission to compromise you."

"What about me?" Flynn asked.

Wolf's eyes widened. "What about you?"

"I'm coming too."

He barked out a laugh. "Uh, yeah, no."

For the first time Nate didn't say anything, clearly unwilling to agree with Wolf on a matter.

"Uh, try stopping me," Flynn said.

"Flynn, you've never even shot a gun before. You could be a huge liability, let alone a target."

"Why would she be a target?" Nate lasered Wolf with a steely glare. Splotches of red had crept up his neck.

Wolf shifted, looking down at his hands. Flynn could feel the friction between them, crackling through the air and zinging against her skin.

"Because they know her from our Magnetic infiltration last year."

"Oh, you mean from taking her hostage, torturing her, blackmailing her, and then killing her best friend?" Nate seethed.

Everyone stared at Nate in shock, waiting for Wolf to react. Something passed over Wolf's face, something Flynn couldn't quite recognize, but it looked like pain—the pain of regret.

"Nate," Kerri snapped, "what did I say when we began this meeting?"

He shrugged. "Only stating the facts."

Flynn sighed. "I don't need you to fight my battles for me, Nate. Now's not the time."

"I didn't know what I was fighting for at the time." Wolf's voice was strained. "I just knew I was fighting to keep her alive."

"Enough!" Flynn practically screamed. "Enough. We're in the midst of planning a high-stakes attack, where all of our lives are at risk. Let's put our feelings aside, shall we? How many times do I have to say it? This isn't about any of us. This isn't about who we are, or where we've been, or what's happened in the past. This is about making it out alive. So, as Kerri said, let's move the fuck on, shall we?"

Flynn stood, pushing past Nate, and then stormed up the stairs, taking them two at a time. She might lose her shit if she sat there any longer. She was so sick of wasting precious energy trying to figure out how to navigate Wolf and Nate. How to placate Wolf so he stayed loyal to them, and how to do that without hurting Nate's feelings or his pride. Going back and forth trying to explain one to the other was exhausting. Resisting the urge to rip her hair out, she wandered into what must have been a well-appointed living room until the previous occupants had shoved all the furniture against the back patio door to barricade that entry point.

"Flynn!" Antonio called after her. "Wait up!"

"I need a minute."

Antonio came to stand next to her, staring through the slots in the crooked blinds. A glimmer of moonlight filtered through, casting a soft glow over their faces. "You don't have to explain anything to me."

"Good. Wouldn't know how or where to begin anyway."

"I get it. It's an impossible situation."

"I don't have it in me to deal with their petty bullshit," she fumed. "And I wind up feeling guilty for all scenarios. Like...it's another thing that's all my fault."

"Hey, they can deal with their shit on their own. It's not all about you. Nate has to process what's happened the past few months on his own, and it's been a lot. It's normal to direct all your anger at the one person who is easiest to attack. You need to release yourself from trying to fix everything as if it's in your control. News flash, it's not."

Flynn scoffed. "Release myself from it until they kill each other."

"Let them then."

"I can't though—that's the problem." Flynn flexed her hands, feeling the scream build in the back of her throat again. The same scream that had been growing for weeks now and might finally explode. "Not when I c-care"—she stumbled over the word—"about both of them." She side-eyed Antonio, swallowing hard and waiting for him to judge her.

"It's okay to care about both of them," Antonio said quietly. "Life is nuanced. People are nuanced."

The tension wound around Flynn's neck eased ever so slightly, helping to steady her breathing. "You really think it's okay to care about someone like Wolf?"

Antonio's lips curved into a small smile. "I think it shows empathy— something the rest of the world could learn more about."

"Empathy or absurdity?"

"Well, it seems like he's trying to change. He's putting it all on the line to help us. I'm not sure how much more of himself he could give. What's your other option anyway? Hate? Are you supposed to hate him?"

Flynn took several seconds to answer. "I guess if this were a math equation, I *should* hate him."

"Hate is so toxic. So exhausting. I hope Nate comes to see that—how it does nothing but burn through us, leaving us with ashes—emptiness. The hardest part of life is choosing to release ourselves from that burden."

"I understand his anger though, because I still struggle with it myself. I feel those emotions too. It's not like I've found it in myself to forgive Wolf, so I don't expect that of him. But I know Wolf better than he does. I see him for who he is and how he was molded into the criminal terrorist he became. I don't think Wolf even knows who he is."

"I worked with PTSD victims in my job before all this went down," Antonio said. "Mostly veterans. I saw men like Wolf all the time. Men who had fought in wars they believed in, and then inevitably realized in the end it was all for nothing. So, their purpose and their commitment to that cause had been for nothing—their entire identity built on nothing. Killing others for nothing. It's why many of them ended up committing suicide after."

Flynn turned to Antonio, sinking onto an overturned ottoman. "You were a therapist?"

"Yup. This fucked up world needs more black therapists—especially men. I learned that early on when I had no one who looked like me to talk to about my life and my past."

"I never even considered PTSD..."

"Why? Because you're living it now? There isn't much that separates Wolf from men in the military. Both asked to do things that are unnatural—killing others because that's what they're told to do, all in the name of something bigger than themselves."

"But Wolf killed innocent people."

"A lot of innocent people die in war too. You just don't see it every day living in this country."

"Do people like him ever really change?" Flynn asked. The question had been weighing on her ever since Wolf saved her from the explosions in the Loop. It wouldn't stop beating her over the head. It wouldn't release her, despite Antonio's advice to let it go.

Antonio sank onto the ottoman next to her and patted her knee. "Trauma literally has the power to change your brain. The only chance a person has at changing and learning a different worldview is when they have a person like you to show them. People can't recover from PTSD without support...and love."

Flynn let the gravity of what Antonio had said settle over her. "But we're both broken. I can't fix him when I don't even know how to fix myself."

Antonio wrapped an arm around her shoulder and squeezed. "You're broken for different reasons. You're broken because you loved. He's broken because he was never loved."

* * * *

When Flynn and Antonio rejoined the group in the basement, Flynn remained standing, refusing to return to the couch. Vic and Kerri were deep in discussion about where to stash the money. Wolf's eyes found hers, but his expression was unreadable once again. She hated how she never had any idea what he was thinking.

"I'm coming with you guys, and there's nothing you can say to stop me," Flynn interrupted. "I get to see this through. You know I'm owed that."

Wolf stood, his hands curling into fists. "No. Absolutely not."

"You always assume I know nothing—that I'm not capable."

He lifted his chin, holding his head high. "It has nothing to do with that. This is about your safety, and the safety of everyone else on the mission."

"You can't stop me from going!"

Wolf maneuvered around the couch and strode toward her. She couldn't take her eyes off the bandage on his neck. She wanted to run her fingers over it and ask what it was he hid beneath it—how it had gotten there.

"Flynn, can I talk to you alone? Please."

Flynn put her hands on her hips, mirroring his defiance. "No. Nothing you say is going to convince me otherwise."

Wolf reached for her and without warning Nate leapt up, diving toward him and throwing him to the ground. Nate slammed a fist into Wolf's face, pummeling him over and over again. "Don't. Fucking. Touch. Her," he growled through gritted teeth.

"Nate!" Flynn screamed.

Something in Wolf snapped. He shoved a knee into Nate's side before swinging a punch straight to his jaw. Nate reeled backward, and both Vic and Antonio grabbed him around his torso to restrain him.

"Enough!" Kerri yelled. "Enough."

Yanking his arm from Antonio's grip, Nate stormed upstairs.

"Alright, that's it, we're done for the night," Kerri said.

Flynn extended her hand to help Wolf up. He stared at her, running his thumb over his already swollen lip. After several seconds he grabbed it, allowing Flynn to help hoist him up.

"You okay?"

Their faces were dangerously close. So close she could feel the heat of his breath against her skin. Her heart pounded against her chest and she resisted sliding her fingers into his damp hair and pushing it back from his forehead.

"Please. That was nothing."

31

WOLF

A week later Wolf waited beneath the walking bridge. Somehow the concrete still managed to hold the stink of urine even after the homeless had vanished two months ago. Wolf didn't know what had become of them. Labeled as "undesirables," they'd likely either fled or were rounded up and killed. If they were lucky, they'd been thrown into the camp. Wolf gripped his rifle, head swiveling back and forth between both ends of the tunnel. Violet shades of twilight dimmed minute by minute, the soft color melting into a screen of darkness. Vic would arrive any second now. Wolf had secured the final round of ammunition and gasoline for the getaway cars. He'd delivered supplies to the Allies in increments over the past week, and tomorrow morning they'd attempt the heist.

The Allies weren't nearly prepared enough, but as each day got colder and shorter, a vigorous sense of urgency burned within Wolf after he'd witnessed the depravity in the refugee camp. The stakes were suddenly higher. No one would be able to survive a Chicago winter without heat, clothes, shelter. Desperation and fear had radiated off the hostages, as strong as the stench of rotting humanity. The little girl's eyes haunted him still, transforming into his mother's when he would finally manage to fall asleep at night.

He still hadn't told Flynn or Kerri what he'd seen. How REDS hadn't done what they promised in their manifesto—transform the weak into an army. How instead of becoming empowered, the hostages became the newly oppressed. If the Allies had even an inkling that children were being detained, they'd be distracted from their current mission, and their own survival was already riding on its success. Besides, what would be the point if they didn't triumph tomorrow?

Despite his growing unease, Wolf felt at peace in the silence of this new world. He didn't miss the constant reminders that he was an outsider. He welcomed the relief of no longer seeing strangers on the street holding hands, wondering what that joining of flesh would feel like. He'd never understood the need for physical connection and touch. The concept of linking fingers or pressing one's body against another person in greeting to show closeness had been completely foreign to him. He'd always been uncomfortable being in close proximity to others, never quite adjusting to someone entering his personal space. But he'd always envied how natural it was for other people when they approached each other. He remembered watching a mother on the CTA on his way into the Magnetic office several weeks ago. She'd shifted her baby on her hip, knowing her child's feel and weight—their smell. What was it like to know someone so intimately?

He hadn't understood that longing until Flynn.

Two shadowy figures appeared at the northern end of the tunnel, now backlit by the moon as they stood in its gaping mouth. One broad shouldered and bulky, one short and slight. Both had hoods pulled high over their heads, but he recognized Flynn's stride, her shape, the way her shoulders hunched slightly inward.

"Didn't expect you here tonight," he said to her when they reached him.

Flynn pulled back her hood and smirked. "Wanted to make sure you weren't going to get cold feet on us."

Wolf's blood heated, but he squelched the feeling. "You should know me better than that by now." He handed a large canvas bag to Vic. "Final weapons delivery." Vic shouldered its heavy weight, nodding in thanks. "See you tomorrow morning?"

"Bright and early," Vic said. "The Old Post Office."

Vic had spent the week scouting and mapping out the tunnel that ran beneath the Chicago River, connecting the post office to the Willis Tower.

The tunnel had been boarded up and in rough shape. It definitely wouldn't pass any inspections, but it would suffice to get them from point A to point B without being picked off like herring gulls floating on the Chicago River.

Wolf addressed Flynn. "Since you're here, mind staying a minute? There are some details I need to discuss with you." To her blank stare, he added, "I can escort you back."

Flynn's lips tightened. She'd remained guarded since his most recent altercation with Nate. She'd tried to walk the tightrope separating Wolf and Nate, and Wolf had the sense she resented them both for it.

"Alright," she said. "Should Vic stay too?"

"Not unless he wants to. It's about your escape route."

Much to Wolf's dismay, Flynn had found a way to convince Kerri to let her join the mission, but on the condition that her only role would be to drive the getaway car. Vic shook his head. "I gotta get back and sync up with Kerri. Start checkin' over all our supplies and preppin' these guns. Make sure we're good to go."

"Okay then, where should we go?" Flynn rubbed her palms together, blew a fog of warm air into her gloves.

Wolf looked around. "Oh, I, uh, just assumed we'd talk here."

Right at that moment a cold breeze forced its way between them, rustling their hair and jackets. "Um, no thank you. We're too exposed out here. It's freezing. Plus, REDS could show up. How 'bout the apartment above the deli? We're super close to there." Wolf, the Allies, Tawny, and Nymph had met there twice this week to finalize plans.

He nodded. "That works."

Flynn's eyes narrowed. "Everything okay?"

"Yeah. I just want to pin down the logistics for tomorrow."

Flynn turned to Vic. "Meet you back at camp."

Vic grunted, checking his watch and pivoting to head in the opposite direction. "Make sure you two get some rest. Gonna be a long day tomorrow."

Wolf hung back awkwardly, unsure of Vic's insinuation. He didn't want Flynn to think he was trying to take advantage of her or even come on to her, for that matter. He'd been on the fence about whether to tell her about the Grant Park hostage camp, and this could be his only chance. What if he died tomorrow? No one else knew about it, and REDS certainly wasn't going to let anyone else see past those gates. Wasn't this technically within his new purview as a double agent?

Flynn bounced up and down on her toes. "Come on, let's get moving, I'm freaking freezing."

The two darted down the three blocks to the apartment, the surrounding mid-rise buildings conspiring with them, standing shoulder to shoulder to disguise them in a cloak of shadows. As they crept between trees and stoops, Flynn would tilt her head back, breathing in the night air and glancing up at the clear sky. It showed off a forest of glittering stars. Wolf reached out and took her gloved hand, intertwining his fingers with hers. Even through the fabric a jolt ran up the length of his arm. She froze, but in the darkness it was too hard to make out her expression. He squeezed once, hoping his rare act of tenderness reassured her instead of alarming her. How could he communicate through his touch that he didn't know how many hours they had left together?

He didn't want to waste them.

This time tomorrow, he would be free from REDS and their expectations. Even if that meant death. For the first time, while holding Flynn's hand, that thought didn't terrify him.

Just past a corner market, they pushed open an old oak door, its once cheerful purple paint peeling away from rotted wood. A ratty shag carpet muffled their footsteps as they made their way up the dark staircase, its moldy wet smell filling the narrow space.

"That deli had the best bagels," Flynn said, glancing over her shoulder. "Cori and I would go there whenever we were hungover." Her grin faltered, then disappeared. She removed her hand from his. "I keep forgetting she's gone—that I'll never get to see her again."

Cori's face flashed before him. How, in her final moments, he'd taken a step toward her, ready to plunge the knife into her back, and he couldn't do it. Maybe Tiger was right. Maybe his inability to kill someone Flynn loved had been the beginning of the end for him and REDS.

Flynn entered the first apartment door on their left, slinking across the room to the window. A glimpse of the lake shimmered in the distance, reflecting back the inky night sky and a slurry of starlight. She stood to the side, behind a curtain, and pulled her jacket tighter around her torso. "Tell me what happened that day she died."

Wolf froze. Rehashing Cori's murder made him instantly nauseous, the sensation building in the back of his throat. Flynn turned to him, her eyes shining. "What do you want to know?" he asked.

She pressed her lips together, searching his face. She took a deep breath. "Everything. I need to hear everything."

Wolf's heart clenched so tight it felt seconds away from exploding into a million pieces. He shook his head. "Flynn..."

Tears spilled down her cheeks, and Wolf fought a wild urge to run away. "You owe me the truth," she whispered.

He crossed his arms and leaned against the wall. He wished it would swallow him whole. He wished he could disappear. He wished he had understood then and there how Spider was using him—twisting and manipulating him to be the perfect REDS soldier.

He wished he had saved Cori.

Hanging his head, he ran his fingers through his hair. "Yeah...I guess I do." He cleared his throat. "Um, when I left your apartment after we escaped from REDS headquarters, Spider gave me an ultimatum. I told him I wouldn't launch the malware targeting the electrical grid if he killed you, so he forced me to pick someone else—someone close to you—to prove my allegiance to REDS. If I refused, then he'd kill us both. Me, I didn't care so much about. You, though..." He swallowed, unable to continue. He glanced up at Flynn, her jaw tight, arms crossed, hands shoved into her armpits. He dropped his gaze back to his feet. "This was the only compromise he was willing to make. He...he could sense me wavering."

"Were you?"

Wolf pushed himself away from the wall, doing anything he could to escape the squirming in his gut. "I mean...I think I was. At first, I thought he wanted me to prove I still had it in me. But now I understand it for what it really was. He wanted to sever us—you from me—force me to do something he knew you'd never forgive."

The tears flowed in a steady stream down Flynn's face, but her fiery stare never wavered. "So, what happened?" Her voice rose, filling the room.

Wolf resisted cringing back. Fear boiled inside him, scalding his insides, numbing his tongue and overpowering his ability to think. This wasn't how he wanted their conversation to go. This wasn't how he wanted to spend possibly their last few hours together.

How could you be so fucking delusional? he cursed himself.

He'd actually believed he could shed his old self like a snake unburdening its body of its outgrown skin. But his old self was still there, snarling in the background, dragging him back. It begged to return to the comfort of his emotional fortress where he'd learned to create barricades against pain. Would he ever get accustomed to this new vulnerability? This constant raw feeling of bareness and exposure?

Except now it was too late.

Flynn had torn down his walls. They lay crumbled around him, beyond repair. He had only one choice: face the consequence of what he'd done. It was the only way to harness the pain welling inside him, a wound kept open by guilt and shame.

"Tell me what happened!" Flynn screamed.

Wolf raised his gaze to meet hers. Her face was set in determination. Her eyes didn't flare with stormy anger, but they held him in their scrutiny, unafraid and prepared for what came next.

"We went to your apartment to wait for Cori to get home, but she was already there. Spider came with me. He wanted to make sure I actually did it...that I would actually kill her. But—" His voice cracked, panic rising in his chest, until he wondered if his sternum might crack open. "I couldn't. For the first time since meeting you, I couldn't. I don't...I don't know what stopped me. Maybe it was seeing her face. Maybe it's because all I could think about when I looked at her was you."

Flynn walked toward him, her limbs trembling. She grabbed his chin, forcing him to look back at her. "So, you let Spider kill her instead? You let him stab her in the back?"

"What was I supposed to do? I didn't see any other way after all we'd already been through. I was trying to protect you."

"You should have killed him!"

"It's not that easy!"

Flynn yanked her hand away as if his skin had burned her. "Bullshit," she spat. "That's bullshit! You always said it was easy for you."

"He was all I had!" Wolf yelled. "I couldn't kill him! Just like I couldn't kill you."

"Why not?" she screamed, rage and grief contorting her face into someone he didn't recognize. "Why didn't you just kill me?!"

"You know why!"

He lunged for her right as she fell to her knees, grabbing her before she hit the ground. Sinking to the floor, he let the sobs wrack her body, holding her to his chest. Pressing his face into her hair, he squeezed his eyes shut. He inhaled her scent, unmasked by perfumes and shampoos and deodorant. Her natural earthy smell with a sprinkle of salt that reminded him of stepping outside after fresh rain.

"I'm sorry," he whispered. "I'm sorry, Flynn. If I could take it back, I promise you, I would. I know you don't deserve me or this. I know you probably hate me, but trust me, not as much as I hate myself."

He tried to take a deep breath but every time his lungs seemed too shallow.

Pulling back from him, she placed her hands on either side of his face. He grabbed her wrists, squeezing tightly, using them as an anchor. He focused on her clear gray eyes, reminding himself she was the only person who mattered. Everything else had gone to shit. He'd spent the last two weeks attempting to unravel himself, discover what was at his core, and then put himself back together. But once again, he'd underestimated how hard it was to let go of everything he'd known. The one thing he could do now was keep Flynn alive.

"I don't... Flynn, I can't keep you safe," he gasped. "I can't keep you safe from them if they kill me. Then it all would've been for nothing."

Flynn pushed herself onto her knees and wrapped her arms around his neck. The wetness from her tears brushed against the scab on his throat. Wolf would never get used to the softness of her touch. Her tenderness called to him, a song from distant memories he couldn't piece together. The rest of the world fell away as she clung to him. His breathing slowed again.

"I don't need you to keep me safe," she said, her voice quiet. "When will you understand that?"

They broke apart. "I dunno," he said. "Maybe it's the multiple times I've had to save you."

Flynn grinned, her teeth white in the darkness. "I could say the same about you, you know."

They stared at each other, both at a loss for what to do next. Flynn began to stand, brushing the dirt off her thighs. Not wanting their closeness to end, Wolf grabbed her hand, pulling her back to him. Flynn fell forward onto Wolf, and as he toppled backward, he kissed her. She pressed him to the floor with her body, kissing him back with unleashed ferocity, as if this could be the last time they touched each other. His thumb traced around her jawline, the other hand cupped her face, determined to never let her go. She threaded her fingers into his hair, angling his head backward for a deeper kiss.

She ripped at his vest, both of them scrambling to yank it off, then his shirt next. Goosebumps bubbled over his chest, his skin responding to the shock of cold. Flynn ran her fingers down his torso, tracing his scars, stopping at his waistband. Straddling him, she sat back, grasping at her shirt, untucking it and pushing his hands under the fabric. A chunk of Flynn's thick hair sprang loose, covering one side of her face. His heart raced. He had never wanted anything so badly in his entire life. He'd fucked women before. Too many women to count. Their attention had always brought him fleeting validation. But this was different. Flynn saw him for exactly who he was. She knew who he was and still, she fought for him.

He unbuttoned her pants and ran a thumb over her hip bone. She inhaled sharply.

"Perfect," he whispered, drinking her in.

She leaned over to kiss him again. Wolf sat up, bringing her with him, their lips locked while he lifted her shirt and pressed her to him. Their skin collided. Pinning him in place with her thighs, Flynn wrapped her arms around him, almost as if they could fuse their bodies into one.

Tires screeching against pavement pierced through the night.

Gasping, they froze as the sound of car engines grew louder. Seconds passed, then suddenly, headlights from the street below filled the room in a brief flash of light, blinding them. Wolf released Flynn and crawled to the window, peeking over the sill as two Humvees patrolled by, their roar announcing their presence to anyone within half a mile. After they'd passed, he slowly rose to his feet.

Patrols didn't usually come this far north at this time of night.

Am I being followed? he wondered. His pulse kicked up another notch as adrenaline flooded his senses. *Are they on to me?*

A jolt of cold prickled his bare chest, reminding him he was half naked. He turned and found Flynn standing behind him, taking him in. Her hair was more disheveled than it had been when they arrived at the apartment. Her cheeks were flushed, her shirt sloped over a bony, exposed shoulder.

"I don't know if we should do this," he whispered.

Her mouth parted, and already Wolf missed her warmth against him.

She lifted her chin, challenging him. Why did she always have to challenge him? Why couldn't she ever just listen to him? "What if I don't want to stop?"

"Of course, I don't want to stop either, but tomorrow—"

"I don't care," Flynn interrupted. She stepped closer, slowly closing the distance between them. "I don't care about tomorrow. I don't care about REDS or our plan. If we're going to die anyway, I want to do whatever the fuck I want."

He froze, prey caught in the path of a predator's hunt.

She stared up at him through thick lashes. Wolf let his forehead fall against hers, any sense of rational logic collapsing along with his willpower. She gripped his shoulders, arching her body against his.

Everything in him screamed to keep going—to kiss her harder and harder until they forgot the world waiting for them outside the apartment.

"Fuck it," he gasped.

32

FLYNN

More. *I want more.*

Flynn's head swam when Wolf kissed her. All the emotions she'd experienced since seeing him again—plus, the whiplash from learning he hadn't killed Cori—had built and compounded until they exploded in a cosmic boom. The rage. The lust. The endless grief. The terror that this could be their last night on Earth.

She sealed her body to his. His fingertips skated up her spine, leaving a fiery trail until they stopped where her shoulder blades met. He pressed against the divot, and for the first time in weeks, her tense muscles relaxed. Until several seconds later a sudden wave of self-consciousness enveloped her—how long had it been since she showered, since she shaved? Did she smell? How long had she been living in this newly acceptable stench? She squashed the thoughts as quickly as they came.

Who gives a flying fuck? she thought. There was something so liberating in tossing aside the expectations and societal norms of beauty in this strange, new, isolated world. Detaching from those insecurities that now seemed so insignificant, a surge of empowerment roared through her.

She grappled with his belt, fumbling over his guns and knife. A smile stretched over her lips at the absurdity of his endless hardware, and they swallowed each other's laughter. He threw off his belt, its many clips rattling, and Flynn yanked his pants over his hips. Wolf let them slide down his legs.

They staggered toward the couch, his hands skimming every part of her as if trying to memorize her body before she disappeared.

They fell backward into the lumpy cushions, launching up a musty cloud of dust. It settled on their skin and in their hair, but she didn't care. He leaned his head backward, exposing his throat. She brought her mouth to the tender part of his skin, grazing it with her teeth, letting her lips soften against the thin scab that had formed. She could feel him swallow, could hear his breath releasing in quick bursts.

Inching up his neck, she grabbed his chin, pulling his mouth back to hers.

His fingers grazed the edges of her tattered, thread-worn underwear. He cupped her ass with one hand and wrapped the other around her waist. From her position she could feel how hard he was. Now, she called the shots. She got to be in control. And she couldn't deny how much that power thrilled her.

"So, did you bring a condom?" She laughed again at the absurdity of what they were doing as the world crumbled around them.

He snorted, grinning with her. "Yeah, since I carry them with me every-where nowadays."

"Well, clearly you brought me here with the intention of seducing me."

"Yeah, right, as if you're seducible."

As she stared into his eyes, they softened in a way they only did when he looked at her—in a way that made her feel as if she might actually be as spe-cial as he made her out to be. She wanted to swim in their green depths. She traced his brows, dragged a finger down the bridge of his nose to his cheek.

Flynn twisted, falling onto her back and prompting another small poof of dust to rise around them. She raised her hips upward to shimmy out of her pants and underwear. Wolf crawled on top of her, pushing up her shirt to kiss her stomach. Kiss her breast. Kiss her collarbone.

Her breath caught, her muscles so tight with anticipation they trembled.

"I'm scared," Flynn whispered. "About tomorrow, I mean. About dying."

Wolf stared at her, his eyes wild and intense. "Me too."

"I don't think I've ever heard you say you're scared."

He lowered his mouth to hers. "I'm scared of being without you."

She caught his lip with her teeth, tugging at it until he groaned. She pulled down his boxers, wrapping her legs around his waist as he lowered into her.

She gasped, allowing him to fill her, allowing herself to melt into him fully.

"Don't stop." She lost sense of where they were as he drove deeper and deeper into her. The room, the couch, the city, the silence disappeared, and all that remained was him. "Don't stop."

"Flynn." Her name washed over her. She loved how he said it—how reverent he sounded. She wanted him to say it over and over again, but then she also couldn't allow her lips to be separated from his for an instant. Grabbing ahold of the back of his neck, she curved against him. She dreaded this moment ever having to end. She allowed herself to sink into their physicality, to shut off her brain and lose herself in every sensation.

He scooped her into his chest, pulling her closer. Their breath and sweat mingled, blending together until Flynn had no idea which inhale was hers and which exhale was his.

"Wolf," she gasped, "let go."

Something in him released. He pushed back into a seated position, bringing her with him. Straddling him, she moved her hips against him faster. They were getting closer, ready to climax at the same moment. No. She didn't want it to end. He yelled out, grabbing and pushing into her, sending her over the edge. She collapsed on top of him, letting the waves roll through her. For several moments her mind went blissfully empty.

She lay against his chest, her body buzzing, both of them panting. After several long minutes, she ran her hands up his abdomen, still slick with sweat, before reluctantly untangling herself. Cold snaked over her once she separated from his heat. Clenching her jaw to keep her teeth from chattering, she reached for her pants and underwear. While she searched for her discarded jacket, Wolf propped himself on his elbows. He grabbed her hand, guiding her back beside him. He smoothed her tangled hair from her face.

"Well...that was fun." Flynn leaned into him.

Wolf wrapped his arms around her. "When I'm with you is the only time I don't feel...broken."

She buried her head into the crook of his neck. His heart beat beneath her ear, strong and steady. It seemed like a lifetime ago she'd wrapped her arms around him for the first time when she'd been drunk and stumbling around her apartment. Was that really four months ago? Or was it five now? She didn't even know what month it was.

She'd changed so much since then, and so had he. She felt hardened, tight as a fist. And he had softened from the rigid, terrifying monster she'd first encountered. Somehow, they'd met in the middle—neither of them vying for the upper hand or seeking to control the other.

"Me too," she whispered. "Trauma bonding at its finest. Now, will you put your shirt back on, please?" His chiseled torso gave her the wild, impulsive urge to jump his bones all over again. "You're distracting me."

A rare smile lit up his face. "At least I have that going for me."

"If this is our last night on Earth, I have no regrets."

"No regrets," he agreed.

"Guess we got a little distracted. Is it too late to ask what you wanted to talk about, or did you really plan to seduce me?"

His body tensed. "I wish. But there's something I need to tell you."

The reservation in his voice made her uneasy. "Don't tell me you really are getting cold feet about tomorrow?"

He sighed. "It's not that."

"What is it?"

"I was on patrol with Tiger the other day, and I saw something REDS kept from me."

"What was it?"

"It was almost like Tiger wanted me to see it. Like he wanted me to know I was officially on the outs with Spider. But instead, it did something else."

Flynn sat up, confused. "Okay... What was it? What did it do?"

"It confirmed I made the right decision in joining you guys."

"Well, that's great, but I still have no clue what you're talking about. Are you going to tell me what you saw?"

Wolf's face shuttered closed, like it always did when he compartmental-ized. "If I tell you, you *have* to agree not to tell Kerri. We have to stay focused on tomorrow's plan."

Flynn's heartbeat accelerated, all moisture vanishing from her mouth. Whatever this was, it couldn't be good. "I don't know if I can promise that." She crossed her legs, tucking her shirt in and shoving her arms into her jacket.

"You have to. There's too much at stake, and we both know if we don't succeed, we're fucked."

"Okay, fine. Fine! Will you spit it out?" Wolf grabbed his pants and pushed himself up from the couch. He took his time putting his clothes back on and Flynn jiggled her foot impatiently. "By all means, take your time."

He raised his brows at her like a parent might offer a warning to a cranky toddler and dug into his pocket to withdraw a hefty protein bar. He handed it to her, a convincing peace offering. Flynn grinned and peeled back the wrapper. "You really know the way to my heart, don't you?"

"You have simple tastes," Wolf said.

Flynn snorted as she stuffed a big bite into her mouth. "Doesn't take much to make me happy." She chewed slowly, staring toward the window, momentarily distracted. "I sometimes wonder if this is what it felt like to live in Nazi Germany." Wolf stood in the shadows, his face partially shrouded in darkness. "I've always wondered how the Nazis could do it—senselessly kill innocent people, all in the name of something that ended up being entirely bullshit. All because one person told them a group of people was evil simply for being different." She studied him, her gaze pinning him in place. "Now I know."

"You're finally learning what I've been saying all along."

Flynn slowly leaned back into the couch cushion so as not to disrupt the dust. "Oh? And what's that?"

"That history repeats itself because people never really change. They all want the same thing—power. They *need* it."

Flynn's eyes narrowed and she stopped chewing. "That's not what I want."

"Well, you're the exception, not the rule."

"Maybe you should stop grouping everyone into one static category." She ate the last of the bar, crumpled the wrapper, and tossed it to the ground. She stared at him expectantly. "Alright, nice detour. Time to spill."

He took a deep breath before beginning to speak. "When we first took over the city and started rounding people up, we set up camps to house people. REDS had their own motivations for this, of course. One, gather hostages to protect our strongholds from military retaliation, and two, win people's loyalty by offering them aid. We needed to build a larger army of our own if we wanted to expand beyond Chicago and convince other states to join our cause. The military bombings were part of our plan. We wanted to provoke an attack to enrage people and show them their government didn't care."

A whisper of dread blew its icy chill down the back of her neck as Wolf paused, hesitating. "Okay...makes sense, I guess. So, what's changed then? What has REDS been hiding from you?"

"After the bombings, REDS consolidated what looked like most of the hostages into a large refugee encampment. They must've built it in only a few days, because I didn't see it or know about it until after they'd imprisoned thousands of people in this camp. I don't know what they're planning to do with them. Maybe use them to negotiate with the military? But I do know they won't be able to survive a winter there."

Flynn's chest tightened. Rage flared inside her like a match set to propane. "A camp? Where?"

"Grant Park."

"So, basically, we *are* living in a Nazi-controlled Germany?"

Wolf tried to keep his voice even, but Flynn knew it had to be bad if he was bringing it to her attention. "It was...desolate. Just thousands of people huddled around. No food. No water. No sewage system. No shelter."

Flynn stood up so quickly blood rushed to her head and stars blinked across her vision. She grabbed her pants. "I thought...I thought you just said REDS wanted to create a giant army or something."

"Maybe that's it, I don't know." Wolf's eyes hardened. "It's clear I'm no longer privy to that kind of intel. They must suspect something. But knowing Spider, he's probably using them as a means to an end."

"A means to an end? We're talking about thousands of people! Wolf, we have to tell Kerri."

"We will. I promise. Right after tomorrow's heist." Wolf grabbed her shoulders, forcing her to look at him. "Flynn. You know...you *know* we can't do anything until we get more firepower from Skulls. And money. And manpower. We get it done tomorrow, and then we tell her and the rest of the group. We'll start planning right away. I wanted to tell you in case something happens to me and I don't make it out of this alive."

The room spun, her knees threatening to give out.

Wolf took her face in his hands. "Look at me," he said. "Focus." She squeezed her eyes closed, trying to lock unexpected tears behind her lids. "Don't panic. Not yet. I have a plan."

"This is all our fault." She gulped, a sob bursting from her chest. "It's our fault. All of it."

He wrapped her in his arms, squeezing her tightly and kissing the top of her head. His breath rustled her hair, his voice so muffled she barely heard him. "This would have happened with or without us. One way or another. Trust me."

"How do you know?" she choked.

"Because I know Spider."

33

FLYNN

Flynn, Nate, Vic, and Antonio departed the Allies' headquarters before dawn. They were able to take tunnels most of the way to the West Loop, but would have to go above ground to meet Wolf, Tawny, and Nymph at The Old Post Office. From there, they would enter another tunnel that would take them beneath the Chicago River and to the Willis Tower. It was a short distance, only a half mile at most, but the thought of moving through an ancient, decrepit tunnel beneath water made Flynn's stomach sour.

The Old Post Office sat on the edge of the Chicago River, nestled among high-rise buildings towering above it. From its steps, they could see the raised bridge stretching upward, as if a beast beckoned them into its awaiting jaws. A tall, vertical stoplight stood guard directly in front of the lowered gate arm that would usually block street traffic from passing, its six lights stacked on top of each other dark and empty.

The post office's limestone walls stretched upward from a black granite base. Flag holders jutted outward at the entrance, but instead of the Chicago or the American flag, REDS had replaced each one with a crimson banner. They fluttered in the breeze next to each other like red soldiers, framing the many doors set along the length of the building and gesturing to the huge windows above.

Wolf waited for them inside the once breathtaking lobby, early morning sunlight streaming through the windows. It seemed surreal to see him amid the crumbling marble columns and cracked checkered floor, giant lantern chandeliers strewn about like landmines after crashing from the high ceiling. Flynn's eyes met Wolf's, and the light caught their brilliant green, making it impossible to look away. Heat burst up her neck and into her cheeks. Even her ears felt warm. He watched her, and Flynn did her best not to squirm under the intensity of his stare. Nate, sensing her discomfort, walked between her and Wolf, which just made Flynn nauseous from guilt. She silently cursed her stupid, thoughtless lack of self-control. Sleeping together had been a bad idea. As much as she wanted to deny it, it changed things. She couldn't pinpoint it exactly, but a connection now bonded them together. Was it chemistry? Lust? She broke eye contact and gnawed at the inside of her cheek. The last thing either of them needed was any sort of romantic distraction, especially when they were perhaps a mere hour from death.

I wish you were here, Cori, she thought. *I need you. Tell me what to do.*

Antonio clasped Wolf on the shoulder and gave him a shake. "You ready to kiss your old life goodbye?"

Wolf finally looked away from her. His lips quirked into a small smile. "No turning back now."

"That's the spirit!" Antonio grinned in return. "If we survive this, we will be drinking tonight to new beginnings."

One of the government bombs had narrowly missed the building, but the blast must have still managed to tear open a huge hole in the wall facing the river, giving them a glimpse of the downtown Loop across the water. Long rectangular windows had once taken up almost the entire length of the wall, but the glass had been blown out, allowing a chill to sweep in. Flynn stared up, mouth agape at the high drop ceilings, intricately adorned in gold. Tile mosaics embedded into the marble walls had peeled away, leaving pockmarks in the stone.

"I went to a wedding here once," Nate said, looking around the once beautiful building. "Depressing how much of the city has been destroyed in such a short amount of time."

He shot a glare in Wolf's direction.

"I've never been to a wedding," Wolf mused. "But whoever it was must've had a lot of money to get married in a place like this. Imagine where all that money could've gone instead of toward a giant party so your ass could get wasted."

Antonio stepped between them in case Nate decided to charge Wolf again.

Nate's face folded in disgust. "Yeah, and that gives you an excuse to blow it up instead, does it?"

Wolf stalked toward Nate, his steps echoing in the empty hall. Flynn grabbed his arm, yanking him back. "You want to continue on without me? Good luck getting into the vault. What else would you like me to do? Look, I can't go back, so I'm doing my part to try and fix this—"

"A little late, don't ya think?" Nate hissed.

"Guys," Antonio interrupted. "What the fuck. Now is not the time. Put it to rest, for the love of god."

Flynn squeezed Wolf's arm before releasing it. Vic, Tawny, and Nymph were halfway across the hall. She gave Nate a small push, and Antonio dragged Wolf ahead of them. "Come on, let's catch up."

Nate ran a hand through his tangled hair. It had grown even longer and more wavy. A stray sandy-colored curl flopped over his forehead, and Flynn resisted the urge to smooth it back. She could tell from his tense posture how much he hated being around Wolf.

"Do you ever plan on letting go of all that anger?" she whispered as they reached an emergency stairwell. She clicked on her flashlight, fighting the claustrophobia that tried to scale her ribcage and close off her throat. Taking a deep breath, she began to descend. Wolf and Antonio had already disappeared into the darkness.

"Nope. Not toward him anyway."

"Well," she sighed, "just don't let it change you." She wished she could hug him and siphon some of the tension out of his body.

"What? Like he's changed you?"

"Yes, I've changed, but not because of him."

"Oh, because of who then?"

Flynn stopped mid-step, whirling around to face him. "Because of *me*, Nate." She pointed to her own chest. "Because *I* decided to. You and I...we've seen what hate can do. I know firsthand how it can consume you. I'm not letting that happen to me anymore. I don't want to live with that."

Flynn caught sight of Wolf through the metal railing, waiting for her by the entrance to the tunnel. Shadows danced over Nate's face, sinking into the hollows of his cheeks. "Even after Cori?" he asked.

Flynn shook her head and continued walking down the steps, leaving Nate behind. "Because of Cori."

34

WOLF

The tunnel was short, but they seemed to shuffle through the cramped wet space for an eternity, the walls so narrow they had to walk in a single file line. Wolf felt his way along, fingers grazing the damp cement, unsure what he might touch at any moment. It was a place of nightmares. Flynn's flashlight beam bobbed in front of him, its light catching on drops of water falling from the ceiling. He kept his focus lasered on her unruly hair, pulled back into a low bun. Skulls' strange military garb looked out of place on her frame, the black fabric sagging around her arms and shoulders. Her axe hung from a belt cinched around her waist, bunching the excess fabric from her jacket and pants.

Wolf wanted to reach out and touch her—to remind himself she was real, that she wouldn't just disappear. He wasn't used to feeling scared. He hated how it hijacked every thought, every sensation. He'd never experienced it back when he was alone and had nothing to lose. He might not be able to protect Flynn from what lay ahead, but he would do everything in his power to keep her alive. He would die trying, because he couldn't live without her.

When they reached the other side, Wolf exhaled. It was quite possible he'd been holding his breath the entire way. Thankfully Vic had cleared the exit ahead of time, creating a small hole for them to climb through, since the tunnel had long been closed off. They walked up a staircase and pushed through another emergency door to the lower level of a sunken lobby. Passing a gift shop with overpriced shirts and souvenirs, they headed toward a pair of escalators frozen in place, connecting three floors sandwiched together. Across from them, a row of now blank kiosks lined the wall for visitors to sign in for the famous Skydeck, a tiny glass box sticking out from the side of the 103rd floor of the Willis Tower. He couldn't believe people actually paid to go up an elevator to see a view. What a fucking tourist trap.

They climbed three flights of escalator steps until they reached the main floor of the lobby. Sunlight streamed through the glass atrium ceiling panels, trapping in the heat and infusing his body with warmth for the first time in weeks. Their whispers halted; every sound became more amplified in the empty space. Strings of glass bowl lights crisscrossed above them. Restaurant storefronts promising donuts and sushi were now empty, their counters and shelves ravaged.

Wolf and Vic threw themselves against heavy turnstile doors, depositing them onto Jackson Blvd. A cluster of trees, barren of leaves, greeted them, somehow still standing amid the rubble, resilient against their city's assailants. He turned around, glancing up at the Willis Tower stretching above him and disappearing into the sky. His stomach dropped at its overwhelming height. The group fell into formation and Wolf led the way, avoiding REDS patrol routes. He glanced quickly at his watch—8:45 a.m. Their timing had to be just right. REDS stuck to the same schedule, and they only had a small window to get from the Willis Tower to the Chicago Board of Trade.

They made their way down Quincy Street, crossing over Franklin into a self-park garage that would allow them to move down the block under cover and without REDS's cameras detecting their movement. No one uttered a word, their breath appearing before them like small ghosts in the dim, decrepit space, now strewn with garbage and pieces of tire.

As they neared the exit, Wolf threw up an arm. An engine revved in the distance, but it sounded as if it was headed toward them. They sprinted to a low wall separating the garage from the street and ducked beneath it. Wolf crouched next to Flynn, her warm exhales brushing his face in quick bursts. He noticed the same springy chunk of her hair had fallen in front of her face, and suddenly Wolf was back in the apartment, pulling her onto the couch.

He blinked, transporting him instead to the tiny café where he'd stared up at her from his table, seeing her for the first time. So much had happened since that day. There was no way he could have known it would change the entire course of his life. He gently pushed the strand behind her ear, letting his fingers linger on her cheek. Two Humvees blew past, their wheels vibrating the ground beneath them. Flynn's eyes widened. She grabbed his hand, squeezing it tightly. A thousand unsaid words crossed between them as Wolf counted backward in his head, waiting for the roar to dissipate into the brisk morning air.

"We got this," he whispered, his voice so low only she could hear him.

A small smile broke across her face. "We got this," she repeated.

A full minute later, Wolf signaled them to stay low and keep moving. They crept toward the exit, bringing them a block away from LaSalle Street. A broken-down double-decker tourist bus blocked their view of the Board of Trade entrance.

Wolf turned to address the group. "Alright. Two minutes until go time. Flynn, wait until we're inside the building and then head for the getaway car. It's parked a block north. I filled it with gas a few days ago. Remember how we practiced jump-starting it. Inside are several weapons, including a grenade launcher. If anyone approaches, open fire and head back to Willis Tower."

"Yeah, right. I'm not leaving any of you," she whispered.

Wolf suppressed an eye roll. The least shocking Flynn response. "Once we're inside, the four-minute timer begins. Be on the ready for me and Nate. We'll lead REDS away from the group in Flynn's car while you escape back to Willis Tower with the cash."

As Wolf said the plan aloud, he couldn't help but think how much it sounded like a suicide mission. His heart squeezed, adrenaline already spiking. A slight ringing in his ears filled the deafening silence. He wanted to take Flynn's face in his hands and kiss her one last time.

Flynn studied him, lips pressed into a determined line. "We got this," she mouthed.

He nodded despite the fact that he was the only one who fully understood what they were up against. He straightened, checking his rifle and ammunition. The rest of the group followed suit, shaking out tight limbs and rolling their heads.

It was now or never.

"Be careful," Wolf muttered to Flynn.

She squeezed his fingers. "Good luck."

35

WOLF

For the first time in his life, Wolf slipped on a mask that wasn't crimson in color. The skull plastered on the thick nylon fabric matched Tawny's and Nymph's. Huddled in the shadows of the Federal Reserve Bank of Chicago's giant cracked columns, Vic, Antonio, Nate, Tawny, and Nymph waited for Wolf's signal. From their position on the corner of Jackson Blvd and LaSalle Street, they had an optimal view of the Chicago Board of Trade building. The group shrank back against a burst of cold wind, their shoulders scrunched together beneath bulky bulletproof vests strapped over their skeleton uniforms.

Wolf's fingers danced across his keyboard. His eyes watered, begging him to blink, as he read the lines of code racing across the screen. With a push of a button, he'd disarm the security cameras inside the building that were connected to REDS's main surveillance center. The second they went dark, REDS would be on alert and their four-minute timer would begin. Flynn had disappeared to retrieve the getaway car. Once they secured the cash, he and Nate would go with Flynn and the remainder of the crew would head back to The Old Post Office to stash the money. Wolf didn't trust Flynn with anyone other than himself, and Nate didn't trust Flynn with Wolf, so together they would form the most dysfunctional getaway trio.

Perched atop the Chicago Board of Trade's pyramidal roof, a faceless statue watched over the street below. Ceres, the Roman god of agriculture, looked tiny against the clear blue sky. The building's massing formed what looked like a rigid throne, with two piers jutting outward. In between them, at the base of the seat, an eagle carved into gray limestone sat atop a round, now inoperable clock. Its hands were frozen at exactly 3:47. Etched on either side of the clock, two unlikely sentinels, a hooded farmer and an Native American dressed in an elaborate headdress, scrutinized their every move with vacant stares.

Wolf's finger hovered over the keystroke that would disable the cameras. This was it. The moment of no return. The moment he could kiss his life and his future with REDS goodbye forever. It would seal his fate as a traitor.

He would always be on the run unless he could kill every single one of them.

Wolf inhaled sharply and did what he'd always done—did what REDS had taught him to do. He disconnected. Smothering his flicker of emotion, he shut down. He trusted his gut. He acted on instinct. Forming a mental tunnel in his brain, he blocked out all thoughts but the outcome he aimed for straight ahead. He made the decision and would move forward like he always did, refusing to look back, refusing to waste energy on things he could no longer change or absolve. It was the only way he'd survived up until this point. It was hardwired into him, just like it was hardwired into any animal predator. They didn't sit around and lament their prey, they killed unapologetically to keep themselves and their families alive.

Click.

"Now."

They launched into action, sprinting across Jackson Blvd and through the building's narrow doors. Wolf led, the others flanking closely behind him. A voice crackled through the radio pinned to Wolf's shoulder, connecting them to REDS's comms.

"Code red at Board of Trade. I repeat, code red. Security cameras disabled."

Remaining in tight formation, they rushed into the lobby. Two REDS guards standing outside an elevator bank saw them a second too late.

Pop.

Pop.

Wolf and Vic took them out, their silencers muting the sound. Swinging their rifles around, they approached the small marble staircase leading to the basement vault. As they descended the stairs, another guard rushed to meet them.

Pop.

Three down.

Gluing themselves to the wall in a single file line, they skirted to the end of the hallway. Vic peeked around the corner only to be greeted by an onslaught of machine-gun fire. He yanked his head back. Wolf's ears rang, unable to clear the sound. Vic nodded to Antonio, signaling to the rest of the group to put on their goggles over their masks. Crouching low, Antonio pulled a tear gas bomb from his pack and flung it around the corner. Strangled yells echoed off the low ceiling.

"Go, go, go!"

They sprinted toward a metal gate, stretching from floor to ceiling, where two guards had dropped to their knees, coughing and gagging.

Pop. Pop.

The guards collapsed, the last layer of protection before they reached the vault's circular door. Nymph slammed the butt of his rifle into the gate's lock while Wolf yanked his backpack from his shoulder, and pulled out his computer. He typed furiously, preparing to disarm the vault. He had practiced over the past few days, timing himself to see how long it would take to get through the firewall, but he'd never been able to practice actually unlocking it. Strings of code jumped down row after row while he typed into the blinking cursor.

"Backup en route to the bank," his radio bleated. "Bear, what's the report?"

Wolf blocked out the voice, tried to block out the body of his once comrade, his blood pooling across the marble floor. Nymph, Vic, Antonio, Nate, and Tawny covered him, guns pointed to the end of the hallway from which they'd come.

"Bear, I repeat, what's the report?"

Focus, Wolf. Focus.

Finally, the groan of gears filled the silence, and the lock slid open.

"We're in," Wolf gasped.

Another voice crackled through the radio on Wolf's shoulder, urgent and alarmed. "Vault door has been opened. Vault is open. All patrols to Board of Trade NOW."

Nymph, Vic, and Antonio shoved their weight against the huge, reinforced door. Inside the vault, all four walls were lined with different sized aluminum lockboxes, stacked on top of each other like bricks. Decades ago, when the vault had been in function, bankers used them to store trading receipts, gold and silver bars, and other precious items. Now, mounds of banded cash filled the room.

"Thirty seconds to take as much as you can," Nymph grunted.

Without thinking they shoveled armfuls of cash into bags.

"Alright, that's it, let's go!" Wolf yelled.

Slinging bags on either shoulder, Wolf sprinted out of the iron gate. Taking multiple stairs at a time, Wolf skidded into the lobby, the others right on his heels. In the distance, the roar of trucks echoed off empty buildings. They raced through the door. Wolf and Nate handed off their bags to Vic and Antonio as they diverted toward Flynn's waiting car. Through the windshield, Wolf could see her white knuckles as she gripped the steering wheel with both hands.

Two cars screeched down LaSalle Street straight toward them and the building entrance. A round of shots unloaded.

"DOWN!" Vic yelled.

They leapt behind one of the large concrete planters lining the sidewalk's edge. Bullets pierced the air above their heads, whistling through withered bushes. In a scattering of distinct pings, the metal shells lodged themselves into the building's façade. The machine-gun fire continued with no sign of letting up, pinning them in place. A small object launched over them.

"GRENADE!" Tawny screamed.

They leapt sideways, right as an explosion ripped the air from Wolf's lungs. Smoke singed his nostrils. Coughing and heaving, they army crawled as fast as they could toward the abandoned double-decker bus several yards away.

Don't stop, a voice whispered. *Don't hesitate. Even a second means life or death.*

"Keep going!" Nymph yelled. "I'll cover you!"

Nymph leapt up, running at a crouch toward a tall planter. Taking cover behind it, he began firing his AK-47 at REDS's armored trucks, giving them time to scramble over the burning debris. Undeterred, REDS released another wave of ammunition. Wolf glanced over his shoulder right as Nymph took a hit to the chest, flinging him backward. Thankfully it looked as though his vest absorbed the bullet. Undeterred, Nymph clambered back to his knees and continued to rain gunfire in REDS's direction. He fired so fiercely that he managed to pull REDS's attention—their focus moving away from the Allies' escape to resolving this new threat.

Wolf, Nate, Vic, Tawny, and Antonio gasped for air as they finally made it to the bus. They watched as five armed soldiers approached Nymph, fanning outward to close in on him from all sides.

Wolf turned to Vic, Antonio, and Tawny. "Get outta here!" he yelled. "Head back to the Willis Tower."

"NO," Tawny yelled back. "I'm not leaving Nymph!"

"You know the plan, Tawny! You have to go!"

All at once, REDS opened fire and Tawny's strangled scream rose above the deafening noise. Surrounded but not surrendering, Nymph charged toward his attackers, managing to take several steps before his towering form crumpled to the ground. Tawny clawed toward him, but Antonio threw himself on top of her.

In a screech of tires and burning rubber, Flynn's car careened toward them. Slamming on the break, she aimed a grenade launcher out her open window. She released a grenade right into one of REDS's trucks. It exploded into a mushroom-shaped fireball. The smell of burning gasoline burnt his eyes and throat. Flynn dove over the center console and pushed open the back door.

"GET IN NOW!"

She twisted around and launched another grenade right as several REDS soldiers scrambled to their feet and unleashed more shots at their car. The grenade blasted a crater into the street, engulfing the other truck in a fiery inferno. Wolf and Nate sprinted toward the car and leapt into the back seat. Flynn yanked the gear into reverse, stomping her foot on the pedal so hard they slammed against the seats as they shot backward. Wolf watched out the windshield as the rest of their crew took off down Jackson Blvd; from there they would take Wells Street straight back to the Willis Tower. Antonio dragged Tawny with him. Nymph's sacrifice and Flynn's grenades had given them precious seconds to escape before more reinforcements arrived.

Flynn turned the wheel sharply. The car spun out, its wheels grappling for traction. They took off in the opposite direction, steering REDS away from their group. Wolf threw his AK-47 into the front passenger seat, clambering up after it. Nate slid over behind Flynn, leaning out the window to aim his rifle at the tires of some quickly approaching REDS reinforcement.

"Not too shabby back there," Wolf said. "Can't handle a gun, but guess you're good with a grenade launcher."

She glanced at Wolf. "Helps when you're aiming at the right people."

Wolf looked over, alarmed at the strain in her voice. Flynn's lips were ghostly white. With a whoosh, all sound and color around them disappeared.

Blood smeared the steering wheel's edge, covering her fingers.

36

WOLF

"FLYNN." Wolf's own voice sounded distant, like he was trying to get her attention from several blocks away. "What happened?"

Flynn gritted her teeth. "I think...I think I got hit." Her hand shook as she covered her side closest to the driver's seat window. When she raised it, fresh blood covered her fingers.

Nate swiveled around. Wolf's eyes darted to the rearview mirror. He knew the panic on Nate's face mirrored his own. Both REDS trucks were gaining on them.

"Pull over," Wolf demanded.

"No!" Flynn also glanced in the rearview mirror. "You know I can't. We stop for no one."

Bullets shattered the glass of their back windshield. They ducked, and Flynn swerved but kept her foot on the pedal. Wolf leapt toward her as they careened onto the sidewalk and toward a building. He yanked the steering wheel toward him, trying to correct their path, but one of their wheels exploded, sending the car spinning. They finally skidded to a stop in front of a parking garage. Wolf stared into its dark entrance, promising them a maze with a myriad of escape routes.

Wolf jumped from the passenger seat. "I'll cover. Nate, get her inside the garage NOW."

Nate scrambled out of the back seat and pried Flynn's door open. Wolf watched from the corner of his eye as Nate pulled her from the car, wrapping an arm tenderly around her waist. Her entire side was soaked in blood. He fought the panic mounting inside him. Pressure rose with each passing second, building like a geyser waiting to erupt.

Wolf walked toward REDS's oncoming trucks. He aimed at their tires. *BANG. BANG.*

One lost control as it careened toward them, its wheel caps screeching along the pavement. Next, he aimed for the other truck's front windshield. *BANG.*

He watched from a distance as his bullet hit its mark, shattering the glass.

He darted into the parking garage and sprinted up the steep ramp right as the REDS truck collided with their car. The crunch of metal and an engine's explosion shook the ground beneath him. It would only be moments before more trucks arrived.

Wolf reached the upper landing just in time to see Flynn and Nate slip into a stairwell leading to different levels. It didn't take long for Wolf to reach them. Flynn was fading fast and Nate was practically carrying her.

Gingerly, Nate set Flynn down on a step to rest. Gasping, her hands shook as she tried to compress her side. Wolf's head swam and a fresh wave of terror gripped his heart. The overpowering smell of stale urine made it hard to think. "Flynn." Her name came out as a raspy whisper.

"I'm...I'm fine," Flynn muttered, clearly unaware of the sickly white shade of her skin. "Just a little bleeding, that's all."

Wolf started digging through his bag. He had stitched her up once before, he could do it again.

"Wolf, there's no time," Flynn said. "We've gotta get out of here. Now."

"I don't know how we're going to get you back to headquarters in time!" Wolf practically screamed. His voice reverberated through the compact space. His mind was spinning out of control, hijacked by pure panic.

"I don't want us to get trapped up top," Nate panted.

Wolf nodded. "Give me a second," he muttered, squeezing his eyes shut. *Think, Wolf, think. Visualize.*

They only had maybe three blocks to cover to get back to the Willis Tower. Wells Street would be their best bet. It had the most coverage from the elevated train tracks and the most disruption in security cameras. He mapped a route through his mind, recreating the map of the city he'd reviewed with Spider over and over again in their headquarters.

"You know how a parking garage works," Wolf finally said. "In one way, out the other. While they go up, we go down. Take the exit to a different street and head toward Wells. It will offer the most protection."

"Just keep going," Flynn whispered. "Don't stop. And if you need to, leave me behind."

Over my dead body, Wolf thought.

"She's losing too much blood," Nate whispered.

Wolf unzipped his vest, tore off his jacket, and tied it tightly around Flynn's midsection. Flynn cried out in pain. Every second counted. Nate and Wolf both lifted Flynn, slinging one of her arms over each of their shoulders. The staircase was too narrow to carry her. They burst through a door to the third landing and headed toward the down ramp.

The shrill screech of brakes on the street below alerted them to the arrival of more REDS reinforcements. At this point, Flynn was barely conscious. "Flynn, come on, stay awake," Nate pleaded, lifting her into his arms. "Stay with us." They set out at a jog.

When they made it to the second landing, REDS voices on the other side of the garage echoed toward them. Crouching low, they crept behind a lone car.

"Keep going," Wolf ordered, slipping back into his vest and reloading his rifle. "I'll hold them off and then catch up on Wells or at Willis Tower. The others should have made it back to the post office by now."

Nate nodded, bundled Flynn to his chest, and took off.

Several minutes later, Wolf heard boots shuffling over cement. They grew louder as they inched closer. He could tell by how they moved there were several of them. Wolf slid behind the car's wheel to avoid being seen. His radio had gone silent, which could only mean REDS knew who they were up against. He held his breath, counting backward in his head.

Five. Four. His finger hovered over the trigger. *Three steps. Two. One.*

He leapt up from behind the car, unleashing a spray of bullets. Two Enforcers crumpled, but two others unloaded in his direction. Wolf ducked, crawling around the side of the car, before jumping over the hood and shooting back, taking out another soldier.

The last REDS soldier came at him from behind, knocking him over. Wolf's rifle slid across the cement. He saw stars, tasted the metallic tang of blood as the soldier landed punch after punch. For several seconds he lay there, unable to fight back, wanting to join Flynn wherever she might be going. Until his instinct to fight back took over. Twisting his body, he threw the soldier off him. Wolf pinned him down with his knees, reaching into his vest and grabbing his knife before slamming it into the Enforcer's sternum.

Gasping for air, Wolf staggered to his feet. He grabbed two rifles from the dead Enforcers and slung them over his shoulder before taking off to find Nate and Flynn. He ran down the last ramp's lip and headed toward Wells Street. For the first time in his life, Wolf silently thanked Nate for being there and keeping a cool head.

When Wolf turned onto Wells, he caught sight of Nate darting behind a staircase leading from the street up to an elevated train station. Intricate gridwork hovered above them, blocking out most of the sun's light and creating an iron tunnel, propped up by beams placed every few yards on either side of the street.

Wolf picked up his pace knowing Nate couldn't run as fast while carrying Flynn. As he approached, he called out as quietly as he could. "Hey! Nate, it's me."

Wolf rounded the corner right as a gust of cold wind greeted them. Flynn shook violently in Nate's arms. Sweat poured into Nate's eyes, visible beneath his mask, trailing down his neck and shining in the muted light. For a brief second, Wolf wondered if they were tears. Tears of desperation. Wolf took Flynn, knowing Nate would be faster without her weight. "You cover for now."

Nate nodded, and Wolf noticed how his hands also shook as he passed her over.

Wolf let the cool air settle in his lungs. They moved as quickly and silently as possible. With every step he tried to channel his thoughts into Flynn.

Stay alive. Stay alive. Keep breathing. Stay alive.

Wolf clutched Flynn in his arms, aware of every single labored breath. "Come on, Flynn," he whispered into her ear. "Flynn! Stay with us."

Focus, Wolf. Focus, he told himself again, trying to ground himself as they sprinted along the path. *Focus on where you need to go and getting there. Get her there alive.*

Wolf paused when they finally reached Franklin Street, allowing Nate to take the lead so he could clear the area. Head on a swivel, his rifle raised at the ready, Nate surveyed the area before summoning them forward with a wave.

"Almost there," Wolf muttered.

Flynn's breath got quieter. Wolf shifted her weight, his arms burning, pulling her closer to his chest. Her skin was clammy and damp from sweat. Multiple scenarios swirled around his brain. She hadn't bled out yet, which hopefully meant the bullet hadn't lacerated any organs or hit a major blood vessel.

Maybe...just maybe we can make it.

Flynn's head brushed his chin, her hair tickling his scruff. It had lost its luster and lilac smell, but every inch of her still felt familiar. He couldn't lose her, not after everything. Not after he had chosen her. Not after he had abandoned REDS by doing so. Something twisted sharply inside him. It traveled to his throat, burning and hurting when he tried to swallow.

They made their way into the Willis Tower lobby, diving down the frozen escalators and toward the tunnel entrance.

Faster, a voice kept whispering. *Faster.*

They slowed when they reached the tunnel. Nate retrieved his flashlight, but the passage was so narrow Wolf had to shuffle sideways to fit both him and Flynn. The occasional drip of water and their rattled breaths, releasing in gasps, echoed off the stifling walls. Wolf picked his way as carefully and quickly as he could over strewn pipes and rocks, his path lit by Nate's light.

"You know," Nate said over his shoulder, "there were moments today I forgot who you were and what you'd done. Do you think the rest of your life will be like that, after all this? People who will forget about your past for a moment, and then remember everything. It'll follow you wherever you go."

Wolf kept his eyes on the ground. He couldn't afford to make one misstep. "I've never cared about what people thought of me. If I did, I would probably be dead."

Nate stumbled but regained his balance. "You care what Flynn thinks about you."

Wolf didn't answer. *Get to the end of the tunnel,* he told himself. *Just get to the end.*

"I love her, you know." Even though he sounded out of breath, Nate said it with assurance. The assurance and confidence of someone who has loved and known love his entire life. He could never know the crater its absence leaves. "I'll fight for her."

"I'll fight for her too." He knew Nate meant it as a threat, but Wolf meant it as a promise. A promise to keep her alive. Right here. Right now. That was all that mattered.

"You really think you can give her what she needs?"

They had almost reached the end of the tunnel, and Nate picked up his pace. Wolf hugged Flynn closer so he could move faster. "I haven't thought that far ahead. I've been a little busy trying to keep us alive. But I know she's worth it. If we make it through this, I'll try to be whoever it is she might need, and that'll probably change. Just like we all change."

"Yeah, well, some things don't change," Nate said.

"I'm coming to see that's the problem."

37

WOLF

Antonio's eyes flared with surprise when Wolf and Nate burst through the emergency stairwell.

"What the—What are you doing—" It only took seconds for him to register an unconscious Flynn in Wolf's arms. Her blood had seeped onto his vest. "Shit..."

"We n-need the car," Nate stammered, trying to catch his breath after their mad sprint. "We gotta get her back to headquarters now."

Antonio nodded, leading them to where Vic and Tawny sat, their backs pressed against marble, surrounded by duffle bags of cash. Tawny stared into space, seemingly unaware of their arrival. Nymph's enormous absence hung among them, waiting to be acknowledged.

"Vic can take you. Tawny and I will follow on foot. How much time..." Antonio's voiced trailed off.

"We don't...we don't know," Nate said. "Not much."

Wolf couldn't speak. His throat refused to produce sound. His mouth had lost the ability to move. He could feel himself shutting down with each passing second.

Vic leapt to his feet, grabbing three bags of cash. "Alright then, let's go."

They rushed to the back entrance of The Old Post Office, where an overflowing dumpster still hadn't been cleared. Its overwhelming stench smacked him in the face. A rusted-out wreck of a van peeked out from behind it and

Wolf climbed into the back seat, laying Flynn on his lap. Nate jumped in the passenger seat, twisting to check on her.

"How is she?"

Wolf shook his head, his fingers searching for a pulse at the base of her throat. She had bled through his jacket tied around her waist. He felt a weak, thready beat. "We have maybe five minutes." It was all he could manage. Nate's face turned ashen. A tremor began vibrating through Wolf's hands.

Antonio tossed the remaining bags of the cash into the trunk and then jogged around to slam the van's sliding door shut. He thew his weight against it, and the hinges rasped in protest. Antonio gave them a final salute, his face grim, as the door finally groaned closed.

"Eyes forward, Nate," Vic grunted. "I need you on lookout."

Nate turned, his jaw so rigid it might snap. To quell his shaking, Wolf pulled Flynn closer, resting his chin on top of her head. Closing his eyes, he tried to channel his strength into her, trying to push it past the barrier of his bones and then through his skin into her body.

"Please, Flynn," he whispered as Vic accelerated onto the street. "Stay alive. For me. Please."

He was barely aware of the sharp turns that flung him across the lumpy bench seat, his shoulders cushioning the impact for Flynn. He was barely aware of the van gaining speed, rocketing down Lake Shore Drive. He was barely aware of the screeching wheels as they veered toward an exit. Flynn's breath had slowed, and with each one, Wolf was terrified it would be her last. Wild desperation threatened to overtake him.

Suddenly, Flynn's eyes flew open and she gasped, choking. Her lips were blue.

Wolf grabbed her face. Her cheeks were icy. "Flynn..." She stared above his head, searching for him, but unable to see him. "Flynn!" he yelled again. "Don't leave me." His voice sounded unrecognizable.

"FASTER, VIC," Nate yelled as the engine revved and took a turn so fast the back wheels skidded out from beneath them.

"One minute," Vic said. "Be there in one minute."

Nate swiveled around. "Come on, Flynn, hold on!"

The second Vic slammed on the brakes, Nate leapt from the van and shoved open the back door for Wolf. Still clutching Flynn, Wolf launched from his seat and bolted into the little bodega. A guard stood above the trapdoor, his gun raised in their direction.

"We need a medic NOW."

The guard immediately recognized them and radioed for Kerri. "Code blue, we have a code blue at the cave entrance. We need a medic stat. We have a code blue, I repeat, a code blue."

Wolf dropped to his knees, laying Flynn among the scattered shelves. She wasn't breathing. His mouth opened into a yell his lungs couldn't release. It was stuck in his chest. He searched for a pulse at her neck. This time nothing. His fingers probed her wrist. Again, nothing.

Wolf tilted her chin and blew into her mouth, starting CPR. He began rhythmic compressions, trying to keep the remaining blood circulating through her heart.

"COME ON," he screamed.

Nate staggered in, dropping to his knees beside them. He grabbed Flynn's hand, pressing it to his lips. "No, Flynn. Flynn, please," he whispered. "Please."

Wolf kept pumping, focusing on each passing count. If he allowed his thoughts to stray from the task at hand, he wouldn't be able to rebound.

The trapdoor flew open and Kerri emerged, followed closely by two medics who carried a defibrillator, some sort of kit, and what looked like a small cooler. "MOVE," they yelled, shoving Wolf and Nate out of the way. "Everyone back now!"

"Her heart's stopped," the female medic said, feeling Flynn's wrist. The male medic began working quickly to set up the defibrillator.

"What happened?" Kerri asked.

"She got shot. Her side," Nate croaked. "She lost a lot of blood."

Wolf watched as the female medic snipped Flynn's shirt away to reach the oozing bullet wound. She resituated Flynn's sports bra and wiped her chest with a dry cloth before placing two pads on her exposed skin. "Ready, set, clear," she said as a shock jolted through Flynn's body.

The male medic resumed compressions. "Alright, again," he ordered.

Something inside Wolf snapped. He couldn't contain it anymore. The scream released. He stood up so fast the room spun. He whirled around and hurled a metal shelf—the first thing he could get his hands on. The scream wouldn't stop; it kept building, and the tiny space blurred together. He reached for another shelf, ripping it from the ground.

"Get him out of here!" the male medic yelled, already at work inserting some sort of IV into the crook of her arm.

Nate leapt at Wolf, trying to restrain him, but Wolf threw him off. All of his anger and grief erupted and nothing could stop him. Nate came at him again, bulldozing him into another rack of shelves. They tipped backward and pain reverberated down Wolf's spine, but he welcomed it.

"WOLF!" Nate grabbed his vest, still soaked with Flynn's blood.

"KILL ME!" Wolf wished his lungs would stop fighting for air. He yanked Nate's hands from his vest, placing them around his neck. "Come on, do it. I know you want to. Kill me instead of her."

Something rested behind Nate's eyes, so familiar Wolf could feel it vibrating through each of his own nerve endings. It was terror. Pure terror at the thought of confronting a world without her.

"It doesn't work that way," Nate said, his voice so quiet only Wolf could hear him. Nate released his fingers.

"Vic, get Wolf out of here," Kerri ordered. "Put him in a cell. I don't want him hurting himself or anyone else while we sort this shit out."

Vic heaved Wolf to his feet, and Wolf let himself be led away. With each step he wondered whether it would be the one where he collapsed, his legs refusing to hold his weight. The female medic had pulled a bag of clear liquid from the small cooler, preparing to hook it to some sort of syringe lodged in the crook of Flynn's arm.

Wolf paused at the trapdoor, his eyes locking on Kerri's.

"Bring her back," he begged. "Please."

She gripped his arm for a brief moment. "We'll give it our all."

38

FLYNN

"Please, Flynn." She heard Wolf's whisper from what seemed like a hundred miles away. "Stay alive. For me. Please."

I can't, she wanted to whisper back. He was too far away. There was no way she could make it back to him.

Black nothingness pulled her toward it, trying to swallow her in its complete finality. It felt warm and promising. Peaceful. Easy. Why was she fighting it so hard? What awaited her back there other than pain and heartbreak? But something primal in her fought against the beckoning darkness, yanking her back toward consciousness. Her brain wouldn't command her heart to stop beating or her lungs to stop searching for air. But with each breath, the pull weakened and the darkness grew stronger—more compelling.

"Flynn."

Wolf's voice whispered on the other side, reminding her to keep fighting. Just a little longer. Just a little harder. She couldn't leave him—not when he had given up everything for her.

Blackness enveloped her and she relaxed into it, finally giving in.

I tried, she wanted to whisper. *I promise. I gave it my best shot.*

Her body jolted, shocking her from the darkness. A thousand stars exploded around her. White-hot pain filled every one of her cells. She tried to scream, but she didn't have the strength.

What's happening? Where did the warmth go?

Then the darkness lapped back around her, its warm waves licking her limbs, splayed on a distant shore.

Suddenly, another jolt tossed her back into the fire, bringing a fresh shock of pain.

No, come back. Leave me be. She reached for the peace so cruelly promised to her, watching as it retreated, curling away like an evaporating fog.

Instead, slow thumps reverberated through her chest, working, struggling.

She fought against it, fought to stop the slow beats of her heart.

"Don't fight, Flynn," a voice whispered. This time it was a woman who spoke to her, the voice so familiar instant tears pricked the corners of her eyes.

Cori?

Desperate to hear her voice again, she tried to search for her.

Cori! Flynn called out. *We can finally be back together.*

"Not yet, Flynn."

I can't fix it, Cori. I can't fix what I've done or who I've become.

"Stop trying to fix the wrong things."

"Flynn!" Nate's voice rang through her head.

Nate. New warmth flooded through her, different this time. She wanted to reach for it, reach for him.

A sob welled inside her. *I don't want to leave you, Cori. Not again.*

"I've been here the whole time," Cori whispered into her ear.

In a burst of bright white light, the darkness exploded.

39

WOLF

Wolf sat in the corner of a makeshift cell, his back pressed against icy cinder blocks. A battery-powered lantern in the corner cast an orb of light that barely reached his feet. Wolf couldn't help but think his new fate had banished him to tiny, claustrophobic spaces.

What am I going to do? he wondered. *What am I going to do without her?*

Maybe the Allies would be willing to keep him there until he withered up and died. No one could force him to eat or drink. It would maybe take a week, or two at most? The length of time didn't concern him; once he committed, he could be patient. Without Flynn, something had broken from his heart and departed, and he knew it would never feel whole again. One could only put themselves back together so many times.

A knock on the door shot him from his suicidal reverie, and Kerri entered, closing the door behind her. "You look…" She stared at him, clearly searching for the right word. "Broken," she finally settled on, her voice quiet.

She leaned against the opposite wall and slid down until she sat facing him. Even with her legs outstretched her toes didn't reach the other side. Wolf, on the other hand, had to keep his knees bent with his feet planted firmly on the floor.

Wolf didn't speak. He couldn't ask the question. He braced himself, letting his head fall back and his eyes close. Something hot and wet pricked their edges, pressing against his lids, begging to be released.

"She's alive," Kerri finally offered. "The doctors are operating on her right now, so I can't promise you that she'll stay alive. But she is...for now."

Something in Wolf's chest eased a fraction, enough to make him realize how tightly it had been squeezed. He opened his eyes, meeting Kerri's knowing gaze.

"You love her, don't you?" she asked.

Wolf swallowed hard and stared down at his hands, clasped atop his knees. Tears started filling his eyes before he could stop them. Tears? Is this what they felt like? He'd never cried, not once in his life. Well, not that he could remember anyway. It did nothing except show weakness. But he couldn't suppress the wave swelling inside him, growing bigger and bigger with each passing second, threatening to sweep him away. Flynn was alive. She was still breathing. For now. She hadn't left him, like every other person whom he'd once loved. One of the tears fell down his cheek. He didn't wipe it away. He let it fall, catching in the scraggly hairs of his unshaven beard, burning a slow path with it.

"I don't...I'm still trying to figure out what it means to love someone," he finally admitted. "Killing people used to be easy, until it's not...until you know..."

Kerri's features softened in the dim light. Shadows erased sharp lines of disapproval, catching on the curves of her lips. Sitting with just him alone, her small stature no longer had to stretch to meet all the people looking to her for answers. It rested, content and at peace in its frame.

"You've changed," Kerri said. "I haven't known you long. Never knew you before this, obviously, but something has shifted in you. And it has to do with her."

"I think I've finally realized...if you don't take control of your own life, others are going to take control of it for you. I'm done giving up control."

Kerri tilted her chin, a small smile lifting her face. "It's true. Except so much of life you can't control. Before this...before the city fell, I mean, I was a janitor. At this venue, actually." She lifted her eyes toward the ceiling, indicating the building above them. "It's how I knew these tunnels existed... to bring people here."

"A janitor?" Wolf couldn't mask his surprise.

She nodded. "Not many people here know that. It's interesting how in times of crisis, people's real colors show—almost like a pressure test. People looked to me because I was calm. I showed resilience. Believe it or not, I've been through way worse shit than this. What I'm getting at is regardless of what you can or can't control"—she pointed at Wolf—"these are your true colors. This—" She made a circle with her pointer finger, "this is who you really are and have always been. A fighter."

Wolf felt a corner of his lips flick upward, her words a warm ember tucked into his pocket on a freezing day. "You've been through worse than this?"

She nodded. "You're experiencing it for yourself at this very moment." Her voice sounded distant, lost in a memory. "Losing someone you love. I lost my daughter when she was only four years old." Kerri tensed, as if she'd absorbed a fresh shock wave. She glanced in Wolf's direction. "There's no greater pain on this planet than losing a child, especially one so young and full of life. That pain never ebbs. It just continues to flow through you, like a constant current. It becomes part of your existence—a part of your biological makeup. But at the same time, you don't forget that love either. It changes you, changes the meaning of the word. It stays with you forever, but then the grief does too. They sit side by side, a reminder of what you had and what you lost."

A burst of guilt flooded through Wolf with nauseating intensity. His stomach clenched to prevent him from heaving up its contents. He had ended lives without noticing who it was he killed. Regardless, that person had always been someone's child. No wonder he'd always kept people at arm's length. So he'd never have to face this type of remorse. So he'd never have to wrestle with this complicated and sickening deluge flooding his insides.

"What happened to her?" Wolf managed to ask.

"Car accident," she said. "I lived. She didn't." She finally met his stare. "Every day I asked myself why it wasn't me. Talk about survivor's guilt. I became an alcoholic. I didn't want to live in a world without her, didn't want to be alive without her. I couldn't stop my downward spiral, so I drank and drank and drank hoping to one day never wake up. And then one day,

I didn't. Someone found me and rushed me to the hospital. So, here I am."
Tears now flowed freely down Kerri's face. She gave him a watery smile.
"My daughter wouldn't let me go to her, and so I finally stopped trying.
I decided it was time to live a life she would be proud of in her honor."
She studied him. "There's no point in wondering why it wasn't us; that's
just another thing we can't control. But I do think the reason will reveal
itself to us eventually, inevitably. We're the real survivors, who've survived
the worst pain imaginable. The question is what you decide to do with
that pain. I channeled it, and it led me to here. Now I think I understand
why I was tested, why she wouldn't let me go. She was preparing me for
this moment."

"*You're* a survivor," Wolf corrected, his skin suddenly too hot. "I'm a
murderer."

"You are." Kerri nodded. "But at the same time, you're also a prisoner.
You've always been a prisoner. A prisoner of a system, a prisoner of an organization, a prisoner of brainwashing."

"I've been struggling with that," he admitted. It felt so good to say it
aloud, as if a crushing weight had eased from his shoulders. "Picking apart
what's real and what's not. Who is using me for their own gain versus who
actually cares. I mean, is there even such a thing as redemption for the lost?"
Wolf wondered aloud, reciting from his own manifesto. "Redemption. Execution. Deliverance and Salvation. Those words justified everything I did.
Almost like some sort of promise."

"I think you'll have to find out," Kerri said. "You'll have to find out why
you're the survivor and not them. Why it was *you* who made it this far."

The weight returned, a yoke fastened around his neck. "I don't even
know if that's possible."

"That's what I thought at one point." A slight smirk quirked Kerri's lip.
"Hence the drinking. I'm not a religious person, but any ounce of faith I had
disappeared after I lost my daughter. Nothing could explain why she was
taken away from me, and every aspect of religion made me so bloody angry
after that. I couldn't handle the concept of sin. How sinners got to live and
be forgiven, while an innocent child died? But after I got sober, I went to a

Shabbat dinner with a friend and heard a rabbi speak about morality from the Talmud. I never forgot it. He said something along the lines of how a prisoner cannot release himself from prison; it takes someone else to turn the key that unlocks that door."

Wolf picked at the split skin on the back of his cracked knuckles. The gravity of what Kerri said sank in. Had Flynn unlocked that door for him? Had she been the one to release him from a prison he never knew how to break free from? Another knock sounded on the door. They both jumped, wiping their eyes with the backs of their hands.

Kerri cleared her throat. "Enter."

Nate stood in the doorway, looking as if he'd aged ten years in a matter of hours. The scruff lining his jaw contained a smattering of early grays, and the cold had chapped the skin on his cheeks.

"They've removed the bullet from her side and stitched her up." Nate spoke to Kerri, but his eyes danced toward Wolf for a brief moment. "The doctor doesn't seem to think any major organs were impacted or that there was a massive intrusion. But they aren't able to test her blood type, and we don't have any stored blood for a transfusion, so her body won't be able to make up for the lost blood. She also needs medications we don't have here."

Wolf's accelerating heart skidded to an abrupt stop.

"They can try to keep her blood pressure stable with saline and fluids, but we need more if she's going to make it through this." Nate leaned against the doorframe, his shoulders hunched inward.

Wolf scrambled to his feet. "Then we raid the hospital."

"There's no way we make it inside unnoticed," Nate said. "They're going to be everywhere searching for us. They're on high alert. We'll never make it."

"They'll be everywhere downtown, not the hospital," Wolf said. "What time is it?"

Kerri checked the watch at her wrist. "It's 9 p.m."

"We leave now. I can get us there. It's only a thirty-minute walk from here. Me, you, Vic, and Tawny. Everyone else stays here to wait for the weapons delivery from Skulls."

Nate crossed his arms, as if bracing for an argument, but after several seconds he straightened. He nodded in agreement. "Alright, let's do it. It's her only chance."

Wolf turned to Kerri. "Before I go, there's something you need to know."

40

WOLF

Wolf slipped into the room serving as a makeshift hospital for the Allies. Only three cots were occupied. The two medics who'd attended to Flynn flitted between patients. Kerri had mentioned that one had been an emergency room physician in Chicago and the other a paramedic. He'd told her everything about the refugee camp and about REDS's plan with the ransomware he had built. Only Wolf knew how to deploy it, and when the time came, he was ready. Now that Skulls was supplying more ammunition, they had options and could start planning immediately.

Flynn lay in the cot farthest from the door. A standing screen created a makeshift curtain around her. It blocked most of her body from view, but he caught a glimpse of her unruly hair spread out around her head. As he approached, more of her face was revealed. Her skin appeared translucent in the fluorescent lights. Her freckles, usually unnoticeable, were more pronounced across the bridge of her nose and spattered across her cheeks. Wolf resisted tracing them with his finger.

One of the doctors came to stand beside him. "How long do we have?" Wolf asked.

The EMT took in his large form, as most people tended to when they encountered him for the first time. She extended her hand. "I'm Bri. I'd say maybe twelve hours, if we're lucky. Blood is most critical right now."

Wolf nodded once. "We'll be back in a few hours."

Bri handed him a tattered piece of paper. "Here are the other medications we're in desperate need of and that Flynn will need to prevent a major infection."

Wolf skimmed the list. "Got it. Keep her alive for me."

"I'd tell her that."

Wolf's heart slammed into his stomach. He understood Bri's coded message. Every minute was critical, and it was up to Flynn to hang on. Bri left to check on another patient, and Wolf sank to his knees beside Flynn's cot. Taking her hand, he brought it to his lips, brushing her icy fingertips against them as if he could breathe warmth back into her body.

"Hold on, Flynn," he whispered. "Just a little longer. For me. I need you."

Tucking her hand beneath the blanket, he squeezed it once more. He would get her the blood, or he would die trying.

* * * *

Wolf, Nate, Vic, and Tawny took the tunnels as far as they could south. When they reached the tunnels' end, they crept into the night through an old swanky restaurant in Gold Coast. Exhaustion threatened to overcome Wolf, both physically and emotionally. He rubbed a knot wedged between his neck and shoulder blade. His damn vest suddenly felt too tight and cumbersome. He wanted to rip it off, but that wasn't an option. Rest wasn't an option. Not when every part of him strained toward the one thing that could keep Flynn alive.

They skirted from one block to the next. The sliver of moon cast intermittent shadows over them from behind thick clouds. Brittle cold snuck past their jackets, hats, and gloves to pierce their cheeks, reaching for any inch of exposed skin. Wolf shifted his pack to the other shoulder, scanning the infinite plain of darkness spanning in front of them. They made it the entire way to the hospital without encountering a single REDS truck. The hairs on the back of Wolf's neck prickled. Something didn't seem right.

"Where is everyone?" Wolf breathed.

"Could be they're still searching for us in the Loop," Vic muttered. "Tryin' to dig us out of the city."

Wolf nodded, but his gut wouldn't release a nagging suspicion that Spider knew exactly where he was at this moment. When they were a block away from Northwestern Hospital, they crept into one of the walk-ups to get a better view of what they were up against and plan a point of entry. When they reached the rooftop, Wolf's stomach plummeted back to the ground floor. Wolf counted fifteen trucks surrounding the perimeter of the hospital, their headlights bursting through the darkness. No wonder they'd encountered so few REDS on their route. They'd all been here, waiting for them, guards at the ready for their arrival.

Spider had known. He always knew. And now he was waiting for Wolf to make his next move.

"Shit," Vic said.

Nate locked both hands behind his head. "They must've seen us on some of the cameras and known one of us was hurt."

A hundred different scenarios raced through Wolf's mind, each playing out in disaster.

"We're going to have to split up," Wolf said. "And enter through the back." He set his pack down and reached inside to extract two makeshift pipe bombs, both full of nails. Hyena's specialty. They'd been a part of the stash Wolf smuggled from REDS's arsenal.

"Tawny, set one of these off. Draw REDS away from the hospital. Vic, you have the best shot. Get as close as you can, take position on the top floor of a building, and start taking them out when they head this direction. Make sure you have a clear exit to escape."

Vic nodded, already removing rounds of ammo from his pack.

Wolf met Nate's gaze. "You're with me. Maybe you'll even learn a thing or two." Nate's eyes narrowed. Wolf couldn't resist pissing him off any opportunity he had.

"I wouldn't count on it," Nate sneered. "But then again, I guess you are a pro at killing people. Clearly doesn't matter what side they're on either."

Wolf clenched his teeth instead of punching Nate square in the jaw.

Would showing restraint ever feel better? Doing whatever the fuck he wanted was so much easier. At that moment, Kerri flashed through his mind and shot him a reproachful glare. His conversation with her had been one of the most raw and honest discussions he'd had with someone other than Flynn—one where he hadn't felt judged, nor had to navigate some hidden agenda. She was a true leader and he owed this to her. Wolf glanced at Tawny. She stared grimly into space, her face and eyes swollen. She'd been silent the entire way to the hospital. Clearly she was still reeling from losing Nymph.

"Hey." Wolf snapped his fingers in front of her face. "You got this? Focus."

She blinked twice, her expression dazed, as if Wolf had smacked her. "Yeah, sorry. I keep thinkin' how we wouldn't be here if we'd just given you the weapons in the first place. It was Nymph's idea to go for the cash. He knew we wouldn't have to worry about shit ever again if we got it."

"Now's not the time to mindfuck yourself," Wolf snapped. "You think Nymph would let this stop him from getting shit done?"

Tawny's lips pressed into a thin line. "Right," she said, nodding. The muscles around her mouth twitched, as if she might cry at any second.

"Channel it," Wolf whispered. "All those feelings, channel them into anger. Now, listen. After you detonate the first bomb to lead REDS away, you're going to have to evade them and wait until the last second to set off the second one. Right when shit is about to hit the fan. Once you do, don't wait for us, head straight for the lake."

Tawny closed her eyes, taking a deep breath. When she opened them again, her look was one of fiery determination. "Alright, I'm ready. Let's do this."

41

WOLF

Nate and Wolf crouched on the periphery of the hospital parking lot, watching two Enforcers patrol outside the curved ambulance entrance. Wolf glanced at his watch. Tawny would detonate Hyena's first pipe bomb any second. His heartbeat thundered in his ears. He had never gone into a mission so unprepared or with someone like Nate, whom he didn't truly trust to help keep him alive. But they had no choice. Not if they wanted Flynn to survive. Thankfully, both he and Nate shared that mutual goal, and thankfully their love for her was stronger than their hatred of each other. It was also clearly strong enough for them to do something as brazen and stupid as this.

A sudden explosion reverberated through the city, and shrieks filled the crisp air as nails embedded themselves in more than a few REDS. One of the perks of Hyena's diabolical invention was its wide hit radius. Machine-gun fire began to unload, and intermittent shots followed as Vic likely began to retaliate and pick off advancing REDS. The two guards in front of them froze, looking around frantically for the source of the explosion. It was now or never. Wolf aimed his rifle, taking down one guard and then the next seconds after.

Wolf signaled to Nate. Pointing their rifles in opposite directions, they charged into the building. Nate led the way down a hallway and Wolf tried not to cringe at the sound of his boots scuffing along the linoleum floor.

"Pick up your damn feet," Wolf hissed through his teeth. "You wanna alert the whole building we're here?"

Nate glanced over his shoulder and sneered. "I'm doing my best. Sorry I'm not a skilled operative like you."

The Allies' doctor had worked in Northwestern's emergency room and sketched a rough map to give them an idea of where donated blood was stored and processed before transfusions. Thankfully, the lab was right next to the pharmacy, where they could get the prescriptions the doctor had written down for them to bring back.

The hospital seemed sparsely staffed. They only encountered two nurses wearing blue scrubs, who ducked into rooms when they saw them coming. Northwestern had never been under Wolf's purview, so he hadn't bothered to investigate how REDS managed it or how they selected medical professionals to continue working there. Before turning each corner, Wolf held out a mirror. A backup power system must be operating because the red glow of emergency exit lights caused Wolf to hold his breath whenever they passed under them. As they crept closer to the heart of the hospital on the main floor, a shot behind Wolf narrowly missed his arm.

"Two in the building, I repeat, two—"

Wolf spun around, taking out the Enforcer yelling into his radio as he charged them.

"Shit," Nate groaned.

"Run for it."

They sprinted down the long hallway, skidding to a stop before a big atrium at the center of the hospital. More hallways sprawled in all directions like spokes on a wheel. Then Wolf saw it—the lab straight ahead.

"This way!" Wolf yelled, heading toward the lab. "We gotta make a run for it."

Shots echoed around them, invisible bullets speeding past and sending pieces of plaster flying. Still moving and positioned back-to-back, Wolf and Nate unloaded back, forcing REDS to jump for cover behind tables, booths, and a help center desk spread throughout the atrium.

Wolf and Nate burst through the swinging lab door, right as a bullet whizzed past Wolf's left ear. Wolf got into position, ready to take out REDS if they followed. Nate hurdled over the check-in desk, running toward the back of the room in search of the giant fridge storing donor blood. Because they'd been unable to test Flynn's blood type, they needed O negative, the universal donor.

When a spray of bullets pelted through the door, Wolf scrambled behind the desk. He rummaged through his bag, trying to calm his trembling hand, but his muscles, possessed by an overdrive of adrenaline, ignored him.

"Take your time back there!" Wolf bellowed, although he doubted Nate could hear him over the chorus of relentless gunfire.

Finally, he pulled a small grenade from his pack. He army crawled back toward the door and yanked it open with one hand. Using his teeth to rip out the pin, he chucked the live grenade into the lobby as hard as he could. He jammed his fingers into his ears right as an explosion ripped through the space, blasting out the glass in the panel above him.

Heading back toward the desk in a crouched run, Wolf waited for what felt like an eternity. A high-pitched ringing reverberated through his head, blocking out all other sound. Seconds later, Nate returned with two lunchboxes packed with ice.

"Okay, got it. Think we can make it to the pharmacy?"

Nate's voice sounded garbled. No one had tried to enter the lab since the grenade, so Wolf assumed REDS had switched tactics and were waiting for them to exit.

"Guess we'll find out," Wolf said. "Still got that smoke bomb?"

Nate nodded, dug around in his pack, and withdrew a cylindrical object. He then shoved the lunchboxes inside so he could free his hands for his rifle.

Wolf took the bomb and inched back toward the door, motioning for Nate to follow. "On the count of three, head for the pharmacy. Stay as low as you can, and I'll cover for you. It's a sharp left across from the help desk."

Each passing second gave REDS more time to bring in reinforcements.

"One. Two." Wolf rolled the smoke bomb out of the room. It sizzled as a cloud of thick smoke billowed behind it. "Three."

Wasting no time, they crept from the room. Shots rang out, embedding into walls and furniture, as they ducked and ran. When they reached the pharmacy, the sharp sting of bile smoldered his throat.

There were no doors.

The pharmacy had an open entrance, also serving as the hospital gift shop with tall turnstiles of stuffed bears and deflated "GET WELL SOON" balloons.

"I'll hold them off as long as I can," Wolf called over his shoulder as Nate slid over the pharmacy counter, toward racks lined with bottles.

Wolf kneeled behind a shelf next to the pharmacy entrance. The onslaught of machine-gun fire built in intensity. Disoriented, he shook his head, trying to clear his hearing. It still hadn't returned from the blast of the last grenade.

Think, Wolf, think, he told himself.

He had one more grenade. Yanking it from his pack, he pulled the pin and tossed it into the atrium. An explosion shook the walls and floor, rattling his teeth and masking REDS's yells. Back pressed against the wall, Wolf clenched his jaw against his heaving gasps.

Come on, Nate. Hurry up! he wanted to scream.

Several seconds later, Nate reappeared. He dropped a big bag of pills over the counter with a clatter. Using his pack as a shield, he followed suit right as more gunfire resumed. Nate dove for Wolf, scrambling as fast as he could toward him while Wolf reached around the wall, blindly firing his rifle to hold REDS off.

Nate knelt next to Wolf. "I don't know how we're going to make it out of here in one piece!" he yelled over the deafening noise. Sweat poured down his face, pasting his hair to his forehead and dragging it into his eyes. "We're surrounded."

Wolf couldn't think, adrenaline still commanding his body but fogging his brain. He did the math. They'd used both grenades and the one smoke bomb they had. There was no way out other than to go straight through REDS.

Suddenly, a blast threw Wolf and Nate backward. A hailstorm of pings and clinks rained over the tile floor.

Wolf turned over onto his stomach and pushed himself back up to his knees.

"What the fuck was that?" Nate gasped.

"Nails. It's gotta be Tawny or Vic. They must've seen REDS reinforcements coming for us." They couldn't miss their opportunity. They had to make a run for it. "Come on, let's go. Head straight for the exit. The one we came from. Keep going. Don't stop until you're back at headquarters."

Without hesitation, Nate struggled to his feet and staggered out of the pharmacy. Wolf had to hand it to him, at least the guy had balls. Hot on his heels, Wolf followed. Smoke from the explosions had begun to clear, rising toward the ceiling and revealing scattered mounds of flesh and debris from behind its cloudy curtain. Nails were embedded deep into the dead bodies of REDS, making them appear as giant pincushions. As they neared the atrium's center the shots began again, but they were quickly disrupted by a roaring engine. Wolf threw his arm over his eyes, blinded by a flash of headlights. One of REDS's armored trucks barreled through the hospital's glass doors with a crash.

"Tawny!" Nate yelled.

Wolf caught a glimpse of smoky hair as Tawny poked her head through the top of the truck where the sunroof opened. She fired her machine gun at the few remaining REDS, who turned on the new threat, advancing toward the truck and taking their attention off Nate and Wolf. More REDS poured in from outside, surrounding the truck. Tawny dropped back into her seat. The engine revved as she threw it into reverse, taking out two more REDS in the process. Nate and Wolf kept running, catapulting back down the hallway toward the ambulance entrance.

They burst outside, and although Wolf thought his heart might explode, he didn't slow down. They hurtled across the curved drive, each step bringing them closer to the cover of the awaiting city. From the corner of his vision, Wolf saw REDS trucks peel away from their positions and take off after them. They'd been spotted.

An engine accelerated behind him, its roar reaching to devour him. He had seconds before it caught up to him. Another truck squealed around a corner, it tires screeching against pavement as it headed straight at them. Vic's and Tawny's faces grew bigger as they got closer. Tawny slammed on her breaks several yards in front of them and threw open the door. Nate dove in. Wolf pumped his arms, closing the space between them.

"WOLF, FASTER!" she screamed. "They're on your tail!"

A bullet embedded into his back. His vest absorbed the blow, but the impact sent him sprawling. He skidded across the ground, his momentum causing him to tumble and roll. He lifted his head and instantly knew.

He couldn't make it to Tawny in time, but he could hold off REDS.

"GO!" he yelled. "Go, go, go!"

Tawny's face paled. She hesitated, looking to Vic for guidance.

"Tawny, GO!" he shouted again.

Yanking the steering wheel, she took off, leaving the smell of burnt rubber in her wake.

Wolf hauled himself to his feet right as two more trucks swerved around him, boxing him in. A small breath of relief coursed through him when they didn't chase after Tawny. Clearly he was their target.

Dropping his gun, he slowly raised his hands over his head, blinded by the headlights.

Truck doors slammed and several silhouettes approached him. As they inched closer, he could make out their rifles aimed squarely between his eyes. Wolf didn't care if they killed him. He just wanted to know whether Flynn was going to make it before he died. His muscles tensed, so taut they might snap. He waited, his instincts kicking in, reading the small movements of each Enforcer to gauge when they were within reach. Wolf leapt toward the closest, twisting the Enforcer's rifle out of his grip. He whacked him in the temple, knocking him unconscious. He pivoted, ready for the next attack.

Suddenly, blinding pain filled his head and his legs lost their ability to hold his weight. His body hit the asphalt with unforgiving force.

"Fucking traitor," a voice growled. Wolf blinked but the night had already become fuzzy. His body relaxed, succumbing to the darkness. "Tell Spider we got him."

Everything went black.

42

FLYNN

When Flynn opened her eyes, the memory of the car chase came rushing back so forcefully she gasped. Someone grabbed her hand, shushing her, smoothing hair back from her clammy forehead.

She closed her eyes again, inhaling deeply through her nose.

I'm alive? She couldn't believe it. *How am I alive?*

She turned her head to the side, noticing how heavy it felt, like a bowling ball. She peeled open her lids and Nate's face swam before her, a small smile curving his lips.

"You're awake," he whispered, his voice hoarse.

She nodded. The last thing she remembered was Wolf carrying her into the tunnel, her ear pressed to his chest, memorizing the sound of his rapid heartbeat. She'd tried to match her own to its rhythm, focusing on the steady thumps to keep her breathing.

"Water?" Her voice cracked. She ran her tongue over her craggy lips, energy already draining from her body like a sieve.

Nate lifted her head with a hand and brought a cup of water to her mouth. She sipped, letting the cool liquid wash down her throat. She looked around. She lay on a cot with an IV on an old stand next to her. Thin tubes connected a bag of blood to the vein in the crook of her elbow. A privacy screen formed a small makeshift room around her, blocking her view of the rest of the space.

A cloud swirled around her brain. "How long have I been out?"

"A few days."

She groaned. "Man. Wish I'd slept through the rest of winter. My side hurts like a motherfucker."

Nate beamed, his eyes shining. "Yeah, always wished I could hibernate."

She sighed. Everything felt weak.

"Do you remember much?" he asked.

"Not really. But I had the craziest dreams." A pang sliced into her, stinging worse than her throbbing side. "About my parents. About Cori. And then...I was in the mountains surrounded by so much green. The type of rich, vibrant green you only find in a forest." Her muscles relaxed as she remembered the thick, feathery ferns carpeting the ground, stretching as far as she could see, until they blended in with the canopy of trees. "I want to move away from here," Flynn said, her chest tightening as she remembered where she was. Trapped in the city, the bleak winter an endless panel of gray.

Nate tucked a loose strand of hair behind her ear. "Where do you wanna go?"

"Somewhere far away. Somewhere away from skyscrapers and traffic. Away from loud noises and claustrophobic spaces. I want to live in a place where quiet is only disrupted by birds."

"Sounds perfect. Sign me up," he said.

"Really? You're in, Mr. Socialite? Could you handle being away from the scene?"

"Anywhere you go, I'll go too."

A brief sense of peace settled over her at the thought of having Nate with her at all times. Until Wolf's face in the getaway car flashed before her, panic etched into each of his features when he realized she'd been shot.

Oh my god.

"What about the others?" she asked. She tried to sit up, but a fresh wave of pain sliced through her entire abdomen. Wincing, she lay back down. "Has REDS found us?"

Nate shook his head slowly, cupping her hand in both his own. "Not yet. Something's happened that has...discouraged their pursuit."

She tensed, sensing he was searching for a way to soften the blow of his next words. "What do you mean? What happened?"

Nate sighed, his shoulders sagging as he exhaled. He squeezed her hands tighter. "It's Wolf."

Flynn's heart stuttered to a stop. For several long seconds she was suspended in time, Nate's mouth moving but no sound emerging.

No. Not after he risked everything to help us.

"...had to raid Northwestern Hospital to get medical supplies." She crashed back to Earth. "...needed medicine and blood we didn't have here. You lost a lot of it. They could get your blood pressure stable with saline, but it was temporary. A blood transfusion was your only chance at surviving."

Flynn tried to breathe, but panic squeezed her lungs so tightly air couldn't seem to get in or out. The room spun.

"...formed a small mission to get the supplies. Wolf...he, um, he sacrificed himself so we could escape. They took him alive, but, uh...who knows. We can only assume what they'll do to him."

Flynn looked up at the ceiling, trying to fight back tears. She wished Nate would leave. She wanted to be alone to process what this could mean. She opened her mouth, then closed it, biting her tongue so hard she tasted a metallic tang. She wanted to scream at the unfairness of it all. She wanted him back here. With her. She finally couldn't hold it back anymore. Her eyes burned as she allowed tears to fall freely down her face. After all Wolf had done to save her, he was now at the whim of the same terrorist group who would destroy him without a second thought.

"What do we do?" she gasped. "It's not fair... Nate, you know it's not fair... After everything..."

Nate raked his fingers through his hair, letting them rest at the back of his neck. "No," he said, "you're right, it's not fair. It seemed like he was the only one they were really after. They stopped chasing us as soon as they took him."

Flynn sat up again quickly. "Ah!" She clutched her side where the bullet had been. She tried to ignore how Nate swayed back and forth. "We've got to get him back."

"Whoa there." Nate placed a hand on her shoulder, coaxing her back to the pillow. "We'll figure something out. Kerri's on it. It'll be super risky. But now that we have Skulls' reinforcements, we might have a chance. I'll let Kerri know you're awake so she can fill you in. She's been asking about you."

Sadness rested behind Nate's eyes, layered with concern and exhaustion. She doubted he'd slept, watching over her since he returned from the hospital. He had also risked his life to save her.

"Thank you," she whispered, bringing his free hand to her lips.

"For what?"

"For saving me."

He lay his head on her lap, and Flynn let fresh tears flow silently down her cheeks. She sank her fingers into Nate's hair, still thick and wavy but hardened with grime. "I'm just sorry I couldn't save him too."

43

FLYNN

Kerri and Tawny came to visit Flynn a few hours later. Nate finally left to sleep for what was likely the first time in days. Tawny seemed like a shadow of herself, resigned to silence with dark circles stamped under puffy eyes. Flynn had watched REDS take down Nymph from her getaway car. When she closed her eyes, she could still see him charging forward, his body absorbing rounds of bullets. A fire had roared up inside her, launching her into overdrive. Without thinking, she'd barreled through REDS's gunfire to save Nate and Wolf. Tawny looked exactly how Flynn felt—lost, uncentered, untethered. Flynn wished she could hug her, as if that would lessen either of their pain.

Kerri pulled up a chair next to Flynn's bed and sat, her green eyes wide. "Blimey, I'm glad you're okay. You really were touch and go there fer a bit."

Flynn nodded. "I'd be dead if it wasn't for our crew. And now Wolf..." Her voice broke. She clenched her jaw. *Get your shit together, Flynn,* she told herself. *Your blubbering isn't going to save him.* "We need to get him back," Flynn finished.

Kerri leaned back in the chair, crossing her arms over her chest. "Look, getting Wolf back is a top priority, but before he left for the hospital, he filled me in on the hostages corralled in Grant Park."

A rush of gratitude poured over Flynn, further weakening her limbs. Wolf had kept his promise to tell Kerri. Her stomach fluttered, thinking about their night together in the apartment. It already seemed like years ago. "Yeah, I guess REDS kept him in the dark about that."

"Well, they were smart to. It gave him time before the bank heist to create pathways through REDS's network, almost like a secret digital entry point."

"What does that mean?" Flynn scrunched her brow in confusion. "He never told me about this."

"Probably too risky, in case you got captured during the bank heist." Kerri shook her head, rubbing her palms along her thighs. "It means once we're ready, we can hand over access to the government to disable the nuclear arsenal under Lake Michigan." She paused, deep in thought.

"It was almost like he knew he would have to give himself up," Tawny said, her voice monotone. Flynn glanced at her. Tawny hadn't so much as moved other than to blink. She stared blankly at the wall next to Flynn's bed.

"I wouldn't be surprised. He has always been one step ahead of everyone," Flynn said.

"And thanks to him, we know REDS's next step in their plan with the ransomware and the decryption key. My assumption is Wolf's still alive and will be until he deploys it for them."

The night before the bank heist, in the darkness of the apartment, their voices muffled by thin, stale sheets found in the back of a linen closet, Wolf had explained the ransomware. How it would take advantage of unpatched software and hijack every smart device in the country. How it would demand citizens turn over their senators as a first step to disbanding their government. How it would share a revolving reel of images showing the government being complicit in Chicago's genocide. It would convince people the government was against them.

In some other time, Flynn wouldn't have believed propaganda like that could work. But Flynn knew now it would be a catalyst to incite civil war. It was too easy for secrets and lies to spread, for them to twist into ugly misrepresentations of the truth that explode with terrifying virality. It might at one time have been impossible to get a group of people to side with terrorists, but not when the terrorists appear to be advocates for everyday people— defending them from the dangers of government corruption.

Not when terrorists can convince other people they're just like them.

A small bubble of hope floated inside her and then burst when she absorbed what Kerri was saying. "You think they'll force him to deploy it?"

Kerri studied her carefully, as if trying to measure her mental state. "Yes, I do. Hopefully he can hold off until we can get to him."

Flynn resisted the urge to throw up all over her cot. Thankfully, she hadn't eaten in days. "He can. I know he can. Okay, so if Wolf created this... this digital pathway into REDS's network, then why hasn't the government deactivated the nuclear arsenal? Why hasn't the military taken back the city already?"

Kerri raised one of her brows. "Well, firstly, Wolf only handed me this information two days ago. We haven't had the opportunity to communicate this new development to the government. As soon as Nate and Wolf left for Northwestern Hospital, I sent a runner out to try to get in touch with them. All that aside, this is uncharted territory. Never before in US history has a terrorist group occupied an area or gained access to US nuclear missiles. They're not deterred by our usual rules of war."

"What rules of war?" Flynn asked.

"You know...you can't nuke us because we'll nuke you right back and destroy your population. If they find out we've figured out how to deactivate their dead man's switch, they might act out of desperation. A group like REDS won't hesitate to launch a nuke straight at Washington, and how is our military supposed to respond? Send a nuke right back straight into Chicago?"

"So, what are we supposed to do in the meantime? Let all those hostages in Grant Park rot in a modern-day concentration camp?"

"I have to assume it all comes down to numbers," Kerri said. "We haven't lost enough yet where it would be comparable to a nuclear attack."

"But if REDS launches the ransomware before we get a chance to disarm it, we might be too late. It could turn the entire country against the government before they can interfere." Fear surged through her, as powerful and numbing as an electrical current. "There could be no coming back from that."

"I know," Kerri agreed. "My only hope is Wolf mentioned tampering with the ransomware. Maybe knowing that possibility, he was able to change the ransom note."

Flynn let the magnitude of what they were up against settle over her. An iron fist clamped around her heart, threatening to squeeze out all hope. She'd naively started to believe Wolf trusted her, but it was clear there was still so much he continued to withhold.

"He tampered with it? He never mentioned that to me either. He just told me what the original message would be."

"Again, he likely withheld information to protect you. He had no way of knowing whether it would work. He couldn't test it, so there are a lot of unknowns," Kerri said.

"He prepared us for this moment," Tawny said, awakening from her daze. "We're indebted to him."

Flynn sat up more slowly this time to avoid the shooting pain in her side. "Then we owe it to him to try to save him. We can't wait on the government."

Tawny looked at Kerri pointedly. "We know where REDS's main headquarters are. Think it's safe to assume, given Wolf's position in the organization, he's there with leadership."

"Hold yer donkeys. You forget we haven't deactivated anything yet. REDS still has their finger on the nuke button. They still have all the leverage. We can't do this alone, even with Skulls and the extra firepower. If we want to neutralize REDS, Homeland Security and the National Guard need a way into the city."

"I still have REDS's truck that I used to escape," Tawny said. "Hid it about a mile from here so REDS won't trace it back to this location if it's discovered."

"So, what? You're just going to attack one of REDS's strongholds and hope for the best? Sounds like a suicide mission," Kerri snapped. "And we've run plenty of those lately. Think it's safe to say our luck has run out."

"Maybe," Tawny said. "We've lived through enough already, why not keep testing fate? It's what Nymph would do."

Flynn stared at Tawny, surprised that she'd snapped back to life. Tawny pulled her backpack onto her lap and withdrew Flynn's axe, handing it to her.

"Where'd you get this?" Flynn asked.

Tawny avoided Flynn's scrutiny. "Vic grabbed it from the van. He drove you, Nate, and Wolf back here while you were bleeding out."

Flynn took it, tears scalding her eyes. She ran a thumb over its smooth handle, trying to channel Wolf's strength.

"Kerri!" Vic's booming voice echoed through the room, causing them all to jump.

"Jesus, Vic." Kerri swiveled in her chair. "What in the bloody hell is it?"

"One of our runners returned from Evanston. They secured a satellite phone."

A huge grin lit up Kerri's face. "Fucking brilliant!"

"Apparently we have a call with the Situation Room in an hour," Vic said.

"Situation Room? As in...the president?"

"Dunno." Vic scratched his cheek, unconcerned. "Not sure exactly who'll be on the call, to be honest."

"Kind of an important detail," Kerri mumbled.

"The runner didn't give *any* details," Vic said. "Just a phone and time."

"Well, I want all three of you on the call with me," Kerri said. "And Nate and Antonio. You were in the field most recently, you have the freshest intel."

Flynn's mind reeled. She'd gone from waking up with a gunshot wound to finding out Wolf was gone to learning of an imminent conference call with some of the most powerful people in the world with less than an hour's notice. She wanted to retreat under the covers until this shitshow was over. Until her parents could rescue her from the city. She missed them and her sister, Fiella, so much it hurt. But now Wolf's life hung in the balance, and she would never forgive herself if he died so she could live. The prospect of that grated against her conscience like an unforgiving scalpel.

Kerri stood and stretched. "Alright, get some rest before the meeting. Maybe this will be the answer we've been looking for."

44

WOLF

Wolf slit his eyes, allowing the blurred cell to come into focus before slamming his lids shut again. He might as well have a block of concrete crushing his skull, and he knew the second he showed signs of awakening, the pain would worsen.

"Ah, Wolf, you decided to rejoin us." Spider's voice drifted over him.

Let the torture begin. The grim thought floated through his sluggish brain.

Wolf rolled onto his back, his hands zip-tied in front of him. Good thing he'd learned how to embrace pain from the best. The irony was laughable, except for the fact that his death waited to descend at any second.

"I guess 'decided' isn't really the right word though, is it? More like forced."

Wolf blinked several times. Spider sat in the corner of the cell on a folding chair, watching him.

"Just fucking get it over with, Spider," Wolf muttered.

"Oh, Wolf, you know me better than that," Spider sneered. He stood with a groan, placing his hands on his hips and stretching his lower back. "I'm not as young as I used to be, but I'm confident I still have it in me." His boots slapped the icy concrete floor as he took slow steps toward Wolf. Wolf stared at the cracked ceiling, waiting until Spider stood over him, staring down his long nose in disgust.

A crushing blow to his side knocked the wind out of him. "That's for the bank." Wolf rolled onto his side gasping, trying to convince his lungs they still had the ability to suck in air. Another blow to his back sent searing pain zinging through his spine. "That's for the hospital." A blow to his shoulder and a crack. "And that's for your brothers whom you killed."

Wolf closed his eyes, shutting down his body's screaming response to the agony. He pictured Flynn's face, remembered the touch of her lips on his skin.

"You know, I had my suspicions," Spider whispered, crouching low, his mouth next to Wolf's ear. "Tiger warned me, of course. But even I didn't think you were capable of such treachery."

Spider stood again and began to circle, like a shark angling to sink its teeth into the soft underbelly of its prey. "Don't worry. Despite how weak you've become, I know your mental fortitude. I remember how you performed during training. You can withstand torture, although I did promise Tiger he could have a little fun. But now I also know what you cannot withstand."

Wolf had the sudden sensation he was free falling from the top of a building, the ground speeding toward him at an unstoppable speed.

Flynn.

Wolf's eyes flew open. "You'll never find her." He contracted his abs to protect his abdomen from an unexpected blow, but even then his voice shook.

"You of all people know I have eyes everywhere. You think I didn't know that bitch and her little cronies were running around the city, playing dress up and war? Those fucking fakes didn't deserve an ounce of our energy." Spider bent over and grabbed Wolf by the throat. "And I waited...waited for you to do what you'd always said you would but never had the balls to do. I watched her toy with you like a cat playing with its food. Did you think you won? After you FUCKED US?" Spider screamed, spittle flying from his mouth, his gleaming teeth bared. He yanked Wolf toward him, wrapping all ten fingers around Wolf's neck. He squeezed, and Wolf waited to die. "I will kill every last one of them until I find her and tear her apart in front of you, limb by fucking limb."

45

FLYNN

In the low light of the room, Flynn watched Kerri's taut shoulders and waited for some sign of movement. They were so stiff and motionless Flynn suspected she could rest a glass of champagne on them and not a drop of liquid would spill. Flynn's tongue prickled at the memory of the carbonated beverage tickling her nose as it slid down her throat. What she would do for a drink right now.

She rubbed her eyes, fighting against the exhaustion sucking away her energy with each passing second. She slumped into her uncomfortable folding chair, its flimsy metal pressing against her shoulder blades. Other than Kerri and Flynn, only Antonio, Nate, Vic, and Tawny were present, sitting in a small circle. As if on an altar, the satellite phone sat on two stacked, over-turned crates. The meeting would be top secret. They couldn't risk anyone leaking any information.

They'd been waiting for over a half hour to be connected to the Situation Room. How there could be more urgent matters taking place somewhere else in the world was beyond her.

Don't worry about us, Flynn wanted to scream. *We're just here, trapped in an apocalyptic nightmare, while you assholes are late for this call from your safe bunker a few states away.*

It was all Flynn could do not to dig her fingers into her scalp. She needed to do something to release her pent-up frustration, its pressure building by the minute. Each passing second brought Wolf closer to death. She decided gnawing on her nail bed would be a sufficient alternative. She knew she'd been growing more attached to Wolf, but hadn't realized the extent until he was ripped away from her and thrown to certain danger, if not death. Now, the thought of living without him felt similar to carving a piece of her away and pulverizing it into dust.

Muffled static came over the line, and everyone shot up in their seats. The sudden movement made Flynn yelp in pain. Nate looked at her, concern creasing his brows.

I'm okay, she mouthed.

They leaned forward in anticipation, straining to hear. A number of harsh, gruff voices talked over each other, mumbling incomprehensible sentences.

"Um, hello?" Kerri ventured.

The mumbles continued, oblivious to their awaiting room.

"Excuse me, some of us haven't got all day, so can we begin now?" Kerri barked. The voices fell silent. "Would, uh, help to know who we're talking to," she continued, throwing up her hands at the phone.

"Of course," a flustered female responded.

They began with a quick round of introductions on both sides. A number of men barked out official titles, and then Flynn counted two women—the president's chief of staff, and the secretary of defense. The president hadn't joined. Masked behind the receiver, Flynn couldn't help but think they sounded like regular people and not some of the most influential policy leaders in the world.

"We'll proceed without the president today. He's decided to distance himself from the issue after the public uproar following the bombings," one of the women said. Flynn was pretty certain it was the chief of staff.

Kerri rolled her eyes. "Yes, I can imagine the government bombing its own citizens wasn't well received."

"The intent was to avoid civilian casualties and eradicate a terrorist group."

"Intent rarely seems like it's fairly interpreted by the public," Kerri snapped.

Silence followed, and Flynn held her breath.

"It certainly seems that way," one of the men said. "Especially with the unchecked nature of all these damn social media platforms. We had to shut down TikTok. It was getting out of hand. Misinformation spreading like wildfire. It can't be contained."

Flynn and Nate exchanged a look. TikTok had been shut down? Flynn could only imagine how much fuel that added to the "wildfire." She wasn't up to speed on any of the intel that Kerri gathered from runners about what was going on in the rest of the country, and frankly she didn't give a shit. Not while Wolf's fate rested so precariously in their hands.

"This *issue*, sir, has been out of hand for weeks and continues to escalate with each passing second," said Kerri.

"We find it in our best interest not to negotiate with a group of terror-ists," another man said.

"Well, that will be at the cost of thousands of innocent lives," Kerri said.

"Alright," said the other woman, probably the secretary of defense. "Please debrief us then so we can establish a path forward. It's our understanding that there has been a development that could allow us to safely launch a ground invasion without the threat of nuclear retaliation."

"Yes," Kerri replied. "We have a double agent working for us. He was high in the ranks with REDS, but he has since been discovered and captured. From him we know REDS plans to deploy a ransomware to every smart device in the US. We don't know when but can assume it'll be any day now."

A claw sank its talons into Flynn's gut. In other words, however long Wolf could withstand torture.

"Before his capture, our agent was able to create a pathway through REDS's network," Kerri continued, "which, from my understanding, should allow us to gain access to the nuclear arsenal under Lake Michigan and nul-lify their threat to deploy nuclear missiles."

"Hold please," a man said.

Silence pulsed throughout the room. Antonio, Nate, Vic, Kerri, Tawny, and Flynn glanced at each other, waiting. Kerri wrung her hands, but the confidence in her voice never wavered.

"We confirmed you are correct," the female voice suddenly chimed, startling them. "If what you say is true about the open network, then we can disable the nuclear weapons."

"There's something else, Madam Secretary." Kerri spoke directly to the person who clearly held the cards. "It seems as if REDS has consolidated all the hostages in Chicago to some sort of encampment in Grant Park."

"How many people?"

"We're not sure. None of us here have witnessed it... Maybe a couple thousand?"

Silence again.

"A couple thousand? Did your double agent provide this intel as well?"

"Yes," Kerri said.

"Let's not raise the alarm to the president yet," a man said. "At least not until we send in a drone to confirm the accuracy of this information. Besides, if we neutralize the nuclear threat, then we can send in military reinforcements to rescue the hostage—"

"We trust our source," Kerri interrupted. "REDS is a fully armed militia. If they realize you disabled the nuclear arsenal, they will use those hostages to remain in control. And if REDS's pattern of behavior remains consistent, they will use it to their advantage and live stream it to the public to see how the government responds."

"So, you're suggesting we rescue the hostages first and then disable the missiles," the secretary of defense confirmed.

"Precisely," Kerri said. "We need to time it perfectly."

"This sounds like a dangerous dance with a number of potentially catastrophic outcomes," another dubious man chirped.

Kerri's mouth pressed into a thin line as she glowered at the phone. "Welcome to our reality for the last several weeks, sir."

46

FLYNN

It had been five days since their conversation with the Situation Room. Due to the blood transfusion, antibiotics, and IVs, with each day Flynn's body felt stronger, but her sanity continued to deteriorate. She lay awake at night thinking about Wolf, wondering whether he was alive or what method of torture REDS was subjecting him to. By the time she would finally stumble into a restless sleep, it seemed as if she would jolt awake only an hour later. She tossed and turned, waiting for the night to swallow her, desperate to scream into her pillow, to open a release valve and vent the frustration from her body before it combusted.

On the day they solidified their strategy with the Department of Defense, Nate wandered into the hospital ward to check on her. They'd come up with a plan, a pincer play, to take advantage of REDS's stronghold in the Loop. The Allies would finally receive reinforcements from the military to surround and trap REDS. The Allies and Skulls would push east from the West Loop and south from the Magnificent Mile. The National Guard had to be strategic about where they would meet them to provide additional support, so as not to alert REDS to their involvement. Meanwhile, the US military would set up a blockade on the 90/94 highway to advance into the city and liberate the hostages when they received the go-ahead.

Timing was critical. Once REDS realized their position, they could attempt to strike any part—or multiple parts—of the country with nuclear missiles. Several aircraft waited nearby, prepared for emergency takeoff in case they needed to shoot down any launched missiles. Once they surrounded REDS and deactivated the nuclear arsenal, more of the National Guard would deploy from Lake Michigan and head up the Chicago River to help finish the job. Deactivating the nuclear arsenal was the key. If Wolf hadn't opened the network and provided the ransomware decryption key, they'd be in the same position they'd found themselves in for the last several weeks—stuck.

Of course, Flynn had been sidelined due to her gunshot wound. After everything she had endured the last few weeks, she was supposed to sit back and watch as the grand finale unfolded. The group of people responsible for destroying her life and city would finally be forced to heel, and she had to experience it from a distance. Fuming, she paced back and forth around her hospital cot, stretching and bending her fingers into claws.

"Figured you'd been in this state," Nate said.

"Can you blame me?"

Nate considered her. "No. But you know it's the right decision. You won't be an asset out there. You'd slow down your unit."

She stopped and turned toward him, closing her eyes. "I know, I know. I'm just so fucking sick of doing nothing." She collapsed onto her cot and tried not to wince when a jolt of pain ricocheted through her torso. "And after everything, I deserve to watch REDS suffer. I want to see them squashed. Especially—" Her voice broke. She swallowed hard, attempting to dam the emotion threatening to spew outward. "Especially when the reason Wolf is in this mess is because of *me*."

"Flynn." Nate joined her on the cot. "You know that's not true. We all understand the risks every time we step outside and into that city."

"I wish he would've let me die. He's useful to our cause. He could have actually helped end this!"

"No." Nate's voice was so quiet Flynn had to stare up at his profile to watch his mouth move. "You didn't see him after we thought we lost you. If you hadn't made it...he would have ended it for himself. I know it." Nate glanced down at her, a corner of his lips lifting into a sad half smile. "I've been playing our escape at Northwestern over and over in my head. I keep trying to figure out some way we could've saved him. That way, I could go back to hating him. And maybe I'd still have a chance of being with you."

Flynn bit down on the inside of her cheek. Nate had no idea she and Wolf had slept together. How they were now inexplicably intertwined. Over the past few weeks, Wolf had guided her out of the hopelessness that had threatened to devour her since Cori was killed. Step by step, in his own imperfect way, he'd changed direction. And in doing so, he'd shown her that change was one of the bravest acts someone could attempt in their life.

"I've always had this deep, strange feeling Wolf and I were the same, but I could never figure out how or why. I think now I finally understand it."

"You really think you're similar to someone like him?"

Flynn nodded. "We've both made mistakes that at times feel..." She paused, searching for the word. "...insurmountable."

"I don't think I'd label his *decisions* as mistakes," Nate said. "And unlike him, you were forced into those decisions. There's a huge difference."

"True. But regardless, decisions, mistakes, whatever you want to label them—if we let them continue to define us or continue to use them as evidence to convince ourselves we don't deserve love, then what's the point?"

"The point?"

"I think what I'm trying to say is if we don't work toward redemption, regardless of whether others feel we're deserving of it or not, if we give up on that hope, then what's the point of this life?"

Nate studied her, his expression unreadable. "Maybe you're right." He placed a palm on her cheek and leaned forward to kiss her forehead. Flynn closed her eyes, relishing in the warmth of his touch. How could both Nate and Wolf make her feel whole in such different ways? When he stood, Flynn sat up so quickly her side screamed.

"Nate," she called after him.

He craned his head to look over his shoulder, his hazel eyes appearing heavy and yellow under the room's harsh light.

"You better not leave without saying goodbye," she said. "I can't lose you too."

"I won't," he promised.

As she watched him walk away, what remained of Flynn's heart splintered in two. It wasn't that she didn't love Nate, because she knew without a shadow of doubt she did.

She just now knew Wolf needed her more.

47

FLYNN

Flynn and Antonio sat in silence. The battered pickup truck they occupied barely seemed like it had the gumption to get them the five blocks it had, so Antonio cut the engine and let the cold seep in through its rusty, dented doors. Flynn sulked, still frustrated she'd been sidelined from participating in the Allies' multipronged advance toward the Loop. Thankfully, Antonio had agreed to join her on the fringe of the action. Although Flynn had a strong suspicion he'd really been assigned to babysit her to ensure she didn't do anything stupid.

"What month is it?" Flynn rubbed her biceps to keep warm. Her side ached, but it was manageable. "I've lost track. Are we in December yet?"

"November." Antonio glanced at her. "This Thursday is Thanksgiving."

"What? Seriously?"

He nodded.

"Thanksgiving," Flynn repeated. "The thought that the majority of our country will be sitting down around their tables while we suffer in this forgotten city is kinda unbearable."

Antonio nodded again and smirked. "Yeah, well, welcome to inequality in America."

Flynn's stomach twisted. "Guess it hits different when you finally experience it for yourself."

"That's the beginning of what we in the therapy world like to call empathy."

Flynn leaned her head back into the headrest and watched the quiet streets. In the distance explosions boomed. Bursts and snaps of machine-gun fire punctuated the eerie calm, calling back and forth to each other like songbirds.

"You're the reason I'm allowed up here right now, aren't you?" Flynn reached over and gave his forearm a squeeze. "Or else Kerri never would've let me aboveground. I have no idea how you convinced her."

Antonio lifted a shoulder into a half shrug. "I may or may not have made a case for you to be there when the city was liberated. Even if we have to watch it unfold from a distance, after all you've done and sacrificed, you've earned that victory. And Wolf deserves to know you're alive once they rescue him. We wouldn't be here if it wasn't for his help and you convincing him to join our cause."

Their radio crackled from the cup holder between them. Voices filled the truck with coded updates.

"Do you think he's still alive?" Flynn whispered.

Antonio sighed. "I know he's not the type to give up without a fight."

"I think I love him."

Deep lines furrowed into Antonio's once smooth forehead. "I think he deserves to know that."

Flynn wiped her nose with the back of her hand. "Yeah, well, looks like I missed my chance."

Before Antonio could respond, a voice buzzed through the radio. "Fox Den, I repeat, Fox Den. Two trucks are advancing north. They diverted around our advancements and are headed your way. Seek cover."

Alarmed, Antonio and Flynn looked at each other. Fox Den was their assigned code name, but no one had actually expected REDS to take an interest in their position. Not with the pressure cooker they'd find themselves in as the Allies and military advanced from all sides. Antonio leaned forward and turned the key in the ignition. Flynn tried to remember the last time she'd seen an actual car key, which probably explained the truck's current state.

The engine protested, turning over.

"C'mon," Antonio muttered, cranking the ignition again. The engine sputtered and coughed, straining to start.

Nothing.

A far-off rumble drew closer. Flynn yanked open the center console and grabbed a handgun. A filmy residue formed on her tongue, sticking it to the roof of her mouth. *Fuck.* She still didn't know how to use this damn thing.

"Fox Den, confirm when you're secure," the radio bleeped.

Flynn scooped up the radio and pressed the button. "This is Fox Den. We hear oncoming vehicles. Our truck isn't starting, so we're going to have to proceed on foot. We'll try to update you shortly."

Flynn wrenched open the passenger door and tumbled out of the truck. Right as Antonio leapt down beside her, the rumble transformed into a roar. As if on cue, two Humvees swerved around a corner, careening toward them.

"Shit! Flynn, RUN!" Flynn took off as a spray of bullets shattered the windshield. Glancing over her shoulder, she saw Antonio dive behind the truck then scramble to his feet. He unloaded his rifle at the Humvees before turning to sprint in the other direction.

Flynn clutched her side, gasping.

The trucks split, one following Antonio and the other speeding after her. She willed her feet to move faster, focusing on pumping her arms, ignoring the searing burn that had wrapped itself around her waist like a corset of fire.

Flynn darted down an alley. She would never be able to outrun a vehicle, especially in her current condition. Skidding to a stop she threw her weight against an abandoned flower shop's back entrance.

The door didn't budge.

"FUCK!" Flynn yelled, giving the door an unsuccessful kick.

Flynn set off again, but right as she prepared to sprint down another side street, a motorcycle appeared from nowhere. Flynn whirled around, heading back in the direction she came from, but the Humvee had caught up, screeching to a halt and blocking her path forward. The motorcycle cut its throaty growl behind her. She staggered to a stop, knowing she was surrounded. She dropped to her knees. A cramp doubled the pain in her side, squeezing harder each time she sucked in frigid air.

Two men approached, their rifles aimed directly at her. Their faces were covered with crimson masks—the color that would haunt her dreams forever.

"Drop your gun," a cool voice from behind her said.

She tossed the handgun to the ground and glanced up at the Enforcer. He still wore his motorcycle helmet, his eyes shielded by its visor. He also pointed a rifle at her head.

Here I come, Cori, Flynn thought. *Somehow fate keeps bringing me back to you.*

"Thought we might find you around here," he cackled. "Didn't take long to get one of your pussy runners to talk."

"Too bad your timing is a bit late," Flynn spat. "Just kill me and get it over with."

"Nahhh. Not yet. Boss wants you alive. We've got someone waiting to see you."

48

WOLF

Wolf lay there waiting to die. He'd done everything he could to give the Allies a fighting chance. A small part of him clung to the hope that it might somehow mend all the damage he'd unleashed. Or maybe it would prove to himself he could relinquish his pursuit of power and seek something else. Loosen his grip. He couldn't reverse time and bring back the people he'd killed, but he could set forth on a new path. He could choose something different this time, and he could make that choice for himself and himself alone.

"Get up." The voice sounded tiny. Distant.

"Get up!" This time the voice gurgled as if someone had submerged his head into a pool.

Freezing water splashed over Wolf, yanking him back to the present. Wheezing, he forced his swollen eyes open. Icy droplets slid down his broken nose, trickling over his chin and onto his neck. Chills shook his body. He tried to stop the tremors, tried to control the overpowering shudders, but he couldn't.

"Oh, come on, Wolf. You're no fun! A few bumps and bruises and you're out of commission?"

Wolf hated that voice. Tiger's voice. Wolf had spent the last few days of his capture imagining ways he could sever Tiger's vocal cords first and then his head. It had been one of the only thoughts that had brought him peace as he'd drifted in and out of consciousness.

The torture hadn't been too bad. Well, maybe it had. He'd blacked out through most of it. But the fact that Tiger had inflicted most of the damage somehow made the suffering worse. Dreaming up all the ways he could kill him once he was free kept Wolf's shreds of sanity patched together.

Tiger leered down at him. "Up and at 'em. You got a visitor. Don't wanna be rude now." Wolf blinked, the gears in his brain finally clicking into place. "Bring her in!"

A door creaked open and the thud of a body landed next to him. "Ouch! Can you at least tell me where I am now?"

No. Flynn. No. It can't be. How had they found her?

Flynn pushed herself to her knees and Tiger yanked a blindfold off her head. When their eyes met, she yelled out and scrambled toward him. He wanted to reassure her, but he was fairly certain his jaw was broken.

"Flynn," was all he could manage to cough out.

"W-Wolf." She choked back a sob. Gently, she smoothed his wet hair back from his forehead. He watched the desperation on her face transform into fury. Without warning, Flynn spun around, simultaneously swinging her cuffed fists upward at Tiger's gnarled face. She landed an uppercut to his nose. Blood gushed everywhere, strangling his gurgled scream.

"You dumb bitch!" He grabbed Flynn and threw her across the small cell. Her body slammed into the cement wall.

Blood spewed from Tiger's nostrils despite his attempt to staunch the flow with his palms. "If you so much as move, I'll fucking rip your teeth out one by one," he warned her. He wrenched open the cell's thick metal door. "Grizzly!" he bellowed into his radio. "Get me a medic NOW."

He stormed out, slamming the door behind him. Flynn shuffled on her knees toward Wolf. She tried to help him sit up, straining her wrists against her cuffs, but Wolf gritted his teeth. His broken ribs protested any movement.

"I've been wanting to do that, but seeing you do it was ten times better. You sure as hell pissed him off," Wolf whispered. He couldn't help but grin. "You're alive."

Her face split into a watery smile. Tears shone in her eyes, turning them the color of an icy puddle. "For now, thanks to you." He could tell from her horrified expression he must look as bad as he felt. "I'm so sorry. You wouldn't be here if it wasn't for me getting shot."

"Typical Flynn, act first, think later. Had to come save the day, guns blazing."

"What was I supposed to do, watch from the sidelines while REDS shot you up like target practice?"

"I know, I get it. I couldn't let you die either," he muttered.

"I didn't think it was possible for me to hate REDS even more than I did before." She took his bloody hands in her own and brought them to her lips, kissing each finger.

"They're going to make me deploy the ransomware. That's why they brought you here. They knew they could torture me to death, but for you, I'd crack."

"Don't do it. Not for me. You know they're going to kill me regardless."

"Did Kerri tell you? I had a feeling it would come to this. So, I made my own ransomware."

"Of course you did." Flynn stroked his cheek, then guided his eyes to hers. "Like I've said, you're always one step ahead. Hold on just a little longer. The military is finally helping us now. They joined forces with us and Skulls. They will crush REDS. I know it."

He reached up to cover Flynn's hand with his own, sealing her warm skin against his. "Flynn, we both know I can't survive in a new world. Who would I be?"

"Who will any of us be? We'll figure it out. Together." Flynn's tears turned murky as they cut through the dirt and grime on her face. "I can't lose you."

He let out a dry, lifeless laugh and then grimaced. "You know what I've always said? This world needs more people like you in it."

"What kind of person is that? One who never knows what she's doing?"

"No. People who are willing to give those of us who are different a chance. You tried to find the best in me when no one else would."

Flynn gingerly lay next to him and scooted her body as close to his as she could. Slipping her cuffed hands under his shirt to press her palms to his skin, she rested her head on his chest. Her touch dulled the pain that filled every corner of his body and helped quiet his trembling muscles. He could feel her soft breath caressing his swollen skin.

She glanced up. "I'm just sorry you never got that chance. You deserved it. Everyone does." Wolf traced the delicate curve of her cheekbone, trying to memorize the pronounced shape her of brows and nose. "I love you," she said, relenting an embarrassed smile.

No one had ever said those words to him before. Not in the context of actually knowing him—all of him—and still somehow being able to love him. He allowed the overwhelming mixture of peace and comfort to grow inside him. He relished it, examining it from every angle, like something cherished and brand new but that might disappear in a blink.

Who could he have been had he experienced this warmth throughout his entire life instead of just in this late moment?

"I think I've always loved you," he whispered back.

"Guess it's my turn to save you now, huh?"

"You already have."

49

FLYNN

Flynn gnawed at her stubby thumbnail while she surveyed their tiny cell. Her heart cartwheeled through her chest. There were no windows and even though she'd been blindfolded, her escorts had definitely dragged her down multiple sets of stairs. Based on the room's size, they must be in some sort of basement closet. A circular drain and an empty cup were all that sat in the corner. She wondered if Wolf had eaten or drank in all the days since he was captured. As he slipped in and out of consciousness, her desperation grew.

Tiger would be returning any second, and she had no idea how they were supposed to get themselves out of this mess. The Allies had to be getting close. But would she and Wolf be killed before help could reach them?

Flynn tried not to panic as she observed Wolf's labored breathing. Gently, she lifted his head and placed it in her lap. Purple bruises covered his face, taking on a greenish hue beneath the single lightbulb overhead. What a full circle moment. Once again locked in one of REDS's cells, waiting to die. Fresh tears pricked the corners of her eyes. Pressing her cuffed fists against her sockets, she willed them back into her body. Her heart splintered with another crack, then another and another. How many more cracks could it withstand before it shattered completely?

Keep it together, Flynn, she scolded herself. *Crying isn't going to change anything. Stay strong. Do it for Wolf.*

BANG.

The door slammed open. Flynn jumped and Wolf twitched awake. Tiger stormed into the cell, gauze and tape wrapped over his nose. Wolf looked up at her. His clear green eyes, netted by long lashes, remained untouched by Tiger's brutality.

Tiger's lip pulled into a sneer, his misshapen scars buckling with fresh fury. Nothing provoked a man more than a damaged ego. Flynn lay Wolf's head on the ground and stood, positioning herself in front of him.

"Don't touch him," Flynn warned, her voice low.

"And what're you gonna do about you it, you little bitch?"

"Guess I could go for your jaw next."

Tiger lunged. Flynn spun out of reach. Tiger's anger had made him impulsive. She skated around him to the other corner of the cell, away from Wolf. He swung, and this time she ducked, managing to land a forceful blow into his side with her cuffed fists. Her knuckles burned, instantly swelling, but dang that felt way more satisfying than she'd expected.

Releasing a strangled yell, he charged her, throwing her into the wall. Neon sparks exploded behind her vision as her head collided against concrete. He shoved his forearm under her chin, pressing it into her neck. The cell tilted. Flynn dug her nails into his skin.

"You're not going to fight, Wolf?" Tiger spat, not taking his eyes off Flynn's face. "Even for your girl?"

Wolf pushed himself to his knees.

"Looks like you need a little more motivation."

Tiger touched his blood-crusted lips to Flynn's ear. She squirmed, trying to escape his rotten breath against her skin. He grabbed her waist, searching for the hem of her sweatshirt. Flynn twisted away to rid herself of his groping fingers. Her bullet wound stitches pulled and she screamed, mainly so she wouldn't pass out.

"Let her go!" Wolf yelled.

"I dunno, maybe you were onto something with this one. She's a lot hotter up close."

Flynn jammed her knee into Tiger's balls. He released a grunt, instinctively crunching inward, and the pressure against her throat eased. She jammed a swollen knuckle into Tiger's eye socket. Reeling back, Tiger clutched the part of his face that wasn't bandaged.

Wolf staggered toward them and swung his cuffed fists into Tiger's temple. *CRACK.* Tiger's head snapped to the side. Taking advantage of Tiger's dazed exposure, Wolf grabbed a knife from Tiger's belt and jammed it hard into his stomach before awkwardly slicing upward. Blood and guts spilled from his open belly.

Flynn pressed herself into the corner, as far away as she could from the waterfall exiting Tiger's body. Tiger collapsed, falling into the ruby pool of innards.

Flynn heaved, unable to catch her breath as the smell overwhelmed the tiny cell. Wolf doubled over, resting a palm on the wall to support his weight. He stared down at Tiger's body and gave it a shove with his toe. "To think this piece of shit actually believed he could replace me."

Flynn sidled over to Wolf and held out her wrists. "Can you cut me loose?"

He angled the blade's tip beneath the zip tie and sawed upward until it snapped. Flynn took the knife and returned the favor. Once they were both unencumbered, she slung his arm around her shoulders. Stepping around Tiger's body, she led Wolf to the opposite side of their cell and helped him sit. They both still breathed heavily. Space rapidly shrunk as Tiger continued to bleed out, the thick liquid reaching toward them.

"This is exactly what I was afraid of," Wolf finally managed, turning his head to look at her. "I knew they would use you against me."

She checked her side, amazed her stitches hadn't ripped. "Oh, please. I held my own." She approached Tiger's body, tiptoeing around his mess. Reaching down, she grabbed a handgun from his belt holster. For the first time, its cool, textured grip didn't incite a shudder. Instead, a thrill crept up her spine.

"You don't even know how to use that thing," Wolf mumbled.

She turned and handed it to him. "That's what you're for."

He raised his brows. "I think it's about time you actually learn."

"Okay, Jedi Master. Teach me your ways."

Wolf ignored her snark. "First, make sure it's loaded. You do this by checking the chamber for a round." He pulled the slide back, revealing the round seated in the chamber. "It's called a press check. Then check the magazine for a round count." Using his thumb, he pressed a button on the upper side of the gun's grip. The magazine slipped from the handle. He showed it to her and then shoved it back into place. He balanced the gun in his palm. "I've been doing this long enough I can tell by its weight if it's loaded or if it has a full magazine. You'll get there eventually."

"Let's hope not."

Wolf held the gun out for her to take. "Let's hope you actually pull the trigger this time."

Slipping it under her jacket and into her waistband, she grinned. "Once again, you underestimate me."

50

WOLF

Wolf awoke to a boom, so close the walls around them trembled. His eyes snapped open. He lay slumped against Flynn, her arms wrapped around him, her cheek resting atop his head.

"What was that?" he murmured.

Wolf struggled to sit upright, but it felt as if a meat grinder was chewing up every muscle and ligament in his body. Even the tiniest movement sent pain rocketing through his limbs.

"Must be the Allies," Flynn murmured. "Or National Guard. Or both. They're getting closer."

Each inhale and exhale burned. Not a good sign for his lungs. Flynn helped ease him into a seated position. His helplessness terrified him. How could he protect Flynn in this state? He'd spent his last ounces of energy killing Tiger.

Wolf glanced over at Tiger's corpse and allowed himself enjoy a brief moment of smugness.

Another boom outside sent shock waves vibrating through the floor and ceiling.

"We're going to get through this," Flynn whispered. "We're going to win."

Wolf could sense Flynn's optimism, but it did little to ease his dread. "REDS will go down swinging. They'll fight 'til the very end."

"My da always used to talk about the war he and his family left behind in Ireland. His mother had to beg his father to immigrate to America. Eventually he agreed, but only for my dad's sake. Sometimes I think children are the only hope of a new life—a new world."

"Just like my dad," Wolf said.

Flynn squeezed his hand. "Exactly."

"Tell me about your parents. What was it like growing up with them?"

Flynn snorted, rolling her head backward. "Well, my mom is extremely overbearing. So opinionated it's obnoxious, especially because my sister and I never seek out her opinion. It's almost like she's never satisfied. The complete opposite of my dad. He never complains about anything. Always sees the bright side. Never quick to judgement."

"Sounds like you."

She shrugged. "I don't really understand what brought my parents together. My dad left behind his entire family for my mom, you know? Because she's Jewish. I've never met his family. They basically disowned him."

Wolf grunted. "I can't imagine missing out on your child's life because of some stupid book you pray to. Especially after all they sacrificed to come to America."

Flynn nodded. "He never seemed bitter about it or seemed to hold a grudge. He just accepted it. Goes to show how little we know about our parents' lives. What led them to each other. How they fell in love. We don't really see them as people, we only see them through our lens of mom and dad."

"True. I don't know anything about either of my parents...about where they came from or, like you said, what brought them together. It's an entire story and history that's now lost."

They sat in silence, and Wolf allowed a new sting of bitterness to spread through him.

"I hate holidays," Wolf admitted. "All holidays, but especially Mother's Day and Father's Day. Days so many people take for granted, but that always reminded me of what I didn't have."

Spider had filled that emptiness. He'd shoveled through the sadness that had hardened around Wolf's heart and replaced it with anger and hatred.

But the thing about anger is it's always hungry. That hunger grows and grows, demanding to be fed, until it consumes everything.

As if on cue, their cell door swung open. Spider strode inside, flanked by two heavily armed guards.

"So, this is where he's been." He prodded Tiger's body with the tip of his boot, sniffing in disgust. He nodded to a guard. The soldier grabbed Tiger's corpse by the arms and dragged it from their cell, leaving behind a slippery trail.

Unfazed, Spider stepped through the bloody puddle, leaving red prints in his wake. Flynn scrambled to her feet.

"Don't touch him," she snarled, positioning herself in front of Wolf again. "He doesn't deserve to die, not after all he's done for you."

"Get out of my way before I make you," Spider snarled. "You've caused enough damage. If it weren't for you, he wouldn't have betrayed us."

"You can get rid of me, but you still need him," Flynn said. "You're nothing without him and you know it. You've only ever used him, twisted his potential in ways that benefit *you*. That's all you do, build your success off the people you've convinced to work for you, and you don't give a shit about any them. Do you even care he's dead?" she asked, gesturing to Tiger's bloody remnants. "Is that how much you care about your people?"

Wolf had never heard anyone speak to Spider that way. He couldn't see her face, but her posture had changed. She stood tall and resolute, shoulders pushed back, like a tree weathering a storm, unyielding and unafraid. As if she understood Spider would blow right by—but could never dictate her worth or strength. A deep respect and profound realization filled Wolf's entire body. That confidence and conviction she had, that was true power. The kind of power that wasn't sustained by sucking it from others, but that grew on its own from a seed planted, tended, lovingly cultivated over time. It was the ultimate protection against the crashing winds and rains of future storms.

"I need no one. Meanwhile, *your* little friends are practically on our doorstep. It's a shame, really. They're so close, but by the time they get here, you'll already be dead. And, yes, you're right, we do still need him. Wolf, it's time to do your job. Deploy the ransomware." Spider looked Flynn up and down. "It won't matter if the military takes Chicago, not once we show the rest of the world what their government has done with the hostages. Besides, how can the country support a government that sends a nuclear missile directly into one of its own cities? The question is which one..."

"So, this is it then?" Flynn spat. "A last-ditch effort because you've lost?"

Spider backhanded Flynn so hard she stumbled backward, clutching her face. Spider yanked a knife from his belt and stalked toward her. Wolf's heart plummeted at the same time his adrenaline spiked.

Spider beamed. "This is exactly how your friend died, you know. Ask Wolf. He saw the whole thing. He was just too pitiful to do anything. He couldn't kill her, but he also couldn't stop me."

"Fuck you!" Flynn screamed. "You've taken everything from me. Everything! I won't let you take him too."

Wolf rolled to his side and pushed himself into a seated position. The room spun so violently he couldn't get his footing to stand.

"If you kill her, I won't deploy the ransomware." It sounded as if his voice was being squeezed from his chest.

Spider shoved Flynn to the ground, and lunged at Wolf. He grabbed Wolf by the throat, forcing his head backward.

"Remember the last time you threatened me? Look where it's led you," he snarled. "We were so close. Together we could've taken over the entire country. You singlehandedly ruined everything we've spent our entire lives working toward. For what? For her!"

Flynn leapt at Spider. "Don't touch him!" A guard grabbed her, pulling her back. "Leave him alone!"

Another explosion shook the cell, this time joined by the muted patter of machine-gun fire.

"I should've known. I should've seen it. You're just like your father. I never should've let it get this far. We killed your mother too, you know. I knew she'd come back for you, and she did. So predictable. She deserved the death we gave her after corrupting your father."

Something in Wolf snapped. He hadn't fully admitted it to himself, but he'd clung on to the tiniest shred of hope that his mother might still be alive—that maybe she was still out there somewhere, waiting for him to find her. He'd even considered, if he survived this, he might try. But Spider's words snatched that hope away, tossed it to the wind and out of sight forever.

Wolf lunged at Spider, allowing the anger roaring through him to reignite a new surge of energy. But the other guard intercepted him and tugged his arms behind his back. His broken shoulder burned, as if a hot poker had been shoved through his skin. Wolf was too weak to fight back. His legs were seconds away from giving out. He coughed up a spittle of blood, tasting its tang in the back of his throat.

Spider bore down on Wolf, his complexion a splotchy red. "I gave you every chance to change," he snarled. "I believed in you. You lost, Wolf. You let love destroy you."

Wolf closed his eyes, ready to die. The end had to be close. "You're wrong," he whispered. "Love saved me." And he believed it in his heart. Finally, he understood what Flynn had been talking about all along.

51

FLYNN

Be patient, Flynn told herself. *You have one shot.*

The cool metal of Tiger's concealed gun pressed against her hip bone, cushioned by her thick winter layers. All moisture in her mouth evaporated, and she realized for the first time how thirsty she was. Her heart thumped against her sternum so hard she wondered if it might explode. Craning her neck to glance over her shoulder, she caught a glimpse of another guard helping drag Wolf up the three flights of steps their decrepit party laboriously climbed. Desperation engulfed her, dragging her like a cinder block to the bottom of a hopeless ocean.

One shot.

Her guard shoved her head. "Eyes forward," he snapped.

Flynn lasered a glare onto Spider's back as they ascended. Her cheek still smarted from where he'd smacked her. More explosions reverberated around them, and the *pop, pop, pop* of gunfire accelerated into a steady stream. Several deafening roars overhead merged together, drowning out any surrounding sound and passing as quickly as they appeared.

Fighter jets.

Another series of blasts followed in perfectly timed succession.

The same small bubble of hope surfaced inside Flynn again, and she focused all her energy on protecting it from bursting. Even if the Allies couldn't rescue her or Wolf, Chicago could still be saved, and after everything, that was all that mattered. At least they could die knowing they'd done what they could to remedy the harm that had occurred at their hands.

Finally, they reached a landing and pushed into a narrow hallway. Although they were no longer belowground, the windowless corridor seemed endless. She tried to glance behind her again, but couldn't see past the hulking shoulders of her thick-bodied guard. There was no way Wolf could still be walking, not after all he'd already been through.

"Move it," the guard grunted, giving her a shove.

Flynn resisted turning around and giving this asshole a kick to his shins. She followed Spider closely as he made tight turns. First left. Then right. Then left again. The sharp, acrid stench of ammunition filled her nostrils. Chills snaked down the back of her neck. She wondered if the labyrinth they wandered through might swallow them, like a giant sea monster snapping them up in its enormous jaws.

Finally, they reached a hallway that widened. REDS soldiers flew past their group, yelling to each other as they sprinted by. Spider's radio chirped with urgent updates and commands. A flurry of chaos spread as the world threatened to collapse around them at any second. If this was the end, Flynn refused to go quietly.

"No matter what Wolf did...it never would've been enough, would it?" Flynn shouted to Spider. He didn't acknowledge her, but she didn't care. Her rage had built and compounded, morphing into something unrecognizable, and it refused to be contained any longer. "You fed him lies! You brainwashed him into believing you would build a better world. You told him *I* manipulated him. But really, it was you all along. *You* used him! Extracting everything you could until he had nothing left. Not even an identity." Flynn's throat burned. But she couldn't stop. She wouldn't stop. She knew Spider was going to kill them at any moment, and this could be her last chance. "You did whatever you could to turn him against the world. To make everyone else the enemy, when it was you all along. *You're* the enemy!"

Spider turned, stroking his chin, unfazed by his soldiers rushing around him, likely heading to their own deaths. "I presented Wolf with a new life. New opportunities and choices. He made those decisions all on his own."

He grinned, his white teeth shining, before continuing down the hall.

"You made him believe he didn't deserve love! That it didn't exist."

"Love? Love is bullshit!" Spider called over his shoulder. "A fickle illusion that lasts as long as the fuck is good. It's foolish. It's selfish. I did him a favor. I kept him alive."

"You stole everything from him! His family. A future. He would've died for you in a second, and you would've let him. You'd sacrifice him without thinking twice."

"Oh, and what've you done? Saved him?"

Flynn could never take credit for saving Wolf. She'd learned by now, no one can really save another person. Not in the way Wolf had needed to be saved. "No. He didn't need me to. He did that all on his own, even after you whittled him into nothing!"

Spider stopped, and Flynn's guard pushed her forward. She dug her heels into the ground, twisting to free herself. His grip tightened, squeezing her upper arms so hard she knew they would bruise. In one last-ditch effort, she dipped her head and sank her teeth into the fleshy top of his hand until she tasted blood. The guard yelled out, ripping his hand away. Flynn yanked her other arm free and spun around, taking off toward Wolf.

"Wolf!" Flynn screamed.

Wolf appeared unconscious, his guards holding his limp body upright between them, his head lolling forward.

"Shark!" Spider roared at her guard. "GRAB HER!"

Shark tackled her to the ground. Her chin busted open in blinding pain. Shark pinned his knee into her back, crushing her wrists in an iron grip.

"Stupid bitch," he mumbled and dragged her to her feet.

Spider stalked toward her until he was so close she could see tiny red spokes splaying around his black pupils. Those bloodshot veins and the dark shadows under his eyes betrayed him, hinting at sleepless nights. His nose was long and angular. She couldn't tell his age, or even his ethnicity. His smooth golden skin stretched over gaunt cheeks and appeared ageless, other than a few flecks of gray smattering the stubble on his chin.

Spider's upper lip curled back into a snarl, exposing his pointed canines.

"*I* saved Wolf from the ugliest parts of this fucked up world. From being abandoned. I taught him he could overcome what had been done to him, and he did. I gave him the tools. He didn't only survive, he thrived in REDS. He could never be a part of your world."

Blood trickled down Flynn's chin and onto her shirt. "But he wasn't abandoned, was he? He was orphaned."

"And what makes you so holy?" Spider's stale breath stroked her face. "You convince yourself you're good. That human nature is good. I know so many people just like you. People who believe they can *pray* the bad away. But it's a story you tell yourselves—trying to convince yourselves we don't all have evil in us, hidden away. We all have dangerous impulses. We're all selfish. Jealous. Greedy. Self-absorbed. We're animals shaped over thousands of years of evolution. Shaped for survival." Spider swiped a finger through Flynn's oozing blood, and held it in front of her. "That little lie you tell yourself is called delusion. That lie is what keeps progress from happening. Our movement—REDS's movement—isn't evil. It's change. Change that keeps being strangled back into submission to benefit people who want to stay in power."

"It doesn't matter if we have evil in us. What matters is choosing good. What matters is the wolf you feed."

For a brief second Flynn could've sworn a hint of pink colored Spider's cheeks. Scrunching his nose in disgust, he looked past her to the other guards and nodded toward the door beside him. "In here."

"Whatever happens"—Flynn tried to stand straighter—"I won't leave Wolf. I'm not leaving his side. I'm not afraid of you anymore."

Spider dragged his finger, tipped with her blood, down her cheek, turning Flynn's insides icy cold. "We'll see about that."

Shark pushed her inside a room lined with small rectangular screens, all flashing footage from security cameras placed throughout the city. She tried to gauge which buildings they were looking at based on the angles, but some had gone dark and there were too many of them to discern. Besides, her jittery brain couldn't focus enough to put a single puzzle piece in place. A desk stretching the length of the room hosted a row of computer monitors and keyboards. Three REDS analysts sat in chairs and didn't acknowledge their entry, as if the screen's blue glow held them in a hypnotized trance. Their fingers clacked against keys, racing against time.

"Ready for your final act, Wolf?" Spider stretched his arms wide. "Come, we've been waiting for you."

As Wolf's guards hauled him toward a monitor, the analysts sitting at the desk finally turned to glance at them. One of Wolf's guards smacked him across the face in a lazy effort to rouse him.

"Spider, we have a code red. We lost access to the nuclear arsenal," a lanky analyst who sat at least two heads taller than the others said. "The government must've found a way through Wolf's firewall. They locked us out."

"That can't be." Spider went to stand behind him and squinted at the screen. "It's impossible."

A tiny analyst, at least in comparison to his taller counterpart, looked at Wolf. "Not if someone had the decryption key."

Wolf finally seemed conscious. He stared straight ahead, eyes unblinking, hands limp in his lap. Spider spun Wolf's chair around to face him. "Tell me you didn't do this."

Wolf remained silent. Flynn's stomach launched into her throat. A strange mixture of pride and fear twisted together. Wolf had done it. He'd armed the Allies and the US military with what they'd needed to take back control from REDS.

"Tell me you didn't give away our leverage!" Spider screeched, clearly starting to panic. "The nukes we had made us untouchable. Without them..."

Spider grabbed Wolf by the shoulders and threw him from the chair. "THIS IS YOUR FAULT!" Spider screamed. "You. Ruined. EVERY-THING!" Grabbing Wolf's empty chair, Spider heaved it over his head and threw it across the room with a crash that made Flynn wince. The analysts leapt to their feet and backed away. Spider crouched closer to Wolf. "I will make you fucking pay!"

Wolf pushed himself to his knees on shaky arms. "You already have."

Flynn watched their exchange, petrified. In an instant Spider could kill Wolf.

"S-S-Spider," the tiny analyst interrupted. "We're surrounded." He scurried back to his computer and clicked through the cameras. On every screen, REDS stood with their arms raised in surrender or lay scattered on the ground. "We can't hold off the advancing military without the threat of nuclear retaliation."

Spider snapped his fingers toward Flynn. Without warning, Shark threw her to the ground. Flynn scrambled forward, army crawling on her forearms toward the door, but she wasn't fast enough. Shark stomped his boot on her ankle.

Flynn heard a sharp *CRACK*. She screamed as loud as she could, as if she could expel the sudden pain flooding her left leg.

"The ransomware. NOW, Wolf," Spider said. "Or else it's her skull next."

Wolf's guard grabbed him by the back of his vest and dropped him into one of the analyst's chairs. Wolf glanced back at Flynn, a sheen of sweat visible over his sickly complexion. He began typing furiously into a blinking cursor. Flynn rolled onto her back, gasping in pain. She tried to scoot backward, away from Shark. He leveled his rifle at her. Flynn clenched her jaw, waiting for the agony to subside, but it continued cleaving into her shattered ankle.

Wolf paused, his finger hovering over a key.

"Shark, I think Wolf needs a little encouragement," Spider said.

Shark released a bullet an inch from Flynn's right pinky. The coarse, cropped carpet absorbed the shot with a metallic thud. She yelled, yanking her hand to her chest, as the three analysts cowered away, as if they could hide amid their computers.

Wolf pressed the final keystroke and slumped back. "Done."

52

WOLF

Flynn's deafening scream echoed through Wolf's brain. All his impulses strained to protect her, but his limbs couldn't respond to their command. He tried to focus, but blackness crept into the corners of his vision, threatening to drown him in darkness. He blinked back the dizzying sensation.

The final keystroke to unleash the ransomware waited, resting beneath his finger. He wasn't even sure he deployed it correctly. He could barely think, let alone lift his arms.

Do it, he told himself. *Your last act for REDS can finally be on your own terms—an act of defiance.*

Click.

"Done."

"This is it, Wolf." Spider's jaw appeared locked in place, so rigid he could barely speak. "We've reached the end."

Wolf swiveled his chair around to face Spider and search for Flynn. He had no idea when Spider would find out the message that would soon hijack smart devices throughout the country wasn't the one he'd ordered. He didn't really care, Spider planned to kill him anyway. Machine-gun fire somewhere outside the room prompted a chorus of muffled shouts and strangled yells. They sounded different this time. Less urgent and more desperate.

He met Flynn's gaze, and for the first time felt a small flame of hope burn inside his chest.

The Allies.

Flynn clutched her ankle, tears streaming down her cheeks. Her brows squished together, fighting against the pain, her face set in determination.

Wolf tore his eyes from her and settled his glare on Spider. All outside noise suddenly disappeared, sucked away like they'd been tipped into a black hole. The two men stared at each other, refusing to blink, as if years' worth of unsaid words could be freed in a matter of seconds.

Using the chair's armrests as support, Wolf rose shakily to his feet. His broken bones protested, but by this point he was numb. "The end of a long road together." Wolf took a deep breath, grounding himself and using his last wisps of strength to balance. "I know you think loving someone makes me weak. I know you don't believe in its power. Neither did I. But that's because I never experienced it before. Not in its purest form. I thought I had, from REDS...but I know now it wasn't real. I was manipulated to believe it was, but no other love has felt right. Worshipping someone has the same effects, I guess. But worship is one-sided. It's *quid pro quo*. It's a reward for obedience, and punishment for deviance."

Spider raised his gun, pointing it at Wolf's forehead. His eyes were inky glass pools. "Redemption for the oppressed. Execution for the unjust. Deliverance for the guilty. Salvation for the lost," he murmured.

Heat bubbled up Wolf's arms—the kind of all-encompassing warmth that soaks from the skin to the core, like basking in the sun. He waited, but Spider didn't move. A slight tremor shook his hand.

A yell right outside the door and more gunshots filtered through their bubble. "SHARK," Spider bellowed. "Get on that."

"What about her?" Shark grunted, jerking his chin up at Flynn.

"Who gives a shit about her? She's next," Spider snarled.

Shark gave Spider a dubious look before he sprinted toward the door, his rifle at the ready. When he wrenched it open, an explosion of shrapnel colliding against concrete almost threw him backward. The floor beneath Wolf's feet trembled.

"You three, OUT," Spider yelled at the analysts.

"B-But, Spider—" the tall one tried to protest.

"OUT!" He turned to Wolf's guards. "You too, all of you. Go help Shark. He'll need reinforcements." Seething, he directed his attention back onto Wolf as his guards shoved the analysts out of the room and into the abyss of explosions. "I did care, you know," Spider said. "It's why I gave you so many chances. It's why I tried so hard."

Something wet slithered down Wolf's cheek. He blinked the tear away, sliding his palm down his face. "I believe you," he croaked. "In your own twisted way, I do believe you cared about me. It was just for the wrong reasons."

"I know your birth name, you know," Spider said, his voice so quiet it was almost a whisper. "Your real name. Your father told it to me before he died. He should've known that was the beginning of the end. Like you should've."

Wolf's throat constricted as the tears began to flow more freely. He wished he could stop them, but he didn't have any energy left to slam down the floodgates. "Who gives a shit when he's already gone? Dead. And I'll be too." A frenzied desperation buzzed through him, a wasp close to its death. It grew more violent and aggressive, almost as if to fight the inevitability of his fate. He supposed now he could finally meet his mother and father. He wasn't sure he really believed in an afterlife, but the thought did bring him a surprising boost of comfort. That, and knowing he wouldn't have to start over.

Wolf glanced at Flynn and instinctively smiled. "Thank you," he said. "For showing me the way."

Spider stepped forward, closing the distance between them, blocking Wolf's view of Flynn. All he could see was the dark, round mouth of Spider's handgun tunneling to his end. Wolf's lungs squeezed so tightly he couldn't breathe.

"I made a mistake saving you," Spider said. "I thought you would be my greatest triumph, but you're my greatest regret. My biggest mistake. You sold us out. Our failure to complete our mission is your fault. I'm doing you a favor. You don't belong in this new world—"

Wolf lowered himself to his knees, his joints no longer able to hold up his weight. He linked his fingers behind his neck, allowing Spider's words to sting. He braced himself, wishing he could fall through the floor and disappear, but he wouldn't give Spider the satisfaction of watching him cower from death.

Spider's gun followed, angling toward Wolf's heart. "Goodbye, Wolf."

Wolf squeezed his eyes closed.

BANG.

A whoosh of air and a thud several feet from Wolf forced him to crack a lid open. No fresh pain ripped through his flesh. Instead, Spider lay on the ground before him, and Flynn sat clutching Tiger's gun.

Flynn tossed the gun to the side and crawled toward Wolf, dragging her leg behind her. Throwing her arms around his neck, she held him as they rocked back and forth. They touched foreheads, breathing in each other's air. Wolf let her closeness sink through his skin, as if she could drink up his pain. She took his face into her hands, hooking her thumbs beneath his chin. His body shook, his sobs releasing a current of grief and leaving behind a wrecked vessel.

"Look at me." Tears smudged streaks of dirt and grime down her face to mix with the blood coating her chin. "You're so brave," she choked. "And you're not a mistake."

"I couldn't do it," he gasped. "I couldn't kill him."

"I know," Flynn finally said, pushing his hair out of his eyes. "That's why I did it for you. So you wouldn't have to."

After what seemed like hours, they released each other, too exhausted to move. They lay on their sides, facing each other, listening to the building explode around them. Even as the gunfire and explosions diminished, neither of them moved. None of the analysts, Shark, nor Wolf's guards returned. Their breathing gradually slowed as they waited for the Allies to find them.

"We've earned this," Flynn muttered.

Wolf stared into her gray eyes, clear as a winter day. The eyes he'd never forgotten since seeing them for the first time in that coffee shop over a decade ago. The eyes that stopped him from pulling the trigger that night at Soldier Field. The eyes that had saved him. "What did we earn?"

Flynn smiled. "Rest."

53

FLYNN

Flynn studied the knots twisting through the wood grain of the walnut bar top. She traced a swirl with her finger, her nail skipping over sticky drink rings left behind and calcified from years of spilled beers. A thin golden strand of spider silk caught her eye, stretching across three beer tap handles. The brightly colored taps alternated in size and shape, spanning the length of the bar's back wall. The web would've remained invisible if not for its delicate thread catching a ray of sunlight streaming in through a window. It glinted every time it twitched and bounced, as if caught on the other end of a ghost's breath. As Flynn watched the light slide along its gossamer surface, she wondered how something could be so strong yet so easily broken at the same time. How its net could remain unseen until just the right angle of light set it aglow.

She closed her eyes, inhaling a lungful of cold December air. Although electricity had been restored in select areas, most buildings were still without heat. Electric crews worked around the clock, and many had been bused in from out of state, but Chicago's destroyed infrastructure slowed its recovery.

Jamming her crutches into her armpits, Flynn hobbled around the bar's vast main seating area. A thick cast on her broken ankle saddled her with a new weight she hadn't grown accustomed to, throwing her off balance. As she looked around the empty room, a heart-shattering pain tore through her chest. The last time she'd been at Old Town Pour House had been with

Cori on a hot summer day. Flynn braced herself for the torrent of sadness that tended to flood through her at the thought of Cori, but as the memory washed over her, for the first time she savored it like a rich, full-bodied stout.

Flynn could still hear the clamor of voices and feel the memory of bodies jostling through the bar's once crowded space. It had seemed much smaller at the time. Instead of winter's dry, knuckle-cracking cold air, hot August humidity had crept inside as a line of people trickled through the door. Flynn's shirt had stuck to her collarbone, damp with sweat, and her hair clung to the back of her neck. She and Cori had graduated college a few months earlier, and Flynn had walked over a mile from work to meet Cori because she'd been too poor to afford a cab.

"Flynn! Over here!" Cori had waved frantically from where she sat on a stool, already surrounded by men.

Flynn had pushed her way through the mass of bodies, undeterred by their unwillingness to let her pass. When she'd reached Cori and her gaggle of men, all of whom were now watching her approach, she instantly flushed under the attention. A new and different heat crept up her cheeks. Scraping her hair off her neck, she dragged it over her shoulder, wishing she could hide behind its curtain.

"Jeez, took you long enough to get here," Cori yelled above the noise.

"You had to pick a bar that has no El stops nearby!"

"Well, I'm glad I did, because these lovely gents are offering to buy us a drink."

Good. Flynn knew neither of them could afford even a happy hour special at this place. Thankfully, she could always count on Cori to work a room, and Flynn benefitted from it.

Flynn plastered on a smile. "How kind of them."

One of the guys leapt off a stool next to Cori and offered it to Flynn. Cori handed her a drink, the glass slick and watery. "Matt here was just telling me he's from Indiana...wasn't sure if maybe you knew him."

Flynn studied the three men, all tall and almost identical in their matching khaki golf shorts and patterned polos sporting different tiny logos over their left pectoral muscles.

"Doubt it." Flynn shook her head. "Despite what you think, Cor, Indiana is a pretty big state."

"Yeah, I'd remember if we'd met." Matt took her in. "You're not someone I would forget."

Flynn blushed, heat rocketing from her cheeks all the way to her scalp. Unlike Cori, Flynn cowered under attention. As if sensing her impending abandonment, Cori grabbed Flynn's arm.

"Shall we celebrate the end of a week with a round of shots?" Cori asked.

"Yes, let's. Another week of survival. TGIF!" Flynn cheered.

When the shots arrived, Flynn threw hers back, then pressed a lime wedge into her mouth and sucked every drop of juice it offered. Her lips puckered at the same time her throat closed, the shock of tequila making her wince. Matt's company instantly became more bearable. After squeezing far too many free drinks out of Matt and his friends, she and Cori left. Flynn had granted Matt a sloppy make-out session to show their thanks, but opted out of giving him her number. Cori had a rule about how to cut a guy loose after a first encounter.

"Always leave them wanting more," she'd say with a wink.

Flynn and Cori rode rented bikes along the lakeshore path, laughing drunkenly as the sky dimmed and the oily black water took on the setting sun's orange reflection.

"You know, being a real adult is a lot different than I thought it'd be," Flynn said as they wheeled their bikes to park them at a station.

"What d'you mean?" Cori asked.

"I dunno. I guess...I guess I've kinda realized no one seems to know what they're doing. Everyone seems to be winging it. Is there ever going to be an age when we have it all figured out?"

"I sure hope not," Cori said with a laugh.

"You mean, you *like* all this unknown?"

"Oh, come on, wouldn't life be so boring if we had it all figured out and knew exactly what was gonna happen?"

Flynn considered this. "No, I think it would be quite reassuring, actually."

Flynn could still see Cori's face as she swiveled her head over her shoulder to look back at her. Cori's cheeks were flushed from exertion and alcohol, and the humidity had coaxed her perfectly ironed hair into a frizzy halo.

"Trust yourself, Flynn."

"Trust myself to do what?"

"To break. To heal. To rebuild. And then to do it all over again."

She thought about all the unknowns she'd faced since that day. The Green Line concert. Meeting Wolf. Cori's murder. Nate. REDS's defeat. She closed her eyes and suppressed the urge to flip the nearest table, but not the tears that began to flow.

"Hey." Nate's voice burst through her memory, and Cori's ghost disappeared. When a hand touched Flynn's shoulder, the reality of a cold bar and a city decimated came back into focus.

"Hey." Flynn wiped her cheeks quickly, maneuvered around as best she could on her crutches, and smiled. "Sorry, I haven't really gotten used to these things yet."

It had taken Flynn and Nate a few nerve-wracking days to find each other after the military liberated the city. Flynn's fear that Nate had been killed during the Allies' advance had kept her awake for three nights, until she'd finally reunited with Kerri and Antonio, who thankfully knew his whereabouts.

Nate pulled back a chair, its legs screeching against the floor, and gestured an arm for her to sit. Flynn hobbled over, and Nate helped ease her into its seat and relieved her of her crutches.

"You clean up nice," Flynn said.

Nate had shaved most of his scraggly beard except for a thin carpet of stubble. He glanced down at his clean jeans, which now appeared baggy on him. "I'd say the same about you. Didn't that first hot shower feel like a million bucks? Coulda stayed in there for hours."

Flynn chuckled. "Same. Took me almost an hour to get all the knots outta my hair. I'd just been accumulating them for weeks. Even then, I had to cut most of them out."

"Might as well start fresh. I can't stop eating either. It's like my hunger will never be satisfied."

"Not surprising, I guess, after not eating a decent meal in months. I've probably gone down a whole size. I can't decide what food sounds best...a hot, fresh pizza or a ginormous salad from Portillo's."

She felt like she'd grown a new skin, one she wasn't comfortable in yet, and a shadow of weariness followed her wherever she went. She had a suspicion she could sleep for days on end and still wake up tired.

Nate turned around and retrieved two steaming Styrofoam cups before joining her at the table. The unmistakable smell of coffee toasted her insides. "Look what I found to celebrate the occasion."

"What occasion is that?" she asked, taking a cup and sticking her nose further into the delicious aroma.

"Uh, surviving."

Flynn gave a small laugh. "I'll cheers to that. Sometimes I catch myself thinking it's amazing we're still alive."

They tapped their cups and took their first sips. "Yeah, well, we all got lucky. Sure came at a cost though," Nate said.

"Yeah... It sure did." Flynn leaned back in her chair and stared out the cloudy front window. Sunlight dimmed as thick winter clouds moved in, circling around a small patch of blue sky like the frozen eye of a hurricane. She sipped the hot liquid, feeling the caffeine course through her and awaken cells she had thought were dead forever. "My god, I missed coffee."

They sat in silence for several long minutes.

"Do you think the city will ever go back to the way it was?" Flynn asked.

Nate shrugged and took a loud slurp. "Might take a long time. This course of events will surely make it into the history books, though."

"Think about all the countries that have endured bombings that destroyed entire towns and cities. Now we're dealing with a destroyed city of our own and events that very nearly caused another civil war."

Nate nodded. "It would've, if it weren't for Wolf."

Flynn looked up from her coffee, surprised. "Wow, changing your tune about him, I see."

Nate gave her the same crooked smile that always made her stomach jolt with excitement. "I figured assuming people can't change is what got us into this mess. When people show us who they are with their actions, we have a responsibility to listen. Plus, maybe his ransomware note had some truth to it."

Instead of REDS's manipulative government propaganda and a call for states to rally together to kill their senators, Wolf had left the country with a different message.

"It only takes one person," Flynn recited quietly.

The two of them let it sit there between them for a moment before Nate continued. "I'm beginning to think we needed something like this to happen. We've been on the verge of it for so long. People never took a threat like REDS and their ideology seriously. But our biggest threat has always been from within—us turning on each other."

"I agree. I just hate how it took so much suffering for people to realize and understand these things." Cori's grin flashed through her mind. "It's always innocent people who suffer most. Even all the news coverage didn't capture the reality of what REDS did."

Nate tilted his head, examining her. "You mean the refugee camps?"

"Those weren't refugee camps, Nate, they were modern-day concentration camps. Or internment camps."

"Yeah." Nate exhaled loudly through his nose. "Can't expect a reporter to summarize someone's experience who has lived among corpses."

Flynn had watched the National Guard and military begin to pick up pieces of the city's wreckage. No record of what happened in Chicago could adequately capture the despair Flynn and so many others felt and that would likely never fully subside. Small embers of rage still smoldered within her, kept alive by the complacency that had allowed REDS to take control.

"I wonder if this is how my great-grandparents felt after World War II ended. Finally free from concentration camps, only to be released back into civilization like wild animals who no longer belonged in a gentile, domesticated reality. They were outsiders, a reminder of humankind's horrors."

The corners of Nate's mouth turned downward. "The parallels are all too real."

Humanity would always dance along the razor-thin line separating the past from the present, the evil from the innocent, forever on the precipice of repeating itself.

"Is Wolf still in the hospital?" Nate asked, interrupting Flynn's troubling thoughts.

"Yeah. REDS did him in pretty bad. Then he'll be detained by the FBI."

This time the pause between them hung awkwardly. "You think he'll be locked up?"

"He'll get a lawyer, but yeah, I don't really see a scenario where he makes it out of this without doing time."

"Well, hopefully he can get his sentence reduced if he cooperates. He deserves another shot at life. Will you visit him in prison?"

Flynn bit her lip. She couldn't ignore the longing that tugged at her heart. "Maybe. I'll definitely write to him."

"What about me?" Nate asked.

"What about you?"

"We never went on that date. I'd say the Cubs game doesn't count, considering how it ended."

Flynn smirked and rolled her eyes, although she inwardly grimaced at the memory of Wolf attacking Nate. "Well, sadly I'm not sure if I'm going to stick around Chicago."

"Sooo...what's your plan?"

She sighed. "I don't really have a plan. I just have too many...bad memories here. My parents are on their way up. I'm going to live at home for a bit to figure out what's next."

"So, that's it then? After all this, you're not willing to give us a shot?"

Flynn's heart clenched again at the image of Cori in her mind, surrounded by her frizzy halo, the sun's electric glow cast over her face. Now she finally understood what she'd meant all those years ago. "I need to heal, Nate. And then I have to rebuild. There will always be something between us, but this has to be my priority right now."

Nate shook his head, his eyes pleading. "I can feel the distance between us. You always find an excuse to push me away. Look, I know it's a lot to ask right now, after all we've been through. But also, that's the same reason I'm asking you to give us a shot."

Despite how she tried, she couldn't erase the night with Wolf from her memory and how it had felt being with him. How Wolf had always found a way to slip into her missing pieces and make her whole again. "I can't give you what you need or want from me. I just need time."

"I love you, you know."

"I love you too." Flynn knew now there were lots of ways to love and be loved by a person. "I never could've made it through these past few months without you."

"But you also love him?"

Flynn considered Nate carefully before answering. His question didn't seem reproachful or accusatory. He seemed earnest. Diplomatic. Almost as if he simply wanted to research all the information to properly weigh his chances of a future with her. "Yes, I love Wolf too." The words tripped over her tongue. Saying them aloud still sounded foreign, like they were in a different language with a different meaning. "But I don't have the capacity to navigate a relationship with anyone right now. I need to focus...on myself. I need to process what's happened to me over these past few months."

"Can't deny that's probably true. And wise."

"What're you thinking about doing next?" she asked, wanting desperately to move on from this conversation.

"Haven't decided yet. I think the city and military will need people here for a while. Gotta help rebuild."

"Always the good soldier."

He smiled wryly, raising his golden brows. He'd styled his hair back but kept its length so the ends curled around his ears. "Nah, just anything to get me out of Magnetic recruiting."

They surveyed the wreckage outside the window, drinking their coffee. Flecks of snow had begun to fall from the now gray December sky.

"I just found out Kerri got an invite to the White House," Nate said.

"What? That's amazing! She deserves it."

"She wants all of us to go with her."

"All of us?"

"You, me, Vic, Antonio, and Tawny. I think she asked to bring Wolf, but not sure if they'll greenlight that."

"They should. Like you said, we never could've made it outta this mess without him."

"Agreed. But we're also in this mess because of him too."

Flynn couldn't argue that logic.

"Would you accept the invite?" Nate asked.

"Maybe. Not sure. I'll let her extend it first."

"You should." Nate gave her a nudge with his shoulder. "We're outta this mess because of you too, you know."

Flynn squirmed. She knew Nate meant it as a genuine compliment, but she had also played a part in the making of all this, even if unwillingly. "No. We're not. I did what anyone would've done and stumbled around blindly for the rest of it."

"Are you crazy? Most people would've given up. You were resilient. Resourceful. You found a way to create a bridge with Wolf when no one else would've dared tried. You never gave up."

"I don't know if I'd say that, but it wasn't until Cori died that I finally started making decisions with my heart. My brain might be more reliable... or more logical...however you want to describe it. But at the risk of sounding cliché, I'm starting to understand how my heart guides me toward decisions that actually make me feel...free." Hot tears burned the corner of her eyes. "And isn't that what life's all about? It's the only thing I can hold on to. Even now, when everything still feels hopeless."

Nate put an arm around Flynn and squeezed. "I think it's normal to feel hopeless in the aftermath of what we've lived through. It's raw. Fresh."

She rested her head on his shoulder and sniffled loudly. "At least now I know we'll make it through this."

"Yup. It won't feel like this forever, and no matter what happens, we'll always be friends, right?"

"Always."

"I think you should go," Nate said.

"Go where?"

"To the White House. Who knows what will come from it. Action always gives me a sense of control, anyway."

Flynn thought for a moment. "Maybe. We'll see. I want to forge my own path...see where it leads me."

Nate pulled back to give her a once-over. A dimple in his left cheek exposed his amusement, despite how he tried to keep his lips pressed into a serious line. "You've changed, you know? Earlier this year, you never would've built your own path."

Flynn squeezed his hand. "Yeah. The thought would've terrified me. But now that I've actually lived through terror—true terror—I realize we build up so much in our heads as scary when really, it's just different. I'm done underestimating myself. I'm lucky to have the chance to build a new path. A new future. It doesn't need to unfold all at once, overnight. It's just one brick at a time. One foot in front of the other."

54

WOLF

Five years later

A heavy lock slid open with a resounding clunk, causing Wolf to bolt
upright as the door to his Special Housing Unit swung wide. A CO
resembling a cave troll entered, carrying with him a heavy waist
chain. Wolf leapt to his feet, allowing a small pop of anticipation to fizz
through him. He'd waited patiently (not like he had a choice) knowing his
visitor would be arriving any day.

The CO wrapped the chain around Wolf's waist, cinching it tight, before
cuffing his hands at his sides.

"Kneel," the CO grunted.

Wolf knew the drill. He turned and knelt on his narrow cot protruding
from the wall like a cliff ledge, permitting Cave Troll to shackle his ankles
and connect them to the center chain.

Another CO waited outside the door, joining them as Wolf and Cave
Troll exited his cell. While Cave Troll was short and stocky, this guard
looked more like the giant beanpole that sprouted from Jack's magic beans.
Wolf shuffled forward, the COs' booted footsteps and his clinking chains
mingling with the constant echoing moans and slamming cell doors of the
maximum-security penitentiary. By now, he'd memorized exactly how many
steps it took to get from his cell to visitation. He passed one barred window

that offered a quick glimpse of Pennsylvania's brown, flat fields and layers of deadly curlicue barbed wire fences stretching until they met a highway. The voltage of electricity running through them could probably fry a human alive, but he didn't plan on testing that theory.

Despite the bleak setting, Wolf would not complain, outwardly or to himself. For his protection, the FBI had placed him in a Special Housing Unit within the prison, separated from the general inmate population. Seclusion didn't bother him like it would other people who weren't used to isolation. The SHU might be torture for some, but for him it offered a much-needed respite from the nuanced prison culture and social dynamics within the wider facility. During his trial, he and his lawyer came to an agreement with the FBI. They would continue to offer him protection as long as he helped thwart notorious hackers on the dark web.

Besides Wolf's lawyer, his only two visitors were Kerri and Flynn. Twenty steps more and he'd catch his first glimpse of Flynn behind the thick plexi-glass. His heart raced, though he kept his face blank of emotion from his guards. With each footfall, the concrete reverberated through the soles of his laceless shoes. Finally, Cave Troll jammed a key into a steel door and shoved it open.

Flynn wore a high-necked cream sweater that complied with visitor rules. She also knew the drill by now. No cleavage. No visible tattoos. No wearing blue to avoid blending in too closely with the inmates' denim uniforms. A thrill shot up his spine, tickling his facial muscles and making it impossible to withhold an enormous smile. A sense of peace settled over him, and he allowed himself to relish the joy of her presence. It might be fleeting, but he would have to cling on to it until her next visit.

Flynn leaned forward, propping her elbows on a shallow ledge, her smile matching his own. She placed a palm on the plexiglass, her fingers stretched wide as if she could absorb him through the clear barrier.

Wolf awkwardly reached for the phone hanging on the wall. His chains restricted his movement, but were still long enough for him to reach the greasy device and press it to his ear.

"You cut your hair," he said.

She'd tamed her coarse waves, her flat-ironed ends now resting a little past her shoulders. "I needed a change. You like it?" Flynn angled her chin to give him the full effect, holding her phone away from her head.

"I do," he said. "It makes you look older. More mature."

"I don't know if aging a woman is a compliment, but thanks," she said.

"You look beautiful, how's that?"

She laughed, and although it echoed through the receiver, he pretended like she was right next him. "Much better."

He wished he could speak freely, but all phones were tapped so they often spoke in coded terms.

"My transfer's in a few weeks," he said, referring to his next home, a minimum-security prison still on the grounds of the Pennsylvania Federal Prison.

"Finally! I'm so happy for you." Flynn leaned back in her seat. "Will it be very different?"

"No perimeter fencing, which will allow me to work more closely off-site with my employers."

Flynn nodded, understanding his meaning. "Sorry it's been so long."

"That's okay. I know you're busy out there saving the world."

Flynn raised a brow. He longed to trace it with his finger. To kiss each of her delicate features. The last time he'd wrapped her in his arms had been before he'd been discharged from Northwestern Hospital after REDS's defeat. The FBI had waited for him outside his room and allowed Flynn one last visit before they took him away.

"How are we going to make it through this?" Flynn had whispered, burying her face into his chest. "Making it through a day feels insurmountable."

He'd inhaled her scent, trying to imprint it on every corner of his memory and lock it there forever.

"Remember what you fought so hard for," he'd whispered back. "That's how."

"Yes, but we had each other. We faced the world together. No matter what it threw at us. Once you're in prison, we'll have to face our new lives alone."

"Trust me, as someone who knows what it means to be alone, this isn't it. We'll always have each other, even if we're not together. Don't get me wrong, saying goodbye is one of the hardest things I've ever had to do. You've grounded me. You've been my foundation as I've tried to rebuild myself piece by piece. But I've realized I have to face my past on my own, even if it terrifies me."

She sighed. "I said pretty much the same to Nate. Still lots to overcome."

"I won't let my future be another burden you have to carry. Not after everything."

Looking back, Wolf fully appreciated how important their separation was. Building a future on the foundation of someone else wouldn't have been reliable. When he faced himself alone, there was nothing and no one to hide behind. No one to influence him. No matter how much he loved Flynn, rediscovering himself wasn't her responsibility.

He had to learn on his own he wasn't a lost cause.

He wasn't a mistake.

Flynn tapped on the glass with her fingernail, yanking him back to reality. "Helllooo. Earth to Wolf. You totally zoned out."

"Sorry." He gave her a sheepish grin. "Was lost in a memory."

"Which memory?"

"The last time I touched you. In the hospital."

Flynn's gray eyes, their clear color muted in the fluorescent lights, softened. "Yeah," she whispered. "I think about that day all the time. What it would be like to go back in time whenever I wanted to hug you again."

"I know. What I would give for that. But it's for the better; I can't rely on you to save me anymore."

"We don't need saving, remember?" Flynn said.

"You're right. We've done enough of that," he said. "Besides, it only takes one person."

"After everything we've been through, you still think it's that simple?"

He shrugged. "Worked for me. Gotta start somewhere. If people think change is impossible and some big undertaking, no one will try."

"Sometimes I don't want to try."

"Remember where that got us," Wolf said.

Flynn nodded slowly. "Alright, alright. I get it, Mr. Revolutionary. I got your letter...about your reduced sentence."

He gave her a look to indicate he couldn't say anything about it yet, but one thing he'd learned about the legal system is no sentence is ironclad. Become a valuable resource and it'll go a long way with a prosecutor and the Attorney General. Especially if Wolf could also help cripple other terrorist networks. His lawyer had told him from the beginning, there have been cases before where guilty felons were given special arrangements. Might as well lean into the skills that got him into this mess in the first place.

"You know me." Wolf gave Flynn a wink. "I've been on my best behavior. They need me, and I need them. I've helped with big enough cases that my handlers are finally starting to understand I'm more useful to them when I'm not locked up here. Too many hoops to jump through. Besides, kinda hard to stay up-to-date with hacking trends from behind bars."

Flynn pinned the receiver between her ear and her shoulder. "You'll be moved to Club Fed in no time."

"I'll fit right in."

Flynn chuckled, wrinkling her nose. "I'm sure you will. A lot's happened in five years. You've turned soft."

"Maybe I have."

Worry sliced a thin line through her forehead. "This is a big move for you. I mean, we're talking a lifelong commitment."

"I'm smart enough to know my options are limited. It's that or blue denim forever." Wolf jokingly plucked his shirt. "Might as well spend the rest of my life trying to make up for my sins. That's all I can do."

A vision of Kerri flashed through his mind. Her daughter. Her grief and the addiction she battled day in and day out. Her commitment to living her life in honor of her little girl, who never got the chance to grow up.

Flynn's eyes roved over his face, trying to read him like a map. "I like that."

"So, I might be a free man someday. Or not." He winked at her again. "Are you waiting for me, Zarytsky?" He couldn't help but tease her, although he asked some version of this question every visit.

"I don't wait for anyone anymore."

Her same response every visit.

"Should I give up hope then?"

"We'll have to see if the timing is right."

Wolf leaned back in his chair, mirroring Flynn's body language. "Good. Because if you know anything about me, it's that I'll never give up." Flynn's cheeks turned pink, although the color had more of a yellowish hue from behind the glass.

"Stop your teasing," she said.

Wolf knew he'd lost the power to make her uncomfortable. He wondered if he'd ever get used to having someone who felt content with him, exactly as he was. As someone who spent almost his entire life intimidating and threatening people, it was as if he'd finally found a home to settle into. One he never wanted to leave. "Who said anything about teasing? Speaking of which, how's working with Nate been?"

Flynn rolled her eyes. "I told you he got promoted to the big leagues. We don't work together anymore, but we help each other out sometimes. We're both so busy, I don't see him much."

"Did you go back to the White House?" Wolf asked.

"What for? Another pat on the back and a gold star? There's work to do." Flynn laughed. "Kerri got the medal and deserved it."

"Yeah. She's pretty brilliant. She stops in every now and then."

"I'm not surprised," Flynn said. "She's always had a soft spot for you. As have I. I miss you. I miss you a lot."

"I miss you too. I've been thinking..."

"Never a good sign."

"With this semiofficial job, getting together all the paperwork has been a nightmare. Especially since I don't have any official records like my birth certificate or social security. So, I think it's time I choose a new name for myself."

"You don't think Wolf will fly in your new job?"

He chuckled. Rare lightness burst inside his chest, a feeling he'd only experienced since Flynn. "I'm looking for something more discreet."

She beamed, her teeth shining. "I just can't imagine you as anything else.

Any boring old name doesn't seem like it would suit you. Like...Andrew? Andy for short?"

"No, nothing like that. I've been studying Hebrew in here—"

"Oh? Thinking of converting, are you?"

He raised his brows at her, making his voice serious again. "For you, I would."

Flynn crossed her arms and gave him a smirk. "You never convert to Judaism for someone else. Every Jew knows that. You have to do it for yourself and your own beliefs."

"Well, I do like how Judaism doesn't focus as much on sin as other religions," he mused. "It's more freeing. Anyway, I was thinking Zev. Hebrew for 'wolf.' More normal, but the same meaning."

Flynn pursed her lips, her perfect Cupid's bow drawing upward. She tilted her head to the side. "Zev," she repeated. "The same, but different. New. It's perfect."

ACKNOWLEDGMENTS

JUSTIN, you are the person who has never wavered in support or belief of this crazy dream of mine. This series wouldn't be possible without you being by my side literally every step of the way, all as we grew into strange new roles as parents, battled a pandemic, moved cities, and changed jobs. With you, life is full of adventure, and I can't wait to continue on this journey together. Wherever it might take us.

To my darling children, thank you for understanding Mommy has a dream and a job she loves. My love for you will always win, but I hope to show you what it means to work hard, lead a life full of what brings you joy, and never lose sight of the long game. Remember, just because it's hard doesn't mean it's bad, and the best things in life are often the hardest.

My favorite part of this journey has been all the incredible thriller authors I've met since *The Rising Order* debuted in 2023. I've never met a group of people more willing to bring me into the fold and help me succeed. I'm so grateful for their friendship, encouragement, and support on this isolating rollercoaster of a ride—the inevitable one that occurs when you release your creative soul into the world.

To Ryan Steck and Jeff Clark, the first eyes on this manuscript. Jeff, thank you for being my weapons expert and a dear friend I trust for advice at all levels.

To Steve Urszenyi, thank you for being my medical expert and consult. I'll never forget your willingness to vouch for me and help connect me to industry professionals.

To Elizabeth Hamilton, who has been a critical part of advancing my career with local exposure. You are my idol, and I can't thank you enough. Your pursuit and championing of literacy in our community is unmatched, and I love you. Every author needs a Liz in their corner.

To John Adams, my forever hype man and the best author friend I never knew I needed. What would I do without you to commiserate with every step of the way?

And to Ilana Berry and Bruce Borgos—wow, what an honor to learn from such talent. What a team, and thank you for being my good friend and literary father figure.

To all my wonderful book clubs who have welcomed me with open arms and thought about this story critically.

To my best friends, who encouraged me to write my first sex scene and who were the first to urge me to look at sex as power and not with shame. Thanks for never getting tired of hearing me whine or complain, and for starring in my TikToks. Your belief in me means everything.

To my extended family, who have cheered me on since I breathed life into these stories and who have continued to scream about them from the rooftop. None of this would be possible without you, and I'll forever be grateful for your love.

To Tanya, who has helped me scour these pages and make them shine with purpose and clarity. I wouldn't be the writer I am without your mentorship, friendship, and love of craft.

To Erika, my life coach, who has talked me off so many ledges, shown me the power of manifesting, and helped me find the creative space I needed to come up with the idea for my next book.

Tenyia and Brian, I never could have done this without you both. Tenyia, thank you for your careful and meticulous editorial eye, embracing my vision while believing in these characters, and all the thought you've put into this story. Brian, your brilliant creative brain blew me away. Editors and designers breathe life into books. They play the most important role of honing words and creating irresistible covers and atmospheres that allow readers to fully submerse themselves into fictional worlds.

And, finally, to all my amazing, wonderful readers who connected with these characters and these pages. Thank you for your reviews and your messages, and for sharing these books with your own networks. You're the reason, day after day, I'm able to make it to my computer. I am here because of you. I'm a firm believer of using stories to change the world, and I hope in some way this one opened your worldview and allowed you to think about life even a little differently. What an honor to have your support, and I hope to never let you down.